"I don't want to hurt you, Lilah," Jesse said.

She laughed. "Law, Jesse, that didn't hurt. It felt plumb good." She wiggled against him. "I want ye to do it again."

"No!" he bellowed, then immediately attempted to soften his outburst with a gentle kiss against her hair. He didn't dare kiss her on the mouth, no matter how much he longed to. "You don't understand what lying with a man is all about."

"But I want to. Will ye show me?" She rained kisses on his neck and chest.

"Stop it, Lilah," he begged, almost at the end of tolerance. When she didn't comply, he pulled away from her. "I mean it. This can't go any further."

"How come? I know ye liked it. I liked it. Ye said I didn't do nothin' wrong." She trailed a hand down his leg, and Jesse bolted from the bed.

"But it isn't right." He plowed a hand into his hair and searched for the right words, words that wouldn't wound. "We're different, don't you see? You're a swamp girl, and I'm from the hills."

"So?"

"So, I don't like the swamp."

"Maybe I would like the hills."

DULCIMER

ELIZABETH LEIGH

ZEBRA BOOKS
KENSINGTON PUBLISHING CORP.

For Michael, Jared, and Whit—
Thanks for all the helpful things you do for me
and the interest you show in my writing.
No mother could ask for more.
I love you guys!

Acknowledgments

Many thanks to Caroline Bourne and Lee Caubarreaux for providing invaluable research information; to my husband, Tawny Hancock, for answering numerous technical questions; and to the members of my two critique groups—Donna Caubarreaux, Vicky Evans, Norma Franklin, Alecia Hulsey, and Jean Walton—not only for catching inconsistencies and technical problems, but also for offering their honest opinions.

They shot the railway-train when it first came,
And when the Fords came they shot the Fords.
It could not save them. They are dying now
Or being educated, which is the same.
One need not weep romantic tears for them,
But when the last moonshiner buys his radio,
And the last, lost, wild-rabbit of a girl
Is civilized with a mail-order dress,
Something will pass that was American
And all the movies will not bring it back.

—Stephen Vincent Benét
John Brown's Body, 1928

Maryville, Tennessee, *Index*, September 18, 1878

Deputy U.S. Marshal Jesse Redford on a recent raid off Cooper Mountain Road, Blount County, a few days since, accompanied by eight men, visited the isolated rum mill of Jack Scurlock, where they seized 11 tubs of beer and mash, 4 tubs of pomice, 130 gallons of brandy singlings, 5 bushels of meal, 2 bushels of rye, 2 bushels of malt. The revenue squad also arrested Scurlock, the engineer of the mill, who subsequently escaped . . .

Chapter One

Medicine Island, Okefinoke Swamp, 1882

Lilah decided not to wait for sunrise.

She couldn't afford to wait, not with Granny Latham wasting what piddling bit of energy she had left trying to fight off the biting flies and mosquitoes that seemed bent on eating her alive. The fighting-bugs-in-her-sleep business amazed Lilah, who figured anything that bothersome ought to wake the dead, but Granny slept right through it.

Must be a real bad case of fever, she thought, swiping at a tear and hoping it wasn't the new mon, which had killed her uncle and a number of other swampers. She took a deep breath and wrung out a clean rag in a gray granite pan. When she'd mopped Granny's clammy face, she folded the rag and held it across the old woman's forehead.

The last thing Lilah wanted to do was leave Granny by herself, but she figured she'd have to eventually anyway, if for no other reason than to check her fish trap. And when she'd done that, she'd gather some yellow tickseed to ward off the bugs.

She hoped the tickseed worked. Bur marigolds would have done the trick certain-sure, but they weren't in bloom yet. Wouldn't be before late summer, and that was more'n three months away. Not knowing what to do reminded her again of how little she knew about taking care of sick folks. She wished she'd paid more attention when Granny was trying to teach her stuff about yarbs and roots, where to find them and what to do with them once you had them.

No one knew about such things better'n Granny Latham. Folks came from all over the swamp to get medical advice, and to trade for bottles of powdered roots and herb penetrates from Granny. That's why they called this place Medicine Island. And when Granny died, her knowledge would go with her.

If only Granny could write, maybe she could put it all down on paper . . .

But what good would that do for someone who couldn't read?

Lilah waved her palmetto fan over the thrashing body one last time, whispering "Shoo now, go on" as loud as she dared, speaking as much to her disturbing thoughts as to the worrisome insects.

"It don't differ how loud I talk nohow," she mumbled to herself, picking up a dented tin bucket and a lighted pine knot, then scurrying out the door into a thick, gray mist. "She's so sick a gran'pappy gator bellering in her ear wouldn't wake her up."

The mist soaked up her voice like a sponge, twirled it through the heavy shroud around the longleaf pine cabin, and spit it back in her face. Lilah ignored the echo and plunged into the mist.

It was the damnedest thing he'd ever seen, this wispy fog that rose from the slick black surface of the water, clung to the bulbous bases of the cypresses, and hovered over the long gray beards of Spanish moss.

Oh, he'd seen mist before. Lots of times. It was a common enough sight in the mountains back home, but that mist didn't look like this. This mist was downright eerie.

He shivered all the way from the top of his head to the tip of his boots, which was a considerable trip for a single shiver to make. He needed a fire—a warm fire and a cup of hot coffee. This close to sunrise, a man needed both.

The fire he could manage. The coffee he couldn't.

Three days he'd been without coffee. Three days with nothing but the clothes on his back, a pen knife, and a plug of tobacco in one pocket, and a tin match safe in the other. The clothes were getting a tad rank and the matches were quickly disappearing. And when they were gone, he didn't know what he was going to do.

Survive, he supposed. That was all he'd done ever since Martha and the boys . . . Jesse blinked back the moisture gathering in his one good eye and tried to swallow the lump in his throat. *You'd think after all this time . . .*

But time hadn't changed anything, nor was it ever likely to, he reckoned. Nearly four years ago, he'd lost all desire to live. Since then, he'd merely survived. And only then because he was determined to see One-Eyed Jack hang from the nearest tree. Once that happened, Jesse Redford didn't know what he'd do. Maybe lay down somewhere and die himself. At least then he'd be with Martha and the boys again.

But that was somewhere down the road for him, or more likely somewhere down the swamp. Heaven only knew where One-Eyed Jack and his band of fugitives had gotten off to. Jesse reckoned they were still in the swamp, probably as lost as he was. He wondered if they had a fire and a pot of hot coffee.

Eventually, he assured himself, he'd find them. And maybe, just maybe, in the meantime, he'd find a populated island, find a family who could give him a change of clothing, a decent meal, and a bed to sleep in. If they didn't kill him first.

He'd heard tales about these swamp people, heard how they'd just as soon shoot you as look at you. They were a clannish bunch, a lot like the hill folks back home. He'd have to be careful not to surprise any of them.

If only he had his badge and his Colt .45 and his Winchester '73 model carbine . . .

Hell, if only he had his coffee!

Jesse shrugged away from the hickory he'd been leaning against and proceeded to collect twigs and small branches for a fire. There were plenty of both lying around, and bigger sticks, too. The trick was finding dry ones.

He made himself a nice little pile from the smaller fare, squatted down, and struck one of his precious matches. He was moving it toward the kindling when the clearest, sweetest voice he'd ever heard came drifting through the mist. Without thinking, Jesse shook out the flame, then cursed under his breath at the loss of the match. Slowly, he rose and crept toward the voice, straining to see through the gloaming, straining to hear each lilting note, certain he'd heard the song before and yet unable to identify it.

Suddenly the mist began to glow, at once both luminous and alive. It swirled around his feet and wafted upward into the trees. And through its shining effervescence strolled a golden-haired angel.

I've died and gone to heaven, he thought. *This isn't mist. It's a cloud. And God has sent this beautiful creature to welcome me.*

At the sharp crack of a twig, Lilah stopped singing, stopped moving, and peered into the dense clump of hardwoods. She caught a glimpse of dark hair, and a cold shiver raced down her spine.

"Is that you, Ol' Codger?" she called around the sudden tightness in her throat. Being scared was just plain silly, she fussed. Ol' Codger wouldn't hurt her, and he surely wouldn't let nothing happen to her. Not if he was around. And if he wasn't, Bob would be.

Then where were they? she questioned, wishing one or

both would show themselves. There wasn't a single critter around anywhere. That was odd . . .

"C'mon out, you sly old rascals," she called again. "If there's more'n one fish in the trap, I'll share with you."

That always brought Ol' Codger and Bob running. But not this time.

Lilah quelled the strange sense of uneasiness as best she could and hurried toward the edge of the lake. The sooner she emptied her trap and gathered the tickseed, the better. Granny needed her anyhow.

The feeling of uneasiness stayed with her all day.

Every time she went out to the rain barrel to collect fresh water, she felt a pair of eyes watching her. Someone was out there. She knew it. Otherwise, Ol' Codger and Bob would a-come begging the second they smelled the jackfish frying. Thinking it would make them show up for sure, she tossed out the head and innards, then watched through the crack in the door, just in case one or both of the critters had developed an unaccustomed shyness. Now it was almost dark, and not even a buzzard had showed itself. Nothing but a passel of flies had taken any account of the smelly castoffs.

At least those same flies weren't pestering Granny no more. Lilah supposed she could be thankful for that, especially since burning the tickseed hadn't accomplished anything more than smoking up the little cabin and making her and Granny's eyes water and their noses itch, proving that tickseed could not be substituted for bur marigolds.

She supposed, too, she should be thankful that Granny had rallied, at least for a spell, long enough to sit up and take a few sips of tonic and a couple bites of fish. She seemed to be resting better, too, and not quite so feverish.

But it was hard to be thankful for anything while this feeling hovered over her—this feeling that someone watched her every move, someone who lingered among the thick trunks of the live oaks and waited for her to give in to the sorely needed rest that tugged at her eyelids.

Stifling a yawn, Lilah closed and latched the door, then dropped the bar over it for good measure. It wouldn't offer as much pertection as Ol' Codger, or even Bob, but it was better'n nothing.

The angel knew he was watching the cabin. That wasn't hard to see. What Jesse couldn't figure out was why her pa or her man hadn't appeared in the clearing. They must be close by. She'd called to both of them several times during the day.

Skulking in the woods had given him ample opportunity to think through this particular situation. Jesse had come to the conclusion that either the angel was tetched in the head, or her menfolk were. No self-respecting man would allow a mere slip of a woman, or anyone else for that matter, to call him "Old Codger." And why wouldn't this husband of hers—Bob—catch his own fish?

Strange. That's what these swampfolk were. Downright strange.

But he needed their help. If he was ever to find his way through the swamp, find One-Eyed Jack—the thieving, murdering, no-account scoundrel—Jesse needed help. He needed a boat or a canoe, and a man to guide him.

They'd tried to tell him that before he'd left Cowhouse Island, on the north side of the swamp. There, he'd discussed the situation with various members of the Crews family, whose numbers dominated the island. They explained to him that Cowhouse wasn't really an island, not like the other islands in the Okefinoke, which they pronounced Oak-fin-oak. Rather, it was an extension of the sandy land of Ware County, separated from it by some swampy ground, easy enough to get to.

"Ye're jest on the aidge here," one of the Crews brothers told him. "A feller whut don' know his way 'round shouldn't go no further into the swamp by hisself. Even swampfolk gets theirselfs a mite confused at times."

"Not lost, mind you, jes' confused," his father quickly clarified.

" 'Tain't no way to ketch a man in the Okefinoke, if he don' wanna be cotched," another Crews chimed in. " 'Sides, ye can't track a man in the swamp."

"That's right," the father said. "It ain't likely ye'll ever find them thar skunks ye's a-lookin' fer, but if yer determined to try, ye best get you a guide. Ye can take one a my boys. Course, hit'll cost you."

But Jesse had waved their concerns aside. In all the dozen or so years he'd been a deputy U.S. marshal, he'd managed to nab close to a hundred criminals, usually without involving a single civilian. He was an expert tracker and a seasoned outdoorsman, and he'd refused to believe the swamp could be as different or as difficult as the Crews men let on. Now that he'd gotten himself thoroughly lost, however, he wished he'd listened to them.

Thank goodness he'd let them talk him into leaving his horse on Cowhouse Island. The creature could never have made it through the dense growths of cypress knees—which were often submerged—without breaking a leg.

Despite his misgivings about the angel and her family, he wasn't about to leave this island without at least talking to them. He considered moving on, taking to the muck again with the hopes of locating another inhabited island, but there was no guarantee that the next people he encountered would be any different. *And heaven only knows how long it'll take to find someone else,* he thought.

No, his best bet was to stay right where he was, until the menfolk came home.

Granny moistened her dried, cracked lips and pierced Lilah with a narrow-eyed stare. "What's wrong with you, gal?"

There was no point in evading the question. Granny had always been able to see right into Lilah's soul. "Some-one's out there."

"How do ye know?"

"I just . . . know."

Granny's warty chin bobbed. "That's good. Always trust yer mother wit." That was Granny's way of referring to in-stincts and a woman's intuition, and it was one of her standard pieces of advice.

Lilah eased an arm behind the old woman's thin shoul-ders and raised her to a sitting position. "Can ye eat some supper?"

"What ye got cooked?"

"Corn pone and the last a them dried beans we traded for last fall. It's most done."

"Fetch me some water and let me study on it."

Lilah dipped a gourd into a wooden bucket. "I was afeared ye was a-goin' to die."

"I am, child, I am."

Lilah's heart lurched, and she fought back the tears that welled in her eyes.

"No need to be afeared of death, gal. It's the only sure thing in life. Ye know that."

Lilah took a deep breath and offered a weak nod with the dipper of water.

Granny took a sip. "We're all a-goin' to die. Sometime. My time's a-comin'. But not yet."

"How do ye know?"

The old woman smiled and handed back the cup. "The same way ye know that man out there means you no harm."

"But I don't know that, Granny. What if he's one of them outlaws, like the ones kilt my folks?"

"Ye afeared of him?"

Lilah plucked a black skillet off a rack in the fireplace,

turned it upside on a plate, and shook out a crisp, brown circle. "Aye."

"Ye afeared he'll take yer life . . . or yer heart?"

"What do ye mean?"

"Ye're a woman now, Lilah, full growed, with a woman's yearnings."

"I don' want a man," Lilah denied with a vehemence that surprised her. "I jest want to stay here in the swamp with you. Take care of my critters and grow some corn and taters, like I've always done."

Granny sighed and closed her eyes. "Yer maw thought that was no life for a pretty girl like you. She tol' me onct she wanted you to leave this swamp. She thought ye oughter go stay with her sister in Homerville and learn to be a lady."

"I ain't a-leavin' you, Granny," Lilah declared, surprising herself again. She couldn't ever recall defying Granny Latham before. She stopped cutting cornbread and held her breath, waiting for Granny's reaction.

The old woman's wrinkled eyelids slowly opened, revealing dark eyes that sparkled in the candlelight, and her thin lips smiled. "We'll see, child. We'll see."

Jesse's mouth watered itself dry over the lingering fragrance of hot corn bread, but he waited until long after the thin light inside the cabin disappeared before sneaking into the small garden plot in search of food. Silvery moonlight filtered through the opening in the trees, revealing a stand of corn that had a ways to go yet and a wealth of creeping sweet potato vines with bright green, smallish leaves. New leaves.

Realizing that was all the garden held, he looked around in some amazement. No cabbage. No greens. Not even an onion. Nothing but corn and potatoes. And neither ready to harvest.

But he didn't lose hope. He'd heard hens clucking,

heard the angel talking to them when she'd fed them earlier. He crept to the far side of the cabin, praying he'd find an egg or two. Hell, he was so hungry, he'd eat them raw. Sure enough, there stood a small wire coop on spindly pine poles, barely visible in the thin moonlight sifting through the trees that grew close to this side of the cabin. Jesse eased up to the coop, twisted the twig latch open, and reached a hand inside, feeling in the dark for a straw nest and the soft down of belly feathers. Instead, his hand encountered course fur.

Fur? he questioned. *What the—*

Before he could finish the mental expletive, a set of sharp teeth sank into the tender flesh on the back of his hand. Jesse yelped despite himself and jerked his hand free. He relatched the door, then peered hard at the animal that had bit him.

A masked face stared back. Damned, if it wasn't a raccoon!

A closer inspection of the wooded area revealed several more wire cages which held a variety of small mammals—an otter, a marsh rabbit, two squirrels, a possum, and a skunk. A skunk! What the hell did they want with a skunk? Why these folks kept wild animals caged up, he couldn't fathom. He considered driving his knife into the breast of the rabbit or one of the squirrels, but the thought of taking such unfair advantage of a caged animal sickened him. Surely, he could find something else to eat.

He found the coop, but the chickens put up such a fuss he quickly abandoned the notion of finding an egg. He supposed the only thing left to do was rob the angel's fish trap, and hope she caught another fish before morning. Even if she didn't, he'd bet she had other food to eat. He didn't. And he was so hungry, he was getting weak.

Jesse's stomach rumbled so loud it startled him, but not so much as the bellow that erupted from somewhere near the water's edge, then rose in an earth-trembling crescendo. Almost immediately, an answering bellow resounded from the other side of the island. This bellow, though almost as loud, carried a different tone.

Gators.

Did they stray far from the water? he wondered, wishing he had somewhere to bed down besides the ground. That thought made him feel downright foolish. Hell, he'd spent most of his adult life sleeping on the ground. But never in a swamp. Here, he felt like a fish out of water. And without his weapons, he felt plumb naked. He couldn't recall ever feeling quite so helpless.

He considered walking up the steps, rapping on the cabin door, and begging entrance. The problem with that was he might very well never get a chance to ask for anything else. For a moment, he stood in the clearing and stared at the door, weighing the chances of being blown away by a shotgun against spending another night surrounded by bellowing alligators and other less noisy, but equally dangerous creatures. Like snakes. But such creatures, as a general rule, proved dangerous only when riled, threatened, or their habitat invaded by a potential enemy.

The same could be said to hold true of people. A knock on a cabin door this late at night could very well be interpreted as a threat.

He chose the woods.

As he left the clearing and headed for the fish trap, he crossed his fingers, knowing it was a silly thing to do yet unable to stop himself. The way his luck had been running, he figured he needed all the help he could get.

As was her habit, Lilah rose before dawn. First, she checked on Granny, who breathed hoarsely in her sleep. Her brow didn't feel quite so hot, though, and her face looked a bit more restful than it had the day before. Lilah let out a long breath, which she realized she'd been sort of holding in ever since Granny took sick the day before yesterday. She knew the old woman wouldn't live forever, but that didn't keep her from wanting to cling to life the way she'd known it for the past six years. Lilah wouldn't allow herself to imagine what her life would be like without Granny Latham in it.

Following routine, Lilah built a fire in the fireplace, collected water from the rain barrel and some leaves from the soap bush growing next to it, and washed herself. By the time she'd put on a fresh dress and apron, the mist was beginning to glow, and Granny was stirring in her bed.

"Did ye get a big fish this mornin'?"

Lilah busied herself by dipping water from the bucket into an iron pot. "I don't know. I didn't check. Thought I'd cook up the last of these oats afore the bugs gets in 'em."

"Ye're not still afeared a that man, are ye? More'n likely, he's long gone by now."

Had Granny been sleeping so hard she hadn't heard the man yelp last night? Lilah wondered. The memory of that yelp sliced through her brain, startling her almost as much as when the noise had awakened her from a sound sleep. It felt like someone had grabbed her heart again and was trying to squeeze it to death. She concentrated on stopping the sudden shaking of her hand before any more water sloshed out of the dipper and back into the bucket.

"I . . . well, I jest don' see no reason to take chances, Granny."

"Sometimes ye have to take chances, child."

Lilah shivered and thought, *Not this time,* but she didn't want to argue with the old woman, who had sheltered her and shared her wisdom and her love ever since Lilah's parents had died. Besides, she didn't want to frighten Granny. "Ye want some red bay tea?"

Granny said she did, and Lilah hoped her companion would drop back off to sleep after breakfast. She didn't.

"Ye better check that there trap," Granny advised while Lilah was washing the breakfast dishes.

" 'Tain't a-hurtin' nothin'." Lilah bit her lip at the harshness in her voice. She supposed she might as well agree, else Granny would harp on it till the swamp dried up. "All right. I'll go see about it in a little while, soon's I finish up here and feed the critters."

She took her time drying the pots and pans and putting them away, then stripped her bed and put on fresh linen.

"Ye plannin' on washin' today?"

Lilah shrugged. "The sun's a-shinin', and it don' look like rain."

"I've got me a hankerin' fer some candyroot. Would ye see if'n ye can find me some whilst ye're out?"

"But, Granny," Lilah argued, "candyroot grows over on t'other side of the pine thicket. I weren't a-goin' that a-way." At the look of disappointment on the brown, wizened face, Lilah relented. "I'll fetch you some—if'n I can find any. But ye've got to promise me ye'll stay in that bed till I get back."

"I ain't a-goin' nowheres," Granny said, her black eyes aglow with something akin to devilment, 'cept Lilah hadn't ever knowed Granny Latham to be guilty of mischief. Whatever could the sick, old woman be planning?

Lilah propped her fists on her hips and gave the glittering eyes a long, hard look. "I mean it, Granny."

Granny made a shooing motion with her gnarled hand. "Go on, now, and git. Time's a-wastin'."

The swamp had taught Lilah wariness, but she didn't fear it. Yet, for some unaccountable reason, she found herself standing poised on the edge of the clearing, waiting for her skin to prickle up. But it wasn't fear that crept over her this morning. It was more like dread. Like she'd told a fib and was about to get caught, 'ceptin' she wasn't the one in trouble. Instead of prickling her skin, it took her stomach and tied it in knots. It was a strange feeling, one she'd never experienced before.

Granny!

Quickly, she retraced her steps, then frowned in total confusion when she spied Granny lifting the kettle off its hook and pouring hot water into the teapot. The old woman couldn't be as sick as she'd made out. Then why, Lilah wondered, did she feel this fearful boding of disaster? Nothing could be worse than something happening to Granny . . .

Before Granny could turn around and catch her, Lilah hurried back across the clearing and into the woods. As she made her way down the path to the lake, she kept an eye out for Bob and Ol' Codger—and for the pair of eyes that had watched her yesterday, the eyes she'd seen with her soul. They were human eyes. A stranger's eyes. She didn't feel them following her this morning, but they were out there. Somewhere. The yelp from the darkness had confirmed it.

Her bare foot sank into a bog up past her ankle. Lilah pulled it free, then gave herself a silent chewing out for not watching her step. What if it had been a water moccasin or a gator she'd stepped on, instead of a patch of bog? She shuddered at the thought and made herself concentrate on where she was going.

There was only one fish in the trap, and it was not big enough to keep. Lilah tossed it back into the black water, lowered the trap, and waved to a cooter basking on a log in the late morning sun. The gentle though usually leery turtle stretched its mottled neck and raised its head, almost as though it were trying to return her greeting. If the cooter sensed no danger, why did she?

Though the going would have been faster if she cut through the cypress bay, Lilah headed back toward the cabin, preferring to take the longer, drier route when wearing a skirt. As she brushed past an inkberry bush, a fox squirrel scampered across her path, startling her. Close on its tail raced another. The two spiraled up a slash pine, their claws scraping harshly against the bark as they played their game of chase. And that's all it was, she assured herself. A game. Two squirrels playing chase. They weren't afraid of anything, so why should she be?

She took a fortifying breath and plunged into the thicket, where the taller longleaf pines grew so close together in places, she couldn't squeeze between their trunks. Only tiny bits of sunlight penetrated the dense upper story, rendering the sandy soil bare of vegetation.

Lilah had walked through the thicket countless times. It was almost always cool in the thicket, and she usually relished the soft carpet of pine needles beneath her feet and the sound of the swamp breathing in the high treetops. But not today. Today, it closed in on her, its darkness blinding, its coolness stifling. Today, she wanted to lift her skirt and run, giving no heed to snakes or rat holes.

Run! her mind screamed. *Turn around and run back home as fast as you can.*

But instinct drove her onward. "Always trust yer mother wit," Granny had said. And Granny was never wrong.

She obliged her feet to slow their haste and her heart to cease the thrashing it was giving her chest. Yet all the while, her right hand sought the small spade in the basket she carried. It wasn't much of a weapon, she supposed, but it was all she had. Its smooth wooden handle rode reassuringly against the backs of her fingers, and helped her fight the urge to look behind her until she burst through the thicket and into a sun-filled clearing.

Lilah fell to her knees, sat back on her heels, and arched her neck toward the sky, letting warmth and light and fresh air wash over her and through her. After a while, she felt plumb foolish for being so skittish. All around her, tall spires of colic root swayed in a soft breeze, the delicate yellow petals branching off the long stems seeming to mock her with their gentleness. An occasional white meadow beauty with its showy, golden anthers bobbed in

the breeze, while purplish pink clusters of swamp milk-
weed added bright spots of color to the grassy field.

Her gaze swept the sea of wildflowers, searching close
to the ground for the dense orange blossoms of the low-
growing candyroot. When she failed to spy even a speck
of orange, she regained her feet and strolled through the
grasses, her eyes on the ground. She made several trips
across the meadow, taking a slightly different course each
time, before she remembered that it was too early for
candyroot to be in bloom. And without the flowers to
guide her, she'd never find the roots.

Granny knew that. Granny knew when *everything* was
in season. Why, then, had the old woman sent her on this
fool's errand?

Lilah recalled the twinkle in Granny's dark eyes that
had accompanied her promise to stay in bed. She was up
to something, though Lilah couldn't fathom what.

"And here I am," Lilah muttered, "mite near a hour
away, clear on t'other side of the island."

There was nothing to be done but to head back home
empty-handed, but the absence of a fish to fry and a piece
of candyroot for Granny to chew on didn't bother Lilah
nearly as much as the feeling of urgency that swept
through her. Something was wrong, her instinct said.
Something had happened, and only she could fix it. Despite the skirt, she was going home through the cypress
bay.

Wishing she'd worn britches, she reached between her
legs, tucked the front of her skirt back and pulled the back
of her skirt forward, up and over the front and into her
waistband, creating a pair of baggy trousers that left her
lower legs bare—and free. Lilah cut across the glade and
back into the pines, entering the thicket near the far side
of where she'd come out.

Within a short time, the pines thinned out, giving way to
the dense growth of massive cypresses, their swollen bases

sitting in shallow water. It was dark inside the bay, dark and gloomy. Lilah allowed her eyes to adjust, then stepped into the water, watching for submerged cypress knees and the slither of the ever-present moccasin as she slogged through the bay.

She almost missed seeing him. He was lying on a protruding tussock of bog moss among a clutch of ferns, his clothes covered in muck. She didn't know what had caused her to look over that way, but now that she had, Lilah couldn't look anywheres else.

The still, lifeless form drew her as surely as flame draws a moth.

Chapter Two

Despite the tug that drew her to him, Lilah approached the man cautiously. He was a big man, bigger'n any man she'd ever seen. Most of the swamp men were wiry, but this man was muscular, broad across the shoulder and narrow in the hip. Tall, too, judging from the length of his legs, which were longer than the tussock was deep. Curiously, one foot wore a boot, while the other was bare. He was lying belly down with his arms folded and his hands under his head. More'n likely asleep, she told herself, although she couldn't figure out why anyone would be foolish enough to fall asleep in a cypress bay.

She wished she had a pine knot to burn, so she could see him better. Since she didn't, she poked the sole of his bare foot with the handle of her spade. He didn't move, didn't make a sound.

Was he dead?

Somehow that thought tore at her heart.

Why she should care that he might be dead was beyond her ken, but she did. She turned the spade around and poked him with the blade end, harder this time, but not hard enough to break the skin. He groaned. Lilah thought it was about the sweetest sound she'd ever heard, but that didn't keep her from fearing this stranger. And distrusting him. He wasn't swamp people, which meant he was up to

no good. Otherwise, he wouldn't a-ever ventured into the
Okefinoke.

She waited for him to say something, to turn over or
raise up. When he did nothing, she tucked the spade into
the waistband of her skirt and crawled onto the fern-
covered tussock, until she was alongside the leg that belonged to the foot she'd poked. Even in the gloom, she
could see the shredded fabric of his trousers, the bandanna
tied around his leg, just above his knee, and the blood-
caked crosshatches bulging from the swollen skin below
the joint. Her breath caught in her throat, and her pulse
thumped hard in her ears.

Snakebite!

She set the basket aside and worked the knot loose in
the bandanna. It was a wonder he was even alive. And if
she didn't move him to higher ground, where she could
tend his fever and poultice his leg, he probably wouldn't
survive. But how was she ever going to move him? There
was no way to get her canoe into the bay, and even if she
could, she doubted she had the strength to put him in it.
Not as big as he was.

She was going to have to drag him out. But first, she
had to turn him over.

Lilah surveyed the tussock, which was nothing more
than a floating layer of peat and humus caught in the apex
of three bald cypresses, just thick enough to support the
shade-loving ferns. The bay was quite shallow here, which
was all that had prevented him from drowning. As Lilah
acknowledged this fact, she felt water seeping through the
ferns and realized her additional weight was forcing the
tussock downward, into the water. If she didn't move him,
and move him fast, he would drown.

She scooted back, closer to the cypress that was directly
behind her, braced her spine against its trunk, and wedged
her feet between his chest and the bog moss. At first, the
fern fronds snagged her toes, but she wiggled and pushed

her feet, until his chest rested on her lower legs and her feet were free. Hooking her feet tightly against his far side and placing the heels of her hands against his near side, she pulled and heaved and pulled with every ounce of strength she could muster.

His moan, low and almost whimpering, cut Lilah to the quick. She hated having to hurt him, but better that than leaving him to drown. In mid-turn, he thrashed out, his fingers curled into claws, raking thin air; then his shoulder hit the tussock with a soft thump, and his hand fell limply to his stomach.

Lilah drew her thighs into her chest, expelled a long breath, and dropped her forehead onto her knees. The effort had taken everything she had to give, and then some. Glittering sparks swam behind her closed eyelids and her muscles burned from the exertion. There was no way on earth she was ever going to manage to drag this giant of a man all the way out of the bay. Why, he was so big, he'd make Ol' Codger stand up and take notice.

She'd barely caught her breath when the tussock shivered and shook and the water sucked it down in one huge gulp, ferns and all, making loud belching noises and sending fat air bubbles to the surface. Lilah sank right along with the peat. So did the giant. The dark water swirled over his legs and sloshed over his trunk. For a moment, his head stayed clear, and then the water covered it, too.

Before Lilah could garner enough energy to move, the man sputtered and coughed and tried to sit up, but the effort was too much for him. He sagged back, propping himself on his elbows, and whispered something that sounded like "angel" in a voice that was hoarse and filled with pain.

Addle-brained, more'n likely. Lilah maneuvered herself around his shoulder and settled down on her heels behind his head, which put her upper thighs completely out of the water.

"Jes' lean back," she said, "and ye can rest yer head in my lap, whilst I figure out how to get you out'n here."

With a groan and a shudder, he collapsed. His head hit her knees, which put his ears in the water. Lilah scooped her hands under his arms and gave a little tug. "Now, wiggle back some. A wee bit more. That's it."

When she got him situated, he heaved a long sigh, opened one eye, and looked up at her. Streaks of soft light sifted through the cypress boughs overhead and drifted across his face, making it difficult for Lilah to see him well. Then, for a moment, a beam illuminated his eye, and its fevered brightness burned into her, searing a path all the way to her heart. His mouth moved, but no sound came out, and he lifted a hand toward her face, then dropped it as though the effort were too much.

"Jes' lie still," she advised. "We both need to rest a spell."

He worked his mouth into a semblance of a smile and closed his eye, but there was nothing else peaceful about his expression. She didn't think she'd ever seen a face so gray, so contorted in pain, which was clearly evident even in the waltzing light. As she raked long, damp strands of dark hair off his brow, she found herself wondering what he'd look like right side up, with the stubble shaved off his jaw, some color in his skin, and a real smile on his lips. For a moment, she relished the thought, imagining this giant of a man whole and hardy, his face scrubbed shiny and his hair combed, a wide smile creasing his cheeks and lighting up his eyes. The vision stirred something deep inside her, something as strange and foreign as this outlander, a sort of yearning for something she hadn't known existed.

No! She shook her head, trying to erase the vision. This man was an outlander, and outlanders who ventured into the swamp were up to no good. He was probably either a deserter from the Army or an outlaw—or, heaven forbid, a hunter or a trapper! In Lilah's estimation, hunters and trappers ranked among the lowest forms of human scum, interested only in lining their pockets with profits from selling animal pelts and hides. For whatever reason he was in the swamp, he probably didn't deserve another minute of her attention. She oughter just leave him right there, in the cypress bay, for the gators to eat.

The outlander moaned again, and, as before, the sound tugged at her heartstrings. She gathered a bit of water in her hand, skimmed it over his hot forehead, and murmured words as soothing as she could manage in her state of indecision, knowing in the depths of her soul that she could never leave him to die. Ever-who he was, ever-what his purpose, she had to do everything she could to help him.

But first, she had to get him out of the bay.

She clapped her hands against his cheeks. "Hey, you! Mister! Wake up."

One lid slid open and his eye rolled back. Part of her acknowledged that he had yet to open his right eye, and she wondered if maybe there was something wrong with it, but that was the least of her worries at the moment.

"Ye're going to have to stand up and walk. Ye can lean on me."

"Angel," he murmured.

So, that *was* what she'd heard him say before. Probably had her confused with someone else.

"My entitlement is Lilah. Lilah Bennett. Watch yer head. I'm a-lettin' it go." She scooted around to his side, squatted, and picked up his hand. "C'mon. Stand up."

His palm lay in hers like a wet dishrag. She folded his fingers over the back of her hand and pulled on his arm. She might as well have been pulling on an alligator's tail, but she didn't let up.

"Ye're gonna die, mister," she screamed at him, "if'n you don' get out'n this bay. I can't stay here and hold yer head forever."

He didn't budge.

"What's the matter with you? Do ye want to die?"

Lilah yanked his arm and hollered until she wore herself out. She was just about ready to sit down and cry when Ol' Codger came splashing through the bay. Maybe, between the two of them, they could haul the stranger onto dry land, where at least he'd have a fighting chance of surviving.

Twilight was creeping into the swamp by the time Lilah, beat all to flinders and looking it, trudged into the little cabin. Fully expecting Granny to light into her the minute she got home, Lilah had prepared a defense, but the old woman lay on her bed, snoring loud enough to wake the dead.

Lilah wanted nothing more than to fall into bed herself, but rest lay a long way off. By some miracle, the man she'd found in the bay still clung to life, though only by the thinnest thread. She reckoned he wouldn't live to see another day-bust, but she couldn't just leave him out there in the woods to die all by his lonesome. And maybe she could bring ease to his final hours.

As quickly as her tuckered-out bones allowed, she stripped off her filthy clothes and washed the grime from her body, relishing the cool water and then the fresh garments she donned. Somewhat revived, she put some clean cloths and a bottle of Granny's fever tonic in one apron pocket and a slice of day-old corn bread in the other, threw an old blanket over her shoulder, then filled a bucket from the rain barrel and headed back to the woods.

"Ever-who ye are, mister," Lilah said, "ye've got a will of iron. I've never seed a body so determined to live."

He grunted, making her wonder if he'd actually heard her. She supposed it was possible. Twice, she'd managed to rouse him enough to get him to take some of the tonic and a few sips of water, but each time he'd fallen back on the bed she'd fashioned from long-haired moss before he took enough of either to do him much good. He spent most of the night moaning and thrashing and calling for a woman named Martha. And all the while, Lilah bathed his fevered skin and talked to him and prayed for him.

"The sun'll be up tirectly," she said, rising to her feet, "and Granny'll be a-wakin' up and a-wonderin' what in tarnation happened to me, so I best go see her. I'll be back soon's I can. Jest hold on till then."

What if he didn't make it? she wondered. What if he didn't live until she got back? For some unaccountable reason, the thought ripped through her, gnashing at her innards and tearing at her heart.

She removed the lantern from the branch where she'd hung it the night before and held it closer to his face. For a long while, she stared down at him, memorizing every feature. The shadow of dark stubble covered his square jaw and trickled up the planes of his cheeks and across the space above his upper lip. For the first time, she noted the way his hairline formed a widow's peak in the center of his broad forehead, and the thin line of untanned skin that angled down from his left temple to the cover of his right eyebrow. There, it bloomed into a full oval that covered his eye before dissolving into another thin line that crossed his right temple and melted into his hairline again. Within the oval gleamed a thin, crescent-shaped scar that held his eyelid permanently shut.

The sight yanked on her heartstrings. Sinking to her knees and bending low over the stranger, Lilah brushed her lips over the scar. "Don' go a-dying on me," she whispered, savoring the salty taste of his skin even while the feel of the ridged flesh against her lips restored a portion of her wariness. There was something unnatural, something almost sinister about a one-eyed man, yet her heart went out to this one.

"Ye jes' get well now, and I'll make you another patch," she promised, touching her lips to his scar again and feeling nothing this time but remorse at his loss.

During his rare moments of nebulous lucidity, Jesse clung to the ragged edge of consciousness, his instinct for survival demanding that he hold fast for as long as he could. Though ignoring the promised comfort of the beckoning darkness required every ounce of mental fortitude he could garner, he knew that his effort kept him one step further from death.

And he must survive. He must conquer death, whatever the cost. He had vowed to hunt down One-Eyed Jack, and see the felon hang for his heinous crimes. Jesse would not allow death to claim him before then.

He fixed his mind on a vision of Jack's black eye patch and his heart on justice; and he gripped both images with ruthless tenacity, until the unrelenting pain vaulted him into the darkness once more.

"Mornin', Granny," Lilah called as she came through the door. "Ye look plumb spry today. I sure am glad. Ye been awake long?"

From her bed, Granny Latham nodded and blew out the candle on the bedside table. "Jes' been a-sittin' here, waitin' for you."

Lilah moved to the hearth and started building a fire. "I hope ye didn't worry none."

"I didn't."

The smile in Granny's voice eased Lilah's mind. "How're ye feelin'?"

"Fair to middlin'. But not good enough to do much stirrin' around. That fever sapped me good and proper."

"I'm glad ye're better," Lilah said absently as the kindling blazed to life. She added a few sticks of wood from the box by the fireplace, then pulled a chair up to Granny's bed. For a moment, she worried her bottom lip, trying to decide where to start.

"That man what was a-watchin' us went and got hisself in trouble," she blurted out.

Granny nodded. "I figured something like that. What'd he do?"

"Got hisself snakebit."

"Where is he?"

Lilah inclined her head toward the door. "Out yonder. In the woods." She frowned, considering Granny's lack of surprise. "Ye knew it, didn't ye? Ye knew he was hurt. That's how come ye to send me for candyroot, when ye knew good and well it weren't in bloom."

The same mischief that had brightened the old woman's dark eyes the day before twinkled there again. "Why didn't ye brang him inside, where ye could take care of him better?"

A shiver coursed down Lilah's spine. "I'm afeared of him." It was a double-edged truth. She was, truly, afeared of him, not only for who he might be, but also for the way he made her feel. She stood up and paced, trying to dislodge her apprehension. " 'Sides, he's too big to move. It was all Ol' Codger could do to tote him out'n the cypress bay."

"That ol' ba-ar toted him? That must a-been a sight to behold!" Granny cackled so hard her sides shook, which threw her into a coughing fit. When she sobered, she asked, "Will he live?"

"Maybe. I been a-bathin' him and a-givin' him yer fever tonic, but I need to poultice his wound. What do I use?"

"Dog-tooth violet leaves."

Lilah racked her brain, trying to recollect the plant, and finally gave up. "I ain't never gonna learn all the yarbs. What does it look like?"

"Not like a violet, that's for certain-sure. It ain't

toothed, neither." Granny snorted. "I've never been able to figure why it ever got called that in the first place. It's a lily. 'Tain't blooming no more, but the leaves're easy to spot. Long and purple they are, with green specks. They grow close to the ground. Ye oughter find some in the woods."

Lilah nodded and started toward the door. "I seed a whole heap of 'em yestiddy. I'll get some water and see if'n the hens laid any eggs."

While they were eating a breakfast of fried eggs and hominy grits, Granny rubbed her chin hard and pierced Lilah with a soul-searching stare. "If ye're so afeared a this man, how come ye're a-tryin' to save his life?"

The stare made Lilah uncomfortable, but she didn't look away. "I don' rightly know. 'Cause he's a helpless critter, I reckon. I jest don' got the heart to leave him to die."

"What're ye goin' to do with him when he's well?"

Lilah blinked in confusion. "What do ye mean?"

"He ain't no wild critter what got its foot caught in a trap. You specting him to jes' go back to the woods when he's all healed up?" Granny's observation hinted at reproof.

"Ye think I done wrong?"

The old woman speared the last bite of egg and chewed on it thoughtfully before answering. "Nay, but there's things need to be considered here, Lilah."

"Such as?"

A conspiratorial smile wreathed Granny's face as she handed her plate to Lilah. "Ye best go gather them leaves and see after yer man-critter." When Lilah hesitated, Granny shooed her along. "Jes' put the dishes on to soak. And don' worry none 'bout me. I'm goin' to take me a little nap whilst ye're gone."

The man-critter was awake.

Lilah stopped short and gaped at the shimmering green

of his good eye. She realized that she hadn't known until that moment what color it was.

"Hello," he said, startling her so she almost dropped the bucket of water.

Her moistened lips suddenly gone dry and willed her shaking limbs to be still. Despite herself, she glanced around, looking for Ol' Codger. There was no sign of the black bear, but Bob crouched on a limb right behind the stranger's head, just out of his line of vision. Knowing the cat was near lent her strength of mind and body. Her legs stopped quivering, and she smiled down at the outlander.

"You *are* real."

"Course, I am." Lilah settled herself on her knees and pressed the tips of her fingers against the swollen, bluish skin around the crosshatches. A shudder racked his frame, and he took a gasping breath. She glanced at his face. Pain crinkled the skin at the corners of his eyes. He'd closed the one functioning lid again.

"I'm sorry. I don' mean to discomfit you none, but I have to clean and poultice this or it's sure to get infected." She wrung out a clean cloth, rubbed a soap bush leaf against it until it lathered, then washed the wound with gentle but firm strokes. His leg trembled beneath her ministrations, but he made no protest. Something dark and sticky lay in the open knife cuts and refused to wash out.

"D'ye put something on this, mister?"

"Tobacco," he muttered through clenched teeth.

"It don' want to come out, so I'm a-leavin' it." Lilah rinsed the wound, slipped a long strip of fabric cut from a flour sack under his leg, then laid several dog-tooth violet leaves over the swollen skin.

"Was it a moccasin what got you?"

"Yes."

She folded the cloth over the leaves and tied the knot on

the inside of his leg, opposite the entry wound. "I'm surprised ye're alive."

"It only got one fang in." Every word seemed a supreme effort for him, and his face looked pinched and drawn.

"Here," she said, sliding her arm under his shoulders. "Drank some water, and then I'll let you rest."

As he took several long swallows of water from the gourd she held to his lips, she felt the burn of his skin and the quiver of his muscles through his shirt. In response, her heart burned and her soul quivered with apprehension, whether for his quite possible death or for her own continued well-being should he survive, she didn't know.

"I have to go now," she murmured, setting the gourd aside and lowering his upper body to the moss bed. "Try to sleep."

Jesse twisted and turned upon the moss bed, trying to find a comfortable position and finally settled for the one that caused him the least discomfort.

He'd hoped she would stay and talk for a while, this golden-haired angel who'd rescued him from the cypress bay. Not physically rescued, of course. Whoever—or whatever—had carried him to safety, had been much larger and far stronger than any man Jesse had ever encountered. He was certain of that. Though he possessed no distinct memory of leaving the bay, the musty smell of a wild animal and the coarse texture of fur filled his senses.

Was it possible? he wondered. Could his rescuer have been a black bear?

The very idea! A bear would surely have torn him to shreds, not saved his life. No, it was the one she called Old Codger who'd picked him up like he didn't weigh any more than a sack of flour. He'd heard her call the man by name. Perhaps Old Codger wore a coat made from a bear skin. Yes, that's what it was. That was what it had to be.

There was so much he wanted to ask this angel of mercy, so much he needed to know—about her, her family, and the swamp. Jesse began to list questions in his head so he'd be prepared when she returned, but before he'd finished mentally forming the third one, he fell asleep.

". . . dangerous, murderin' thieves, that's what they is. As soon cut yer throat as look at you."

Lilah stood on the porch, listening to Colin Yerby, who was inside the cabin talking to Granny. She didn't much like Colin, mostly because he'd caught her alone in the woods one day a few months back, and kissed her before she realized what the varmint was up to. At least, she supposed it was a kiss. The only other person who'd ever kissed her on the mouth was her mother, whose kisses had been sweet. Colin's was slobbery wet and perfectly disgusting.

As Lilah rubbed her mouth with the back of her hand in an effort to wipe off the memory, she considered going right back to the woods and staying there until Colin left. But the subject of his conversation with Granny both intrigued and frightened her. Colin wouldn't be a-scarin' Granny with talk about "dangerous, murderin' thieves" unless there was a band of 'em loose in the swamp. What if the giant was one of them? She had to find out what Colin knew.

Creaking hinges announced her entrance. Colin spun around and grinned broadly. "Lo there, Miz Lilah," he said, his tone so full of long-sweetnin' it turned her stomach. "I'm glad ye're back."

Lilah attempted a smile she was certain looked as fake as the wax fruit Granny kept in a bowl on the table. Someone had traded Granny the fruit for remedies, and neither she nor Lilah knew the names of most of the pieces.

"What brung ye to Medicine Island?"

"Why, the pleasure of yer company, a-course. Yer'n and Granny's," he added hastily, shooting her a grin designed to charm, but it didn't quite make it.

Lilah moved toward the fireplace. "Ye hungry, Colin?"

She hated asking him. If he stayed for the noon meal, he was likely to stay most of the afternoon, and she needed to get back to the sick man out in the woods. But she had to eat something, and so did Granny. Besides, knowing Colin, he'd probably stay anyway. He'd be in his punt boat so he wouldn't have to worry about trying to get home before dark.

"A little bit. Thanks for the invite. What ye got to eat?" He bent and picked up a burlap sack.

"Nothing much. Some beans from t'other night. Thought I'd rustle up some spoon bread to go with 'em."

"Colin brung us some fatback, Lilah," Granny said, the corners of her mouth twitching. "Maybe you could fry some a it up."

He handed her the bag, a sheepish grin on his lean face. "I know you don't eat meat, Miz Lilah, so I brung you a jar of blackberries my maw put up last summer. They oughter still be good."

Lilah removed a greasy, brown-paper-wrapped package and a blue Mason jar with contents so cloudy she wouldn't a-been able to identify 'em had Colin not told her what they was. She pushed back the frown that threatened to spoil his offering. "I'm sure they is, Colin. Thank yer maw for me."

There was something else in the bottom of the bag, something that smelled suspiciously like fresh meat. Lilah made a face and threw Colin a half-questioning, half-accusative glance.

"A squirrel," he explained, "fer Granny." He took the

sack from Lilah and set it in the enamel dishwashing pan. "He was old. Probably tough. I'll put it on to boil later."

His words brought tears to Lilah's eyes, and she quickly set about building up the fire to hide her vexation with him for killing a helpless old squirrel.

"It's not that Lilah don' eat meat," Granny said. "She eats chicken and pork and fish, but she don' have no truck with killin' wild animals for food or fer their hides."

"Oh," Colin said, his voice and demeanor contrite. "I'm sorry, Miz Lilah. I didn't know. I won't do it again."

You mean you won't let me know you did it again, Lilah thought, knowing full well Colin wasn't about to stop killing wild game just because she didn't like it. Deep down, she was almost glad he'd brought the squirrel. The broth would be good for the giant. Remembering the man in the woods made Lilah pay closer attention to the conversation going on behind her.

"Like I was a-sayin', ye'uns need to be real cautious-like till they catch them murderin' thieves. Ye really oughter have a gun."

"Don' need no gun," Lilah said. "Not s'long as we got Bob and Ol' Codger."

"Them two ain't no better'n watch dogs," Colin sneered. "Two bullets would be the end of 'em both, and then what would ye have fer pertection?"

"It'd take more'n one bullet to brang down Ol' Codger!" Lilah argued. "Why, he's got healed-up places all over him where he's been shot, and he jest went right on a-livin'."

"Tell us more about the thieves," Granny said, probably to stop the argufyin'. Lilah immediately tensed, certain the man she'd found was one of 'em, yet hoping with everything in her that she was wrong.

"Don't know much 'sides the fact that there's at least three of 'em. Judgin' from the size of the tracks Pa found, one's got ter be a big feller."

"When was that?" Lilah asked.

"Couple days ago."

Lilah prayed Granny would keep her mouth shut about the man in the woods. Regardless of what he might've done, he was sick, and she didn't want Colin hauling him off to Billy's Island and keeping him in chains until some lawman came to fetch him. Or until he died, which was more'n likely to come first.

"How old was the tracks?" Granny asked.

"Purty fresh, Pa said."

"Then how come he didn't catch the varmints?" Lilah twisted her head to see Colin's reaction. His pa was known for having a yellow streak as wide as Chesser Prairie, but she couldn't help goading Colin. Sure enough, his face burned bright red and his right pointer finger worried his collar.

"Tried to, but they got too fur a jump on him."

"How d'ye know they's dangerous?" Granny asked. "Could be they's jes' hunters or turpentiners lost in the swamp. Happens all the time to furinners."

Colin shook his head. "Naw, they's outlaws, all right. Old Cyrus McIntire come by yestiddy and ast if'n we'd seed 'em. Said he went up t' Cowhouse Island to collect his stock and run into this marshal feller, who follered 'em into the swamp. 'Cording ter the marshal, they was four or five of 'em, but Pa only found three sets a tracks."

Lilah nearly dropped the crockery bowl in her hands. To cover her sudden uneasiness, she set it on the enamel shelf of the Hoosier cabinet, putting her back to Colin. "What happened to t'others?" she asked, dismayed at the tremble in her voice.

"No one knows, Miz Lilah. Maybe gators or snakes or a ba-ar got 'em. Maybe the marshal did. Maybe they split up or got separated fer some reason. But this marshal says they kilt a woman and some children up yonder in Tennessee. They's bad men, that's fer sure and certain."

Chapter Three

As Lilah made her way across the clearing and into the woods, she fretted at the thin rays of sunlight slashing across the earth. In a few minutes, darkness would swaller the swamp in one mighty gulp, and she shivered at the thought of being caught with the stranger after nightfall.

Last night had been different. Last night, the giant had been harmless as a just-hatched gator—and she hadn't known then that he was a murderin' thief.

Just 'cause she'd suspected as much didn't make the knowledge any easier to take now. She'd suspected he might be a whole lot of things, any of which named him a scoundrel of the worst sort. But to be a murderin' thief, like those horrible men who'd kilt her parents . . .

Lilah shivered again and hastened her steps, thinking she oughter turn around and go back to the cabin. She oughter forget about him. She'd done everything she could. Either he'd live or he wouldn't.

She'd just check on him one last time, she told herself, make sure he had everything he needed and give him the jar of squirrel broth. Then she'd tell him she spected him to get off the island soon's he could travel. In the meantime . . . well, in the meantime, she'd have herself a little talk with Ol' Codger and try to make the bear understand she needed him to stay around Medicine Island for a spell.

Yep, that was exactly what she needed to do—no, what she *had* to do in order to pertect Granny and herself. There was no telling what danger she'd already put them both in. If anything happened to Granny 'cause of it, she'd never be able to forgive herself.

Tell the truth, her inner voice chided. *It's not Granny ye're so worried about. It's you. It's yer own woman's heart ye're afeared for.*

"Hesh up, ye hear?" Lilah muttered to the voice. "I *am* afeared for Granny's sake." But she knew, deep down, that the voice was right. The stranger might be a thief, probably was, but he weren't no murderer. Lilah didn't know how she knew that, only that she did. She knew it the same way she knew the setting sun would rise again come mornin' soon. She might not know where it went at night, but she knew it'd be back.

Being so certain in her heart didn't erase her fear, though. It was as firmly snagged as the hapless, red-eyed fly caught in the spiderweb she almost ran smack-dab into in the quickly disappearing light.

"Howdy do, Mistress Spider," she crooned, reaching up and gently stroking the large spider's back with the pad of her finger. "This is quite a web ye done spun since I come by here last. Enjoy yer vittles."

Feeling somewhat more lighthearted, though wary still, Lilah ducked under the web and took three more steps before stopping short. Slowly, cautiously, she turned completely around, her gaze raking the murky woods before coming to rest on the silken threads gilded by an almost horizontal shaft of sunlight. The web had been there before. She'd watched it glow in the sunlight that morning whilst she sat with the stranger ... but from the opposite side.

"Where'd ye go?" she breathed, not really expecting an answer. Her heart in her throat, Lilah ducked back under the web and surveyed the pile of squashed-down, long-haired moss that had been the giant's bed. The blanket was gone, but there sat the water bucket and the basket of clean rags she'd left in the woods.

"Lord a-mercy!" she prayed aloud, snatching up her skirts and hightailing it back to the cabin. "Watch out after Granny till I get there."

Half-expecting to find the old woman brutally murdered, Lilah burst across the threshold, her lungs burning from her flight and her eyes stinging with unshed tears. Deep shadows swathed the corners of the cabin, the only light that of the cook fire, the only sound that of the squirrel stew bubbling as it simmered. Panic seized her.

"Granny!" she called. "Granny Latham, where ye be?" Her voice caught in her throat and she choked on the question.

"Right here, child."

Lilah whirled around to face the voice, her eyes blinking back the moisture that blurred her vision. She swallowed several times, but she still couldn't manage clear speech.

Granny bustled through the open door, a fistful of yarbs in one hand and a pail of water in the other. She brushed past Lilah and headed to the fireplace. "What's ailin' you, child?"

Lilah's heartbeat skidded back to normal, but her limbs took to quivering and her head felt light. She plopped down in the rocking chair and scooted it closer to the old woman, who was adding snips of the aromatic yarbs to the stew. "He's gone," she said, "and I was fearful worried for you."

The old woman didn't look up, just kept fiddling with the stew. "I ain't never heared of a body a-gittin' over true snakebite that fast. Are you certain-sure?"

A heaviness settled in Lilah's stomach. "Yes'm. He's gone."

"Then 'tain't nothin' left for you to do 'ceptin' to pray."

Lilah nodded. "Ye don' reckon he was one of them murderin' thieves Colin was telling us about, do ye?"

The old woman didn't answer right away. She busied herself tying the stems of the remaining yarbs together and hanging the bundle on a rack with other drying herbs, before pulling a chair up to the hearth and sitting down. Lilah held her breath, waiting for Granny to answer.

"I reckon that's what he was, all right, 'cause he shore couldn't git very far on his own."

"What d'ye mean?"

"More'n likely, they come and taken him whilst Colin was here."

Since Colin had lingered the whole afternoon, Lilah didn't doubt that possibility, but she still couldn't believe the stranger was an outlaw. "If the man-critter was bad, how come ye not to feel it? Ye never was afeared of him."

The old woman shrugged. "There's both good and evil in ever'body. Maybe it was the man's goodness I felt, 'stead of the evil. That don' mean the evil 'tweren't there."

"Ye reckon I'll ever see him again?"

"A body can't be certain 'bout nothin'. Not in this life, no ways."

For a long while, the two sat in silence, Lilah rocking in her chair, Granny poking the fire and stirring the stew from time to time. Lilah didn't know when she'd felt so empty. Not since her parents had died, she supposed.

No matter how hard she tried, Lilah couldn't recall the events of *that* day, but that didn't keep her from rememberin' how she felt. She tried again to drag up the memories that lay buried deep within her. They were there. She knew they were. She'd told Granny that two bad men she'd never seen before had kilt Maw and Paw, but that was all she knew. Maybe, that was all she'd ever know . . .

"Don' you want to try some a this stew?" Granny asked, drawing Lilah out of her reverie. "It's awful good."

"Nay, you eat it," Lilah said. "The hunger bug's done left me."

Nightmares riddled Lilah's sleep.

Three men roamed through the nightmares. One carried a smoking six-shooter. Another wielded a bloody knife. And the third, who was much larger than the other two, wore a black eye patch. Evil distorted their indistinct features, and the stench of vileness clung to their wavering forms. A scarlet sheen overlaid the images, a sheen that grew brighter and brighter until it blocked out everything except a field of red, intent on burning itself into Lilah's brain.

Someone pushed on her shoulder. Lilah pushed back, then screamed when her palm encountered the heat from the red field. Through the fog of sleep, she heard a woman's voice calling to her, begging her to wake up. At first, the voice rang as clear as her maw's, but as she came more fully awake, it deepened into Granny Latham's aged voice.

"Wake up, child. Ye got comp'ny, and ye done burnt yer hand on the lamp."

The light made Lilah blink, and her scorched palm throbbed with pain. Her mouth was so dry she could hardly talk. "What? Who?"

"Ol' Codger. He brung the furinner back."

Lilah struggled to sit up in bed. She couldn't possibly have heard right. Ol' Codger? The furinner? "I'm dreamin'," she rasped. "Go 'way."

" 'Tain't no dream," Granny said. "Ye have to get up and let the man-critter have yer bed. Ye can sleep with me. But first, we got to git that man dry."

When Lilah didn't respond, Granny snatched the light bedcover back and tugged on Lilah's arm. "C'mon, now. It's rainin', and that stinkin' ba-ar is a-drippin' all over the floor."

Although she was close to being fully awake, Lilah re-

fused to believe what she was hearing. Her bed sat against
the back wall, and the light from Granny's lamp failed to
reach the area near the door. But then Ol' Codger stepped
into the circle of light. As big as he was, the bear was all
stooped over from the weight of the stranger in his arms.
The man's head lolled back and his outside arm hung
limply, his fingers almost touching the floor.

Her feet hit the floor and she rushed toward Ol' Codger.
"Is he breathin'?"

The bear grunted and Granny snorted. "Jes' barely."

Suddenly wide-awake, Lilah snatched the blanket off
the foot of her bed, snapped it open, and spread it on the
floor. "Put him down, Codger. Granny, put the kittle on
the fire."

"Ye put the kittle on," Granny countered. "Ye don' have
no binness laying yer innocent eyes on this man's necked
body. 'Sides, ye don' need to be dippin' that burn in hot
water. Put some lard on it. And git that ba-ar out'n this
house!"

Lilah turned apologetic eyes on Ol' Codger, but the
huge black bear had already dropped to all fours and was
making his way toward the door. "A thankee don' seem
like nearly enough," she told him as she opened the door
wide. "I don' know how ye fount him, but I'm beholden
to you for a-brangin' him to me."

Ol' Codger grunted and loped out onto the porch. Lilah
closed the door behind him.

For the next hour, Lilah hauled and heated water and
fetched towels for Granny, while the old woman bathed
the stranger and repoulticed his wound. Lilah caught
glimpses of the man's furred chest and his long, muscled
legs, but Granny was careful to hide everything else with
the blanket. When she was done, Granny folded the blanket around the man like a sling, and the two somehow
managed to lift the giant into Lilah's bed.

"This man's burnin' up," Granny said, her open palm

stroking his forehead. "I give him some of my fever tonic, but I don' know as how it's gonna be much help to him, as bad off as he is. His clothes ain't nothin' but rags, but they's all he's got to wear. If he lives, he's goin' to need 'em. I reckon I best wash 'em out and hang 'em to dry afore ye go back to bed."

The last thing Lilah wanted to do right then was go back to sleep. Partly because of the nightmares, but mostly because she knew she couldn't sleep so long as the stranger hovered so near death's door. She wasn't sure why his living instead of dying meant so much to her, but it did. "I'll stay up with him, Granny."

The old woman nodded. "But no peekin'. It ain't fitten."

Though Lilah agreed to Granny's bidding, she wished Granny hadn't thought of it. In truth, Lilah hadn't even considered peeking, until the old woman told her not to. Because she did, Lilah's natural curiosity prodded and poked, whispering, "Look. See what's under the blanket that ye're not supposed to see till ye're married. Granny's asleep and so's the man. No one will ever know."

I'll know, Lilah told the voice. *'Sides, I been a-knowin' what makes a man a man for a long time.* But try as she might, she couldn't quite imagine Ol' Codger's privates attached to the stranger.

"Tetchin' ain't the same as seein'," the voice goaded.

After a while, Lilah couldn't stand it anymore. She slipped the hand she hadn't burned up under the blanket and skimmed her palm over the giant's ribs. The incredible softness of his skin amazed her. She didn't know quite what she'd expected, but not skin as soft as goose down. It set her palm to tingling.

The voice urged further exploration. One of her fingertips plunged into his belly button, and her thumb caressed a stream of coarse, curly hair that trickled down toward his legs. Suddenly, his stomach contracted, then relaxed, the muscles rippling beneath her hand. A shiver coursed through him, and a soft moan escaped his throat.

Lilah jerked her hand back and plopped it into her lap. When it didn't stop tingling, she buried it in the folds of her nightdress, wrapping it in the cotton fabric and making a fist. She could hear her maw's voice reciting poetry: "My wanton thoughts enticed mine eye to see what was forbidden." Feeling quite shameful, Lilah glanced toward Granny's bed, but it was encased in darkness. Had the old woman seen her? Lilah wondered. Worse, had the stranger felt her hand upon his stomach?

Lilah chanced a look at the giant's face. His one good eye remained closed, but she thought she detected the merest hint of a smile on his lips. Dadblame it all, he had! Lilah was sure of it. Her only hope was that he wouldn't remember it later.

Regardless, his smile firmly squelched any further desire to discover how he was put together. At least for the moment.

"I thought you was plumb crazy when you put up that rope and strung that ol' quilt on it," Granny said, using a bob of her head to indicate the makeshift partition since her hands were busy drizzling honey over a fat johnny-cake. "But I surely am glad now you taken a shine to modesty."

Lilah turned her head to glance at the stranger, who was sleeping, though fitfully. "Does lookin' at him discomfit you?"

"Naw. 'Tain't that a-tall." The old woman paused long enough to chew a goodly bite, which she followed with a swallow of tea. "I ain't never knowed nobody could make johnnycake good as you."

"Maw could." The admission stirred up a wealth of emotion and a world of memory. Lilah fought back both by joshin' the old woman with tease-talk. "You know,

Granny, ye're as bad 'bout a-cuttin' off down the wrong trail as one of Colin's no-'count ba-ar dogs. Course, that's a good thang fer them dogs. Keeps 'em alive."

"You got a point to make, gal?"

Lilah grinned. She had a purty good notion where Granny was taking her observation, but the conversation helped fill the time—and ease the pain her mention of Maw had caused. Besides, Lilah enjoyed playing these verbal games with Granny. "I thought *ye* did. What about the curtain?"

"It'll hide him, a-course."

"And ever-who do we need to hide him from?"

Granny laid down her fork and rolled her eyes back. "Ain't you got a lick a sense? Why, ever'one, 'ceptin' us."

"You spectin' comp'ny?"

"No one in partic'lar, but ye know we don' never have no warnin'. Folks jest show up here."

That was true. Sometimes, weeks went by without a single swamper visiting Medicine Island. Other times, folks showed up one right behind t'other.

"I'll keep the curtain closed," Lilah promised.

"Just a percaution."

Lilah nodded. "You want I should hide his clothes?"

"Don' have to. They's dry. I'm fixin' to put 'em back on him, what's left of 'em, anyways." Granny sopped up the honey on her plate with the last bite of johnnycake. "What you reckon happened to his other boot?"

"I spect it's out there som'eres, if'n a gator ain't et it yet."

"Or yer ba-ar. I swear, that ba-ar'll eat most anything."

Lilah started gathering up the dirty dishes. "I'll go look fer it, soon's I wash these up."

"I'll do the washin'," Granny said. "Yer hand ain't healed yet. Git anything else the man-critter might've drapped, and fetch me a cattail stalk—a fat un. Hurry up with you, now. I need you to hold him whilst I open up them blisters. That shore ain't goin' to cause him no pleasurement."

A flurry of activity so thoroughly consumed the next three days that Lilah lost track of time.

Lilah combed the woods, the bay, and the edge of the lake looking for items that might belong to the stranger, especially his boot. All she found was the remains of a fire he'd built; she buried the ashes and bits of charred wood, leaving nothing for prying eyes to question. She destroyed the mound of long-haired moss, and hauled home the bucket and gourd she'd left in the woods. Not far from the moss bed, she found the blanket, which she took home and washed. Granny had been right. The man-critter hadn't gone far.

Besides her searching and the regular chores, there was the man-critter to see to. Granny laid his leg on a shadow pan and used a piece of the cattail stalk as a tube, inserting it directly into the wound.

"It's all I know to do to drain out the pizen," she explained to Lilah, who came close to gagging on the smelly pus that slowly seeped through the hollow stalk and collected in the pan. Every few hours, Lilah cleaned the pan, and several times a day, she went to the woods to collect fresh dog-tooth violet leaves for the poultices.

They doctored him with tonic and Granny's herb penetrates, and they bathed his fevered skin. They ladled broth into his mouth, and talked to him low and gentle-like to calm his restlessness. They changed his poultices and lanced his blisters. Despite their attention and Lilah's constant prayer, the giant seemed to be slipping closer and closer to death.

"He ain't a-goin' to make it, is he?" Lilah asked, bracing herself for Granny's answer.

"Are ye givin' him up?"

Lilah thought about that for a minute. Sometimes, she almost lost hope, but never completely. "Nay."

"Good. Me neither," Granny said, but her voice lacked enthusiasm. She bit her bottom lip, then sighed loudly. "Ye're not goin' to like what I'm fixin' to say, but I don' see no way past it. We're goin' to have to gag that man and tie him to the bed."

Nothing could have surprised—or shocked—Lilah more. "How come?"

" 'Cause he's out'n his head, that's how come. Hollering for somebody named Marthy all the time, and thrashing about so. Right fitified, he is. Why, he's liable to fall right out'n that bed. Ye want him to do that, or call out when someone's here?"

"But, Granny—"

The old woman pulled Lilah against her thin bosom and hugged her tight. "I don' like it no better'n you do. We've had three quiet days, but someone's bound to come a-visitin', child. We got to be ready. We got to do what's best all the way 'round."

Reluctantly, Lilah agreed. The next day—which marked the fourth sunrise since Ol' Codger showed up with the giant—proved Granny right.

Mistress Chesser came with one of her younger boys to purchase spirits of bayberry bark, St. John's wort, and saw palmetto berries, as well as several of Granny's herbal penetrates, a large bottle of red bay mouthwash, and some scented candles. Because Mistress Chesser wasn't much of a talker and seldom stayed longer than it took Granny to fill her order, she was usually one of Granny's least favorite customers. Since their visitors were few and far between, Granny liked to hear all the latest goings-on from every one of them. That day, however, Lilah and Granny were glad Mistress Chesser wasn't one to tarry.

But that day, Mistress Chesser seemed in no hurry to

leave. "I'll take me a cup a that red bay tea ye're always offerin' me," she said, pulling out a settin' chair at the small, rough-hewn table and sitting herself down. While Granny set the tea to steep, Mistress Chesser turned her attention to Lilah. "Ye been out on the perairies lately?"

"No'm. Been too busy."

"Ye should take advantage of this glorious weather, Lilah. Why, it's so bodacious wondrous out there, I jes' couldn' stand to stay cooped up in the house no longer. The water lilies is a-bloomin', and the bonnets, too. I do love them yaller bonnets, don' you?"

A thump resounded from behind the quilt curtain. Lilah felt herself jerk from the inside out, and hoped Mistress Chesser hadn't noticed either the noise or her reaction to it.

She did. "Whut was that?"

Lilah attempted a nonchalant shrug, but vexation made her too stiff for the gesture to be truly effective. "Oh, prob'ly jes' one of my critters a-tryin' to get out."

"You and yer critters! I reckon that's where my Allen got off to—out there a-lookin' at yer critters. He's ferever brangin' home strays an' orphans and a-tryin' to doctor 'em up, jes' like you."

"Yes'm," Lilah said, her mind on the man-critter hidden behind the curtain. Another thump echoed through the cabin.

Mistress Chesser turned her head toward the hanging quilt, and narrowed her eyes as though she was trying to see through it. She seemed a mite narvious to Lilah, who chanced a look at the quilt. Except for the thumping, everything seemed normal.

"Ye got one of them critters in the house?" Mistress Chesser asked.

"Here's yer tea," Granny said, setting a tin cup on the table. "Maybe it'd pleasure ye to drank it out on the porch, it being such a glorious day an' you not a-wantin' to be cooped up."

Sending Granny a grateful look, Lilah picked up the cup. "I'll tote it for you," she offered, heading toward the door.

Mistress Chesser drank three cups of tea, while twelve-year-old Allen plagued Lilah with questions about puny animals. All the while, Lilah felt as caged up as one of the critters they discussed, but keeping the Chessers occupied outside was far better than having either of them in the cabin, poking their eyes and their noses where they didn't belong. She kept waiting for one of them to say something about the outlaws—a subject she didn't dare raise herself, lest she give something away and make Mistress Chesser even more suspicious about what was behind the quilt curtain. Fortunately, the subject was never mentioned.

At long last, Mistress Chesser and Allen went back to their punt boat, and Lilah and Granny went inside to see to the stranger. Almost immediately, the boy's shout brought Lilah running back out.

"I 'most fergot to give you this," Allen said, holding out the stranger's boot. Without thinking, Lilah breathed a sigh of relief and accepted the soggy boot. "Ever-where'd ye find it?"

"A-floatin' out on the lake. I tol' Mama it weren't yer'n, but I s'pose 'tis."

"It was, uh, my paw's." Lilah almost choked on the lie. "Thankee, Allen." She stood in the clearing and watched until the boy disappeared into the woods, and then she stayed a spell longer, just to make sure he didn't come back. When she finally went inside, the first thing she saw was the toe of the boot's mate sticking out from under the quilt-curtain. No wonder Mistress Chesser had looked so suspicious! Suddenly, Lilah was glad she'd lied about the boot, but to be on the safe side, she tucked the boots well under the bed.

Though not fully awake, the outlander fought the binding ropes so hard he lifted the bed off the floor every once in a while, which accounted for the thumps they'd heard earlier. Granny gave him a big dose of her tonic.

"That oughter make him sleep like a ba-ar in winter," she said. Lilah said she hoped it worked.

They had barely gotten the stranger's poultice changed, when three members of the Lee family from Billy's Island showed up. The Lees owned the only store in the swamp. Old Daniel Lee, who had sixteen offspring, sent some of his boys to Medicine Island periodically to trade staples for Granny's remedies. Before they left, Jacob Crews, who was suffering with stomach complaint, arrived, which kept the Lee brothers from leaving.

Before too long, a couple more swampers emerged from the woods. Luckily, the men preferred the sunny May weather to the confining walls of the pine cabin. They stood in knots in the clearing, propping themselves on stumps, and talked about the gang of outlaws loose in the swamp. Each of them cautioned Lilah and Granny to take "extree keer."

"We worry erbout you two womenfolk all by yer lonesome here," Jacob Crews told Lilah. That made her wonder if his stomach hurt for true, or if he'd just used the ailment as a convenient excuse to pole over to Medicine Island and assure himself all was well with her and Granny—him and all t'other men gathered in the clearing.

By the time the sun started to disappear behind the towering pines, more'n a dozen swampers representing seven families and an equal number of islands had passed through their door. It was by far one of the busiest days they'd had in recent memory—and a day they were both glad to see draw to a close.

"Whew!" Granny declared, falling into her rocking chair and laying a hand over her heart. "I know we got a monstrous heap a work left to do, but I got to ketch me a breath first."

Lilah had already grabbed a lamp and was disappearing behind the drawn quilt that hid her bed. "Just sit there and don' trouble yerself for a spell," she called. Within a heartbeat, she came barreling across the room and dropped to her knees in front of Granny's chair. She blinked back a sudden rush of tears and tried to swallow the lump in her throat.

The old woman took one of Lilah's hands and squeezed it. "Yer man-critter's dead?"

Lilah shook her head. "Nigh on to. The blisters done spread, one of his arms is a-swellin', and the wound's turnt black. I don' want him to die! What else can we do?"

Granny closed her eyes and took a deep breath, which she slowly expelled. Her withered lips moved, silently at first. Then she gave voice to words that Lilah had never heard before—strange, foreign-sounding words that rose and fell in a chanting rhythm that was almost song. Fascinated and yet frightened, Lilah watched the old woman's face twist into features she didn't recognize. Granny's shoulders started to twitch, and then her arms and trunk and legs, until her whole body was in motion. Her hand squeezed Lilah's so hard their bones cracked.

Certain Granny was suffering some kind of fatal attack, Lilah let loose the tears she'd been holding back. Her chin fell to her chest and she sobbed—deep, mournful sobs that wrenched at her innards. For the second time in her life, someone she loved dearly was dying right before her eyes. And for the second time in her life, she felt completely helpless.

She might not remember the details clearly, but she remembered how she'd felt watching her parents die. She'd desperately wanted to do something then. She desperately wanted to do something now, but she didn't know what to do.

Chapter Four

"Lilah ... Lilah! Hesh up!"

At the sound of Granny's clear, strong voice, Lilah snapped her head up and quit crying so fast she got the hiccups. Between burbles, she said, "I was so afeared. I thought ye was dying."

"Well, I ain't."

"What was ye a-doin'?"

"Callin' up the speerits. They give me a idee."

Lilah perked up then. She'd heard the old woman talk about the spirits, but this was the first time she'd been present when Granny called them up. Lilah wiped her tears away and held her breath to stop hiccupping. "For true?"

Granny nodded. "For true. Tell me, child, what would ye do for a deer that'd been snakebit?"

"Shucks, I'd go get me some moss out'n the bog and pack it over the bite."

"And the deer would get well?"

"Ever' time. Ye don' think—"

"Why not?"

Hope rushed through Lilah with gale-wind force. She jumped up, snatched a lantern off its nail by the door, and headed to the fireplace, where she lit the lantern with a straw.

"Ye be keerful out there," Granny said.

"I will." Lilah adjusted the wick, then picked up a pail to put the moss in.

"How'd you know to use bog moss?"

"I've watched wounded critters roll theirselfs in it, till it sticks to their sores. If they's real bad off, they lay down in the bog an' stay there till they's all healed up."

The old woman clucked her tongue and shook her head, then rose from her chair and ambled toward the quilt curtain as Lilah dashed out into the night.

He'd been wrong. He hadn't gone to heaven. Heaven couldn't possibly be so hot.

He'd heard circuit preachers holler about fire and brimstone all his life, but until now, Jesse Redford hadn't possessed a clue as to how truly hot fire and brimstone could get—or how thoroughly it could burn. It smoldered in his belly, as though he'd swallowed it. It scorched his lungs, parched his throat, and seared his skin. And as if that weren't enough, the fire melted the brimstone and sent it coursing through his veins. Yet, it didn't consume, just kept eating at him from the inside out.

Only hell could be this hot.

He'd tried to get away, tried to escape the bonds that held him hostage in a land that knew no mercy. But the ropes were too strong, the knots too secure. He'd called out to Martha, begged her to come down from heaven and rescue him. But she hadn't heard his pleas, just as he hadn't heard hers the day One-Eyed Jack and his band raped her, then mutilated her, and left her to bleed to death.

Afterwards, Jesse heard her cries. He heard them in the soughing wind and the caw-cawing of the crows. He heard them in the plaintive lowing of a cow caught in a berry vine, and in the mournful call of the doves at twilight. The cries resounded in his head when he was awake, and

haunted his dreams when he slept. They kept him going
when he wanted to give up and reminded him of his purpose when he lost his focus. He'd sought retribution,
hoped that bringing One-Eyed Jack to justice would as-
suage his guilt, if not his sorrow. But he hadn't lived long
enough.

This was his punishment for not being there when Martha and the boys needed him. The day of their funerals,
Jesse had tried his case and found himself guilty. His guilt
had caused him nothing but misery while he lived. Now
that guilt smoldered in his gut, and he supposed it would
continue to do so for all eternity . . .

It rained again that night and all the next day.

For Lilah, the rain brought a mixed blessing. While it
kept the swampers away, it also made it difficult for her to
get to the bogs to collect fresh moss, and that she knew
she must do if she was to save the stranger. She was preparing for another moss-gathering trip when Granny
stopped her.

"Come lookee here," she said, folding back the moss
dressing.

Lilah set her pail down and moved slowly toward the
bed, half-afraid to look. "It didn't work?"

"Didn't work?" Granny's voice practically crackled with
enthusiasm, putting Lilah's worries temporarily to rest.
"Why, I ain't never seed anythang work like this."

Lilah moved closer and stared in amazement at the dry,
clean moss. Defeat sliced through her. "It ain't workin'
a-tall," she moaned, almost as disappointed in the old
woman's glee over the giant's certain death as she was in
the inability to save him. "Soon's it quits rainin', I'll go
dig his grave. It's li'ble to take a spell, big as he is."

"No need for that. This man's gonna owe his life to
you, gal."

"I don' understand."

One of Granny's gnarled fingers gently separated the moss to reveal tiny, hairlike tubes. "See how these strands is thicker? The peat's soakin' the pizen right up and a-storin' it inside. I been studyin' on it, and I think it's actually drawin' it out. Look at how clean this part is." Her finger tapped the portion that had been next to his skin. "This moss ain't like cotton. It's more like a sponge. See how even-like it absorbs? We don' got t' change it so much. And lookee here at his wound. It ain't all black no more."

Lilah gazed at the reddened flesh, which did look a sight healthier than it had the day before. "But the moss is all dried up. Don' we need to put some wet moss on his leg?"

Granny shook her head. "Seems to work jes' as good dry—maybe better."

Lilah still wasn't convinced. "Do ye really think . . ." She bit her lip, unable to finish the question.

"He's gonna live?" Granny finished for her. "Yep, I do."

"What about the blisters? They don' look no better."

"I been studyin' on that, too. Let's start bathing him with water from the bog and giving it to him to drink, too. It can't hurt and it mought holp."

With each day-bust, the stranger appeared a bit stronger, but each bout of the fevered restlessness that continued to plague him chipped at Lilah's hope for his full recovery. She seldom left his bedside, and then only to snatch a few hours of rest, or to see to the other critters in her care. As one day bled into another, her energy waned, and she found herself nodding off in her chair from time to time.

Late one afternoon, almost a week after they started the bog moss treatment, Lilah jerked herself awake to see his one good eye open and a weak smile tugging at the corners of his dry lips.

"Ye must be hunger-bit somethin' fierce." She helped

him sit up in bed so she could spoon-feed him some
chicken broth, the first real sustenance he'd had in more
than a week.

"Ye come all 'round dyin', mister," she said, the lilt in
her voice belying her fatigue.

"I thought I was dead," he said between spoonfuls. "I'm
sorry."

She didn't know what she'd expected from the stranger,
but it wasn't an apology for living. She propped the spoon
in the tin cup and frowned at him. "Ever-what are ye sorry
for?"

"Everything. You're worn to a frazzle."

Jesse watched her self-consciously tuck several loose
strands of curly hair behind her ears, and smooth her
palms over her bodice. He wished he could take the words
back.

"I reckon I do look a fright."

"You look beautiful." The admission surprised him, for
she did honestly look a fright. Yet, she was the most beautiful person he'd ever seen. Even more beautiful than Martha. There was something about the way her curly hair sort
of stood out from her head that dredged up a memory—a
memory of a halo, of all things. "You're the angel."

Smiling, she filled the spoon and moved it toward his
mouth. "Ye're disremembering my entitlement. I s'pose
you was right addlepated when I tol' you afore. It's Lilah."

"Lilah. Lilah." He rolled the syllables around in his
mouth and relished the way the *l*'s tickled his tongue. "A
most pleasant-sounding name. Lilah."

She bobbed her head. "And what be yer'n?"

"Jesse."

She repeated his name in much the same way he'd repeated hers. "I'm awful glad ye're on the mend, Mr. Jesse.
I was some mindable about you."

Her use of language reminded him of the hills. "You
from Tennessee?"

The glow left her face and her mouth pinched up. She gave him a narrow-eyed glare. "Naw. Never been there. That where ye're from?"

"All my life."

She shifted her weight from one foot to the other and set her gaze on a point over his head. "How come ye to think I was from Tennessee?"

"Mindable. My pa used to say that when he meant worried or concerned. That is what you meant?"

"Yeah." She stood the spoon in the cup and turned to leave.

"Must you go?"

Without turning back around, she said, "I got work t' do. 'Sides, you need to rest."

"Please stay with me a spell. There's so much I want to ask you."

"It'll keep." She pushed the quilt aside and was gone.

Jesse watched the quilt fall back into place behind her and wondered what he'd said to upset or offend her. He'd surely managed one or the other, but for the life of him, he couldn't figure out why talking about the words a body used could be distasteful, not when those words weren't distasteful in themselves.

He soon tired of trying to figure it out and decided it was high time he looked at the snakebite. Whatever the angel Lilah had done had accomplished wonders. Why, he'd been at the point of death. No question about it. And death, as he remembered it, meant hell for him. That was a subject he didn't think he wanted to explore at the moment.

The simple act of folding the covers aside proved more of an effort than Jesse would have believed possible. He lay back against the pillows, waiting for his arm to stop quivering and his head to clear. How long had it been, he wondered, since the moccasin had bit him? He'd lost all track of the passing of time, but it must have been several days. Maybe longer, as weak as he was.

After a while, he sat up again and peered at his leg. Although the hanging quilt effectively closed off the light from the cabin, the fading rays seeping through the window enabled him to see the blisters on his thigh and the pink, puffy skin on each side of the clean, white bandage. It wasn't much to see, but it did assure him he still had his leg.

Losing his leg was something he hadn't stopped to consider, but he realized then that the possibility had existed. He'd known many a man who'd lost a limb when the flesh started to rot. He realized, too, that he owed Lilah more than his life. Not that he couldn't have survived without the leg. Hell, he'd survived without an eye for most of his life. But he didn't need the eye to mount his horse or chase after outlaws on foot.

He covered his leg back up and took advantage of the meager light to survey his surroundings. The small, almost square window was set high in the wall at the foot of the bed, which, though narrow, took up more than half the space in the enclosure. On his right side, the bed sat against a solid log wall. He didn't see a single crack in the chinks. Apparently, Lilah's husband was good for something. At his left shoulder was a small twig table with a plain white cloth laid over its top and hanging down on both sides. The only item on the table was a candle lamp. A slat-back straight chair with a plump cushion on its seat sat near the foot of the bed, while a tall, skinny chest-of-drawers occupied the wall space between the window and the quilt curtain.

Jesse could hear voices from the other side of the curtain. Two distinctly different voices. Both women. One voice definitely belonged to Lilah; the other sounded like a much older woman. His first thought was that Lilah had company, but the more he listened, the more certain he became that the second voice was familiar. He was sure he'd heard it often in the past few days.

He'd heard men's voices, too. He was sure he had. He recalled Lilah calling out to Bob and Ol' Codger that first day he'd seen her. While he lay there, listening for them to come in, the memory of a smelly fur coat filled his senses. Ol' Codger. The man who'd hauled him out of the cypress bay, then brought him to the cabin later. Jesse could almost see the old woman's face, but for the life of him, he couldn't put a single feature to Ol' Codger, outside of the odor and texture of animal fur.

The blue-eyed angel said he needed to rest, but Jesse had done more resting recently than he'd ever done in his life. He wasn't tired or sleepy, just weak. And bored. He wished Lilah would come back and talk to him, or at least open the quilt curtain so he could see something besides the shadows collecting in the corners.

A part of him wished, too, that he could hear what Lilah and the old woman were talking about. Jesse gave himself a good fussing for wanting to eavesdrop, but he knew he needed something to occupy his mind, lest the memories come back to haunt him.

Lilah couldn't think about anything except the stranger—Jesse, she reminded herself—being from Tennessee, but she waited until she and Granny were washing up the supper dishes before she mentioned it. Lilah hoped the clatter masked their conversation.

"He's one of them outlaws," she said, just loud enough for Granny to hear. "I know it now for sure and certain."

"What makes ye so sure?"

"He tol' me he was from Tennessee. Colin said them outlaws kilt some folks up in Tennessee. So he's got to be one of them outlaws."

With her thumbnail, Granny scrubbed at a bit of chicken

skin stuck to the inside of a pot. "Did he say he was a out-law?"

"Course not."

"Did he say what he was a-doin' in the swamp?"

"No."

"Did ye ast him?"

"No-o-o."

Satisfied that the pot was clean, Granny handed it to Lilah to rinse. "Then ye can't be so sure, can you?"

"But, Granny—" Lilah protested.

"If one of the swampers come here and tol' you a ba-ar'd kilt his pig, would ye think it was Ol' Codger done it?"

"Course not."

"How come?"

" 'Cause it could a-been any bahr. Codger ain't nearly the only one in this swamp." Lilah chewed her bottom lip for a minute. "I see yer point."

Granny swished her hand around in the dishpan and came up with a spoon. "It don' mean he *ain't* a outlaw. It jes' means he mought not be. He don' seem mean, and he's too weak to get out of bed anyways. I don' think we need to be afeared of him, jes' afeared *for* him."

"Ye reckon someone knows he's here?"

"It's possible. Mistress Chesser was awful s'picious, and there's the question of where Ol' Codger fount him and how he got there. 'Sides, he could a-been with them outlaws or anybody else when he got hisself snakebit and they left him t' die."

Lilah dried the spoon and put it away. "I s'pose I need t' go talk to him some more."

"I s'pose ye do."

Though Jesse wasn't asleep, boredom had him nodding off when the light hit his face. He opened his one good eye and smiled when he saw Lilah standing just inside the quilt curtain. The tray she held bore a lamp and a tin cup with the air coming off it.

"More chicken broth?" he asked, sniffing as he sat up and scooted back against the headboard. It didn't smell like chicken. It smelled like sassafras.

"Red bay tea," Lilah said, setting the small wooden tray on the twig table. "Granny swears by it. She dranks a cup ever' morning and ever' night and sometimes betwixt the two. Says that's why she's still a-livin'."

So, he was right about the other voice being familiar. "Ah. The old woman." He accepted the cup and nodded at the chair. "Why don't you sit down and keep me company? This tea is so hot, it's liable to take me awhile to drink it all."

It sounded like a poor excuse. She could always come back for the cup. Probably would if he didn't say something else fast, something more logical, perhaps more cordial, definitely more compelling. Jesse was forming another reason when he realized she'd already sat down. She looked so tiny, even in the small chair. And so fragile, with the lamplight bouncing off her curly blond hair and casting shadows that made her cheeks look hollow. But strength shone in her clear blue eyes. It was a strength of character, a strength of purpose, a strength far greater than anything physical. It was also a strength she hadn't yet fully realized she possessed. Jesse didn't know how he knew that, but he did.

"Ain't ye gonna drank yer tea?"

He answered by taking a sip of the greenish amber liquid. "This is good. What did you call it?"

"Red bay tea. I hope I didn' put too much honey in it for you. I like mine sweet."

"No, it's fine. Just fine." *And this conversation is getting me nowhere fast.* He lowered the cup to his lap and angled his head toward the front of the cabin. "You mentioned Granny. She lives here with you?"

"I live here with her."

Jesse allowed her comment only brief digestion before plunging ahead. "And Bob and Ol' Codger live her, too?"

She laughed. "Ever-what give you that crazy notion?"

Since he didn't feel comfortable telling her he'd spied on the cabin before he got snakebit, Jesse ignored her question and asked another himself. "But it was Ol' Codger who carried me out of the bay, right?"

A look of surprise crossed her delicate features. "Ye mem'ry that? I figured ye was too fur gone to know what was happenin' to you."

"I don't recall much of anything very well," he said, proud of himself for leading her right into giving him more specific information. But she didn't take the bait.

"Ye mem'ry Ol' Codger travelin' you here t' the cabin?"

"What?"

She leaned toward him and propped her elbows on the edge of the mattress. "Ye was in the woods, then ye disappeared, then Ol' Codger brung you here. I don't know where he fount you, or how ye got there."

"Why didn't you ask him?"

Her smile made him think of the way Martha would look at one of the boys who'd asked her a ridiculous question, but for the life of him, he couldn't find anything foolish about his question at all. Nor could he make much sense out of her answer.

"It wouldn' a-done no good. He don' never do nothin' but grunt and growl."

Everything he could think of to say to that sounded hateful to Jesse, so he didn't comment. Instead, he said, "I suppose I owe the old man my life."

Lilah frowned at that. "Partly, I s'pose. Mostly to Granny, I reckon. Usin' the moss was her idee." She pointed to the cup. "Ye ain't dranking yer tea."

He wanted to ask her more about her family, but while

he was taking another sip, she regained control of the conversation.

"I don't know how to ast you this, mister. Straight out, I s'pose. Are ye one a them outlaws?"

Jesse almost choked on the tea.

" 'Cause if ye are—"

He waved his arm at her while he tried to swallow the burn in his throat. Tears stung his eye, and he couldn't catch his breath. Lilah rushed out, then came right back with a gourd dipper filled with water. After several sips, Jesse fell back against the pillows and took a deep, cleansing breath, then another one for good measure. Still, his voice rasped when he tried to talk. "No" was all he could manage.

She handed him the gourd and sat back down. "Drank the rest of that."

Jesse wasn't sure he liked the way she ordered him to do things, but he supposed her heart was in the right place. The cool water soothed his throat and settled his breathing.

The girl picked up right where she'd left off. " 'Cause if ye are, ye're leavin' this island soon's ye can get around. And if ye're thanking about a-tryin' anythang in the meantime . . . well, I wouldn't if'n I was you."

Jesse found himself so absorbed with the lyrical quality of her voice that he didn't pay much attention to what she was saying. Thinking about her voice put him in mind of their previous conversation, when he'd mentioned his pa and Tennessee. It was then, he realized, that she'd clammed up. What could she possibly have against Tennessee, he wondered, especially since she'd never been there? Maybe it wasn't Tennessee. Maybe her aversion had something to do with fathers or language. He wanted to ask her, but he was afraid she'd clam up again.

". . . folks is afeared a Ol' Codger. I reckon they oughter be. Course, I'm not. He wouldn't ever hurt me. But I reckon he could tear a body up—if'n he taken a mind to it."

"Hm-hm," Jesse halfheartedly agreed, pulling himself back into the conversation without stopping to give her statements any real consideration.

"So, I wouldn't be thankin' about tryin' to hurt me or Granny."

"The thought never crossed my mind, I assure you. As you've already pointed out, I owe the three of you my life. Only a scoundrel would want to harm the folks he's beholden to."

As though she'd been holding her breath, her chest deflated, and a brief smile curved her lips, but her voice still carried a hint of apprehension. "Are ye a-tellin' me ye ain't no scoundrel?"

"That's what I'm saying."

"Then what was ye a-doin' in the swamp?"

Her question seemed innocent enough, yet Jesse detected accusation in it. He supposed he did owe her an explanation, but would she believe him?

"Chasing outlaws."

He watched closely for her reaction. She pinched up her lips and narrowed her eyes at him. "Tell me about the outlaws."

"They're bad men."

"All outlaws is bad men. That's why they's outlaws. What makes the ones ye're a-chasin' so bad?"

Talking about what One-Eyed Jack and his band had done to Martha and the boys hurt too bad—even after all these years—to talk about it. He closed his eye, trying to make himself focus on the bare facts. Instead, he saw three bloody corpses. His inner eye fixed on the woman's face, and for the first time in four years, it wasn't Martha he was looking at. It was another woman, a younger woman with delicate features and blond hair.

His breath left him in a *whoosh,* and fear for the angel

Lilah gripped his heart. As long as One-Eyed Jack was loose, no woman was safe. Including Lilah. He should have caught him by now. Hell, he'd had four years to bring the barbarian to justice. And he might have been successful, had other duties not interfered with the chase. He'd come so close to catching the scoundrel several times. If he'd just been a little quicker . . . If he'd just been a little smarter . . . And then, just when he thought he'd figured out Jack's next move, he'd get pulled off the trail and assigned to another case.

But not this time, he vowed. This time, he was going to stay on Jack's trail until he caught the devil. No matter how long it took. No matter if he lost his badge in the end, which was a very real possibility. He hadn't contacted Dan Whitcomb, the U.S. Marshal Jesse worked under, since he'd picked up Jack's trail over a month ago, and he didn't plan to contact Dan again until Jack and his gang were behind bars. He just hoped he could catch them before they raped and mutilated another woman . . . before they got to Lilah.

The vision of her bloody face emblazened itself on his inner eye again—and Jesse knew, deep in his gut, that the angel's life was in danger, a danger she was entirely too naïve to comprehend. What if it had been One-Eyed Jack she found snakebit? The scoundrel could be lying here, claiming to be a lawman, and she'd probably believe him. And then one night, while she and Granny were sleeping, Jack would get up and slit their throats. Jesse shuddered at the thought, then opened his eye and glared at Lilah's innocent face.

"What did you mean taking me in?"

She winced at his attack and her voice lost some of its spunk. "Ye was hurt, and I—"

"You don't know who I am. I could very well be an outlaw of the worst sort!"

"But ye said ye was a-chasin' outlaws—"

"I know what I said! And when I said it, you assumed I was a good guy. What if I was just trying to catch up with them? It was foolish of you to be so trusting. You don't know what bad men can do—"

She jumped up from the chair, her fists clenched at her sides. "I should a-left you in the bay. I should a-left you for the gators to eat."

Though her voice was low, it was laced with bitterness, anger, and regret. Bright spots of color flamed upon her cheeks, and she fairly shook with the intensity of her emotions. A part of him questioned the potency of her reaction, but his own anger, coupled with his firm belief in her gullibility, commanded his immediate attention.

"That would have been the smart thing to do," he said. "Bringing me here was dangerous."

"Ye ain't no deer," she said, turning to leave.

"Wait! What in the name of all that's holy are you talking about?"

Ignoring him, she disappeared behind the quilt curtain. And though he called to her until he was hoarse, she didn't come back.

Chapter Five

On a small island deep within the dark primeval swamp, an old woman stood before a small, bright fire. Her gnarled hands gripped the neck of a cloth bag, which she shook with the fierce strength of one long-used to rigor and hard work. The contents of the bag clanked together, the noise commingling with the chorus of toads and frogs—a veritable mélange of screams, drones, squeaks, grunts, and bleats emanating from within the tangled footings of the cypress and magnolia that edged the island, rising to echo off the tall, slender trunks of pines that grew farther inland.

The old woman lifted her painted face skyward, her rheumy eyes seeming to see right through the heavy drapes of long-haired moss, right through the thick canopy overhead, right through the murky darkness, straight to heaven. Her own voice lifted in a song as old as the swamp. The chant played high, almost wailing, then plummeted in tones low and earthy when she bowed her head and plunged her hand into the sack, immersing the withered length of her lower arm all the way to her elbow.

The hand twirled the clanking pieces, then removed a thin, straight bone from the bag. This she twisted and turned in the light of the burning peat until, ostensibly convinced of its purpose, she bobbed her warty chin and bent low, carefully placing the slender leg bone upright on the sandy earth. Again and again, she stirred the pieces, removing them one at a time, placing them with care. And all the while, her ancient voice forever rose and fell, asking the spirits to bind the bones, which were gradually gaining shape and form beside the flickering fire.

When she placed the final bone, the old woman straightened her crooked spine as best she could and moved on to the next task, that of gathering long streamers of longhaired moss. Over and over, she tugged the silvery moss from its fragile moorings, stuffing the curly strands into the sack until it was full once more.

Back to the skeleton she went, her voice now warbling like that of a songbird. The moss she draped over the bones, tucking some pieces, letting others hang as they would, using every tiny bit of moss from the bag. Then she held the sack by its gusseted bottom and shook it out. Fine white powder spilled downward, wafting like fairy dust onto the moss-covered skeleton.

The woman became a fairy herself, lifting her knees high and prancing around her creation, singing all the while. Round and round she went, with no one but the creatures of the swamp to hear her resonant voice or see the knobs of her knees slicing through the long fringes of her skirt.

After some time, she stopped dancing and sank to the earth, where she crossed her legs, pulled her bare feet under her thighs, and leaned forward until her forehead touched the sand, mere inches from the animal-like form. The low hum of her voice, which had yet to fall silent, droned on through the night.

At long last, she slowly raised her head and stretched her knotted hands outward, splaying her fingers and reaching for the skeleton, but not quite touching it. Like tiny crystals, the beads of sweat on her painted brow shimmered in the light from the fire, for neither moonlight nor *starlight could penetrate the dense growth of cypress, magnolia, and pine.*

"*Su-Wan-Nee, daughter of the sun,*" *she chanted,* "*I am La Loba, the Wolf Woman. I have searched for the bones of she-wolves among the creek beds, made dry by winter. I have sifted the sands of many islands and stirred the dry needles from many pines. Long have I searched. Long have I gathered the bones.*

"*I have mixed the colors in the ways of my ancestors, I have painted my face with red for blood and courage, with yellow for hair and laughter, with indigo for sight and wisdom. I have worn the dress of many colors and many pieces, the dress of my mother, who was La Loba before me, and her mother before her.*"

She paused, humming, lifting her all-seeing eyes heavenward again and beginning to move her hands in a side-to-side motion.

"*Su-Wan-Nee, daughter of the sun,*" *she sang,* "*pour thy spirit into this creature of bone and moss. Make her a daughter of the Eckenfinooka. Give her the courage of the wolf, the strength of the alligator, the grace of the deer, the cunning of the fox, the voice of the mockingbird, and wisdom of them all.*"

Returning her gaze to the form of moss and bone, she rose to her feet, raised her hands over her head, and sang out loud and clear. "*Su-Wan-Nee, daughter of the sun, I am La Loba.*"

As flesh began to cover the leg bones and rib bones, La Loba's voice grew stronger. "*Su-Wan-Nee, daughter of the sun, pour thy spirit into this creature of bone and moss.*"

The moss became fur, and a shaggy tail curled upward. Eyes of the darkest blue glittered from the twin holes in the skull. "*Su-Wan-Nee, daughter of the sun, blow the breath of life into this creature.*"

The creature's nostrils twitched, and the hair on its

breast trembled. *"Su-Wan-Nee, daughter of the sun, make this creature a true daughter of the Eckenfinooka."*

A shudder racked the lean frame of the creature, and it turned its head toward the deep, dark recesses of the pine forest. La Loba sang louder, and the creature crouched, then sprang, its movements as graceful as a doe's, its legs as powerful as the jaws of an alligator, its fur as slick and shiny as the water of the river on a sunny day, its body that of the too often hunted swamp wolf.

Away from the light of the fire and into the dark pine thicket, the she-wolf ran. But the light seemed to follow it, or perhaps the moon found an open space in the thick canopy. Through eyes moist with thanksgiving, La Loba watched the silvery light frolic on the gray coat, watched the she-wolf stretch her front legs upward as though it were a panther leaping into a tree, watched as the paws became hands, the claws long fingers, the legs arms. The fur became a mane of golden hair, and the mouth softened into lips and chin. The teats became breasts, the back legs lengthened, the tail disappeared, the fur fell away—and that which had been nothing but moss and bone, now looked back at La Loba with eyes that were filled with apprehension.

"Go, my daughter," La Loba cried. "You were born of creature and have no need to learn their ways. Now you are human and must learn the ways of mankind. Go and learn well. Su-Wan-Nee has breathed her spirit into you, and she will protect you and mother you until that time when you shall return to me."

Understanding replaced the apprehension, and the young woman turned and fled into the forest.

"The dream come to me again last night."

As she always did when presented with this news, Granny merely nodded and smiled.

"Ever'time it comes," Lilah continued, "La Loba looks

more like you, and the woman she makes from the bones
and moss looks more like me."

Again, Granny nodded.

"And this time, I heared ever' single word La Loba
said. Some a them words sounded a awful lot like the ones
you was a-usin' when ye called up the speerits. What does
it mean?"

The old woman stirred her tea. "In time ye will know."

Lilah sighed. "That's what ye always say. I wish I could
tell the dream the way I see it, but I don' have the words
in me."

"Ye would if'n ye could read."

"I know I'm a dull-wit." The admission hurt Lilah far
worse than she'd thought it would.

Granny stretched an arm across the narrow table and
laid her gnarled hand over Lilah's. "Nay," she said with
gentle but firm assurance. "The good Lord give ye a full
measure a smarts. Book-learnin' don' make a body wiser.
Ye've tol' the dream to me well, child."

"But I can't tell it the way I see it."

"I want ye t' promise me something."

"Ye know I'd do anything for you."

Granny shook her head. "Ye ain't gonna like this, child.
Ye ain't goin' to want to promise me, but ye got to. 'Sides,
this ain't for me. It's for you."

Lilah waited, at once both eager to hear what the old
woman had on her mind, and dreading it. With her free
hand, Granny stirred her tea some more, then set the spoon
aside. Her other hand pressed down against Lilah's, not
hard, just warm and reassuring. When the old woman
spoke again, the words seemed to be pulled from her
throat, as though she didn't want to give voice to them.

"I've tol' you afore, yer maw thought ye oughter leave
the swamp."

"No, Granny!"

"Please. Let me have my say."

Lilah clamped her lips together, and though she tried to open her heart and her mind to Granny's request, she made little progress. She wasn't leaving, no matter what reason the old woman could give her.

"She thought ye oughter leave the swamp and go stay with yer maw's sister in Homerville." Granny's brow furrowed. "I disremember her name."

"Agnes." Lilah said the name with distaste. Once, long ago, Agnes had come to visit. Despite the years, Lilah remembered her aunt well. She was a tall woman, taller even than Paw, and with large, bulging, almost lidless eyes that reminded Lilah of a snake. The thought of sharing a roof with Agnes gave Lilah the heebee-jeebies.

"Wouldn't ye like to have some book-learnin'?"

Lilah thought about the way Jesse had talked to her, like she didn't have good sense, and wondered if he'd like her better if she could read. She looked down at the britches she was wearing, and thought about what Maw had told her about the way fine ladies dressed. She did want to know how to read and write and talk properly. Sometimes she even dreamed about living in town, riding in a carriage and going to afternoon teas and Saturday night socials and church on Sunday. But not if it meant leaving Granny. And not if it meant living with Aunt Agnes.

"Ye can learn me ever'thing you know. This time, I'll try harder. I'll learn all the yarbs and roots. I promise I will. Jest please don' send me to Aunt Agnes."

"What're ye gonna do when I'm gone, child? Marry up with Colin and raise a passel of younguns?"

Lilah found that prospect almost as repulsive as going to live with Aunt Agnes. "No," she murmured, feeling suddenly lost.

"A body has a need to belong," Granny said. "Right now, we'uns belong to each other. Who ye gonna belong to when I'm gone?"

"I'll belong t' myself."

"That's a awful lonely belonging. I know, better'n most." Her dark eyes glittered with unshed tears, and her hand trembled upon Lilah's. "Ye're already eighteen out. In a few years, it'll be too late. Ye need to leave the swamp now, while ye're still young."

"I ain't a-leavin' you, Granny."

A look of resignation mixed with a measure of sadness came over the old woman. "Life on this here earth don' be everlastin'. When I'm gone, promise me ye'll go to Homerville. See what the world outside the Okefinoke is like. If'n ye don' like it, if'n it don' suit, then ye can come back. This swamp ain't a-goin' nowheres."

Lilah felt torn. She loved Granny Latham with all her heart. Until she came to live with Granny, she hadn't known a body could love another so much when the two wasn't blood kin. She'd been sincere when she told Granny she'd do anything for her. But Granny, in all her wisdom, was asking Lilah to do something for herself, something that went totally against the grain. If she promised, then she'd have to do it.

"Promise me ye'll give it a try."

"I ain't a-makin' promises I mought not keep. I'll study on it." That seemed to satisfy Granny, at least for the moment.

About that time, the man who called himself Jesse started raising a rookus. After he'd upset Lilah so the night before, Granny had insisted on being the one to change his dressing, and Lilah had put off seeing about him that morning. Confronting the outsider now, however, seemed mild in comparison to Granny's attempt to extract Lilah's promise to leave the swamp.

"I spect the man-critter's gettin' hunger-bit," Lilah said.

Granny scooted her chair back from the table. "I'll brew him up a cup a tea. Ye toast some a that sodie bread. Not too much. His belly ain't ready for real food yet."

Moments later, Lilah carried a tray in to the stranger.

This time, when she pushed the quilt curtain back, she didn't close it. Avoiding the stranger's gaze, she set the tray down on the twig table, then moved to the side wall and opened the shutters at the window.

"Ah!" he sighed. "Fresh air, sunshine, and food. What more could a man ask for?"

"A clean bed and a empty chamber pot," Lilah quipped. "It's beginnin' to smell plumb ripe in here." Still not looking at him, she slid the enamel jar out from under the bed, picked it up by the handles on its sides, and hauled it outside. When she returned, the outsider was sitting up in bed, sipping his tea. The toast had disappeared, all but a few crumbs sprinkled over the dishtowel, which he'd laid across his lap. A wide grin dimpled his cheeks beneath a beard that got darker and heavier by the day.

"Ye liked the toast?"

"Immensely. Did you make it?"

Lilah replaced the lidded pot, then folded the dishrag with the crumbs inside, and tucked it into her apron pocket. "Granny made the bread. I jest browned it a bit."

"Well, I'll just have to tell Granny how much I enjoyed it. She and I had a nice little chat last night. She seems a right knowledgeable woman."

"She is." Lilah wondered what all Granny had told him. Suddenly, she wished she'd stayed in the cabin while the old woman changed Jesse's dressing, instead of going outside to tend to her critters. There was no telling what Granny had told him—and no certainty Granny would divulge the entire contents of their conversation. To cover her agitation, Lilah surveyed the wrinkled bed linens, then she flipped the covers back with more energy than she'd intended.

Immediately, she saw her error and felt the blush of embarrassment on her cheeks, yet she was unable to remove her gaze from the spot where his long, hairy legs met his hips, especially the spot his rumpled shirt failed to cover.

She swallowed hard and muttered, "Are ye able to get up?"

"I think so," he said in measured tones, a hint of amusement in his voice, "so long as I don't have to go very far."

"Jest to the chair."

As Jesse slid his legs off the mattress, he fought the urge to laugh out loud—and to voice the thought that was uppermost in his mind that moment: *You'd think the girl had never seen a man in the altogether before!* But such a thought was ridiculous. After all, she was married.

Or was she? When he'd questioned her about Bob and Ol' Codger living there, she'd asked him where he got such a ridiculous notion. He'd tried to get Granny to talk about Lilah last night, but the old woman had adroitly skirted each of his questions. Maybe he'd been wrong about Lilah all along. There was only one way to find out. His previous visits with her had taught him to tread lightly. He'd have to be just a bit devious.

"Where's Bob?" he asked, settling himself in the chair and stretching his wounded leg out straight. Trying to bend it hurt like the devil, but at least it had accepted his weight, the slight amount he'd put on it anyway.

She hesitated just the slightest bit, but it was enough to make him doubt the veracity of her response even before she voiced it. "How should I know?"

"But you do know, don't you?"

"Not really." She folded the cover and sheets into a neat bundle. "He goes where he wants to go. I spect he's stretched out somewheres, sound asleep."

"In the daytime?"

Gathering the linen up against her bosom, she turned to look at him as though he'd lost his mind. "Wouldn't you, if'n ye'd spent the whole night a-huntin' for food?"

While he pondered that, she trotted away, then came back momentarily with a neat stack of clean sheets and a fresh blanket. When she popped a sheet open, the fragrance of blue-eyed grass filled the room. Surprised yet pleased to learn that this tiny flower so abundant in Little River Gorge back home also grew in the swamp, Jesse closed his eyes and took a deep breath. He realized that the longer he stayed in the Okefinoke, the more things reminded him of the Smoky Mountains—the early morning mist, the quaint language, the suspicious, clannish nature of the residents, and now the flowers.

When he opened his eyes, Lilah was tucking the final corner of the bottom sheet. "Did he kill anything?"

"Did who kill anything?"

"Bob."

"How should I know?" she snapped.

"You haven't talked to him this morning, then?"

Lilah whirled around, planted her hands on either side of her waistline, and stood staring at him for a moment, her mouth agape. "That fever must a-burnt yer brain, mister."

Jesse couldn't see anything the least bit peculiar in his question, but he decided to try a different angle. "I need to hire a guide, someone who has a boat. Can you recommend someone?"

"Depends on how come ye to need one." She went back to making the bed.

"For one thing, I need to get out of this swamp."

"Ye ain't yet ready to travel."

She was, by far, the most exasperating female he'd ever met. Jesse bit back a retort and tried again. "When I am ready to travel, Mistress Bennett, I shall require the services of a guide. Since you know far more about the swampfolk than I do, I'd appreciate hearing your recommendation."

"How come ye t' entitle me mistress?"

He shrugged. "Just common courtesy, I suppose."

"Would be, if'n there was a Mr. Bennett to go with it. There ain't."

So! She wasn't married. He wondered, though, if maybe there hadn't been a Mr. Bennett at one time. Jesse gave the girl a long, hard look, and decided she might be old enough to be a widow. Sometimes womenfolk back home were married and had babies before their sixteenth birthdays. He told himself he didn't honestly care one way or the other, except that her admission still left a big question in his mind. "What about Bob?"

"What about him?"

"If he isn't your husband, then who is he?"

She dropped the blanket and collapsed in a fit of giggles on the bed. Between crackles, she howled, "Husband! He thinks Bob's my husband!"

Jesse was quickly losing patience with her. "Devil's washboard, woman! What in tarnation is so funny about that?"

When she sobered enough to talk, she gasped out, " 'Cause he's a bobcat."

A bobcat! That possibility was one Jesse had never considered. As he considered it now, another possibility struck him. "If Bob's a cat, then what is Old Codger?"

"A bahr."

She laughed again, and this time, Jesse laughed with her, long and hard. So long and hard Granny came to investigate. "He thought Bob was a man," Lilah tittered.

"Worse than that," Jesse added. "I thought he was her husband. I wanted to hire him as a guide."

Granny joined in the merriment.

"And I thought Old Codger was a man, too," Jesse said. With this verbal acknowledgment, his laughter skidded to a halt. He wiped the tears from his eye, and pierced Lilah with a soul-searching gaze. "You said Old Codger brought me here."

Granny stopped hooting and Lilah gulped on a giggle, then started hiccupping, so Granny answered for her. "He did."

The incredulity of it all walloped Jesse with a good measure of awe, mixed with a bit of horror and a dash of repugnance. A bear? First, the animal had dragged him out of the bay. Later, the critter had picked him up and carried him to the cabin. That meant the bear had walked upright. Jesse supposed that was possible, if not quite natural. But the bear had been so gentle! So human-like. It was too much to comprehend all at one time.

"A bear," he murmured. "Old Codger is a bear."

"Shore is," Granny said. "A big 'un, too. Biggest black ba-ar I've seed in all my born days, and I've seed many a ba-ar." For the first time since she came in, she looked at Jesse, then moved closer to him and yanked his shirt down over his lap. "We'uns got t' get ye some clothes, mister. Yer britches was ruint, and that shirt ain't got too many more wearin's left in it."

Jesse noted that she didn't mention the lack of undergarments. He wasn't about to, either.

"Them thangs you was a-wearin' looked store-boughten to me."

"They were."

"Well, there don' be no store anywheres 'round here, leastways none that sells clothes, so ye're gonna have to settle for homemade. Lilah there ain't too handy with a needle, and I ain't never stitched no britches for a man, but I reckon I can try."

"I surely will appreciate the effort, ma'am. And I'll be glad to pay you."

That got Granny and Lilah both to laughing again. "What ye thankin' on payin' us with?" Lilah asked. "Matches? Terbacki?"

She definitely had a point. He'd used his pocket change to buy the tobacco and his folding money was in his saddlebags, along with virtually everything else in the world that he owned. Or used to own. Besides, he doubted Granny and Lilah ever needed much cash. Nevertheless, his code of honor refused to allow him to accept the clothes without some sort of payment.

"Maybe you've got some kind of work I can do, while I'm laid up," he suggested.

Granny studied on that while Lilah finished making up the bed. Suddenly, the old woman's dark eyes took on a glint, and she almost smiled. "You speak right good," she said.

Jesse nodded, wondering where she was going with that observation.

"You got any book-learnin'?"

"Yes, ma'am. I can read both English and Latin and cipher with the best of them, but I never was very good at history or geography."

Granny slapped her thigh and a wide smile wreathed her wrinkled face. "Then ye can learn Lilah to read."

That was the last request he expected her to make, and he wasn't the least bit certain he could manage it. "I've never taught anyone to read," he said, hearing the reluctance in his voice and hoping he didn't sound too unappreciative. It wasn't just the teaching that bothered him. It was mostly trying to deal with Lilah. Being in the same room with her for a matter of minutes was enough to drive a man to drink. Spending hours with her was unthinkable. He flashed Granny a smile he hoped was charming. "Perhaps there's something else I can do."

"Yes," Lilah agreed. "Thank of something else, Granny."

Despite his aversion to the idea, Jesse winced inwardly at the hopefulness in Lilah's voice, his pride stung. But the old woman seemed to have her mind made up. Granny pursed her lips and shook her head hard enough to loosen one of the braids from the knot they made at her nape.

"Ye ain't worth much right now, won't be for another week or so, till ye heal up proper. A-learnin' the gal to read is the absolutest perfectest thang for ye to do. Ye can start today."

"I'm not staying in this bed for another week," he said. Granny pursed her lips and didn't comment. Lilah scrubbed her bare toe on the floor and looked off toward the window. "Besides, I don't have any books or other teaching materials," Jesse continued, hoping Granny didn't have any either. After all, he reasoned, if she could read, she would have taught Lilah already. Logically, two women who couldn't read wouldn't possess any books. There was one book, however, that virtually every family owned, whether they could read or not. A bible. His heart sinking, he watched Granny retrieve hers from the mantel-shelf.

"This be the onliest book ye need," she said, laying it reverently on the twig table. "Lilah, ye go feed yer critters, whilst I holp Mr. Jesse wash off. Then he can start learnin' ye to read."

Chapter Six

"Quit squirming and pay attention!"

Lilah winced at Jesse's harsh tone and tried to put her mind back on the lesson. She wanted to learn to read, honestly she did. And if this man could teach her, then maybe Granny would stop pestering her about Aunt Agnes and Homerville. But this man discomfitted her—bad. She wanted nothing more than to be as far away from him as she could get.

She reckoned that wasn't exactly his fault. He couldn't help having only the one good eye. He hadn't done one thing or said one thing to make her believe he was one of the outlaws, yet a man his size wearing a black eye patch haunted her dreams. He didn't choose to be naked under the covers, but Lilah knew he was. Every time her gaze hit the counterpin, she saw right through it, saw his long, muscled legs and the patch of curly black hair between them. That patch of hair and the private parts it clung to frightened her almost as much as the one-eyed man in her nightmares—frightened her and exhilarated her at the same time, which served to thoroughly confuse her.

His voice, not quite so gruff as before, pulled her out of her ruminations.

"What's this letter?" He tapped one of the symbols he'd written with charcoal on a piece of faded newsprint

Granny had taken out of the cupboard. The paper was old and yellow with two corners missing and a long brown streak down the middle, but it was the only paper in the house.

She looked at it hard and tried to remember what he'd called it. "I think it's a *b*."

He blew out a loud breath. "No, Lilah. It's a *p*. The stem goes down, not up."

"I don't know how ye can spect me t' learn all them letters in a heartbeat."

"We've been at this an hour," he said, his tone growing more impatient by the minute, "and we haven't made it through the lower case letters yet."

She stretched her eyes wide open and stared at him. "You mean there's more?"

"Twenty-six in all, but each has both upper and lower case symbols."

Lilah frowned then, quite confused. "Case? The onliest case I know about don' have nothin' t' do with letters."

Some of the irritation left his face, and his voice lost a bit of its agitation. "Then we're expanding your vocabulary, aren't we?"

"I got all the words in me I need t' know!" she protested, knowing full well that just that morning she'd told Granny she didn't have the words she needed to describe her dream.

"But can you read and write those words, Miss Priss? 'Cause if you can, you sure as thunder don't need me!"

Lilah didn't think she'd ever seen thunder as black as his face was at that moment. "Oh, all right," she relented. "Ye've made yer point. That there next letter's a *q,* and then it's *r* . . ."

As she recited the remainder of the alphabet, the thunder gradually left his face. After a while, she got so wrapped up in what he was teaching her she forgot about feeling uncomfortable around him. When Granny came bustling in with a tray of chicken soup and toast, Lilah couldn't believe it was already midday. "Where'd the mornin' go?" she murmured to herself.

"Did ye learn a passel a words?" Granny asked.

"Not yet, but I memorized the whole alphibet, both cases, and I learned *cat* and *bahr* and *swamp* and about a dozen other words, and we ain't even got to the bible yet."

Granny smiled real big at Lilah, then turned her attention to the stranger-turned-teacher. "I been workin' on yer britches, Mr. Jesse. Oughter have 'em done by the time the sunball goes down. Mornin' soon, ye can start stretchin' yer legs a mite."

"Thank God for that. I'm growing mighty weary of this bed." Jesse accepted the dishtowel from Granny, who waited for him to tuck it into the neck opening of his shirt before she set the tray on his lap. "Mornin' soon," he said, drawing out the *o*'s. "That's another expression I'd almost forgotten."

"What d'ye call it?" Lilah asked, twisting around in the chair so that she faced Jesse.

"Tomorrow morning. But I like *mornin' soon* so much better."

Lilah remembered that he'd said his pa used to say *mindable*. "Did yer pa say *mornin' soon?*"

His mouth full of soup, Jesse nodded. He swallowed, wiped his mouth with the towel, and smiled real wistful-like. "His use of language closely resembles yours."

"Was he a swamper?"

"No. A mountain man."

"Tell me about the mountings, Mr. Jesse. I ain't never knowed nothin' but swamp land. Is the mountings right big, like I've heared?"

"C'mon, child," Granny said, "and eat yer meal afore it gets cold. Ye can pester Mr. Jesse with all them questions later."

Somewhat reluctantly, Lilah followed Granny to the table. There was a passel more questions she wanted to ask the stranger, but she figured they could wait till they'd both finished eating. After all, they had the rest of the day and several more besides to talk about the mountains and Jesse's pa and all the other things Lilah wanted to hear and learn about from the foreigner.

For the first time since the night Ol' Codger brought the stranger to the cabin, Lilah was glad the man had come into their lives. She pondered this as she ate her soup, and she found herself wishing he didn't have to leave.

The day was warm and humid, with a mass of dark clouds gathering in the south. When Lilah came back from the rain barrel with water for dishwashing, she left the door standing open, so what little breeze there was could blow in. Granny, who had moved back to the porch to resume her sewing, told Lilah she'd holler if anyone came. Just to be on the safe side, Lilah pulled the quilt curtain almost closed.

"Sorry to have to do this to you," she said, standing in the narrow space between the curtain and the partial wall, "but we'uns got to take percautions."

"I understand. We wouldn't want your neighbors to think badly of you and Granny."

"Oh, 'tain't that a-tall! It's that swampfolk knows what t'other outlaws done up in Tennessee. If'n they find you here, they's li'ble to kill you first and ast questions later."

He frowned. "The *other* outlaws? Do you still think I'm one of them?"

His question made her uncomfortable, and she dropped her gaze to the floor. "Ye said ye was a-chasin' 'em."

"*Chasing*, Lilah! Why do you think I was chasing them?"

She shrugged, her heart and mind in a turmoil. "I reckon 'cause ye wanted t' ketch up with 'em."

"Yeah, I want to catch up with them. But not to join them."

She ventured a glance at his face, which mirrored his anger—and his disappointment. "Then how come was ye chasin'—" The truth hit her head on, but Lilah refused to believe it. Her mouth fell open and she shook her head. "Naw. Ye ain't the marshal."

"And why not?" Now he sounded truly wounded.

" 'Cause marshals has both their eyes." She said it without thinking first and felt herself blush with shame. "That must a-sounded plumb ignert," she admitted, hoping he didn't hold her hasty words against her. "If ye be a marshal, where's yer star? All marshals has them stars. Elsewise, anyone could say they was a marshal, and there wouldn't be no proof in it one way or t'other."

Jesse sighed. "I lost my badge. And my pistol and my rifle and my saddlebags. But I am a deputy U.S. marshal."

Though a part of her continued to rebel at the idea, Lilah conceded the possibility that he was telling the truth. Still . . .

"How'd ye lose yer marshalin' star?"

"The Crews boys convinced me to leave my horse on Cowhouse Island, so I was carrying my saddlebags and my rifle and wearing my pistol. My badge was on my vest, which I had taken off and put in my saddlebags."

Though Lilah hadn't ever seen a horse, she'd heard about them. But she didn't know what saddlebags were, so she asked him. In the end, he had to describe a saddle, bridle, and reins, as well as saddlebags, and explain to her how they were all used.

"Anyway," he continued, "on my way here, I got into water up to my armpits. There I was, trying to hold my rifle, holster, and saddlebags up over my head to keep them dry, and I guess I stepped into a hole. All I know is one minute I was slogging through the water, and the next thing I knew I was in it over my head. I dropped everything."

"How come ye didn't jest dive down and get it?"

"Do you know how dark the water is in this swamp?"

"But ye was standin' right there."

He shook his head. "I panicked. All I could think about was getting my head out of the water, and by the time I did, I didn't know where I'd gone under. I looked for a while, but it was getting late and the alligators were waking up, so I figured I'd better get to a little island I could see up ahead and resume my search the next morning."

"And ye never did find yer things."

"No, but the gators did." A wry smile curved his lips. "At least, they found the holster and the saddlebags."

"Ye saw 'em?"

"Yep. When the first one surfaced with my holster in his jaws, I shouted for joy. Stupid me, I honestly thought he was going to bring it to me. Then another one popped up with the saddlebags, and the two went swimming off into oblivion."

Lilah laughed at that. "If'n ye'd had a boat, ye wouldn't a ever lost nothin'." That reminded her that he'd been on Cowhouse Island. "How come ye didn't get a boat or a canoe from the Crewses?"

"They tried to tell me I needed both a boat and a guide, but I wouldn't listen. I guess I didn't want to believe this swamp is so big. I figured it wouldn't take more than a day to find Scurlock and his gang. Lord, was I wrong!"

"Them men ye was a-chasin'. What'd they do to put theirselfs on the wrong side of the law?"

Something akin to pain washed over him, pinching the corners of his mouth, turning his eye to a grayish green and flattening the mellow out of his voice. "What did they do?" He closed his eye and the glimmer of tears dewed his dark lashes. "What did they not do?"

Whatever they'd done obviously affected him deeply. It

was just as obvious to Lilah that he didn't want to talk about it. Quietly, she stepped back and slipped the quilt all the way to the wall.

If she needed proof of the man's innocence, she supposed his tears provided it. And yet, she still found it difficult to believe the stranger was the marshal Colin had mentioned, the one who'd talked to Cyrus McIntyre and the Crews boys up on Cowhouse Island. Although she'd never met a real lawman before, she'd heard many a story about sheriffs and marshals and revenuers from the swampmen. According to the tales, lawmen were almost as hard and mean as outlaws, sometimes harder and meaner. This man who called himself Jesse didn't seem hard or mean a-tall.

Lilah was pouring hot water over the dishes in the pan when she heard a male voice holler from the woods. Hollering a greeting upon approach was a custom swampers had adopted to avoid getting themselves shot. Course, everyone knew she and Granny didn't keep no weapons, but folks generally hollered anyway—and not, Lilah suspected, out of courtesy as much as out of just plain liking to hear themselves holler. Otherwise, they wouldn't stand in their clearings and holler of a morning and an evening, and that's what most of 'em did. In some spots in the Okefinoke, you could hear a whole chorus of hollerin' at those times.

This voice sounded like Colin's. If it was, she could forget her afternoon lesson with Jesse. Muttering under her breath, Lilah dashed to the back of the cabin and poked her head around the quilt curtain. The stranger was lying on his side with his back to her.

"Psst! Mr. Jesse!" she hissed. When he didn't budge, she assumed he was asleep and hoped he had enough sense to be quiet when he woke up. There was no time to wake him up and warn him now. Already, she could hear footfalls on the porch and Granny's voice raised in welcome. She stepped away from the quilt and hurried back to the dishpan.

Sure enough, it was Colin Yerby she'd heard. He was asking Granny if Miz Lilah was to home. Having him inside the cabin all afternoon wouldn't do a-tall. She wiped her hands on her apron and hurried out to the porch to cut him off.

"Why, if it ain't Colin Yerby," she crooned, amazed at how sweet her voice sounded when in reality she felt quite fractious. "What brung ye to Medicine Island today?"

"The fancy of yer comp'ny, a-course," he returned, a broad smile wreathing his not unpleasant face. He thrust a fistful of paintroot stems at her, seemingly unmindful of the fact that his lack of care had dislodged most of the tiny white blossoms from their tight clusters.

"Thankee, Colin," Lilah said, taking the tangled bunch from him and picking off the lower leaves, while trying to think of some way to get rid of this unwelcome visitor.

"Ain't ye goin' to put 'em in water?" Colin asked.

Seeing no way out, yet certain Colin would follow her inside, Lilah threw a silent appeal to Granny, who was busy making a bundle of the butternut fabric she'd been stitching. Lord, Lilah thought, if Colin realized that the garment was men's britches, they'd really be in for it.

"Give me them flowers," Granny said, taking the bunch from Lilah. "I was a-goin' inside anyways."

Lilah breathed a bit easier, then realized Granny's help had only served as a temporary solution to her problem. She had to get Colin away from the cabin and she had to do it fast, before he invited himself in for a cup of red bay tea and stayed all afternoon again. That prospect was entirely too chancy. One moan from the stranger, or even a loud snuffle in his sleep, could mean his death. She remembered how much noise he'd made when Mistress

Chesser was there, and how suspicious the woman had been.

Granted, she and Granny might be able to stop Colin from hurting the outsider, but it wouldn't take him long to round up some of the other swampmen. And if she had so much difficulty believing the outsider was a marshal, there was no way the suspicious swampmen would ever be convinced.

"Let's go fishin'," she said.

"What?"

Lilah almost laughed out loud at Colin's stunned expression. He'd asked her to go fishing with him numerous times before, but she'd never accepted his offer. Suggesting the activity herself must truly appear odd, but it was all she could think of. She ignored his gaping mouth and plunged ahead.

"I been a-wantin' to ketch me a big ol' warmouth. They's too big for my trap. Ya got t' go out in the lake to ketch a warmouth. I've been afeared to go by my lonesome with them outlaws on the loose, what'n'all. Then today, I been a-hearin' the woodpeckers jest a-chatterin' in the piney woods. That's a sure sign the fish is bitin', and now I'm a-rarin' to go. Will ye take me?"

He gave her a partial bow and smiled shyly. "A-course I will, Miz Lilah. I'd be proud t' take ye fishin'."

"Good." She took his elbow and headed him toward the steps, but he balked.

"Don' ye want to tote a bite to eat, Miz Lilah? Fishin' makes me hungry."

"We'll pick some huckleberries when we get out on the lake. They oughter be a-ripenin', and I've had me a hankerin' for high bush huckleberries."

Colin chuckled and started walking. "Sounds to me like ye've got more'n yer share of hankerin's, Miz Lilah. Be there another sich ye oughter tell me about?"

Lilah chanced a look at Colin's face. "Ye can quit yer smirkin', Colin. I ain't a-askin' for no kisses."

"Now how'd ye know I was a-thinkin' 'bout kisses? Maybe I had something else in mind."

His light, teasing voice didn't fool Lilah. Colin always had kissing on his mind. And maybe some other things, too. Looking at the stranger had set her mind sniffing at a trail of notions far beyond anything she'd ever imagined, notions Lilah hadn't even fully acknowledged. She'd never thought much about womanish things, and she didn't aim to start now. Not with Colin Yerby, noways. She had to set him straight, before he took her silence as acquiescence.

"If'n ye don' want to pick huckleberries and ketch some fish, then ye can take yer worthless hide home and leave me be."

Colin hooted and slipped an arm around her shoulders in a way that was a mite too familiar to Lilah. "Ye're a reg'lar spitfire, Miz Lilah. I swear ye are. That's one a things I like about ya." He squeezed her closer to his side and kissed the top of her head. "One of a whole passel a things."

Lilah jerked loose and traipsed ahead of him. "I ain't a-razzin' ye," she said, turning her head and throwing the words over her shoulder. "Happen ye don' believe me, then ye need to get on home, like I said. Me, I'm goin' a-fishin' and a-berryin'. If'n ye want t' come along, ye'll have to behave yerself."

He pulled a straight face and barked, "Yes, ma'am!" Though she could hear the grin in his voice, she reckoned she could handle Colin well enough. She reckoned she'd have to.

Jesse worried his bottom lip. It was good dark and still Lilah hadn't returned. Several times over the past couple of hours he'd stifled the urge to call out to Granny, who'd told him not to concern himself when she'd brought him a cup of tea and his new britches.

"That gal-woman knows this swamp," she'd said, "and ye can rest assured Bob or Ol' Codger is a-watchin' out for her. One or both a them rascals follers her ever'where she goes. They won't let nothin' happen to her. Now, put these britches on, and let's see if happen they fit."

They did fit. Perhaps too well. Granny stood back and rubbed her warty chin as she inspected her handiwork. "I wouldn't bend over if'n I was you," she advised, "but I reckon they'll serve till I can stitch up another pair."

"I'll be glad to have a change," he said, taking care to sound grateful for her labor, even if it was less than satisfactory.

"I told ye I hadn't never made a pair of men's britches afore. Only made 'em for Lilah. Yer'n needs some extree room up front I hadn't counted on."

For the first time, Jesse realized that Granny probably wasn't the widow he'd assumed she was, but that was none of his business. Getting better real fast was all he needed to concern himself with at present. While he was out of bed and partially dressed, he decided to try walking. Taking short, painful steps, he made it to the quilt curtain before Granny stopped him.

"Where d'ye think ye're a-goin'?"

"Just around the cabin."

"Not till Lilah gets back and we know for sure Colin's gone. Can't take no risks."

Jesse scowled at her, but he got back in the bed.

"Talkin's chancy, too," she said. "They oughter be back anytime now, so ye keep quiet and stay put."

He'd promised he would, but that was a long time ago. He was bored and hungry and ready to exercise his legs again.

But most of all, he was worried about Lilah.

It was the first time he'd been personally concerned about anyone's welfare since the day he'd buried Martha.

"Ye got us in one fine mess, Colin Yerby," Lilah fussed. "How're ye aimin' on gettin' us out?"

"I'll think a something," he replied, but his voice lacked conviction.

The two sat in his canoe, each end firmly entangled in separate webs of huckleberry vines and each side flanked by large gators. They'd been trying to get loose for what seemed like an eternity, with Lilah working at one end and Colin at the other. Several times, they'd freed one end, only to push the canoe deeper into the opposite tangle.

In the meantime, the sun had all but disappeared, leaving the cavern beneath the overhanging vines in virtual darkness. The hoot of a barred owl camped in a tree nearby seemed to be the signal for the frogs to start their croaking and squeaking and chirping, and the katydids to start their droning. They filled the swamp with their voices, hushed occasionally to enjoy the echo, then started up their chorus again.

"If ye'd a-listened to me," Lilah said, "we'd a-been all right. That little ol' bahr weren't goin' to hurt us. He didn't have nothin' on his mind 'ceptin' gettin' hisself a mess a huckleberries, same as us."

Colin snorted. "That warn't no little ol' bahr. That there was a great *big* bahr. I was jest bein' polite, tryin' to get out'n his way."

"Yer jest bein' polite was what got us snagged."

"If ye'd brung some real food like I ast you to, we wouldn't a-been pickin' berries, now would we?" he countered. "We'd a-been out in the middle a the lake ketchin' warmouth. And we'd a-been home by now."

"Well, I didn't and we didn't and we ain't." In her voice, Lilah heard not only her irritation at Colin and her frustration at their situation, but also her near surrender, and she silently vowed to stand up to this bit of adversity.

"I can get us out."

He'd said that before. About a dozen times before. But every time he tried, he managed to get them more firmly ensnared. "You ain't never goin' t' get us out lessen ye get out'n this here canoe," she said.

"And get et by one a them gators?"

"They's jest restin'."

"If ye're so dadblamed shore, then why don' ye get out?"

"I'm studyin' on it."

Colin snorted again. Lilah thought hard about hitting him, but she couldn't see how that would solve anything.

"Gators ain't like rabbits and coons and deer," he said. "Jest 'cause ye get along with critters better'n most folks, don' mean them gators won't eat ya."

"I know that. Light the lamp."

"How come?"

"Colin Yerby, don' argufy with me, jest do it."

"But I barely got enough coal oil to see me home."

Lilah curved her hands into tight fists and pushed her frustration down. "If we don' get out'n here, you won't be a-goin' home tonight, will ye? Truth is, if either one a them gators wanted to have us for supper, he'd a-done flipped this canoe over with his tail. Course, we could jest keep sittin' here, a-waitin' for one of 'em to get hunger-bit." She paused long enough for that to sink in. "Light the lamp."

He did. Lilah took the lantern from him and held it at arm's length over first one side of the canoe and then the other. As she'd expected, the light glistened on the ridged backs of several more gators. The one that was lying closest to shore opened his jaw wide and bellowed. Another bellow sounded from across the lake, and then another and another, until the air resounded with their bellows.

"Lookee what ye done now," Colin grumbled. "Got the whole lot of 'em stirred up right good and proper."

Lilah handed the lantern back, unfastened her skirt, and pushed it down over her hips. Even over the loud bellowing, she heard Colin's sharp intake of breath.

"What're ye a-doin'?"

"I'm goin' in the water," she said, hoping her voice sounded more confident than she felt. She set her jaw and looked up at Colin, whose face had gone quite white. "The longer we set here, the wider awake them gators is goin' to get. And the hungrier." She slipped her skirt down her legs and over her feet, then folded it lengthwise. Folding it over again, she wrapped it around her rib cage and tied it.

"Ye can't do it," Colin said.

"Yes, I can. I can and I will." Lilah untied the thin muslin strip that held her petticoat closed and wiggled out of it, too. No man had ever seen her bare legs before, except maybe her paw, but this wasn't a time to be troubled with modesty.

"I ain't goin' to let you."

She folded the petticoat and wrapped and tied it around her hips. "Ye can't stop me."

"Lilah, please," he begged, using her name without the requisite title for the first time ever. "One of them gators is li'ble to snap you in half."

"Maybe. Maybe not. I'll take my chances." She surveyed the sizes and positions of the gators, and realized she'd have to get out on the lake side and swim. The narrow strip of water on the shore side was simply too crowded. "Can't swim with the lamp," she said, more to herself than to Colin. "But having a paddle might be a good idee." She propped one up on the side of the canoe. "Ye stayin' or goin'?"

"Give me a little more time to study on it. I'll think of something."

"Suit yerself. But if ye change yer mind and decide to come after me, be quiet and move slowly."

Colin reached forward and laid his open hand on her shoulder. It was a gentle, friendly gesture, yet Lilah flinched. "Don't do this, Lilah. Ye ain't thinkin' straight," he said. "Ye're tired. Ye need to rest."

For a moment, Lilah wondered if he was right, and she almost relented. Then she heard Granny telling her to trust her mother wit, and she *knew* the water was safer than the canoe. No matter how unreasonable that seemed to Colin, she knew somewhere deep inside that it was true. She closed her eyes and called up all the inner strength she could muster. It filled her up with determination and courage and a strange sort of peace.

Quickly, before she lost her nerve, Lilah turned around and slipped feet first over the side of the canoe.

Chapter Seven

Holding on to the side of the canoe with her left hand, Lilah eased the paddle into the water with her right. A gator brushed by her, its powerful body wrenching away her grasp. Her heart thumped wildly, her breath caught in her throat, and she sank to the floor of the lake. When she popped up, she discovered that the lake was shallow enough there for her to walk, which would make carrying the paddle easier than trying to swim with it.

"Please, Lilah," Colin wheedled, "come back afore it's too late."

She shook her head and started to slog away. "If happen ye decide to come after me, don' go makin' no sudden moves."

"How come ye're takin' the paddle?" Colin asked.

"Jest in case."

"Jest in case of what?"

"Jest in case I have to hit a gator on the hose with it."

He laughed at that, but it was a hollow laugh devoid of mirth.

The open lake wasn't quite so dark as it had been under the huckleberry vines, the fading light allowing her to make out the bulky lengths of the gators floating on the water. She successfully passed one gator and was approaching the head of another, when she heard a muffled

curse and then a splash behind her. Not daring to take her
eyes or her concentration off the gator just ahead, Lilah
froze, fully expecting to hear Colin's screams of agony.
When something hit her hard in the back, her own scream
rent the air.

"Hesh up!" Colin hissed in her ear. "It's jest me."

"Lordamercy! How come ye not to warn a body?" she
snapped. "Ye sceered me half to death." She reached behind her and found his hand, which she clasped firmly in
her own. "Are ye travelin' t'other paddle?"

"Yes."

"Good. I wasn't joshin' 'bout hittin' gators. If one
comes at you, knock him."

"I'm not about to hit a gator. If one comes at me, I'll
stick him with my knife."

"Ye dasn't stab one of 'em, Colin. Gators gets plumb
fitified over spilt blood. Ye poke one of 'em, and we'll
wind up gator vittles for sure." She gave him a tug and
they started walking again. Lilah chose their watery path
carefully, giving the alligators as wide a berth as she
could, while meandering slowly toward a spot on the bank
presently uninhabited by one of the big reptiles.

Just when Jesse thought he would scream from utter
frustration, Lilah's hallo resounded from the clearing. He
had a good mind to get out of bed and spank her for causing him so much worry. He might would have, had he not
also heard Colin's shout of "Whoopee" right behind her
call. It was only Lilah's and Granny's warnings concerning
his safety that kept him abed.

Relieved that Lilah was safe and thinking he'd hear
nothing more now than muffled conversation, he relaxed,
closing his eye in preparation for a nap. But Lilah's voice
remained strident as she came into the cabin.

"Colin's got t' stay the night," she announced, which
perked Jesse's ears right up. "We'uns got the canoe stuck

and had to walk out'n the lake, so Colin can't get home afore mornin' soon."

How in the world did she expect to keep him hidden all night long? he wondered. And quiet? He was hungry and thirsty, and he sure as hell couldn't go all night without relieving himself. Regardless of the imminent prospect of discomfort, though, Jesse couldn't help sympathizing with Colin, whoever the man was. Jesse'd spent a few nights alone in this swamp, and he reckoned he couldn't blame a man for wanting walls around him while he slept. Nor could he fault him for not wanting to set out to home in the pitch black, without benefit of a boat or a canoe to keep him safe from moccasins and gators.

Moccasins and gators!

Sakes alive, Lilah said they'd walked out of the lake. The lake that was plumb full of big, ugly alligators with massive jaws and nasty-sharp teeth. Jesse had seen them basking in the sun and rolling in the bogs, and he'd walked past a few of them himself. Why, there must be hundreds of gators in the lake. And Lilah had gotten in there with them. Jesse shuddered and vowed to spank her yet.

He could hear the three of them moving around in the cabin, scraping chair legs across the floor and clattering dishes and spoons as they ate the stew Granny had prepared. They talked, too, a-plenty, but too soft for him to make out much of what was said. Jesse's stomach was rubbing itself raw against his backbone, his throat was getting parched, and his full bladder was beginning to cause him considerable pain. He tried putting his mind on other things, knowing he'd never manage to be still and quiet if he kept dwelling on his bodily aggravations.

Without purposely setting his mind to the subject, he realized he'd started thinking much the way Lilah and Granny talked, which wasn't too difficult to do. He'd grown up using virtually the same vocabulary, the same

speech patterns, but then he'd worked very hard at elimi-
nating those words and the outdated syntax from his
speech. He'd worked very hard at sounding educated, at
wearing his book-learning like he wore his badge. He'd
denied this part of his heritage, deeming it beneath him.
Surprisingly, though, Lilah's soft voice was charming him
right back to his roots, and he wasn't sure a-tall how he
felt about that.

Suddenly, Jesse noticed little scratching noises coming
from beneath the bed. At the same time, his nose started
itching. He rubbed his nose and listened harder for the
scratching, which got louder and steadier. Convinced that
he was no longer alone in his alcove, he slipped off the
mattress and got down on the floor, where he stretched out
full length, since his knee still didn't want to bend.

It was too dark under the bed to see anything, but the
wild animal odor that assaulted his nose, combined with
more itching inside his nostrils, confirmed his suspicions.
A rat. He'd bet his life on it.

He was about to climb back into bed when he sneezed. It
wasn't an insignficant little sneeze, but a loud *ha-choo*
that reverberated in its aftermath.

"What was that?" It was the man Lilah called Colin
talking.

"What was what?" Lilah asked, but not quite innocently
enough.

"Somebody sneezed," the man said. "Ye heard it,
didn't you, Granny?"

"My ears is a-givin' out on me." Jesse almost chuckled
at the old woman's reply, which was neither confirmation
nor denial and still probably not true. He hadn't noticed
Granny having a problem hearing anything.

"Well, I heared it. It come from back there, behind that
hangin' quilt."

The man's footfalls accompanied this last sentence,
prompting Jesse to scoot under the bed, rat or not. His shin

connected with something hard, which turned over, thumped against the floor, and came to rest alongside his leg. Before he could give much thought toward identifying the object, a cold, damp nose pressed itself against Jesse's whiskered cheek.

He froze.

The rat sniffed his cheek, then it snorted. But that wasn't possible. An animal couldn't feel disgust. Not nearly as much as Jesse felt anyway.

But there was no time to explore the subject. Someone was fast approaching, and if he didn't hide himself better, the man Colin was sure to see him. Jesse didn't dare move, however, until he'd secured whatever it was he'd knocked over. He slipped one hand down his leg and cautiously touched the object lying there. A boot, of all things! He mentally shook his head and felt for its mate. Quickly, he nabbed them both and pulled them into his chest, along with his knees. The pain made him want to shriek. He clamped his mouth firmly shut and wiggled further under the bed. Fortunately, the rat scurried out of his way.

Almost immediately, the swishing of the quilt curtain being moved and a loud huff proclaimed the man's entrance. Jesse thought he heard an exhalation of breath as well, and wondered if maybe it was a sigh of relief from Lilah.

"See?" she said.

"Yer bed's all mussed up." The man didn't sound in the least convinced.

"I disremembered to spread it up," she said. Jesse heard her heart pounding and her breath coming in short spurts, then realized it was his own heartbeats, his own panting that resounded in his ears. He took a deep breath and held it.

"That don' explain the sneeze."

Oh, Lord, he's going to look now. I'm done for.

There was, quite simply, nowhere else to go, nothing else to do except lie still and wait. Wait for a shotgun blast to his back at the worst, a strong hand on his arm at best. He couldn't fight. Not effectively. He was still too weak. Jesse braced himself for the inevitable and waited. Already, the man Colin was dropping to his knees. Jesse felt the vibrating thud against the pine floor.

He also felt sharp little claws dig into his bare hip as the rat bounded over him. For a split second, the rat's weight balanced on Jesse's hip, and he was amazed at its size. It had to be the biggest rat he'd ever encountered.

"Come here, Bandit," Lilah said, her voice full of joy and hope and relief all at once. "How'd ye ever get out, you rascal?"

Jesse could mentally see her scooping the rat into her arms and ruffling its fur behind its head. He thought he was going to be sick, right there under her bed, with Colin mere inches away.

"See?" Lilah continued. "It's jes' my coon. He must've chewed his way out'n the cage. Reckon that means he's all healed up and ready to go back to the woods."

A raccoon. Probably the one that had bitten him the night he'd been looking for eggs. Jesse supposed he and the coon were even now.

"Coons don' sneeze," Colin argued, his skepticism still evident in his voice.

"Course they do. All furry critters sneezes."

Lilah's explanation must have done the trick, because they moved back toward the front of the cabin then. Jesse slowly expelled the breath he'd been holding, but he didn't move. At long last, things began to quiet down, and Jesse managed to turn over without making much noise. When he'd moved the bed cover back, he'd left an opening. Through it, he could see a thin stream of light snaking along the floor all the way to the partial wall, which meant Lilah had closed the quilt curtain. Crawling out might be safe, and then again, it might not. He didn't think he wanted to have to attempt another effort at hiding himself, so he stayed put.

After a while, someone pushed the curtain back a foot or two. Jesse was relieved to see Lilah's slender bare feet in the opening. "You can come out'n there now," she whispered.

"Thank God!" he said, worming his way out and starting to stand up, oblivious to his near nakedness.

Lilah gasped and turned her head to the wall. "Sh-h-h," she cautioned. "Colin's on the porch, but he can still hear you. I'll get yer supper."

It was a long night of furtive movement and much whispering within the cabin. Although her bed was as far removed from the porch as it could be, Lilah insisted on keeping the window shuttered. "If happen he passes," she explained. Jesse didn't think Colin—or any other man—was tall enough to see through the high window from a casual passing by, but he didn't argue. Despite the salvation of the raccoon, the swampman might very well retain some suspicion. To get a clear view of the bed from outside, all anyone had to do was stand on an upturned bucket. Like it or not, Jesse knew Lilah was right about the window.

Between the stuffy air and nerves stretched to the limit, Jesse didn't sleep a wink. Judging from the shadows under Lilah's eyes the next morning, she didn't either.

"He's gone," she told him, her voice weary, when she brought his breakfast.

"Take it to the table," Jesse said. "I'm getting up."

Her gaze darted to the counterpin where it covered his legs. "But ye—"

"Granny finished my pants and I found my boots last night. I'm getting up."

"Ye need some holp?"

Though he wasn't sure whether he needed help or not, Jesse didn't think he wanted to feel Lilah's hands on his body or witness another one of her shocked, innocent looks. Both stirred something deep down inside him that he wasn't quite ready for. "I can manage."

"Are ye certain-sure?"

He nodded. "I have to start doing things for myself again. I can't keep lying here, letting you and Granny wait on me hand and foot like I was some helpless invalid."

"The man-critter's gettin' stronger ever' day," Lilah told the fawn, who was eating dried corn out of her right hand while her left stroked its back. "Jes' like you. Yer leg's most healed up. Soon, it'll be time for you to go back to yer maw—and he'll go back to chasin' them outlaws."

An unaccustomed emotion filled her, preventing further speech. Lilah gave herself a mental fussing. This wasn't the first time she'd had to let go of a sick or injured critter, and it wouldn't be the last. That was all the man was, she told herself—another injured critter healed by her hand. Why, then, did this particular critter matter so much to her? Why couldn't she just give him a goin'-away hug and be done with it? Like it or not, that was what she had to do. When the time came.

Until such time, she aimed to spend every minute she could with the man called Jesse, which wasn't hard, since he was teaching her to read. She'd never dreamed she would enjoy anything so much, but she didn't try to fool herself into believing it was only the lessons that thrilled her so that her soul fairly sang with a pleasurement unlike any she'd known before. No, it was the man-critter himself who was responsible, only he didn't seem to know it.

Or perhaps he did. This was a new thought for Lilah, a different look at the situation. She stopped rubbing the fawn's back and let her memory ramble back to their session earlier that day, when she'd reached out and laid an

open palm on Jesse's bearded cheek, with the intention of
asking him if he wanted a shave. Before she could say
anything, he'd jerked his head away as though she'd
slapped him. He'd reacted much the same way yesterday,
when she'd tried to slip the gator-skin eye patch she'd
made him over his head.

She couldn't fault him for not being appreciative or
gentlemanly-like, 'cause in all other instances, he was. He
just didn't seem to want her to touch him. And oh, how
much she wanted to do that! She wanted to run her hands
over him the same way she stroked the fawn. She wanted
to touch every part of him so that she could remember him
better later—not just the way his green eye sparkled sometimes and got an odd faraway look about it at others, like
he was seeing things that weren't actually there. Not just
the pleasant resonance of his voice and the strange way he
talked. Not just the feel of the thin ridge of his sealed eyelid against her lips, or the crispness of his beard against
her palm. Those things in themselves were not enough.
There was more, much more, to this man-critter, and Lilah
wanted to gather it all into her memory to take out bit by
bit later, much as the squirrels put acorns by to see them
through the winter months.

And the winter months were coming. They always did.
Except this year, they were coming early for Lilah.

"Where are ye goin'?"

Jesse winced at the sharpness in her voice and attempted
to dislodge the sudden sharp pang in his chest. It wouldn't
budge.

"Away." He knew he owed her more than that. God, he
owed this angel of mercy more than he could ever give
her. Maybe someday he would come back to Medicine Island and tell her how much he'd come to care for her. But
not today. Today, he couldn't even look at her, much less
talk to her. To cover his discomfiture, he shoved the first

pair of britches Granny had made—the too-tight pair—into a small deerskin pouch and started folding his old shirt.

"Do ye have to go?" The edge was gone. In its place was a plaintive sweetness that was harder to take than the abruptness.

"Yes."

"But Granny's out collectin' yarbs and roots. She'd want to bid you farewell."

Didn't she realize how hard it was for him to go? At least this way, he only had to tell one of them good-bye. "You tell her for me. Tell her I really appreciate everything she did."

"What about the canoe and the guide ye said ye needed?"

"You said I shouldn't trust the swampers, since I don't have my badge and papers anymore. I'll manage."

"Ye could take me."

He shook his head. "No, angel. I won't expose you to that kind of danger. Besides, Granny needs you."

"At least let me fix you up some vittles, so's ye won't go hunger-bit again."

"No! I told you I'd manage." God, there he went again, barking at her. But how could he explain to her how he felt, when he didn't really understand it himself? He supposed part of it was male pride, but the most part came from his not wanting to carry anything extra with him that would remind him of Lilah. If he could have figured out how to replace them, he'd leave the deerskin pouch, eye patch, and new clothes behind. He gave her a long, hard look, and wondered if maybe he shouldn't tell her that, if for no other reason than to make this break as clean and final as he could.

"Watch out for snakes."

"I will."

"Will I ever see you again?"

"Don't count on it. I've hated this swamp since the first

moment I stepped into it. I don't ever want to see another swamp again as long as I live."

There. He'd said it. But immediately, he wanted to take the words back. She was already walking away. He couldn't blame her. Without thinking about what he was doing, Jesse dropped the pouch, seized her shoulders, and turned her to face him. Although she stared straight into his chest, he could see tears swimming in her wide blue eyes and the telltale quiver of her full lower lip. Gently, he tilted her chin up and lowered his mouth to hers.

Jesse realized his mistake instantly, but he could no more stop himself from kissing her than he could take back his harsh words. Sensation washed through him, setting his heart aflutter and igniting a fire in his loins. With eager innocence, her supple lips met his, and when he moved his mouth on hers and skimmed his tongue along the seam in her lips, she gasped softly, opening her mouth and allowing him entrance.

She tasted as sweet as sourwood honey, and she smelled like a meadow in summer. The combination intoxicated him, sending his senses reeling and his reason flying off into oblivion. Moaning, he deepened the kiss, pulling her lithe body into his and thrusting his tongue into the hot cavern of her mouth.

Jesse felt as though he'd found a precious treasure, like he'd opened a common oyster and discovered hidden there a rare pearl. For a long moment, he wallowed in the richness of her warm softness, the lushness of her breasts crushed against his hard chest, the luxuriance of her silky hair and satin skin beneath his callused palms. For a long moment, he forgot why he'd come to the Okefinoke. He forgot about duty and justice. He forgot about catching One-Eyed Jack.

And then, with the swiftness of the viper that had bit him almost two weeks before, reason struck. With more effort than he'd ever thought to employ, Jesse ended the kiss, but he wasn't quite ready to let her go. He set his chin on to top of her head and wrapped his arms around her, holding her close, feeling her heart beat in harmonic cadence with his own.

"Don't you understand, my golden-haired angel?" he whispered, his voice suddenly hoarse. "I don't want to go." She trembled in his arms and sagged against him. "God, I don't want to go!"

"But ye must."

Those three little words were the most difficult she'd ever spoken, and they returned to haunt her over and over throughout the remainder of the day. She heard them in the hoot of the barred owl and in the wind soughing through the tops of the pines. She heard them in the hiss of the cook fire, and in the drone of the black bee that flew through the open window and hovered over her shoulder as she hung the kettle over the flames.

The edge of dark would be on them soon. Time for tea and a spot of supper. The very thought of food turned Lilah's stomach, but she knew Granny would be hungry after her foray in the woods for roots and yarbs. Time for her to come home, too.

Lilah walked out onto the porch and sat in a rocking chair to wait for Granny. She didn't know when she'd needed the old woman so much. Not for a long, long time. Not since she'd lost Maw and Paw. The realization that losing Jesse hurt as much as losing her parents hit her hard. Had she really come to love him so much? How was it possible, she wondered, to come to love anyone that much in such a short time?

But she'd loved Granny Latham from the minute she saw her. As she sat and rocked, Lilah thought back to the day she'd met Granny. She'd been six years old and worried about her mother, whose stomach was so swollen she looked like a cow that had eaten a heap of pea vines. And

Maw must have felt as bad, 'cause she took to the bed and moaned and clutched her stomach from time to time. Paw acted narvious, buzzing around Maw like the black bee that had followed Lilah out onto the porch.

When Maw told Paw it was time to get the granny woman, he said he didn't want to leave her alone. "But I won't be alone," Maw said. "Lilah will sit with me. Go on, now, and hurry."

Lilah sat on the side of the bed and held Maw's hand until Paw came back with Granny. He told Lilah to go outside and play, but Granny said to let her stay, that she needed her to hold Merrie's hand for a spell longer. When Paw went outside to fetch water, Granny explained in hushed tones that Maw was fixin' to have a baby, and that she was there to help her.

If Maw heard, she was in too much pain to object. Eventually, Paw did pry Lilah loose and sent her to pull weeds in the garden. After what seemed like hours to Lilah, Paw came outside and started digging a hole at the edge of the clearing. His shoulders were all slumped over, and Lilah thought she heard him sniffle. Terrified that something had happened to Maw, she rushed inside the cabin to find Maw crying softly and Granny wrapping a tiny body in a clean sheet.

Paw made a small cypress box and Granny dressed the baby—Maw kept calling him Little Jacob—in one of the embroidered white gowns Maw had made. They had a little ceremony before they covered up the box. Maw cried and Paw pretended to read from the bible, but Lilah knew he was just reciting verses he'd heard before. Paw couldn't read a-tall, but Maw could—a little. Lilah wondered why Maw hadn't taught her the little bit she knew.

Granny Latham stayed with them for nigh on to two weeks, until Maw was able to get up and around again. During that time, she shared Lilah's pallet on the floor at night and filled Lilah's days with stories about the swamp.

Afterwards, Paw started taking Lilah with him when he went over to Medicine Island, which was only once or twice a year. With each visit, the bond between Granny and Lilah strengthened.

The day Paw and Maw died, Lilah fled to Granny, the only true friend she had. Granny went back with her, helped her clean and dress the bodies, construct simple coffins, and dig the graves beside Little Jacob's. Once the bodies were laid to rest, Lilah went home with Granny, and she'd been living with her on Medicine Island ever since.

Over the years, Granny Latham's gnarled fingers had stroked away many a tear, and her sagging bosom had provided a comforting pillow for those times when the tears didn't want to stop. Lilah could feel one of those times coming on now, and she ached to bury her face in Granny's bosom. She ached for Granny's healing touch. Though long shadows crept across the clearing, the old woman still hadn't returned.

The black bee buzzed by Lilah's face so close its vibrating wings tickled her cheek. She swatted at it absently and it flew off toward the woods, then came right back and hovered in front of her, mere inches from her nose.

"Go 'way," Lilah fussed. "I don' need you to tell me someone's a-goin' to die. He's gone and he ain't never comin' back. He mought as well be dead."

Her voice caught in her throat and a tear trickled out of her eye. She wiped it off her cheek and stood up, intending to go inside and start the red bay tea to brewin' for Granny. But a movement at the edge of the woods stopped her. Lilah held her breath, waiting, hoping it was Jesse coming back, but knowing in her heart it was Granny coming home. She narrowed her eyes, peering into the gloom, then rushed forward when the old woman broke clear of the trees.

"Granny!" she called. "Oh, Granny, he's gone. My man-critter's gone."

Her heart was breaking, but Granny—dear, wonderful Granny—would fix it. With a brush of a fingertip, Granny would heal the wound.

Granny stood in the shadows, her arm twitching so that she let go of the basket she'd been toting. Lilah watched it fall, watched the fruits of Granny's labor spill onto the sand, watched Granny's body crumple to the ground.

For a second, Lilah froze, recalling the black bee, knowing in her heart that she'd misunderstood the message it was trying to deliver. It wasn't the death of her relationship with Jesse that the bee foretold. It was Granny's death. And now the old woman was lying in the shadows.

In a hip and a hurry, the shadders could take you.

Lilah snapped to and ran to Granny's side, shoving her forearms under Granny's armpits and tugging with all her might.

"Stand up," she cried, "and lean on me. I'll get ye to the bed and brang you some tea, and ye'll be fit as a fiddle in no time."

"Nay," Granny said, her voice so scratchy Lilah barely understood her. "Lay me down here."

"No!" Lilah wailed, her voice echoing in the clearing. "Ye can't lie here in the shadders, Granny. Ye must get up."

"I can't."

Lilah sat down, laid the gray head in her lap, and stroked back wisps of hair that had fallen over Granny's wrinkled forehead. "That's right. Jes' ketch yer breath, and then we'll go inside."

"I ain't long for this world," Granny said, raising her hand. Lilah took it and gave it a gentle squeeze.

"Hesh up, now. Ye're a-goin' to be fine."

The gray head moved just a bit to one side and then back. "It's my heart. It done give out on me."

Lilah squeezed Granny's cold hand tighter. "Ye can't—"

"Promise me," Granny said.

"Anything," Lilah whispered.

"Promise me ye'll go to Homerville and learn to be a real lady. It was what yer maw wanted for you. Promise me, so I can die in peace."

"Ye can't die. I won't let you."

"Promise me."

For the second time that day, Lilah forced herself to give voice to words she didn't want to say. But they were words that had to be said. She closed her eyes, forcing back the tears, forcing back the grief, forcing forth the words.

"I promise."

Chapter Eight

Within twenty-four hours of leaving Medicine Island, Jesse knew he'd made a big mistake setting out on his own, and he'd be a consarned fool not to admit it. His leg was stiff and sore, his stomach was growling, he hadn't slept much the night before . . . and he was hopelessly lost.

At the least, he should have borrowed Lilah's canoe and accepted her offer of a grubstake. Deep down, he wished he could have taken her with him as well, and not only because he needed a guide.

Why did he have to go and kiss her? Why couldn't he have just told her good-bye, and maybe settled for a friendly hug? But no, he had to kiss her. He had to go and ruin everything.

Now, he couldn't seem to take his mind off her. No matter how hard he tried, no matter how much he concentrated on getting through the swamp and finding One-Eyed Jack, her sweet face or her soft voice or the feel of her body pressed against his invaded his thoughts. He'd never felt so funny inside, so strong and sure of himself, and yet so empty—not even when he'd fallen in love with Martha.

Fallen in love . . . with Lilah? Who was he kidding? He wasn't in love with the angel. Not him. Not Deputy U.S. Marshal Jesse Redford. There was no room in his life for a woman. Not now. Not ever again.

Hadn't he learned that lesson before? If he'd never married Martha, if they'd never had the boys, none of them would be dead. They were in their graves, though, and it was all his fault. One-Eyed Jack would never have come after them—hell, the felon would never have known they even existed—if it hadn't been for Jesse busting up the still.

In the mountains, retaliation was considered a virtue. Jesse knew that. Yet he'd gone blindly about his work, as though he was the only one whose life was ever in danger, as though any retaliation would be directed solely at him. And he was smart and strong. He could take care of himself.

What arrogance! What stupid, blind arrogance!

He wasn't arrogant anymore. Not since the snakebite. And surely not now, when he'd gone and gotten himself hopelessly lost. He was beginning to wonder if he'd ever get out of the swamp, much less find One-Eyed Jack. *And if I do luck up and find him, how am I ever going to get the scoundrel out of the swamp and into a town, when I have nothing to back me up but my fists? If he's alone, maybe there's a chance. But he wasn't alone before, and he won't be now.*

Hopeless, that's what this situation was. Virtually hopeless. He might as well dig a grave for himself right here, 'cause the possibility of needing one was getting better all the time.

Lilah finished driving the cross into the ground, then stepped back to take one last look at the grave.

She'd tried to do Granny proud, first by selecting a spot in the sun-filled clearing where she'd looked for candyroot, and second by fashioning the cross from two sturdy cypress limbs and a piece of stout rope. In time, she knew, the weather would rot the rope, but the wildflowers would be there forever. And Granny did so love flowers.

"Farewell," she whispered, the wind catching her voice and swirling it among the swaying blossoms, holding it, Lilah hoped, for Granny to hear through all eternity.

She turned away to find Ol' Codger and Bob patiently waiting for her at the edge of the thicket. Lilah didn't want to think about how she would have managed the past day and night without these two friends. Without a single grunt or growl, they'd suffered both her rantings and her hugs, and when she'd harnessed a slide to Ol' Codger, he'd pulled Granny's body across the island to the clearing like it was something he did every day. Though hampered by his limp, Bob kept the buzzards chased away until she could finish burying Granny Latham.

The two followed her back to the cabin, where she removed the harness and slide from Ol' Codger and put them away before turning all her caged critters loose, including the chickens and the goat. She told them she hoped they all fared well, then made one last tour of the cabin. Assuring herself that the shutters were secure and the fire was out, Lilah picked up her go-away satchel and headed to her canoe, leaving her home behind her once again.

Jesse slogged across the wide expanse of the grassy prairie, which wasn't a prairie in the Midwestern sense, but rather a flooded, open area choked with water lilies, ferns, and sedges. Although the trek left him highly visible and totally unprotected, he basked in the fresh, clean air, in the panorama of open sky, and in the warmth of the May sun beating down on his bare back.

He'd stuffed his shirt into the deerskin pouch Lilah had provided and threaded a vine through the loops at the top of his boots, then tied it securely. Both the pouch and his boots hung around his neck, and he'd tied the vine so the boots couldn't just slip off.

Most of the water in the swamp, he'd discovered, was

shallow, usually no more than waist-high, and sometimes lower than that. Here, in this prairie, it barely came up to his knees. This discovery had caught Jesse by surprise, simply because the open water was so dark and the prairies so clogged with vegetation, it was impossible to see how deep the water was. That was how he'd lost his guns and his saddlebags, and he wasn't about to take any chances with losing what little he had left.

Walking the swamp, as he'd learned when he left Cowhouse Island weeks ago, was slow and tedious. Only determination and sheer willpower kept him moving. The peat bottom sucked at his feet with every step; sometimes he sank past his ankles, and once he'd thought he was a goner when he sank almost to his hip. Luckily, the sturdy aquatic plants had long taproots. By gathering several stems in his hands, he'd been able to pull himself out.

As he walked, he scanned the line of trees surrounding the prairie, watching for movement as well as for other signs of human occupancy: smoke, a boat or canoe, a bit of fabric caught on a briar. He watched, too, for animals, especially the predatory varieties, specifically for snakes and alligators.

Lilah had recounted her tale of wading through the passel of gators the day she and Colin got the canoe stuck. "Ye jes' can't make no sudden moves," she'd said. "There's a-plenty for gators to eat in the swamp, so they generally ain't hunger-bit. When one gets you, it's 'cause ye've threatened him some kinda way. He's as sceered a you as ye are a him. Same's true of snakes. Some folk says to freeze up when ye see a snake. But that's not right Ye got to run from 'em. Ye got to let 'em know ye respect their territory, and then they'll leave you alone.

"Gators is different," she'd continued. "Ye got to run from them, too, but they'll chase you. Snakes won't, 'cept moccasins. If'n a gator ever chases you, ye got to take a crookedy path—ye know, go first one way and then t'other. Gators can move faster than ye can run, but they can't turn fast. A-runnin' crooked's the onliest way to beat 'em."

Jesse didn't think he ever wanted to find himself running from an alligator, but he'd catalogued the information, just in case. He spied a couple of the huge, ugly reptiles floating on the prairie, and several more taking the sun atop logs nearer the cypress bay he was approaching; he gave them all a wide berth. Though he'd never seen one in action, he had a pretty good notion of what those massive jaws could do, and he wasn't about to be fooled by their placid appearance.

He wished he could avoid the bay as easily as he could the gators, but it stretched out so wide, he'd lose most of the afternoon going around it. It didn't look quite as deep or as dark as the one that abutted Medicine Island, maybe because this one faced west and was, therefore, catching the afternoon sun. He'd be more cautious this time and keep a close lookout for moccasins.

About halfway through the bay, the cypress knees got so thick, Jesse could barely get through them—probably couldn't have had someone not chopped some of them out. Jesse silently blessed the soul who'd kept him from skirting the thick growth, and when he saw one of the axed-off knees hung in a mound of bog moss, he wanted to shout for joy. The way sound carried in the swamp kept him quiet.

He'd been wanting a weapon, and there was one for the taking. He made his way to the mound and extracted the knee, using extra care on the outside chance a water moccasin was hiding beneath it. The knee had grown a long, slender crown that fit perfectly in his palm. He tested its weight and balance; although it was hollow, as cypress knees are, he decided it would make a decent club.

It was about time his luck changed. Now, if he could just find a nice, dry spot, maybe he could get some rest.

Hopefully, an island lay on the other side of the cypress bay.

A few minutes later, he walked out of the bay and into moist peat covered with saw palmettos that grew too close together to provide a place to stretch out. Jesse sighed, put his boots back on to protect his feet and lower legs from the sharp-pointed palmetto leaves, and moved onward. After a while, the palmettos gave way to a stand of pines. Oblivious to the damp sand, Jesse lay down. Within minutes, he fell asleep.

Lilah leaned over the side of the canoe and studied her reflection in the dark, glassy surface of the lake. The face that stared back at her only vaguely resembled the one she carried around inside her head. She never thought of herself as pretty, but certainly more pleasant to look at than the shimmering image of herself. Was her nose really so long, her eyes so widely spaced, her lips so pouty? Or was the image a distortion? She hoped so, but she couldn't deny everything she saw.

"Hell's banjer!" she muttered, only marginally noting her rare use of a swearword. "Do I look a fright!"

Another face appeared beside hers, a furry face with whiskers and a neck ruff. Without moving her gaze, Lilah laid a steadying hand on the bobcat's back. "What do you think, Bob? Ain't we'uns a pair? Why, my hair's a-stickin' out from my head, same as yer'n, but with these dark circles 'round my eyes, I look more like Bandit than you. I don't know how come Jesse ever to want to kiss the likes of me."

While Jesse had been on her mind a-plenty, it was the first time she'd allowed herself to say his name since he'd left Medicine Island. Like the swearword, though, the name flowed off her tongue with such ease that she barely noted the utterance. Her whole being was simply too full of the memory of that kiss for anything else to matter.

She supposed that all the time she'd ached to touch Jesse, she'd known, without really knowing, how it would make her feel. That was why she'd had the ache. That was what Granny had meant when she told her she was a woman full-growed, with a woman's yearnings. All the time, she'd been yearning for the fire that leapt to life inside her when Jesse put his mouth on hers.

But once, she'd discovered, was not enough. She wanted Jesse to kiss her again and again. If someone had told her before that she'd enjoy having a man's tongue thrust into her mouth, she would a-laughed herself plumb silly. Now, she longed for his tongue, his lips, his hands, touching her, caressing her all over.

Just thinking about it got the kindling to going in her belly. She shivered so hard her reflection shimmied, which served to remind her of her frightful appearance.

"Jesse's out here sommers," she told Bob, "and I'm aimin' to find him. But first, I've got to clean myself up a bit. I sure don' want to sceer him half to death." Lilah straightened up and dug in her go-away satchel until she found her comb. "Soon's I get these tangles out, I'm a-goin' to find myself a soap bush and take myself a bath. And then I'm a-goin' to put on the skirt I brought, 'stead of these here britches. Skirts gets in the way, but if'n I want Jesse to thank of me as a woman full-growed, he's got to be able to see the womanish side of me."

"Drag him over here," Jack called to Red Watkins, his cohort in mischief since childhood, and in crime since their chins sprouted whiskers. Where Jack had grown up, Red had grown out, leaving him with a stocky neck sitting on wide shoulders over a barrel trunk that was connected to short legs. They called him Red for the overabundance of red-gold hair that grew all over his body, except for a bald patch at his crown. Hamp Riley, who was the only one of the bunch ever to go to a zoo, said Red looked like "one a them hairy apes." After that, Jack took to calling Red "Apeman" when he wanted to see him get riled up. Now was not one of those times.

They'd had nothing but trouble ever since they stepped foot in this dang-blasted swamp. First, a bear got Hamp, and then a gator got Scooter. That left Jack, Red, and Smiley, and now another gator had taken off one of Smiley's legs about mid-calf. Despite the leather strip Jack had tied above the stub, blood was pouring out of the stump. If they didn't cauterize it soon, Smiley was going to bleed to death.

"Be just as well," Jack muttered to himself as he scouted the area for firewood. "Ain't no good to us like he is." If it hadn't been for Red, Jack would have already put Smiley out of his misery, but soft-hearted Red insisted they try to save him.

If they'd had a boat, this wouldn't have happened. And they would have had a boat if the fellows had been smarter about stealing one. But these swampfolks kept dogs, and the minute the dogs took to barking, the men came running with loaded shotguns. Jack got a few of the dogs with his knife, but there were too many dogs and too many shotguns to get them all with only one weapon.

Now, though, they had a gun. And not just any gun, but Jesse Redford's gun. They'd found it just a few minutes ago. The long barrel was sticking out of a pile of leaves and twigs out in the middle of a bog. They sent Smiley out to get it, then hollered at him to dig through the mound and see if he could find the holster. Sure enough, it was in there, too, but it was chewed up so bad you couldn't buckle it on anymore. At least it still held a dozen or so bullets.

"Wonder how it got here?" Smiley asked as he started back toward them.

That was when the huge gator came out of nowhere and

charged at Smiley. Before he could get out of the way, the
monster snapped his leg off.

Jack shook his head in disgust and started building a
fire.

A high-pitched scream ripped Jesse from a sound sleep.

For a moment, disorientation reigned, and in the stillness that followed, Jesse was certain he'd dreamed it.
Then it came again, a wail that was high and long and resounded in the eerie stillness. A wail such as he'd never
heard before.

A panther? Maybe, but this scream sounded different
somehow. Not necessarily more human. A body didn't
have to hear a panther scream but once to know how human it sounded. No, it was the sharp edge of pain that
made the difference.

Jesse picked up his cypress knee club and moved cautiously toward the sound, hurrying as much as he could in
the dense undergrowth, while attempting a silent approach.
He had no idea what he would find, but the last thing he
needed to do was burst upon a mauling and have the wild
animal turn on him. For the moment, he was moving into
the wind, which should keep the bear or big cat from
smelling him. He didn't imagine that the club would be a
very effective weapon against a large, dangerous animal.

So why was he even bothering to see what was making
someone scream? he asked himself, knowing he'd have to
make some effort to save the man, if he wasn't already too
late. The screaming had abruptly ceased.

Jesse smelled the smoke before he saw the fire, and he
heard muttered curses before he saw the faces that the
voices belonged to. There were at least two distinct voices.
Quickly, he dropped to all fours, his skin prickling up as
he realized a man was responsible for inflicting the pain,
and not a wild animal at all. The wind brought another
odor then, the acrid smell of burned flesh.

For a while, he crouched, remaining very still, listening so hard he didn't notice the pain in his left knee until it started throbbing. He stretched his legs out then and slowly wiggled forward until, at last, he reached the edge of a small clearing that was almost completely surrounded by a thick growth of bushes. Using the bushes as cover, he watched two men hovering over a third, who lay on the ground close to the fire. The hovering men had their backs to him, but in his gut Jesse knew who they were.

One-Eyed Jack and Red Watkins.

What luck. What incredible luck!

Red stood up and rolled his shoulders back. "Dammit, Smiley! What'd you have to go and die for?"

"He ain't dead, you fool," Jack said, rising himself and wiping a long, nasty-looking blade on his pants. "He fainted."

"I'm glad. I wouldn' a-wanted to drag his sorry ass all the way here for nothing. My shoulders is sore."

"And my belly's empty. Why don't you go rustle us up something to eat? Maybe a rabbit or a squirrel."

Red started to move away from the fire, toward the opposite side of the clearing from where Jesse lay. Nevertheless, Jesse looked around for a better place to hide, in case Red came back his way.

"Don't you come back with frogs again," Jack called after him. "I've et all the frogs I aim to. Don't brang no lizards, neither."

Jesse had to stifle a chuckle at the image of One-Eyed Jack eating frogs and lizards. As empty as he was, he wasn't *that* hungry. He spied a spot on his left where three bushes formed a triangle with a small bare spot in the middle, but he waited until Jack busied himself with the fire before he moved. When he got settled, he discovered that he couldn't see as well from there, but he really didn't have to see, so long as he could hear. All he had to do now was plan his strategy. He wasn't sure exactly what he was going to do, but whatever it was, it would be under the cover of full darkness.

A shot rang out and Jesse flinched. Damn! They had a gun. He'd have to be extra careful when he made his move.

It was almost day-down when Lilah beached her canoe on a small island that no one lived on—as far as she knew, anyway. It had been a good spell since she'd traveled this way.

Although she knew she oughter be a-tellin' folks that Granny had died, she simply wasn't ready to talk about it and had purposely avoided the inhabited islands. 'Sides, swampfolk carried on something awful when it came to funeralizin' a body. They'd fuss at her for diggin' the bury-hole herself and building the coffin herself, for not affordin' Granny the privilege of a wake, and for not allowin' them to sing and pray over Granny's grave, just like they'd fussed when Maw and Paw died.

Shucks, it would a-took them nigh on to three days to put Granny in the ground, countin' a extree day after the actual buryin' to eat up all the vittles they'd a-brung with them. And, law, if it a-been winter 'stead of near summer when she died, they would a-stretched the wake out another day or two.

Lilah didn't think Granny would have wanted all such to-do made over her. If she had, she would have said so. All she'd asked was for Lilah to leave the swamp and learn to be a real lady, and that was something the swampfolk would never understand. Lilah hadn't understood it herself, until she'd started learning to read. She just wished she didn't have to stay with stuffy old Aunt Agnes while she was learning to be a real lady. Even now, she didn't understand the "real lady" part, but if learning to be a lady was as much fun as learning to read, she reckoned she wanted that, too.

But it wasn't just her going away the swampfolk wouldn't understand. They wouldn't understand about private grief, either. They'd want to take her into their homes, to pass her around like she was a new recipe, sympathizing with her and talking about how sad it was that she'd lost her maw and paw and now Granny. A week would turn into a month and a month into a year, and she'd never get out of the swamp. She'd never get to Homerville to finish her schoolin'. She'd never learn to read more than the few words she already knew. And she'd never see Jesse again.

He was the true reason she wanted to leave. Jesse hated the swamp. Hadn't he told her that when he got out of the Okefinoke, he wasn't ever a-goin' to venture into a swamp again? She'd made up her mind she wanted Jesse, and if she had to leave the swamp to have him, then that was just the way it had to be. And if she just happened to find him on her way out, then she'd be a step ahead.

It was funny, she mused as she started walking inland, dragging the canoe behind her, how she'd thought just a few weeks ago that she'd be devastated without Granny Latham. She'd loved Granny, and a part of her would always grieve for the old woman, but in her death, Granny had given Lilah's life a new purpose.

A few weeks ago, she wouldn't have believed she would ever want Jesse in her life. At first, she'd been discomfited when she was around him, but that had changed, too. So much in her life had changed in such a short time . . .

When Lilah caught a whiff of wood smoke, hope filled her breast and she turned a smiling face to Bob, who was hobbling along beside her, favoring his mangled paw as he always did. Ol' Codger had disappeared sometime back, which was just as well. The critters didn't need to follow her out'n the swamp. Come tomorrow, she'd have to try to shake Bob from her trail, but for the present, she was glad to have his company. And maybe now, she'd have Jesse's as well.

"Maybe I've found him a'ready," she said, pulling the canoe with renewed energy, moving toward the source of the smoke as quickly as she could.

"We-l-l-l, lookee here," Red said from the shadows, his voice brighter than Jack had heard it in some time. It was the brightness that made him draw his roasting stick from the fire and turn his head, 'cause Red never got excited over little things.

At first, he didn't see anything, partially because the contrast of yellow flames and the dark shadows surrounding him proved temporarily blinding. Then he heard a timid voice, coming from over near a clump of tall bushes.

"Jesse? Is that you? Who you got there with you?"

It was a sweet voice, with a sweet body to go with it, he'd bet. "Get her!" he hissed.

And Red did.

Chapter Nine

When Lilah heard the stranger's voice hissing the command to get her, she froze. Not only would her legs not move, but her mind got stuck asking what was going on and refused to budge. Before she knew it, the short-legged, long-bodied man snatched her up and started toting her toward the fire.

Bob's snarl jerked her back to reality. Fearful of the cat's safety, she hollered, "No, Bob. Stay back." Then she let loose with her arms and legs, thrashing the man's upper body with her fists and kicking his shins with her feet. He yelped and almost dropped her, his arm slipping from around her waist down to her hips, where he secured his hold again. He hoisted her up, tossed her over his right shoulder, and slapped her bottom hard with his free hand.

Lilah barely felt the blow. Lickety-split, the memory of the two men attacking her maw ripped through her. She knew the answer to her question now. These men were two of the outlaws, the ones who'd killed those folks up in Tennessee. The grisly possibilities of her immediate future obliterated physical feeling, while hurling her into renewed action against her foe. She pummeled his back and rammed his stomach with her bent knees, her gaze on Bob, who followed them into the firelight, his head up and his mouth open. As much as she wanted to scream, she

dared not. That would bring Bob pouncing for sure, and
the crippled cat would be no match for two able-bodied
men, who were, more than likely, armed.

He sprang anyway, digging his front claws into the
man's back and his teeth into the man's left shoulder. Desperate to save the cat, Lilah grabbed him around the middle and tried to tug him loose. The man hollered and bent
forward, throwing her off balance and making her let go of
Bob. Before she could regain her hold, she fell hard on her
back, mere inches from the blazing fire. Golden flecks
marred her vision, and she gasped for the breath her fall
had knocked out of her.

"Get him off me!" the short-legged man cried, the firelight illuminating his contorted features. His hands were
now on Bob, pulling at him, yanking on his fur, but Bob
had a strong hold and merely sank his teeth in deeper. The
other man, the big one with the eye patch, the one she'd
thought was Jesse, sprang forward, a long-bladed knife in
his fist.

"No!" she rasped, forcing her reluctant body into a sitting position and diving for the man's ankles. She managed to catch the one nearest her. He lost his balance and
fell to his knees.

Her victory was only momentary. In a thrice, the big
man twisted around and grabbed Lilah by the hair on her
head, yanking her forward and sending her headlong into
the grass. Intense pain burst through her nose; blood
gushed out of her nostrils and over her lips. She gasped
for air again. The man snatched her hair, pulling her head
up and complicating her breathing problem. She sputtered,
spitting out blood and grass and sand. And when she tried
to jerk her hand away, he pulled harder on her hair and
planted a knee in the small of her back.

"You ain't going nowhere, so you might as well quit
fighting," the man sneered.

Lilah jerked one more time, but the edge of cold steel

pricking the back of her neck successfully ended her struggle. Her life was over and done for. She couldn't save Bob
and she couldn't save herself. And she was going to die
without seeing Jesse again.

Jesse swore under his breath and plunged through the
bushes, holding his cypress knee club high and praying his
strength held out and his agility sufficed. The long hours
he'd spent lying perfectly still, watching Red and Jack and
waiting for the cover of darkness, had made him stiff, thus
compounding the ever-present throb in his left knee.

Lilah would have to show up when he'd taken a break
to answer nature's call. What was she doing here anyway?
He'd had a plan. A good one. But it didn't involve Lilah.
The notion of anything happening to her muddied his
thinking, and Jesse knew he needed a clear head to suc-
ceed.

As he moved toward the fire, he supposed he should be
grateful that the bobcat was keeping Red thoroughly occupied. The hairy man twisted and turned, his attention
seemingly focused on dislodging the cat, his cries covering
the faint noise of Jesse's approach. The moment Red saw
him, though, Jesse would have two adversaries to deal
with.

Going after One-Eyed Jack first might not be the better
thing to do, but Jesse had to get the man off Lilah. He had
to remove the threat of Jack's knife as quickly and deci-
sively as possible. As he raised the club, Jesse reached
deep down inside, not for physical strength as much as for
soul strength. With a *whoosh,* he took one last leap, bringing the cypress knee down and left in a wide arc. The club
caught Jack squarely on the side of his head, but it barely
fazed him.

Before Jesse could swing the club again, Jack was on
his feet, his blade still grasped in his fist, his one eye blazing with wrath. Jack came after Jesse with a vengeance,

slashing out at him with the knife while backing him out of the firelight.

Jesse tried to concentrate on Jack and the knife, but his thoughts were running amuck. Was Lilah all right? Where was Red? Was the man on the ground conscious and, therefore, another possible threat?

A slash of the knife burned a trail across his belly, wrenching him back to the only reality he could afford to ponder—his survival. He took a step backwards and swung the club again, landing the blow solidly on Jack's left ear. The man hollered this time, but he still kept coming. Jesse walloped him again with the club, this time aiming for Jack's right wrist.

The blow successfully knocked the knife out of Jack's hand and he lunged at Jesse, the force of his body hurling both of them to the ground with Jack on top. Jesse blocked Jack's fist with the club, then grabbed the open end of the cypress knee with his left hand, slipping his fingers inside and leaving his thumb on the outside for leverage. He shoved the club up under Jack's chin and, in one fluid motion, pushed against Jack's neck with the club and against Jack's body with his own. Jack rolled over, giving Jesse the advantage of position. Jack filled his fists with Jesse's hair and tugged hard. With all the strength and focus he could muster, Jesse pushed the club down against Jack's neck. Gradually, Jack's fists began to relax, but Jesse didn't let up.

Just about the time he thought Jack was passing out, strong hands grabbed Jesse's upper arms and pulled him away. Jesse brought the club with him, then found his arms so firmly held that he couldn't maneuver the weapon.

"We got you now, you son-a-bitch," Red hollered in Jesse's ear. "Gimme that club you got there."

At first, Jesse refused to let go, but when Red snatched Jesse's right arm up and back, he dropped it.

Jack groaned and started to get up. Jesse braced himself

for the blow Jack was certain to lob as soon as he got his breath back, but the sharp report of a pistol firing stayed Jack's fist.

"Let go a-him!" Lilah screeched.

Red whirled Jesse around so that he faced Lilah. "Go ahead an' shoot, little lady," Red jeered.

Undaunted, Lilah turned the six-shooter on Jack, who was inching closer to Jesse and Red. Her arm was shaking so much she couldn't hold the gun steady. Jesse cringed inwardly at the way she waved the .45 around. If she wasn't careful, she'd shoot him.

"Let go a-him," she repeated, her voice much softer and far more deadly this time, "or I'll shoot yer partner. And then I'll sic Bob back on you."

Red let go of Jesse.

"Go on now, both ye, and get out'n here."

"No!" Jesse cried. "You can't let them go!" He took a step toward her. "Give me the gun, Lilah."

Something hit him hard on the back of the head. For a second, sparks swam before his eyes, and then everything went black.

Lilah packed damp bog moss over the severed stub of the man the outlaws had left behind, her mind only half-occupied with her ministrations. After all these years, she'd finally remembered how her parents died, and now that she had, the memory wouldn't go away.

It happened on a hot, steamy day in her twelfth summer. Maw always said the heat made her fractious, and that day was no exception. The fact that it was wash day added to Merrie Bennett's crankiness.

Lilah wondered if, perhaps, her parents might still be alive had her maw not been stirring clothes over a hot fire when the two men emerged from the woods. She wondered, too, what might have happened if she'd been standing beside Maw. Maybe she could have stopped Merrie in time . . . maybe she'd be dead herself now . . .

On wash day, one of Lilah's jobs was to haul water from the lake. That was what she was doing when the men stepped into the clearing and started riling Maw. Getting on Maw's bad side was a mighty dangerous thing to do. Most times, Merrie Bennett was sweet as ripe huckleberries, but get her riled up, and she turned into a thistle thorn. 'Course, those men couldn't have known that when they started whistling at her and calling her "sweet thang" and "purty girl" and using words Lilah had never heard before or since. But Maw must've known those words, 'cause that's when she started giving 'em what-for.

Lilah heard the commotion on her way back to the cabin. Paw must've heard it, too, 'cause he come a-runnin' from the hogpen. Something made Lilah stop while she still had the dark woods to hide in, something grounded in either cowardice or smarts. Lilah didn't know which. She just knew she stood there, holding the heavy buckets, not even noticing how their weight tried to tug her arms from their sockets, while she watched the two scraggly men approach Maw.

"Go on an' git out'n here," Merrie screeched. "We ain't got nothin' worth stealin'."

One of the men—the shorter one—bobbed his head as he looked Maw up and down. "Oh, you got sumpin worth the takin', little lady. An' I aim ter git me some."

"I mean it," she warned. "Go on back where you come from."

The men ignored her. Lilah watched, mesmerized, as they sauntered closer to Maw, who just kept stirring the clothes. Then, as quick as a moccasin strikes, one of Paw's shirts come flying out of the big black kettle and right into the face of the shorter man.

After that, everything happened so fast Lilah had trouble separating it all. The man howled and flailed out with his arms, snatching the shirt away. The taller man jumped on Maw from behind, while she and the shorter one struggled over possession of the stirring paddle, which was then free of the shirt. Paw came tearing around the corner of the house and jumped on the taller man, yanking him off Maw. A gun exploded, and Paw fell into the boiling pot. Maw screamed and crumpled to the ground, a knife buried in her chest up to the hilt. The shorter man pulled the knife out, wiped its blade on his britches, and shoved it back into the scabbard that hung from his belt. And all the while, Lilah stood as stiff as the trunk of a mighty live oak, unable to move, unable to feel.

"Now, what'd you go do that fer?" the one with the gun said. "We cain't have no fun with no dead woman."

Something in Lilah snapped. She dropped to her knees and crawled behind a bush. She didn't know what kind of fun the man was talking about, nor was she a woman yet, though she was getting there fast. She just knew she didn't want the men to see her. She didn't want to find out what these two scoundrels had in mind, lest they decide to try it with her.

"She burnt me!" the shorter one wailed. "And I think she done broke my smeller." He grabbed a damp towel off the clothesline, wadded it up, and pressed it against the blood spurting out of his nose.

Lilah raised up enough to see the activity in the clearing. She tried to keep her gaze on the men and not Maw and Paw, but it was hard. It was hard, too, to be still and quiet when she wanted to run to her parents. But that something she never could name held her in the woods. She stayed put while the men ransacked the cabin. She stayed put when they came out, their haversacks bulging and their pockets overflowing. She stayed put while the men made good their escape . . . and for a long time afterwards.

Now that she remembered, she was plagued with guilt.

Over and over, as the events of that day replayed themselves in her mind, she changed the circumstances so that
she became a player rather than an observer. In one such
version, she saved her parents' lives. Another ended with
her lying on the ground next to Merrie Bennett, her life's
blood flowing out of her chest right along with Maw's.

Lilah felt bad. She could've done something . . . she
should've done something . . .

As Lilah bathed the outlaw and tended to his stub, she
kept an eye on Jesse. He'd been out cold most of the night,
and she was starting to get worried. The moment he
moaned, relief washed through her, and she scooted over
beside him.

"Ye're awake," she said, smoothing a palm over his
forehead. "I was beginnin' to think ye mought not come
to."

He moaned again and tried to sit up. Lilah gently
pushed against his head. "Jes' lie still. Yer belly wound
weren't too deep, but it's li'ble to be sore for a spell. Yer
head, too. That man knocked you good."

"Red," Jesse mumbled.

"Ye're seein' red?"

He moved his head to the side, and a sharp pain shot
from his nape to his forehead. "No. Red's his name. Red
Watkins."

"Ye know him?"

Jesse resisted the temptation to nod. "Been chasing him
for four years. That was the closest I ever came to getting
him."

Lilah flinched at the bitterness in his voice—and the im-
plication of his words. It was her fault the two men got
away. She'd really mommicked things up, more than he
knew. Jesse wasn't going to like what she had to tell him,
but she figured she might as well get it over with. He'd

find out when the sun came up anyway. "They taken the canoe."

Her hand didn't stop him from sitting up this time. "They did *what?*"

Lilah gathered moisture in her suddenly dry mouth. "They taken the canoe."

"Why didn't you stop them?"

"How was I suppose to do that?"

"You had the gun. Why didn't you shoot them?"

"I didn't know they was doin' it when they did it. It was dark."

Jesse rubbed the lump on the back of his head and tried to make sense out of what she was telling him. "It's dark again. I can't believe I slept the sun around. Red must've really hit me hard."

"Not that hard. It's still a couple a hours till day-bust."

"If they took the canoe in the dark and it's still dark now, then how do you know it's gone?"

" 'Cause it ain't where I left it"—she nodded toward the stand of bushes she'd emerged from earlier—"over yonder."

Jesse's gaze followed her nod, and he squinted up his eyes in an attempt to make out the outline of the canoe. Hell, it was so dark he couldn't even make out the outline of a single bush! How could she see that the canoe was gone? "How do you know for sure?"

" 'Cause it ain't there no more."

The man next to him moaned, snagging both Jesse's and Lilah's attention. She wiggled over and inspected the stump. Jesse bit back his frustration and watched her tamp at the mess of peat moss covering the stub, a slew of other questions suddenly vying for position. What was Lilah doing here, on this island? How did she know that Red and Jack were really gone and not lurking somewhere in the shadows? Where was the knife? The gun? Hell,

where'd she get the gun in the first place? For that matter,
where did she get the bog moss?

"Where did you get the bog moss?"

Lilah looked up and blinked at him, wondering if he'd
lost his mind. "The swamp's full of it."

"I know that!" He rubbed his temples, trying to ease
both the pain in his head and his raw nerves. "But there
isn't any close by."

"I got it from the aidge of the lake. That's how come
me to know the canoe's gone."

"Damn, woman!" He had to stop barking at her. Even
quiet words jarred his head. Screaming intensified the pain
to an almost intolerable level. Jesse forced himself to
speak calmly. "You're telling me that you walked down to
the lake? In the dark?"

"Since I ain't got a pine knot or a lantern, what was I
suppose to do?"

"You were supposed to sit right here with the gun in
your hand. By the way, where did you get that shooter?"

"Took it off'n Red, whilst Bob had him occupied."

"Good for you!" Jesse was truly impressed with her ini-
tiative, but he'd feel better once he had the .45 firmly in
his waistband. He looked around for it but didn't see it
anywhere. "Where'd you put the gun, Lilah?"

She bit her lower lip and looked away, fixing her gaze
on the dying fire. "I throwed it in the lake."

"You did *what?*" His anger overrode the pain his outburst caused.

"I throwed it—"

"I heard you."

She turned her head sharply and glared at him. "Then
how come ye to ast me again?"

He sighed. "I didn't mean to ask you again. I meant,
why did you do it?"

"Then how come ye not to say so? Ye're always a-doin'
that."

"Doing what?"

"Sayin' one thang and meanin' t'other."

Patience, he cautioned himself. "Why did you do it, Lilah?"

" 'Cause I don' have no truck with guns."

"We needed that gun."

"I kep' the knife."

"Well, well. Will wonders never cease!"

She turned back to the wounded outlaw, ignoring his sarcasm. Jesse took a good look at the man and recognized him as the one Jack called Smiley, whose real name, according to Jesse's sources, was Adam Shaunessey. From the looks of it, Smiley had suffered a run-in with an alligator. *Serves him right,* Jesse thought. He watched Lilah bathe Smiley's face and listened to her coo to the felon until he couldn't stand it another minute.

"Stop it! He isn't worth your concern."

"He's sick," she said matter-of-factly.

"Will he live?"

"Prob'ly not."

"Then why bother with him?"

Lilah dropped the scrap of cloth into the bottom section of a coffeepot and turned sad eyes on Jesse. "I didn't think ye would live when I found you."

"Then why'd you bother with me?"

" 'Cause I ain't never left a critter to die, and I'm not aimin' to start. Takin' care of wounded critters ain't no botheration. Not for me."

For reasons Jesse didn't think he wanted to explore, her answer wounded his pride. He let his gaze wonder, searching for something else to focus on, and spied the coffeepot.

"Where'd that come from?"

"Where'd what come from?"

"The coffeepot."

"They left it here."

That made Jesse's spirits take a turn for the better, but he didn't dare hope too much, not the way his luck was going. "Did they, perhaps, also leave some coffee?"

Lilah shrugged. "I ain't got no use for the foul-tasting stuff myself."

"I do!" he bellowed.

"Then look in the haversack." She waved an arm to indicate a tarred canvas bag sitting on the ground near Smiley's head.

Jesse snatched up the bag and carried it closer to the fire. Inside, he found a skillet and a small pot with a bail, a copper match safe half-full of dry lucifers, a few strips of jerky, small, half-empty bags of flour and cornmeal, some short-sweetnin', a metal tripod, and—glory be!—a bag of coffee beans. His enthusiastic "Whoopee" startled the croaking frogs and chirping insects, creating a moment of silence before the swamp came alive again with noise.

While Lilah nursed Smiley, Jesse gathered more wood and built up the fire, then went down to the lake to get some water. He'd rather have used rain water, but his hankering for coffee was too great to quibble about the purity of the water he made it with. All the way to the lake and back, he kept a close lookout for One-Eyed Jack, as well as for snakes and gators, which wasn't easy in the close darkness. He supposed he should have found a pine knot first, but the light would have alerted Jack to his movement, and Jesse still wasn't convinced Jack and Red were really gone. Besides, if Lilah had made the trip without mishap, he supposed he could, too.

When he got back, he proceeded to parch the coffee beans in the skillet. "I need the coffeepot," he told her.

She poured the dirty water out and handed it to him, surprising him with her calm cooperation.

"Aren't you going to tell me you need it back?"

"No."

"Why not?"

" 'Cause he's dead."

Though Jesse found this news heartening, he could tell Lilah wasn't happy to supply it, so he busied himself setting up the tripod and building up the fire, hoping she'd change the subject. He should have known better.

"Ain't ye goin' to say something?"

What could he say? He considered trying to explain to her that now they needn't concern themselves with attempting to transport Smiley, which would have proved difficult without her canoe. Nor did they now have to share their time, energies, or food with an outlaw whose final destiny was the end of a rope. Telling her those things would only make her angry. She would never understand how Smiley's death unencumbered them.

Jesse settled for the most noncommittal answer he could come up with. "Oh."

"Ain't ye sorry?"

"Leave it alone, Lilah," he warned.

"Ye ain't sorry a bit, are you? A man's dead, gone forever, and ye ain't feelin' the least bit sad."

"No, I'm not," he agreed, fighting for control.

Lilah stared at Jesse and realized she didn't know him at all. "I thought ye was diffrunt." Her voice caught in her throat, but she plunged ahead anyway. "I thought ye had a heart."

"I do!"

"I don' believe it."

"He was scum, Lilah. Pure-dee scum. As low and vile and worthless as they come. The world is better off without Smiley Shaunessey in it."

"And what makes ye sich an authority on this here man?"

"He murdered my wife and children!"

Immediately, Jesse wished he could take back the words. Now that he'd opened the proverbial can of worms, he'd have to elaborate, and he just didn't feel up to it.

Through several moments of tense silence he waited for her to ask him another question, then she surprised him by rising and walking away from the fire, toward the bushes.

"Where are you going?" he called.

"Over to here."

"Come back. It's dark over there."

She kept walking. "I know it."

Damned exasperating female! "Look. I'm sorry for screaming at you. I had no reason—"

"Yes, ye did."

"Then why are you mad at me?"

By that time, the shadows had completely swallowed her—and Jesse was beginning to panic. He wanted her back in the light, back where he could see her and protect her from harm. But it didn't look like she was coming back. He stirred the coffee beans, then rose, aiming to go after her, then realized he needed a light to find her. He was extracting a good-sized pine branch from the fire, when she spoke again.

"I ain't mad."

She sounded close. Jesse relaxed a bit. "If you're not mad, why did you walk away?"

" 'Cause."

" 'Cause why?"

He waited for her answer, trying to be patient, then gave up. He lifted the flaming branch and hoped it didn't go out too quickly. "I'm coming after you," he called.

"Stay there!" She sounded distressed. A dozen possibilities raced through his head, none of them pleasant.

"No. Something's wrong, and I'm coming over there to find out what it is."

"Nothin's wrong. I'll be back tirectly."

The real panic in her voice negated the assurance of her words. Something was definitely wrong. He was sure of it. His head filled with a vision of One-Eyed Jack holding a knife blade at her throat. His stomach knotted up and his heart jerked.

"I'm coming," he called again, taking a step away from the fire.

A hand fastened around his ankle and squeezed, halting both his movement and his breath.

"You ain't goin' nowheres, mister."

Chapter Ten

"Damnation!" Jesse barked. "I knew it. I knew it."

What a predicament he was in. Lilah had the knife—he supposed, since she never had told him what she did with it—and she'd thrown away the .45. All he had to defend them with was the blazing stick in his hand. Jesse prayed it was enough. He started to twist around to see which one of the two bastards was holding his ankle, but Lilah's voice stopped him cold.

"What'd ye know, Jesse?"

There wasn't an ounce of concern evident in her cheerful voice. Simultaneously amazed and confused, he whirled back around to see her come tripping merrily into camp. *The little fool!*

"Run, Lilah!"

She laughed at him. "Run? Ever-what for?"

"Don't argue! Run! Run for your life. Now, before it's too late." In his fear for her safety, his heart was beating double time and sweat was pouring off his brow. But just as calm as midday in August, she kept walking toward him. She walked right up to him and laid an open palm on his damp forehead.

"What's got into you?" she said. "Ye're pale as a haint."

"They're back!" he hissed. "They probably never left."

She gave him an indulgent smile, then shook her head ruefully. "Shet yer worryin', Jesse. They's gone, I tell ye."

"Can't be. One of 'em's got me—" Suddenly, he realized the handhold on his ankle wasn't there anymore. He felt like a consarned idiot. "I swear, someone grabbed my ankle and told me I wasn't going anywhere."

She broke into gales of laughter that quickly became a fit of giggles. Dreaming this situation up was bad enough, but to have her laugh at his anxiety was, well, it was just too much. Jesse took her by the shoulders and shook her. "Stop it! This isn't funny."

"Yes, it is," she tittered, pointing to a spot on the ground behind him. He let go of her and turned around, then broke into laughter himself. Smiley's open hand lay right beside Jesse's foot, and a lopsided grin softened the pain etched on the outlaw's face.

"Sceered ya, didn't I, Marshal?"

"What are you doing alive? I mean, you're supposed to be dead. I mean—"

"He never says what he aims to," Lilah interrupted, moving over and bending down next to Smiley. "How're ye feelin'?"

"Piss poor. I mean—"

Smiley's face turned red, but Lilah smiled sweetly and said, "I'll bet you do," which put him completely at ease. Jesse watched all this in some amazement. Most women would have thrown a hissy fit at hearing such language and demanded an apology.

"They went off and left me, didn't they?" Smiley whined.

Jesse winced at the resignation evident on the man's face, then mentally fussed at himself for weakening. Smiley didn't deserve his pity. He didn't deserve anyone's pity. He sure as hell didn't deserve Lilah's, but she seemed bound and determined to feel sorry for the outlaw.

"Yes, they did," she said, "but we're here with you now. We'll take real good keer of you."

No, we won't, Jesse thought, but he didn't have the heart to say it. Instead, he asked the question that had been plaguing him for several minutes. "Just exactly what were you doing over there in the bushes, Lilah?"

She shot him a look that made him wonder if he'd suddenly grown two heads, and then he knew what she'd been doing and why she'd wanted privacy. Nature was calling him as well. He gave her a nod of understanding as he rose to leave. When he came back, she was still fawning over Smiley, telling him not to worry, that they weren't going to leave him there.

Like hell we're not! The two of them had to get a few things straight. "We need to talk," he told her.

Without even turning her head his way, she offered the merest nod of acquiescence. "Jesse says Smiley is yer entitlement."

"Yes, ma'am."

Ma'am? Jesse wondered if Smiley had ever said the word before.

"Well, Mr. Smiley, ye need to rest."

"Yes, ma'am, but don't I smell coffee beans parchin'? I shore would like to have me a cup of coffee."

Damn! He'd forgotten the coffee beans. And they smelled like they were burning. Jesse snatched the skillet off the fire and shook it, tossing the beans, then he set them aside and dug in the haversack for a grinder. When he couldn't find one, he took off his shirt, laid it out on the ground, and dumped the beans onto the back side of it.

"What are ye a-doin'?" Lilah asked.

"I have to crush these beans in order to make coffee," he explained, making a bag out of the shirt and looking around for a good-sized stick. He found one, set the makeshift bag on a fallen log, and proceeded to clobber the shirt with the stick. As he worked, he watched Lilah tuck the blanket around Smiley and listened to her talk to the scoundrel just the way she'd talked to him after the snakebite. He'd thought she actually cared for him, that he held a special place in her heart, but he realized now that this was the way she treated all wounded critters. He was no different than all the rest.

The acknowledgement hurt worse than he'd ever thought possible, sort of curling around his heart and squeezing it for all it was worth. He beat the beans harder.

The plaintive cry of a bird he couldn't identify floated through the clearing. Just as it faded away, a similar cry rang out, and then another and another. Jesse looked up and saw the distinct though still dark outline of the bushes surrounding them. Daylight was fast approaching.

When he'd set the coffee to boiling, he returned his attention to Lilah, who was digging in the knapsack.

"There's flour here, and a tin a-lard. I think I'll whoop up some biscuits."

As hungry as Jesse was, talking to Lilah was more important at the moment, especially since Smiley appeared to be sleeping again. "They'll wait," he whispered, taking her arm and pulling her to her feet, then guiding her toward the bushes.

Lilah didn't like the way he was manhandling her. She jerked her arm away from his grasp and marched ahead of him. She'd known this time was coming, and though a part of her actually relished the idea of being alone with Jesse, a larger part dreaded it, since he was sure to scold her for the way she'd mommicked things up.

When she reached the bushes, she stopped and turned around. Surprisingly, Jesse walked right past her, heading on toward the lake. She hurried to catch up with him.

"Where're ye goin'?"

"To get my .45 back."

"*Your* .45?"

"Yes, mine!"

Though it was still too dark to see his face clearly, she could hear his utter irritation. He was even madder than she'd thought. "But I taken it off'n—"

"Red. I know. But it's mine. He must have found it somewhere. It's a wonder that alligator didn't eat it. It sure chewed up the holster. Dammit, Lilah! Why did you—oh, never mind." He took another couple of steps, then stopped suddenly and turned around. "You *do* remember where you threw the gun away."

"Yes."

"Are we headed in the right direction?"

"I think so." She surveyed the immediate area. "I know I took one of these gator trails."

"But you aren't sure this is the one?"

"Not certain-sure. I can tell better when the sunball comes up."

"You can answer my questions in the meantime," he said, leaning against a laurel oak sapling and crossing his arms over his chest. Figuring she might as well make herself comfortable, too, Lilah copied his stance, using a sapling opposite him for support.

"First of all, what are you doing here?"

"I live here."

Jesse rolled his head back and stared at the lightening sky for a moment. When he looked at her again, she could feel the intensity of his one-eyed gaze. "What are you doing on this particular island?"

"I stopped here to rest, same as you."

"How did you know why I—" He paused, shaking his head. "You're getting me off track."

"I don' aim to."

"The same way you don't aim to misunderstand me?" he accused wryly. "Just tell me, plain and simple, why you left Granny and came here."

Lilah squeezed her eyes tight, trying to squelch the sudden rush of tears, then found she couldn't speak past the lump in her throat.

"Tell me, Lilah! Why did you leave Granny and come trailing after me?"

His unfeeling roar made her jump, and she pinned him with a glare of her own. " 'Cause she's dead."

Jesse didn't know what he'd expected her to say, but it certainly wasn't that. How she must be hurting inside, and he'd treated her with callous disregard ever since he'd come to that morning. In two long strides, he crossed the space between them, then folded Lilah into his arms. She collapsed against him, her arms going around his waist, letting his chest absorb her sobs. For a long time they stood there, Jesse holding her against him, one hand smoothing her hair and the other rubbing her back, while he murmured gentle, consoling phrases.

The sunball, as Lilah called it, made its daily appearance on the eastern horizon, its pink-gold radiance setting her blond hair to shimmering. Jesse couldn't resist touching his lips to the sun-kissed mane, and before he knew what was happening, his mouth was devouring hers.

Lilah melted against him, savoring the feel of his hard, muscled chest against her soft breasts, and the thrust of his tongue as it explored the deeper recesses of her mouth. The flame leapt from her belly and into her veins, scorching her from the inside out and making her shiver all at the same time. His heart thumping in rhythm with her own and the searing heat of his mouth told her he was as deeply affected by the kiss as she was.

This was what she'd hoped for, what she'd dreamed about ever since Jesse had kissed her the first time, the day Granny died. And yet, this wasn't right somehow. Not now. Not like this.

She pulled away from him, disengaged herself from his embrace, and started walking toward the lake again.

"Wait!" he called after her.

Though she kept moving, he quickly caught up with her, halting her with a tender hand laid upon her shoulder. He stepped in front of her and tilted her chin up. "What's wrong?" he asked, his voice hoarse.

"I don' want yer pity."

"Pity? Is that what you think?"

She nodded.

A hint of a smile touched his wide lips, but the green tint of his eye remained dark with passion. "I've never kissed a woman out of pity, Lilah."

"Then—how come?"

He rubbed his thumb back and forth across her bottom lip. His touch raised gooseflesh, but she refused to give in to the urge to fall into his arms again. "Because . . ." He let go a heaving sigh, lifting his gaze and staring at something over her head. "I don't know how come, Lilah. But I assure you, pity never entered into it."

Then he drew her to him again, but this time he held her in friendship rather than passion. "I'm sorry," he said after a while. "What happened?"

Lilah swallowed hard, gathering inner strength. "The day you left . . . you mem'ry Granny was out gatherin' yarbs and roots?"

She felt his chin bob against the top of her head, indicating his recollection. "It was late when she come home. Almost day-down. I was a-waitin' for her, a-wonderin' what was keepin' her. She—" Lilah swiped at the moisture on her cheeks and swallowed again.

"Did a snake—"

"Naw. It were jes' old age, I guess. She said her heart give out."

Jesse thought his heart would surely break, right along with Lilah's. He pulled her closer, recalling his own misery the day he'd found Martha and the boys. For a long time, he'd merely sat in a stupor, his mind refusing to accept the reality of their deaths. If James McDougall, who owned a farm less than a mile away, hadn't come along, he might be sitting there still. Thank God, he'd had James to help him build the coffins and dig the graves. Thank God, he'd had Sally, James's wife, to dress the bodies, and Owen, their oldest boy, to go get the preacher. He didn't want to think how he would have managed without the help and support of his friends . . . all the way through the funeral.

The funeral. Less than three days had passed since he'd left Medicine Island, barely enough time for word to get around, surely not enough time for folks to gather for Granny's funeral.

"Who came to the funeral, Lilah?"

"No one. Ye're the first person I've tole." *And that was the first time I've cried,* she mentally added. With the same cleansing effect as the tears, the dam in her heart opened up and the words spilled forth, almost tripping over themselves in her rush to share her grief. When she finally ran dry, Jesse held her close for a moment longer, his hands tenderly caressing her head and back. Until that moment, Lilah hadn't known how much she needed to tell someone, how much she needed the comfort and understanding of a friend. She tried to imagine talking to Colin this way, having his arms around her instead of Jesse's, but the very notion rang false.

As Jesse held her, he tried to imagine how she must have felt digging the grave, constructing the coffin, and preparing the body all by herself, and he realized she was made of much sturdier stuff than he.

The gun, he decided, could wait. He looped an arm around Lilah's shoulders and walked her back to the camp.

Lilah's biscuits were hard and the coffee tasted burned, but Jesse enjoyed every bite and every swallow. Smiley woke up long enough to drink some coffee, then fell asleep again. Jesse helped Lilah gather up the dirty dishes and haul them to the lake to rinse clean.

"Yer gun's yonder," she said, pointing across the lake to a thick stand of maiden canes growing close to what appeared to be a nearly solid bog. Here, the lake ran finger-like between the island and the bog. Jesse estimated the canes lay some twenty yards from where Lilah stood in the shallows.

"You threw it that far?"

She nodded. "I heared it rustle in the canes as it sank."

He eyed the dense growth again and wondered how he'd ever find anything in it, even something as large as a Colt .45. The dark side of him wanted to make Lilah go find it. After all, she was the one who'd put it there. But he couldn't do that to her, no matter how outdone he was with her for throwing the gun away.

Lilah sensed his reluctance. "Snakes don' hide in the maiden cane," she said. "Jes' fishbait critters."

"Such as?"

"Oh, little ol' turtles and frogs, sal'manders, beetles—nothin' that'd hurt you."

Hoping she was right, Jesse stepped into the lake and slogged across to the stand of canes, which stretched out on either side of him for what looked like miles now that he was up close. "Am I even close to the spot?"

He watched her gaze sweep the expanse of dense growth, then she shrugged. "It was dark."

Since he saw no sense in combing the same area twice, Jesse figured he needed to mark the spot where he'd started looking. He grabbed a fistful of the slender cane and yanked. Surprisingly, it came right up. Something crawled across the back of his hand and a yelp jumped into his throat. Jesse managed to swallow the sound, but not his trepidation. When he saw that it was just a bug, he felt plumb foolish. Breathing easier, he tossed the canes over his shoulder and grabbed another handful. The cane was so thick, it took a dozen or so such yanks to make even a small dent.

"Ye aimin' to take it all out?" Lilah asked, her voice incredulous.

"Nope, though that may be a good idea."

She deposited the skillet she was washing on shore, then slogged across the lake herself. "You go that away, I'll go t'other."

"You're going to help me?"

"I s'pose, elsewise ye'll take all day. Or pull up all the canes."

Jesse watched Lilah deftly separate the canes and slide her extended arms all the way down to the peat bottom, then move over a bit and repeat the actions in reverse. He tried to imitate her movements, but he couldn't bring himself to think of the cane as totally harmless the way Lilah seemed to. He didn't like putting his arms into places he couldn't see, especially when this place literally crawled with creatures that seemed bent on crawling on him.

Maybe talking would take his mind off this odious task.

"Let's review our situation here," he began.

Lilah laughed. "Not much to review. Ye're way behind me."

"I'm not talking about *this* situation. I mean the whole kit and kaboodle."

"Oh. Like the canoe's gone and Smiley can't walk. That what ye're talking 'bout, Jesse?"

Her voice rang with a cheerful optimism that rankled Jesse, who didn't see anything the least bit humorous in their predicament. "You know something I don't?" he asked.

"Yep."

Jesse waited through a silence that seemed to stretch out forever. Finally, he said, "You gonna tell me?"

"Ye don' have to be so fractious."

"And you don't have to be so damned reticent!"

"What does that mean?"

"Reserved. Quiet. Unwilling to share this tidbit of knowledge with me."

"All ye want's a tidbit? All right." She inclined her head to the southwest. "Yerby's Island."

"So?"

"That's my tidbit."

"Don't play with me, Lilah. Tell me what's so special about Yerby's Island."

She snorted. "Oh, it ain't so special. Jes' a little island, not big as Medicine Island. Got a goodly sized hummock, though."

"Hummock?"

"Ye know, a passel a-trees a-growin' all close t'gether-like."

"A hammock."

"That what ye call it?"

She's going to be the death of me yet. "Yes. What's so special about this hammock on Yerby's Island?"

"Oh, it ain't much of a hummock anymore. The Yerbys done cleared it so's they could grow some corn and ta-ters."

"The Yerbys. You know these people?"

"Sakes, alive, Jesse. I been a-knowin' the Yerbys, long as I can mem'ry."

"Will they help us?"

"More'n likely."

"How far is it to Yerby's Island?"

"Walking? Half a day."

"Let's go." Jesse pulled his arms out of the cane and started back to the shore. Lilah made no move to follow him. "Come on."

"Now? I thought ye wanted to find yer gun."

"I'll borrow one from the Yerbys."

"They don' keep no extree guns, Jesse. 'Sides, they'd know somethin' was up if'n I ast for a shootin' iron. That'd be like me sittin' down and eatin' a rabbit or a squirrel. If'n ye're so set on havin' one, then ye'd best keep a-lookin' for yer'n."

Reluctantly, Jesse went back to the cane. He hadn't paid much attention to what Lilah ate, but her comment made him ask. "What do you have against rabbits and squirrels?"

"Oh, I don' have nothin' agin 'em. I like 'em. I jest don' eat 'em."

"Why not?"

"They's forest critters and they's yard critters. God made yard critters for man to eat."

"But you eat fish," he pointed out.

"Fish is water critters."

Jesse could see himself getting nowhere fast with this subject, besides which he was far more interested right now in the Yerbys than in Lilah's eating habits. "Just how do you think the Yerbys will help us, Lilah?"

"They got theirselfs one a Josiah Mizell's punt boats and a canoe, so I figure I can borry the canoe. And Miz Mamie'll give me some food and maybe some clothes. All I got's this here skirt and blouse. My go-away satchel was in my canoe."

It was funny, Jesse thought, how she kept talking about asking for things in a singular sense, as though she was planning to go to Yerby's Island by herself, which wouldn't do at all. He started to ask her if that was what she intended, but she let out a squeal that plumb near stopped his heart altogether and made him completely forget everything else. Damn snakes! He knew the cane wasn't safe.

"Hold on, Lilah! I'm coming."

But already the water was rippling out from her descent, and before he could reach her, the dark water engulfed her head.

Chapter Eleven

As Jesse rushed headlong for the spot where Lilah had disappeared, he stepped into a depression on the floor of the lake and plunged forward, completely submerging himself in the dark, acidic water. For a moment, he knew total and utter panic—not because he feared drowning, but because his stumble delayed his reaching Lilah.

He popped up, sputtering and coughing, unable to see through his burning eye, unable to hear through his water-clogged ears. Before he could collect himself, something warm and surprisingly soothing encircled his rib cage, then drew him forward. His chest collided with cold, wet fabric, but he could feel the warmth and feminine softness of the human body beneath it.

Lilah!

But that wasn't possible. He rubbed his eye and tipped his head first to one side and then the other, to drain the water from his ears before chancing a look at his captor. Even then, he couldn't believe Lilah was actually standing there, looking up at him without even the tiniest bit of pain or discomfort on her face.

"You're not hurt?" he asked.

"No. Are ye?"

"Just wet." He wrapped his arms around her and squeezed. "God! I thought you were—I thought you had been—" He pushed away, holding her at arm's length, not about to release his hold on her. She grinned at him, her blue eyes alight with glee. "I swear, woman! You scared me half out of my wits. And what do you do? Smile about it."

Lilah didn't allow his gruff scolding to spoil her good mood, not when she'd just made the most delightful discovery. He cared what happened to her, really and truly cared. The knowledge filled her with wonder and humbled her at the same time. She wanted to see him smile, too, and she possessed the object to make that happen.

"I found it!" she crooned, drawing the .45 from the water and dangling it in front of his face.

She waited for the smile, but it didn't come. Instead, the hunger-bittenest look she'd ever witnessed overtook his features. Why, he was practically drooling—and it wasn't over the gun. He wasn't even looking at it. His one good eye bored into her chest, his gaze so intense that Lilah grew warm and flustered all of a sudden, without knowing why.

Until she glanced down. Both her cream-colored bodice and the thin cotton chemise she wore beneath it clung like a second skin to her breasts, which were thrust out as proudly as a pair of coon dogs' noses. The wet fabric left nothing to the imagination, not even the dark crests and the tight round nubs that were growing harder by the second. That full-growed-woman yearning blossomed deep down inside, and she ached for Jesse to touch her in places she'd never imagined being touched before.

She lifted her gaze to his face and saw that he was watching her. A niggling voice told her that she should feel ashamed, but the longing on Jesse's face and the warm, wet rush that seeped down her inner thigh told her otherwise. Without taking his eye off her, he took the gun from her hand and tossed it toward the island, then he laid his open palms on her breasts and moved them back and forth over her throbbing nipples.

The ache built to a fevered pitch so fast it took Lilah completely by surprise. Suddenly, she wanted more. A lot more. The trouble was she couldn't pin down what she wanted. All she knew was that it was something wild and wonderful, something that would ease the ache and satisfy the yearning, something that was meant to be, not only between a man and a woman, but between the two of them.

She moved toward him until her toes bumped into his, and when she leaned her head back and parted her lips, his mouth descended on hers with the swiftness of a hawk swooping down on a field mouse. His beard brushed her face, at once both soft and bristly, and his moustache tickled her lips. His tongue raked her teeth, begging entrance, while his thumbs teased the hard crowns of her breasts. Without the slightest hesitation, she offered him the treasures of her mouth, and when he took her tongue into his mouth and suckled gently, she thought she would surely scream with pleasure.

Jesse marveled at her trembling response. He would have sworn she was a complete innocent, yet the way she pressed her breasts against his hands and moaned into his mouth suggested an unleashed wantonness contrary to his image of her. He marveled, too, at his own response to her. He'd grown long and hard the moment he laid his eye on the dark crests of her breasts, and now he wondered how much longer he could hold out without making her wholly and completely his woman.

Too many years had passed since he'd allowed himself to combine caring with passion—so long that he'd almost forgotten the surge of energy that rushed through him, making him feel whole and handsome and wonderful in a way lying with soiled doves never did.

The unwelcome image of such liaisons slapped him hard. God! What was he doing? Despite her fiery re-

sponse, Lilah was innocent. He'd bet his one good eye on
it. And here he was, taking unfair advantage of that innocence. No matter how much he wanted her right then, no
matter how much his heart longed for the companionship
of a good woman, no matter how much his body ached for
release—he couldn't do it.

With as much restraint as he'd ever been required to
employ, Jesse cooled his ardor, but he did so with tenderness, relaxing his kiss and slipping his hands around to her
back before finally pulling his mouth from hers and taking
a step backwards. Still, he felt her stiffen and knew she
didn't understand. Somehow, he had to make her understand, but this wasn't the time to do it, not when they both
had to deal with unsatisfied passion. Not now, with his
throat too full for words.

"I'm sorry" was all he could manage.

Lilah didn't know what to say, what to think, what to
feel. Her mind was in a turmoil and her full-growed-
woman yearning screamed to be eased. She might not be
the prettiest girl he'd ever seen, but he seemed to be at-
tracted to her. He seemed to enjoy kissing her, and he'd
seemed to enjoy looking at her breasts. This last she
wasn't certain-sure of, since now he kept his gaze leveled
on her face. She must be doing something wrong—or
there was something wrong with her body, though for the
life of her she couldn't imagine what it could be. All she
knew was that she'd never hurt quite so bad inside.

Unbidden tears welled up in her eyes. She stepped out
of his embrace and turned away, heading for shore and
hoping Jesse hadn't seen the tears swimming in her eyes.
Once her back was to him, those tears spilled forth, but
she refused to wipe them away. Her intuition told her that
she couldn't let him know how much power he wielded
over her emotions.

She had to get away from him for a while. She needed

time to calm herself, to sort things out, to regain her perspective. But first, she needed time to cry.

With a heavy heart, Jesse watched Lilah, her back rigid, step over the .45, which had landed safely on the boggy earth, and take off down the gator trail.

He'd hurt her—again. That he'd done it unintentionally didn't matter. That he'd tempered his rejection with tenderness didn't matter either. He didn't see his withdrawal as rejection, but he was sure Lilah viewed it that way.

He supposed he could traipse off after her and try to explain, but he still didn't think he was ready to do that, nor did he think she was ready to listen. Regardless, his gut instinct told him this was one of those times she needed to be alone. He didn't figure she was too different from him deep down inside, where it mattered, and there were certainly times he required absolute solitude.

Lilah understood that, probably better than he did. He recalled the time she'd asked him what the outlaws he was chasing had done. The memory of One-Eyed Jack's unspeakable deeds had filled his soul, preventing explanation. He'd answered her with a question of his own—*What hadn't they done?*—and she hadn't said another word. Lots of folks would have pushed for a definitive answer, but not Lilah. She'd quietly left him to deal with his misery alone, which was the way he wanted it, only he hadn't realized it until after she was gone.

He'd caused her enough misery for one day. The least he could do now was allow her to deal with it in her own way.

The fact that she was angry with him for not following her didn't make sense. She wanted to be alone, she told herself. She didn't want Jesse there to see her tears or hear her sobs. She didn't want Jesse there to ask questions or to tell her again that he was sorry.

What did he have to be sorry about anyway? Was he sorry he'd kissed her? That didn't make sense—since he'd already kissed her once before. If her mouth had a-tasted bad or something the first time, he wouldn't a-kissed her again. He had too much smarts not to remember.

Was he sorry he'd touched her breasts? That didn't make sense, either. It wasn't like they was prickly or thorny or anything like that. Nope, it couldn't be her breasts. If there was anything wrong with them, he wouldn't a-kept on feeling of 'em. Just to make sure, Lilah ran her palms down her breasts and over her nipples, which served to elicit that warm, golden glow in her belly all over again. Self-consciously, she folded her hands in her lap and forced herself to concentrate on why he'd said he was sorry.

But that was a mistake, too, since it put her hands almost on top of her most private place, the place that had throbbed and ached and got all wet while he was kissing her and rubbing her breasts. Without conscious direction, she pushed the heel of her hand against the feminine mound and moved it back and forth until it started to throb again. Before she'd stopped to think about what she was doing, the throb turned into a spasm and then exploded into flinders of earth-shattering sensations that caused her to arch her back and rub harder.

As the sensation melted away, rational thought returned. The blush of shame and embarrassment burned her cheeks, and she scrooched her eyes tightly shut, trying to block out the reality of what she'd just done. No one had ever told her it was wrong to touch herself this way, but she couldn't quite imagine either Maw or Granny telling her it was right.

Was this why Jesse was sorry? Because he'd lit the fuse and then stomped it out before it had a chance to set off the explosion?

Hell's banjer! Didn't he know all he had to do was rub her a little bit down there to make it happen?

She bet he didn't know! That was why he was sorry, 'cause he didn't know what to do to make her feel so good. Well, she could fix that easy enough. All she had to do was get him alone again, and then explain it to him.

Smiling, Lilah rose from her perch on a fallen log, brushed her skirt off, and set her feet on a hasty path back to camp.

Jesse heard her coming before he saw her. She was singing, her sweet, clear voice trilling over the notes of a song about dancing around a maypole.

Maypoles! Dancing! Whatever had gotten into her? He could have sworn she was upset when she'd left him back at the lake. If he was right, she surely had gotten over it fast. He supposed he ought to be glad, but he wasn't. There he was, wallowing in his own misery, while she was as happy as a bee on a buttercup.

Determined not to let her see his frown, he returned his attention to oiling the pistol and listening to Smiley ramble on about how he'd first gotten hooked up with One-Eyed Jack, and how sorry he was now that he'd ever met the scoundrel.

"I didn't have nothin' to do with killin' yer wife and boys, Marshal," Smiley said, his voice and expression so sincere Jesse almost believed him. "I heared you tellin' Miz Lilah that I done it, but swear I didn't. All I ever did was make a little moonshine. I ain't never kilt nothin' that wasn't something to eat. I ain't never even aimed my shotgun at a man. My paw taught me not to aim my gun lessen I planned to pull the trigger."

"My family wasn't shot," Jesse said, his voice tight. The look of confusion that crossed Smiley's face, followed by a sick expression as understanding dawned,

made Jesse wonder again if, perhaps, he hadn't mis-
judged the man.

Lilah's voice drew closer, and then she practically burst
into the clearing. In spite of his resolve, Jesse couldn't resist glancing up. The broad smile she cast him dusted the
frown right off his face and made him forget about his
wounded pride. There was just no way he could be angry
around someone that happy.

She ended the lighthearted song on a high, clear note,
then hugged herself and spun around, her full skirt flying
up to expose trim ankles and slender bare feet. Like a
wreath of diamonds, sunbeams sprinkled themselves atop
her blond head, but the sparkle in her blue eyes came from
within. In fact, her entire face glowed so much she looked
like she'd swallowed the sun.

"Ain't this day jes' bodacious wonderful?" she cried,
throwing her arms wide and slowing her pirouette to a
gradual close.

Neither Jesse nor Smiley agreed with her, but she didn't
seem to notice. She plopped herself down directly in front
of Jesse, folding her legs and settling her skirt over them,
then leaned forward at the waist, which put her head mere
inches from his. He tried not to notice, but a pleasant fragrance wafted up from her hair to tickle his nose, and her
head cast a shadow on his lap, and therefore on the dis-
mantled pistol. She didn't seem to notice the shadow, either.

"Is it goin' to work now?" she asked.

"I don't know yet," Jesse said, wiggling backwards. Just
about the time the shadow disappeared, she scooted forward, shutting off his light again. "Do you have to get so
close, Lilah?"

He heard the impatience in his voice and reckoned
he'd gone and hurt her feelings again, but when he
looked up, she was still glowing. He couldn't imagine
what had put her in such a good humor, but he was sud-

denly glad of it. Walking on eggshells had never been one of his talents.

She moved out of his light, but still not far enough away to suit him. If she would just watch and not talk, then maybe he could concentrate on his work, instead of thinking about how he wanted to kiss her again.

"Did anybody ever tell ye what strong hands you got, Jesse?"

"No."

"Ye do. They's kindly broad acrost the beam, but yer long fingers keeps 'em from lookin' too common."

"Thank you, I guess."

"Oh, I was aimin' to pleasure ye with my talk," she hastily assured him. "I ain't much at speechifyin'. Never had much of no one to talk to, 'ceptin' Maw and then Granny. And my critters. Course, critters can't talk back, so's a body can't truly know what they's thinkin' about what ye're a-sayin'. Sometimes, folks acts the same way."

Though she didn't elaborate, Jesse suspected her comment was directed at him. "Sometimes folks don't know what to say, Lilah. Sometimes they do know, but they can't bring themselves to say it, for one reason or another."

For a few minutes, she watched him in silence. She'd seemed so irrepressibly talkative, this pause surprised Jesse, but it pleased him, too. He was beginning to think *he* was the one who'd needed solitude, not Lilah. Then she started up again. At least now she was directing her "speechifying" to Smiley.

"Ye ever had any critter-friends, Mr. Smiley?"

"Jest dogs," he said, a smile in his voice.

"I ain't never had me no dog. Never had much truck for the critters. They ain't no good at takin' care a theirselfs. Not much credit to their wolf brothers, dogs ain't."

"What kind of critter-friends do you have, Miz Lilah?"

"You've opened the door now, Smiley," Jesse said amiably, glancing up and catching a wistful gleam in Lilah's blue eyes. "She's liable to talk your ears plumb off."

"What else I got to do? I shore ain't going nowheres," Smiley said without even a trace of bitterness. "Go 'head, Miz Lilah. Tell me erbout yer critters."

"Well, sir, first there's Ol' Codger. He's a bahr. The biggest bahr ye ever did see. Maybe the biggest bahr ever there was. But for all his size, he's got a heap a gentleness about him. Why, he toted Jesse out'n the bay when he was snakebit."

"When the bahr was snakebit?"

"Naw. When Jesse was snakebit."

"What kind of snake was it, Marshal?"

"A cottonmouth."

"Swampfolks calls 'em moccasins," Lilah said.

"How'd it happen?"

"I wasn't watching where I was going," Jesse said.

"It's a wonder you lived to tell erbout it."

"Probably wouldn't have, if it hadn't been for Lilah and Granny."

Lilah explained who Granny was and told Smiley all about the snakebite treatment. "That's how come me to put the bog moss on yer stump," she said. "It worked on Jesse. 'Course, ye don' have no open wound no more, so ye prob'ly don' need it."

"I'm glad you did it anyway, Miz Lilah. I 'preciate you taking such good care of me. But you was telling me erbout yer critter-friends."

She nodded. "Like I said, there's Ol' Codger. He jest showed up one day with a thorn in his paw that was all festered-up, and we've been bestest friends ever since. He watches out after me. Sorta set hisself up as my pertector. I reckon he'd tear a body to flinders, if'n he thought I was in danger."

Jesse snorted. "I wish he'd been here to get Red and Jack, but I guess Bob did a pretty good job of tearing up Red's back."

"Bob's a bobcat," Lilah told Smiley, "what got hisself caught in a mean old swamper's trap, but I fount him afore the trapper did. Good thang, too."

"You saved his life," Smiley said simply. "But I think you're being unfair to the swamper, calling him mean. Trapping's jest a way of life for some folks. Pelts and hides brings good money."

"Critters needs their hides worser'n folks needs 'em. But Bob's hide wasn't what the trapper was after."

"'Tweren't? Then what? I never heared of a body eating a bobcat, though I s'pose you could, if'n ye was hungry enough."

"Naw. 'Tweren't food neither. Most swampfolks is mean to bobcats. They trap 'em jes' to torment 'em."

Lilah had thoroughly claimed Jesse's attention now. The disassembled pistol fell to his lap, and he watched her animated face with rapt attention.

"Torment 'em? How?"

A cloud of despair shadowed Lilah's face, erasing her earlier happiness. "There's the poor bobcat with at least one leg already mangled up, it bein' sore and hurtin' him and him not bein' able to move 'cause of the trap. The swampers come along and beat him with sticks till the cat's plumb give out, then they let him out'n the trap and take turns shootin' at him, aimin' for his rump, till he can't run no more. Then, they jes' leave him there to die."

The torment she described so closely paralleled One-Eyed Jack's treatment of Martha and the boys—in intent if not execution—that Jesse thought he was going to be sick. Quickly, he excused himself, then walked purposefully into the bushes. He didn't stop until he'd reached another small clearing some distance from the camp.

There, he fell to his knees, and gave in to the first truly
cleansing sobs he'd allowed himself since that day almost
four years ago when he'd come home and found his family slaughtered.

When several minutes passed and Jesse didn't come
back, Lilah got up to follow him.

"I wouldn't do that if'n I was you," Smiley cautioned.

"How come?"

" 'Cause you don't know what he's doin'. Maybe it's
private. You wouldn't want to embarrass yourself and
Jesse, too, now would you?"

Lilah gave Smiley's counsel brief consideration. "Naw,
but I wouldn't want him to go get hisself in trouble again,
neither. He was near dead when I fount him in the cypress
bay."

Smiley shuddered and glanced around nervously. "This
swamp is crawlin' with snakes," he mumbled.

"Ye don' have to worry," Lilah assured him. "One's not
likely to come slitherin' along and bite you, not here in the
clearin'. If one does, knock him silly with this here skillet." She moved the iron vessel right up next to his right
hand.

He nodded but he didn't appear convinced. "Maybe you
better go see erbout the marshal."

Jesse had left behind a trail of smashed-down grass and
broken twigs. He really must have been in a hip and a
hurry to get away from camp, Lilah thought. She was beginning to wonder if, perhaps, Smiley had been right about
Jesse's immediate need for privacy, but she figured anyone
in that big a rush should a-been through with his personal
business by now. Nevertheless, she called out to him occasionally, but the only response she ever heard was either a
bird calling or a frog croaking.

And then she broke through a stand of hardwoods and

saw him kneeling there on the ground, his face in his hands, his whole trunk shaking with his sobs.

Her heart wrenching, Lilah sped to his side, dropping to her knees and looping an arm over his shoulders. At first, he took no note of her presence, and then he uncovered his face and turned his head toward her. Lilah didn't think she'd ever seen a face so haunted.

She pulled him into her. His head sank to her bosom and his arms went childlike around her back and squeezed her tight. While she attempted to comfort him, Lilah fished her memory for a reason for his distress. Just before he disappeared, she'd been talking about how the swampers torment bobcats, but she couldn't believe Jesse was so tenderhearted he'd a-run off and cried over some bobcats. Maybe her tale had struck a memory spark in him, making him think of something else, something about somebody being tormented and then left to die. Somebody he cared enough about to grieve for. And then she recalled his reason for not caring about what happened to Smiley: *He murdered my wife and children!*

Not wanting to believe it, she'd refused to explore the subject, but now she took it out and tossed it around in her head. No matter how hard she tried, however, she couldn't see Smiley as a murderer, but those other two—the ones Jesse called Jack and Red—they were different. She had no doubt either one was capable of killing a woman. Maybe even children, too.

"Oh, my god!" she breathed, tears springing to her own eyes. How could she have been so blind? So utterly stupid? She could hear Colin's voice as clear as though he were standing right there speaking to her: *This marshal says they kilt a woman and some children up Tennessee way.*

Not just a woman and some children. Jesse's woman. Jesse's children.

Lilah's tears flowed unchecked down her cheeks, puddling at the corners of her mouth and then spilling onto the top of his head. She clutched him tighter. "Oh, Jesse," she whispered around the knot in her throat, "I'm so sorry."

Chapter Twelve

"Ye mought as well shet yer argufyin'," Lilah said for at least the twelfth time that morning, " 'cause ye're not goin' with me."

And for at least the twelfth time, Jesse told her she was the most stubborn individual he'd ever encountered. "You're not going without me," he insisted—again. "With One-Eyed Jack and Red on the loose, it's entirely too dangerous for you to be out there alone."

"Ye're disrememberin' that they've got theirselfs a canoe now," she reminded him. "Shucks, the sunball's done rose twicet since they left here. I 'spect they's long gone by now. 'Sides, we'uns got the gun and the knife."

He could feel himself weakening, but he wasn't about to let her know it. He glared at her even harder. "It's still too dangerous."

Her blue eyes spitting fire, she glared right back, planting her fists on her hips and tilting her chin up in total defiance. Damn, but she was determined to do this thing herself.

Jesse had reluctantly agreed that Smiley was too sick to be left alone for as long as it would take to get to Yerby's Island and back. His reluctance to agree with Lilah on this particular point had nothing to do with Smiley. Jesse was convinced now that Smiley had had no part in the deaths of Martha and the boys. Rather, it was the idea of becoming separated from Lilah that had made him balk.

"When I agreed to the separation," he told her, "it was with the understanding that I'd be the one to go."

"*Yer* understandin', not mine. Ye'd never get to Yerby's Island by yerself," she said. "And even if ye did, the Yerbys wouldn't holp you. I've tole you how s'picious swampfolks is of outlanders. 'Sides, what's the diff'runce in whether I stay here or go, long as we're apart? Smiley ain't in no shape to do nobody no good, so it's all the same, one way or t'other."

"No, it's not. Jack and Red aren't likely to come back here."

"Says who? Them two don' know this swamp no better'n you do. They could be goin' 'round in circles."

Jesse grinned and verbally pounced. "Exactly!"

Lilah frowned. "So?"

"So, they're not necessarily long gone, are they?"

She picked up the deerskin pouch and slung it over her shoulder. "Ye ain't a-goin' to win, Jesse, so ye mought as well give up."

"What if I follow you?"

"And leave Smiley here by hisself? I don' think ye'll do that."

He knew he wouldn't—knew he couldn't, but he wasn't quite ready to give in to her yet. "Maybe if we just wait here another day or two, someone will come along and help us."

She raised up on tiptoe and planted a kiss on his chin, which was as close to his mouth as she could reach. He felt like a cad for not making it any easier for her, but kissing her back would put his stamp of approval on what she was doing, and he refused to believe this was the best way.

"I'll see you in a day or two," she said.

"I thought you said it was only a half-day's walk to

Yerby's Island. It ought to be much faster coming back in a canoe, and it's still early. You could be back by nightfall."

"I could, but there ain't no way the Yerbys will let me leave without feedin' me and makin' me stay the night." She adjusted the pouch, glancing over at Smiley, who was sleeping soundly. "Don' let nothin' happen to you or Smiley whilst I'm gone."

He stood perfectly still, watching her traipse off across the clearing, her hips swinging in a pair of Red's britches she'd found in the knapsack. He grinned at the way her bottom filled out the pants, even though she'd had to cinch up the waist with a rope. And then she was gone, leaving nothing but the twitch of a limb to indicate she'd passed through the bushes—and leaving him with a heart full of lead and a head full of misgivings.

Lilah missed Granny, but the old woman's death hadn't left a big, empty hole the way Lilah had thought it would. She pondered this as she made her way across lakes and bogs and prairies on the way to Yerby's Island, finally coming to the conclusion that purpose was at the center of it all.

For six years, her life had revolved around Granny Latham. Oh, her critters had been important to her, still were, but not in the same way as Granny Latham. The critters didn't need her the way Granny did—or the way she wanted to believe Granny needed her. A human critter needed the love and companionship of another human. Just as important, a human critter needed to feel needed by another human. She and Granny had loved and needed each other. Granny had been her reason for getting out of bed every morning.

But then she'd found Jesse in the cypress bay, and suddenly another human critter needed her. Not that Jesse could replace Granny Latham. No one could do that. Finding him, however, had opened up all kinds of possibilities Lilah had refused to consider before. Just *thinking* she'd lost Jesse had hurt almost as bad as *knowing* she'd lost Granny. Now that she'd found him again, she wasn't about to let him go. If she had to, she'd dog his steps all the way to Tennessee.

Remembering how hard he'd tried to talk her out of going to Yerby's Island made her laugh. Didn't he know how hard it was for her to go off and leave him, even for just a day or two? Didn't he know she'd fight gators and snakes and outlaws tooth and nail to get back to him? Didn't he know how important he was to her now?

He was her purpose, her reason for getting out of bed every morning, and she wasn't about to let anyone or anything prevent her from collecting what she needed from the Yerbys and getting back to Jesse in a hip and a hurry.

"Turn around," Jack said. "We're going back."

"Back?" Red echoed. "But they've got the gun and the knife now. That marshal will kill us for sure."

"Not if we're careful. We shouldn't a-left Smiley alive."

"Smiley won't give us up, Jack."

"Sure, he will. He'll sing like a bird the first chance he gets."

"But what if they're already gone?"

"We've got the gal's canoe. Remember? They're still there. And maybe we'll hit it lucky and get the gun back. Maybe we can even get the marshal this time."

"And the gal?" Red asked.

"I've got plans for the gal." He licked his lips. "Yes, sir. I've got plans for that gal."

When the noon sun beat down on him and Smiley the next day and Lilah still hadn't returned, Jesse told himself not to worry. She'd said a day or two. Later, when dark storm clouds amassed in the western sky and lightning flashed dangerously close to the tall trees, Jesse told himself not to worry. Yet, all the while he worked at making a lean-to out of the square of canvas from the knapsack, he worried. Throughout the long, stormy night, he worried. Throughout trying to stay dry and attempting to keep Smiley warm, he worried.

"You're gonna worry yerself sick," Smiley told him.

"So what if I do? It's not hurting you."

"Suit yourself, but she'll be back."

"How can you be so sure?"

" 'Cause her critter-friends went with her—that big ol' black bear and the crippled bobcat. They'll keep her safe."

Jesse shot Smiley a disbelieving look. "How do you know? You were asleep when she left."

Smiley grinned. "Naw, I was jest playin' possum."

"Why?"

"So's you and Miss Lilah could give each other a proper good-bye. It didn't make no nevermind, though, 'cause you went and mommicked it up."

"Good lord! Now you're talking like Lilah."

"I always talk this way," Smiley insisted. "What's that got to do with anything anyway?"

Jesse ran his palm over his head, smoothing his damp hair off his forehead and hearing his father, who'd grown up and lived his life in the same hills as Smiley, say *it don't make no nevermind* and *mommicked*. "I don't know. Nothing, I guess."

"Why don't you lie down and try to get some sleep?"

Jesse looked off into the dark, rainy night and shook his head. "You go to sleep, Smiley. Me, I'll just sit here for a spell. The ground's too wet and my mind's too busy. I'll sleep when Lilah gets back."

Smiley mumbled something about fools, then was snoring a few minutes later. Jesse tried to relax, which meant getting his mind off Lilah, but every time he closed his eyes, he saw One-Eyed Jack pinning her to the ground and pressing a knife against her neck.

In the middle of Jesse's own wide-awake nightmare, a scream rent the air. Before Jesse could reorient himself, Smiley's forearm smacked him hard in the ribs.

"What the hell!" Jesse bellowed, finding himself competing with Smiley's screams. "What is it?" he bellowed louder.

Smiley just kept screaming. Without a light, Jesse had no idea what was going on, but whatever it was had frightened Smiley witless—or was killing him. But the man was fighting back. His flailing arms prevented Jesse from getting very close.

Not that he wanted to get too close. But he had to help Smiley. He had both the pistol and the knife, since Lilah had refused to take either, but weapons were no good if you couldn't see what you were shooting or slicing at. Jesse scooted as far away as he could get and still have the protection of the canvas, then fished his match safe from his pocket and struck a light. It might only be temporary, but it was better than nothing.

With a trembling hand, Jesse moved the match closer to Smiley. The man was sitting up. His wide-open eyes darted wildly in their sockets and his arms battered thin air. "Get him off me!" he screamed. "Jack ... Red ... help me!"

The gator! Of course. Jesse figured he'd be having nightmares, too, if one of those ugly monsters had taken off one of his legs.

The flame burned the tips of his fingers. He shook the match out and tossed it aside, then felt around until he found the pot, which he'd set just outside the canvas shelter to catch rainwater. He hated to douse Smiley, but he didn't know any other way to wake him up. He took a swing with the pot, praying he didn't miss in the dark.

"Son-of-a-bitch!" Smiley hollered, sputtering. "What'd you go do that fer?"

Jesse smiled and set the pot down. "You okay, Smiley?"

"Br-r-r! That water's cold and now my blanket's all wet."

"I'm sorry." Jesse didn't know what else to say.

"I was having a dream, huh?" Smiley's teeth were chattering so he could barely talk.

"Something like that."

"Thanks, Marshal."

"You're welcome."

Jesse heard the rustling of the blanket and reckoned Smiley was trying to rearrange it. "I wish I could build us a fire, but there can't be a dry stick of wood anywhere. I really am sorry, Smiley. I didn't know what else to do."

"Don't trouble yerself. You did what you had to do, but I don't think I can go back to sleep," Smiley said. "Fact is, I don't think I *want* to go back to sleep. You know any good haint tales?"

Jesse laughed. Why a man who'd just had one helluva nightmare wanted to hear a ghost story was beyond reason, but he was willing to humor him. "I know a few."

"Tell me one." With the rain pouring down and the thunder rumbling. Jesse and Smiley swapped stories until they'd both talked themselves hoarse. The longer they talked, the more personal the stories became. Jesse told Smiley about losing his gear and the gators hauling it off, and Smiley told him where they'd found the .45 and how he'd lost his leg retrieving it. Jesse wondered aloud if maybe his saddlebags were in a gator nest somewhere.

"Could be," Smiley allowed, "but I'd be real careful about trying to get 'em back, if'n I found 'em. There can't be anything in those bags worth losing yer leg or yer life over."

"I'm sorry about your leg," Jesse said, surprising himself.

"Me, too. But I'll get used to it. I know a man what lost his leg in the war. He wears a wooden leg and gets around purty good. There's a feller back home whittles out wooden legs with feet on 'em, and be damned if you can't hardly tell 'em from the real thing. Course, you walk with a limp, but that's better'n being in a grave somewhere. Thanks for taking care of me, Marshal."

"You're welcome."

"I reckon I'll have to spend some time in jail, but when I get out, I promise to behave myself. And if'n you ever catch One-Eyed Jack and I can help out at the trial, I will."

The storm blew over before sunrise, but it left behind a mist so thick it made seeing very far impossible. Although such mists weren't uncommon to the Okefinoke, as Jesse had discovered, the sun usually burned them off by mid-morning. By Jesse's reckoning of time, which was more instinct than anything else without either a watch or the sun to go by, noon came and went without a significant change in the denseness of the fog. This mist seemed determined to stay.

If Lilah hadn't started back the day before—and Jesse prayed she hadn't—she certainly wouldn't come back today, not in this heavy fog. At least, he hoped she wouldn't.

"Where you reckon we are, Colin?" Lilah asked.

His terse reply carried his frustration. "Lost."

"Swampers don' get theirselfs lost in the Okefinoke."

"Shore they do. They jes' don' own up to it. Many's the time I've heared my pa say he ain't never been lost, jes' mighty confused sometimes. Well, I ain't never been so confused as I am right now."

A good twenty-four hours had passed since the two had left Yerby's Island in the punt boat with the canoe tied behind. Aiming to go back alone, Lilah had been ready to leave at day-bust, but the Yerbys wouldn't hear of it. Too dangerous, they said. Jes' give Colin the morning to do his chores, and then the two could travel together. Later, they would split up. Colin would travel Smiley to Billy's Island in the punt boat, while Lilah and the marshal would take the canoe on out of the swamp. That way, they said, she'd never be alone—and defenseless.

Now, looking out into the thick mist, Lilah didn't know when she'd felt so defenseless. They had come so close to getting back to Jesse and Smiley, probably were no more than an hour from the island where the two waited, when the storm hit yesterday afternoon. Colin had wanted to tie up to a tree until the storm passed, but Lilah had insisted they could make it. She'd been wrong. The winds had blown them so far off course that she doubted they could get their bearings if they could see, which they couldn't. The fog left them no choice but to stay where they were and wait for it to clear up.

As Jesse made his way down to the lake to collect water, he hoped the mist wasn't masking any surprises. Like moccasins or gators. For that very reason, he'd put off going all day, but the rainwater he'd caught in the pot was long gone, and both he and Smiley were getting mighty thirsty.

He made it to the lake without mishap, and he set back for their campsite with a little more confidence than he'd left there with. Getting lost didn't occur to him, until he realized that he should have already reached the clearing. For an instant, panic gripped him—until he remembered hearing Smiley holler from clear across the island. All he had to do was call out to Smiley, then follow the man's voice back to the clearing.

Jesse's hollering raised a ruckus among the wildlife, stirring up chirps and croaks and yowls all around, but the only human sound he heard was the echo of his own voice. As if that weren't enough frustration for the moment, his rambling had taken him into a marshy bog he couldn't seem to find his way out of. He stepped onto a mound of decaying vegetation and sank up to his knees in muck. *Damn the mist. Damn the swamp. Damn the—*

Gator!

A big monster of a gator, with its lethal jaws snapping inches from his knees, and the glint of malice in its hard black eyes evident even through the gloomy mist. Jesse dropped the pot, snatched his pistol from his pants, aimed, and shot. The alligator didn't even flinch.

Without pausing to question the fact that he couldn't have missed, not at such close range, Jesse shot the gator two more times. Rewarded with the sight of blood on the reptile's head and neck, coupled with an abrupt clamping of the gator's jaws, Jesse hauled himself out of the muck and onto firmer ground. He felt like he was sweating blood himself, his heart was pounding so hard it made his ears ring, and the strong, musky smells of the alligator and Jesse's own fear assaulted his nostrils. But at least he'd escaped harm.

The snap of jaws at his heels quickly wiped that notion away and sent Jesse scurrying forward. Both the alligator's scent and the sound of the snapping jaws followed. In a panic, Jesse ran, his long legs pumping, his feet fairly sailing over the soft ground. Despite his speed, he didn't have to glance over his shoulder to know the gator was gaining on him. He knew how Smiley must have felt when he was trying to get away from the alligator that took his leg off.

Then, like a flash of lightning, he recalled Lilah's advice: *Run a crookedy path. Gators can't turn fast.*

Jesse angled out to the left, took three long leaps, then turned to the right. A half-dozen turns later, he allowed himself the luxury of a look backwards. Though the gator was still coming, it was lagging behind now. Barely cognizant of his labored breathing and aching left leg, Jesse plunged ahead, continuing his zig-zaggedy route while keeping a keen eye out for other gators. The last thing he needed right now was another monster on his tail.

After a while, he realized that the gator no longer followed. He slowed to a jog and then a walk before finally stopping to rest, bending forward and resting his hands on his thighs, while his breathing and pulse returned to normal. When he straightened up, he could clearly see a clump of hurrah bushes a good ten paces in front of him. Finally, the mist was burning off—now that the day was almost gone.

The glitter of sunlight restored his bearings, and within a short time, Jesse walked into the clearing. With a light head and an even lighter heart, he made his way toward the makeshift tent and the pile of charred wood and ashes beside it. Maybe he could manage to build a fire. And then he'd take the coffeepot back to the lake and get some more water.

"Hey, Smiley!" he called. "I'm back."

Smiley didn't answer. And when Jesse reached the lean-to, he understood why. Smiley Shaunessey lay flat on his back, his hazel eyes open and staring at the canvas canopy over his head, a dark pool of blood on his chest. A buzzard plucked away at Smiley's outstretched hand, while another swooped down and landed just inches from Smiley's head.

Jesse's breath caught in his throat and a tear welled up in his one good eye. "Shoo now. Go on!" Jesse told the buzzards, waving his hand at them. When they ignored him, he found a stick and swatted at them, until they flew off and perched in a nearby tree, waiting.

"Now, why'd you go and kill yourself?" Jesse asked the corpse. "You were going to be all right. Losing a leg's no reason to—"

But Smiley hadn't committed suicide. If he had, the knife Jesse had left with him would be sticking out of his

chest—or maybe clutched in his fist. It wasn't. In fact, it
wasn't anywhere in sight. Nor was the knapsack.

A cold sense of dread wiggled down Jesse's spine, and
he forgot all about building a fire. He forgot all about everything except hunting down One-Eyed Jack and making
the felon pay for each and every one of the innocent lives
he'd taken. He prayed Lilah's wasn't among them.

Sometime that night, Jesse finally went to sleep. He
hadn't intended to, not with Jack and Red probably lurking
nearby, and certainly not with Smiley's canvas-wrapped
corpse a mere six feet away.

It wasn't that he was afraid of a corpse, Jesse assured
himself. The haint tales he and Smiley had shared the
night before were just that—tales. Jesse doubted there was
a bit of truth to them. Cats didn't wallow in hot coals, and
a man with his head half-cut-off couldn't walk and talk.
They were just stories people made up to explain away
strange noises and illusions.

No, it wasn't that he was afraid of the corpse. He just
didn't want anything to happen to Smiley's body before he
got it buried. The buzzards still perched nearby. By nightfall, their numbers had increased to six, and he expected
several more had arrived since then. And there were other
predators, he was sure—panthers, bobcats, wolves, maybe
even an alligator or two—just waiting for him to leave the
corpse unattended long enough for them to move in and
tear at Smiley's body.

As long as the light lasted, Jesse had worked at digging
a grave in the soft ground, but with nothing except a good-
sized hickory stick for a tool, he hadn't been able to scoop
out more than a foot or so of soil. All he could do was
guard the body and wait for sunrise, which wasn't going to
be easy, considering the fact that he hadn't slept at all the
night before. Several times, he caught himself nodding off

and jerked himself awake, until finally, despite his good intentions, he nodded off and didn't catch himself.

He was still asleep when Lilah and Colin arrived the next morning.

Chapter Thirteen

The sight of Jesse sitting there next to the canvas-wrapped body, his heels pulled in to his buttocks and his head resting on his knees, ripped at Lilah's heart. She wondered what had happened to Smiley, but she was more concerned about Jesse at the moment. He looked as gray and worn as the day she'd found him in the cypress bay.

Before she could stop him, Colin hollered a greeting. Jesse's head snapped up and his right hand, which clutched his pistol, flew out, then slowly fell as a half-smile tugged at the corners of his mouth.

"I've been worried about you," he said in a scratchy voice. He unfolded his long legs and tried to stand up, but his legs didn't seem to want to support his weight, so he settled back down on the ground.

Lilah rushed to his side and threw her arms around his neck. For a long time, they hugged each other, neither aware of Colin until he cleared his throat, which served to remind her of Smiley.

"He was jes' too weak to make it, huh?" she asked, turning her head to stare at the length of lumpy canvas.

Jesse hadn't considered telling her anything except the facts as he knew them, but he hadn't thought about her having someone with her when she came back, either. Eventually, he'd have to explain what had happened to the knife and the haversack, but for the moment her companion's wary stance and distrustful glare stayed the truth. Jesse offered a nod of agreement and looked straight at the young man by her side. "You bring any coffee with you, son?"

Lilah watched Colin flinch. Not even his pa called him "son" anymore. She braced herself for his angry retort, then was relieved when Colin seemed to shrug it off and started unpacking the long canvas bag he'd brought with him from the punt boat. At first, she didn't think much about Jesse's request for coffee. After all, there hadn't been that much in the first place, and he'd had ample time to use it up. But when she looked for the pot to haul water in, she realized the haversack was nowhere in sight.

By that time, Colin was busy gathering firewood and kindling, too far away from the campsite to overhear her whispered question. "Where's the haversack?"

Jesse put a forefinger on his lips and shook his head. More than a little confused but reluctant to pursue the subject, Lilah took a pot from Colin's bag and headed down to the lake. When she got back, Colin was attempting to light a pile of damp pinestraw and small sticks.

"Dadburn rain," Colin snapped. Lilah couldn't recall Colin ever being so short-tempered over something as insignificant as damp kindling. Did he suspect Jesse wasn't being completely truthful?

When the fire sputtered to life, Colin set the coffee beans to parching and water to boiling, then he sat down in front of Jesse, crossing his legs Indian-style and eyeing the six-shooter in Jesse's hand. "Ye're the marshal?"

Jesse nodded. "Jesse Redford's the name."

"Mine's Yerby. Colin Yerby."

Lilah watched Jesse's eye pop and wished she'd prepared him better for this meeting, but until that moment, she'd forgotten that he'd never actually met Colin, just heard his voice the night Colin stayed at the cabin after they got the canoe stuck in the huckleberry vines. She supposed she should have told Jesse that Colin was a Yerby before she left, but her mother wit had told her that wasn't a good idea.

"What happened here?" Colin asked, bobbing his head toward Smiley's body.

"He died," Jesse said.

"I can see that. How did it happen?"

"I don't know. I wasn't here." Jesse told them about his encounter with the gator. "He was dead when I got back."

Colin snapped his fingers. "Jes' like that?"

"No, not just like that."

Colin narrowed his eyes at Jesse. "Ye're shore ye're the marshal?"

"Of course, I'm sure! Why wouldn't I be?"

"Where's yer star?"

"I lost it."

"Colin, I done tole you 'bout ever'thang what happened to Jesse," Lilah said. "This here's the marshal."

"How do we know he ain't One-Eyed Jack pretendin' to be the marshal?"

" 'Cause I met up with One-Eyed Jack," Lilah declared. "He's a mean 'un."

"Some marshals is mean. Don' ye thank it's mighty peculiar that a one-eyed marshal's chasin' a one-eyed killer?"

"What are you getting at, Yerby?" Jesse asked, his jaw clenched.

Colin's gaze dropped to the pistol, which still lay limply in Jesse's right hand. "Aw, nothin', I guess." He fidgeted with a piece of grass for a minute, then rose. "I'll make the coffee, and then we'd best get on with digging that bury hole. I'll get a spade from the boat. Oughter make the job easier."

Colin's mentioning the boat reminded Jesse that Jack

and Red had stolen Lilah's canoe while no one was watching. "Somebody needs to go down and stay with the boat," he said. "Did you bring a gun with you, Yerby?"

Colin smiled. "A swamper always takes his gun with him. I got mine right here." He pulled a rifle out of the long canvas bag he'd brought back from the punt boat.

"Good. You watch the boat. I'll dig the grave."

Two hours later, Jesse wished he'd reversed the tasks. He was so weak from lack of sleep that Lilah had ended up doing most of the digging, and though she didn't seem to mind, watching a woman labor so hard bothered him. Added to that was the knowledge that this was the second grave she'd dug in a matter of days. No one should have to do that, much less a woman.

A woman. God, she was definitely all woman. Even in the britches she insisted on wearing. Suddenly, Jesse found himself very uncomfortable. He started to talk, had to clear his throat first, and then tried again.

"That's deep enough. Help me drag his body over there."

When they'd wrangled Smiley into the grave, Jesse picked up the spade and started filling the hole, all the while trying to concentrate on what he was doing instead of thinking about how, in a short while, he and Lilah would be alone again. The prospect frightened him. This realization frightened him even more, for he was not a man easily frightened. Yet with each spadeful of earth, he felt as though he were burying himself instead of Smiley Shaunessey.

Perhaps he should hire Colin to guide him, and send Lilah back to Yerby's Island to stay with Colin's folks. Yes, that's what he'd do. That way, Lilah would be safe from One-Eyed Jack. Or would she? The dream image of her bloodied face assailed him, reminding him of the sick feeling he got every time they were apart—and he knew he couldn't allow her to be separated from him again. He hadn't been there for Martha, but he could be there for Lilah. No, the only way he could guarantee her safety was to keep her with him, whether he liked it or not.

"Pore ol' Smiley," Lilah said, drawing his attention. She was sitting on the ground tying two sticks together with a piece of vine to make a cross. Beside her lay a bunch of wildflowers. "He should a-had a buryin' box and a bit of funeralizin' to send him off to his Maker." She looked up then, and he saw the tears that washed her blue eyes. "Ye *did* dress his body, didn't you, Jesse?"

He hadn't done anything except wrap the canvas around Smiley's body and tie it up with vines, but he hated to tell her that. Cleaning the body up hadn't even occurred to him. Besides, he didn't have any water or another shirt to put on Smiley anyway. He thought he'd done quite enough by guarding the body from preying animals.

"Thank goodness for that," Lilah said, apparently taking his silence for agreement. Jesse saw no need to correct her. As soon as she put the cross in place and laid the flowers in front of it, he hustled her away from the clearing. He was beginning to feel uneasy, whether from her talk of dressing dead bodies or because he had the sneaking suspicion that Jack and Red were lurking somewhere nearby, watching them, he didn't know. If the latter was true, he didn't know why Jack and Red hadn't ambushed them yet, but he couldn't discount the possibility that this would happen. Perhaps it already had, but with Colin Yerby as the target.

As Jesse hastened Lilah onward, the pistol in his right hand, he watched both sides of the trail for movement, grateful that every step brought them closer to the punt boat, and yet troubled by what they might find when they reached it. It was with tremendous relief, therefore, when Colin's voice hailed them even before they broke through the trees at the edge of the lake.

Without breaking stride, Jesse stepped onto the flat-bottomed boat behind Lilah, handed Colin the spade, and picked up a pole. "I don't mean to seem unappreciative," Jesse told Colin, "but we need to get out of here as quickly as we can."

"Yeah," Colin agreed. "I've got the heebee-jeebies myself."

With Jesse on one side and Colin on the other, they pushed the punt boat out into the lake, then turned it westward. Lilah sat down in front of the cabin, and for a long time, no one spoke. Silently, they moved through choked masses of water-loving shrubs and vines. The gentle splashing of water against the hull coupled with the songs of a multitude of birds gradually soothed Jesse's nerves, but he refused to let the tranquility lull him into total peace of mind. Both One-Eyed Jack and the creatures of the swamp posed an ever-present threat, and Jesse knew he couldn't afford to let down his guard even for a minute.

After a while, Colin stopped poling. "This is where you turn south," he said. "Lilah can guide you from here."

"I can't thank you enough for what you've done, Yerby. I'll see that you get your canoe back."

"Jes' see that Lilah is took care of." He paused, looking down at his feet and obviously wanting to say something else. "I still ain't certain-sure in my heart that ye're a marshal," Colin finally said, "but Lilah here seems to thank so, and she knows a heap more about you than I do. The onliest reason I agreed to this here plan of her'n is 'cause she's so bound and determined to leave the swamp with you." His head snapped up then, and his eyes flashed with zealous confidence. "But if ye hurt her—if ye harm one hair on her head, I'll come after ye, marshal or no. Ever' man in this swamp will come after ye. Prob'ly ever' critter, too."

"I won't hurt her, nor will I allow anyone else to," Jesse assured him.

Colin gave a jerky nod, then threw his arms around

Wish You Were Here?

You can be, every month, with Zebra Historical Romance Novels.

AND TO GET YOU STARTED, ALLOW US TO SEND YOU

Historical Romances Free

A $19.96 VALUE!
With absolutely no obligation to buy anything.

YOU'RE GOING TO LOVE GETTING
4 FREE BOOKS

These books worth almost $20, are yours without cost or obligation when you fill out and mail this certificate.
If the certificate is missing below, write to: Zebra Home Subscription Service, Inc., 120 Brighton Road, P.O. Box 5214, Clifton, New Jersey 07015-5214

4 FREE BOOKS!

Yes! Please send me 4 Zebra Historical Romances without cost or obligation. I understand that each month thereafter I will be able to preview 4 new Zebra Historical Romances FREE for 10 days. Then, if I should decide to keep them, I will pay the money-saving preferred publisher's price of just $4.00 each...a total of $16. That's almost $4 less than the publisher's price, and there is no additional charge for shipping and handling. I may return any shipment within 10 days and owe nothing, and I may cancel this subscription at any time. The 4 FREE books will be mine to keep in any case.

Name _____

Address _____ Apt. _____

City _____ State _____ Zip _____

Telephone ( ) _____

Signature _____ LF1095
(If under 18, parent or guardian must sign.)

Terms, offer and prices subject to change without notice. Subscription subject to acceptance by Zebra Books. Zebra Books reserves the right to reject any order or cancel any subscription.

A $19.96
value.
FREE!

No obligation
to buy
anything, ever.

ZEBRA HOME SUBSCRIPTION SERVICE, INC.

120 BRIGHTON ROAD

P.O. BOX 5214

CLIFTON, NEW JERSEY 07015-5214

Wish You Were Here?

You can be, every month, with Zebra Historical Romance Novels.

AND TO GET YOU STARTED, ALLOW US TO SEND YOU

Historical Romances Free

A $19.96 VALUE!

With absolutely no obligation to buy anything.

YOU'RE GOING TO LOVE GETTING
4 FREE BOOKS

These books worth almost $20, are yours without cost or obligation when you fill out and mail this certificate.

If the certificate is missing below, write to: Zebra Home Subscription Service, Inc., 120 Brighton Road, P.O. Box 5214, Clifton, New Jersey 07015-5214

4 FREE BOOKS!

Yes! Please send me 4 Zebra Historical Romances without cost or obligation. I understand that each month thereafter I will be able to preview 4 new Zebra Historical Romances FREE for 10 days. Then, if I should decide to keep them, I will pay the money-saving preferred publisher's price of just $4.00 each...a total of $16. That's almost $4 less than the publisher's price, and there is no additional charge for shipping and handling. I may return any shipment within 10 days and owe nothing, and I may cancel this subscription at any time. The 4 FREE books will be mine to keep in any case.

Name _____

Address _____ Apt. _____

City _____ State_____ Zip _____

Telephone ( )_____

Signature _____
(If under 18, parent or guardian must sign.)

LF1095

Terms, offer and prices subject to change without notice. Subscription subject to acceptance by Zebra Books. Zebra Books reserves the right to reject any order or cancel any subscription.

AFFIX
STAMP
HERE

ZEBRA HOME SUBSCRIPTION SERVICE, INC.

120 BRIGHTON ROAD

P.O. BOX 5214

CLIFTON, NEW JERSEY 07015-5214

Lilah and held her tightly against him. She hugged him back. A sharp pang of jealousy sliced through Jesse. The pang intensified when Colin whispered "I love you" against her hair.

"Don' wait for me, Colin," Lilah said, pulling back, her blue eyes glittering with unshed tears. "I mought never come back here."

"You'll be back." Surety rang in his suddenly husky voice. "The Okefinoke is yer home."

She broke away and stepped into the canoe. Jesse followed, and Colin passed them the long canvas bag. Jesse set the bag down, then turned and clasped Colin's hand. "Thanks again. For everything."

"Jes' be extree keerful," Colin said. "And take good care of Lilah. I hope ye ketch them rascals soon."

"Me, too."

Colin untied the canoe and tossed Jesse the rope, then stood on the stern and waved good-bye until the myrtles and the hollies swallowed him up. "Ye can tell me now," Lilah said.

"Tell you what?"

"What happened to Smiley."

He nodded. Slowly, almost painfully, Jesse related the events of the previous afternoon, concluding with his belief that One-Eyed Jack had come back and plunged the knife into Smiley's breast.

"How come him to want to do that?" Lilah asked. "Mr. Smiley was a nice man."

"Jack hasn't ever left a witness," Jesse said, his voice tight. Lilah recalled his story about his family, especially the part about his two little boys gettin' their throats slit, so they couldn't ever tell no one what had happened to their maw, and she shivered.

"But if Smiley was part of Jack's gang," Lilah argued, "he must've witnessed a passel of Jack's bad deeds afore now. It don' make no sense."

Jesse shrugged. "Nothing Jack Scurlock's ever done made any sense to me. The man's got the blackest heart of any I ever met, and I've met some bad men in my day. I just wish I'd been there."

Lilah heard the pain in his voice and figured he was feeling guilt and regret all over again, just like he had when he'd come home and found his wife and boys dead. She knew how he felt. She wished she could see his face, but he was sitting in front of her and he didn't turn around.

"Ye can't be ever'where at once, Jesse," she said, trying to soothe him. "Ye was here for me when I needed you."

"If it hadn't been for that gator chasing me, I would have been there for Smiley. Of all the times I've walked right past alligators in this swamp, I don't know why that one decided to make me its supper."

"Ye stepped on its nesty," she said. "Female gators piles up leaves and sich to make a big ol' mound in the marsh. They lay the eggs on the mound, then covers 'em up with more leaves, and watches the nesties till the babies hatch. Coons and skunks jes' love to eat gator eggs. That gator thought ye was after her eggs."

"It would have gotten me, too," Jesse said, turning around and taking one of Lilah's hands in his own, "if you hadn't told me how to run from a gator." His hand trembled, then clutched hers tighter. "Is there anything else I need to know about the monsters?"

"Not 'less ye're aimin' on huntin' 'em."

He laughed, a short, snorting sort of laugh. "I don't think so. You know what kind of hunting I want to do."

"How come ye didn't want Colin to know what happened to Smiley?"

"I'm not sure. Gut instinct, I guess. You could see that he didn't really trust me. I have no proof that Scurlock came back and killed Smiley, but I know he did. It had to have been him. When I found Smiley dead and with blood all over his chest, my first thought was that he'd commit-

ted suicide. But the knife and the haversack were both
gone. A man can't kill himself and then dispose of the
weapon. Besides, Smiley told me he'd get along all right.
He was already planning to have someone he knows carve
him a wooden leg. And he was also planning to testify
against Scurlock. I think Jack figured that out and came
back. It's the only thing that makes sense. I just didn't
know if it would make sense to Yerby."

For a spell, they paddled in silence. All the while, jealousy was eating steadily away at Jesse's heart.

"How close are you to the Yerby fellow?"

"Colin? Oh, we'uns have been friends all our lives, I
guess."

"Just friends? Nothing else?"

"If'n Colin had his way, we'd get hitched up and raise
a passel a kids."

"But that's not what you want?"

"No, Jesse. That's not what I want."

He considered asking her what she wanted, but he was
half-afraid to hear her answer. On the other hand, he supposed he'd be relieved to know she wanted him, while on
the other, he knew he couldn't make her any promises. He
wasn't even sure he wanted her. He just didn't want anyone else to have her.

"We're comin' to Big Water," Lilah said, "the beautifulest part of the Okefinoke."

Jesse smiled at the reverence in her voice and marveled
again at her ability to see beauty in what he considered supreme ugliness. "No part of this swamp is beau—"

A sudden awareness of his surroundings stopped him
cold. They had entered a narrow lake flanked by a forest
so thick and so close to them on either side that the
branches of the trees created a cathedral-like ceiling overhead. No wonder Lilah had sounded so reverent. Jesse felt
as though they'd entered a church. Even the wildlife
seemed to hold this part of the swamp in awe. Nothing

moved except the canoe. Nothing made a sound outside of the *swish* of the oars in the black water.

"I was wrong," he said, and heard his voice reverberate with a strange echo.

Lilah stopped paddling. "You can jes' sit here," she said, "and listen to the swamp breathin'."

They drifted for a spell, the gentle current pulling them along as it moved on a southwesterly course. Up ahead, the lake widened, allowing golden sunlight to spill through the trees into a chaotic pattern of splashes and dashes that adorned an army of aquatic plants. Jesse recognized maiden cane and water lilies, a profusion of yellow and white blossoms, some as big as dinner plates, glorifying the broad leaves. A slender-bodied black bird with white wingtips and a bright red beak and brow tripped lightly across the leaves, then stopped and used its beak to turn up a lily pad.

"Watch him," Lilah said. "He's eatin' the insects off'n the underside of the leaf."

"What a balancing act! Do they ever fall in?"

"No."

"What are those?" he asked, pointing to a bright clutter of long, wide leaves and red-bodied, golden-tipped spikes striving skyward.

"Neverwets."

He laughed at the ridiculous-sounding name. "Neverwets?"

"Watch." Lilah guided the canoe closer to the plants, scooped up a handful of water, and sprinkled it over a leaf. Like quicksilver, the water rolled off. "See? They never get wet, so we call them neverwets."

"And those spikey things are the flowers?"

She nodded.

An osprey swooped downward, squawking at them, then swept away to a dead cypress. "See the nesty?" Lilah sked. "No two osprey nesties is exactly the same. If'n ye memorize the nesties, ye won't never get lost."

"Like landmarks," he mumbled, rubbing his chin. "What if you can't see the nests?"

"The ospreys always builds 'em in dead cypress trees right on the aidge of the lake or the perairie, so ye can always see 'em."

The long, narrow finger that was Big Water seemed to stretch out forever in front of them. "How long is this lake?" Jesse asked.

"I don' know. Forty, fifty acres, I s'pose."

Jesse mentally calculated that to be five or six miles. He twisted around to look behind them. There was no sign of another canoe, no sign of life at all except the occasional dip of a bird or dragonfly. Even the path their canoe cut through the plants was quickly closing up. How had he ever thought he could track anyone through a swamp? He found small comfort in realizing that meant no one could track them, either.

"They's back there," Lilah said.

Jesse's heart skipped a beat. How did she know what he was thinking? "How do you know they are? I can't see them."

"Me neither, but that's 'cause Bob and Ol' Codger are such good trackers."

Jesse didn't tell her he had two other critters in mind. "Where are we headed?"

"Where do ye want to go?"

He thought about that for a minute, then made a decision he hoped he didn't live to regret. "Out of the swamp—the quickest way."

"I thought ye wanted to catch One-Eyed Jack."

"I do. And I will one day. But I don't think it'll be here." When she didn't comment, he asked, "Do you?"

"The swampers say that if'n a man wants to get hisself lost in the Okefinoke, there ain't no way to find him."

Jesse nodded. "I have a feeling Jack Scurlock doesn't like this swamp any better than I do. If that's the case, he'll find his way out eventually. I want to be on the outside when he does." A few minutes passed before Jesse spoke again. "You feel up to paddling by yourself?"

"Sure. What're ye aimin' to do?"

"Take a nap. I haven't slept the past two nights. Besides, one of us needs to be awake at all times. You can sleep tonight." He handed her the pistol. "Don't fire this unless you have to. We're low on bullets."

She nodded, laying the six-shooter across her lap. Jesse moved the canvas bag to the bow, plumped it up, then slid into the bottom of the canoe, which wasn't nearly long enough to accommodate his legs. He pulled his knees toward his chest, and after a couple of twists and turns and replumping, he decided he was as comfortable as he was going to get.

He was almost asleep when a terrible thought struck him. Almost in a panic, he raised his head and looked at Lilah's lap. There lay his Colt, right where she'd put it. "Thank goodness," he muttered, breathing a huge sigh of relief.

"What's that ye say, Jesse?" she asked.

"Nothing." He settled down again, then popped right back up. "Tell me you aren't going to throw my gun in the lake again."

She gaped at him. "Course, I ain't."

"Are you sure? Maybe I should hold on to it." A broad smile wreathed her face, and Jesse heard himself say, "Never mind."

God, he was in trouble, he thought. Big trouble. Yet, he didn't know when he'd felt so at peace.

As Lilah paddled down Big Water, she watched Jesse sleep and thought about how lucky she was to have found him that day in the cypress bay. They were meant to be to-

gether, not just for the present, but for all eternity. She
didn't think Jesse understood that yet, but he would. Eventually.

He looked so peaceful, lying there asleep with his dark
head on the provisions bag; his back all curved around like
a baby sleeps, and the sunlight dappling his tanned skin.
His beard now covered his jawline and neck, the hair curly
and thick with just a sprinkling of gray here and there to
give it character. He'd turned his good eye into the pillow
of the bag, and the golden light glistened off the alligator
hide she'd used to make the eye patch. Lilah found herself
wanting to slip the patch off and put her lips on the thin
scar that connected his eyelid to his cheek.

She closed her eyes for a moment, dredging up the
memories of the feel of the ridge against her lips, the taste
of his mouth on hers, the softness of his long black hair
slipping through her fingers. The memories made her feel
all warm and golden inside and wondrously happy. She
ached to kiss him again, to teach him how to make her
feel good, so's he wouldn't be sorry no more.

At the south end of Big Water, the canoe trail narrowed,
winding back and forth through glades and thickets. Further on lay Minnie's Lake and Billy's Island and the ridge
of land swampers called the Pocket that led southwestward
out of the Okefinoke. It was the easiest route out of the
swamp, as well as the most traveled. And it led right past
a number of homesteads, where they could get food and
shelter and information about the outlaws.

Suddenly, Lilah didn't want to go that way. It might be
the quickest way, but it wasn't the best, at least not for her.
Not for Jesse, either, though he didn't know it yet. But he
would, just as soon as she could get him by himself for a
few days, get him rested up and his mind off chasing Jack
and Red.

She turned the canoe due west, heading straight into the
sun, straight into the open territory known as Big Water

Prairie, straight toward an island she hadn't seen in six years, an island she'd never thought to see again. For six years, she'd thought of the island the same way she thought of a bad omen, but now she thought of it the same way the osprey thought of her nest—as a haven. They would be safe there—and completely alone.

Chapter Fourteen

Twilight was slipping down the trees and seeping into the bushes when Lilah woke Jesse. He raised his head off the lumpy bag, rubbed his eyes, and blinked several times. "Where are we?"

"On a island." She stepped out of the canoe and into a bog.

"I can see that! Which one?"

"Ye sure are tetchy. Ye must not a-rested as good as I thought ye did. It's jest an island. Ain't got no name. Pass me that bag, and ye can drag the canoe."

"First, you pass me the gun."

He tucked the Colt into his belt, then stepped into the marsh and picked up the bag. "The bag's heavy and you're shorter. You drag the canoe."

"Then walk behind me. Ye don' know the way."

"The way? Where are we going?"

She moved into the hardwoods that lined the edge of the bog. "Ye want to sleep here . . . with the gators?"

Jesse suspected Lilah wasn't telling him everything. "Does anyone live on this island?"

"No."

"Did anyone ever live here?"

"Onct 'on a time."

"But not now?"

"No."

He had to slow down to keep from tripping over the canoe. "You knew the people who lived here?"

"Yep."

"What happened to them?"

"They died."

"You amaze me, you know it?"

"How come?"

"Sometimes, there's no shutting you up. Other times, getting information out of you is like pulling teeth."

"Or gators' tails."

He liked her analogy better. He told her so, then fell silent, concentrating on watching her back in the fading light.

As darkness fell, the swamp started to come alive, as it did every night. Although he'd been in the swamp several weeks now, Jesse didn't think he'd ever become accustomed to the sudden onslaught of croaks and chirps and scratchings and splashings that were an integral part of the swamp at night. The noises made the hair on his nape curl up, and sent a creepy-crawly shiver down his spine. Even having Lilah as a companion failed to temper his adversity to the dark swamp.

The marshy ground turned to damp sand, and still Lilah trudged ahead. Through the treetops, the sky blazed apricot and lavender, but below dense gray shadows swathed the woods. Jesse wished they'd hurry up and get to wherever it was they were going.

Suddenly, a huge monster loomed directly in front of Lilah. Jesse had scoffed at tales of swamp creatures—half-animal, half-vegetation—but here was one of them, growling, raising its arms and flexing his muscles like a man, and coming right at Lilah. It was as bloodcurdling a sight as ever he'd seen.

With the heavy bag over his right shoulder and the Colt shoved into the right side of his belt, getting to the pistol proved difficult. By the time he dropped the bag and had the gun firmly in hand, the monster had picked Lilah up in its forepaws. From where he stood, he couldn't shoot the creature without shooting Lilah.

Sweat poured off Jesse's brow and his stomach dropped to his shaking knees. He had to do something, and he had to do it fast. But first, he had to move around to the monster's side.

"I'll save you!" he hollered. In his haste, Jesse forgot that the canoe lay between him and Lilah. He stubbed his toe on the pointed end and lunged forward. Instinctively, his hands went out to absorb his fall.

The gun went off. Lilah screamed. Jesse cursed.

Weakened by frustration, fear, and anger, he fought to right himself while regaining his hold on the pistol, but when he tried to stand up in the canoe, it tipped onto its side. Jesse jumped out, brought the Colt up—and blinked in total confusion.

Lilah was standing on her own feet again, and the creature had dropped to all fours. Quite calmly, she patted the monster's head while she spoke soothingly to the beast, whose shudders were visible even in the dim light. "He didn't mean no harm," she said to the swamp creature. "Ye know him, but he don' know you. He was jest tryin' to pertect me."

God! It wasn't a swamp creature. It was a bear . . . Ol' Codger!

Recognizing his mistake didn't erase the turmoil of emotion that continued to rage inside him. "Dammit, Lilah! You scared me half to death! You could have told me!"

"Ye didn't give me a chance! How come ye to shoot? Ye could've hurt Ol' Codger, Jesse. And he saved yer life!"

"How was I to know? He had you in his claws. I thought . . . I thought . . . hell! I thought he was going to

rip you to shreds right before my eyes! I thought he was
a swamp creature or something. What's that stuff all over
him, anyway?"

The pain in his voice curbed her vexation with him, but
she refused to let it go completely. "Shucks, that's jest
Codger's way a-stoppin' the flies from bitin' him. Bahr's
bites big chunks out'n pine trees, lets 'em bleed a good
long spell—maybe half a day—then rubs theirselfs against
the trunks till they's covered in pitch. Then they rolls in
sand or leaves. The flies don' come near 'em after that."

Jesse shook his head. "I don' blame them. Look, I'm
tired and you're tired and we're both hungry and the
light's going fast. When were you planning on stopping?"

"Up yonder a piece." She pointed in the general direction they'd been heading, then started pulling on the canoe
again. Codger grunted and ambled off into the woods.
Jesse picked up the provisions bag again, but this time he
carried the gun in his left hand instead of in his belt.

A moment later, they entered a clearing similar to the
one around Granny Latham's cabin. Though the house appeared to be somewhat larger than Granny's cabin, its lack
of care was obvious even in the gloom. Shutters hung
askew on their rotting wooden hinges, the porch roof
sagged where a limb had fallen on it, and an abundance of
weeds grew in rampant abandon in the yard. Around and
beyond the house, Jesse spied an assortment of outbuildings and livestock pens, testimony that an active, produc-
tive family had once lived and worked and loved here. A
host of questions begged to be asked, but Jesse decided
they could wait until he and Lilah were settled in the
cabin.

She slid the canoe under the porch and picked her way
up the steps, taking care, he noted, to watch where she put
her feet down. The boards popped and groaned even under
her slight weight, but they didn't break. Jesse followed her

example, holding his breath until they were safely through the door.

"Give me a match," she said. Jesse fished the safe out of his pocket and handed it over. He heard the match scrape against the striker, then a candle sprang to life, its meager flame penetrating only a few feet into the dark interior of the house. As he watched Lilah locate and light additional candles, he realized that she was quite familiar with this house. Almost as though she'd lived here . . .

"Was Granny Latham your mother's mother or your father's?" he asked.

Lilah set a candle on an eating table surrounded by four chairs, then flicked her fingertips across its surface. "Neither."

He waited for an explanation. Instead, she opened a cupboard and removed a large, black iron pot with a bail. A big rat darted out of the cupboard, then scurried across the floor and out the open doorway. She watched the rat without even blinking an eye, much less screaming like most women would, then returned her attention to the cupboard. "Come on out'n there, the rest a ye critters. Come on, now."

Like dutiful soldiers obeying a drill sergeant, six mice, another rat, and three raccoons tripped out of the cupboard and marched out of the house. One of the coons made a detour by Jesse, sniffed at the toe of his boot and snuffled, then poked its nose in the air and got in line behind the other critters. Jesse's mouth dropped open in amazement. What was it with raccoons? he wondered. They didn't seem to like him at all.

Lilah thrust the pot into his hands. "There's a rain barrel sittin' next to the porch. Brang in some water."

"Yes, ma'am!" He wasn't at all sure he liked this take-charge attitude of hers, but he couldn't argue that they needed water—or that he was the logical person to fetch it.

"And be sure to rinch that pot," she called as he was going out the door. "No tellin' what's been a-crawlin' in it, but I spect it's a durn sight cleaner'n the bucket sittin' out there on the porch."

He started to ask her how she knew about the bucket and why she didn't have him use one of the clean pots from the provisions bag, then decided he'd just play along and see what she was up to. Taking one of the candles with him, he picked his way across the porch to the rain barrel. Sure enough, a wooden bucket sat near the barrel. Jesse held the candle over the bucket. It was full of cobwebs and dirt-dauber nests.

When he came back with the pot, Lilah told him to set it on the table, where she'd piled up some dingy-looking rags. She handed him an enamel dishpan. "Fill this up, too. Rinch it first."

"I know," he said, smiling.

She followed him outside this time.

"Where are you going?"

"To get some soap."

He raised his eyebrows, then clamped his mouth shut. She seemed to know exactly what she was doing. "Be careful."

"The bush is jest around the corner."

Of course. The soap bush. The swamp provided almost everything a body needed to survive, even soap.

A short while later, he'd hauled in half of the water in the barrel in a dozen or more containers, each of which Lilah had reminded him to "rinch." After the first time, he mentally questioned the importance of this "rinching," since the water in the barrel smelled suspiciously stagnant and shone green in the candlelight. In the meantime, she cleaned the ashes out of the fireplace and hauled them outside, using the nasty bucket from the porch as a vessel to carry them in.

"Now go out there and dump that barrel," she said,

transferring firewood from a box on the hearth into the clean fireplace.

"Why?"

" 'Cause it's li'ble to rain tonight. Don' ye want fresh water?"

He snorted. "I sure as hell ain't gonna drink any a-that I brought in."

"Listen to yerself, Jesse! Ye're a-startin' to talk like me."

"Heaven forbid!"

For the next hour, he followed her orders, using a pine knot she provided to search out dry firewood, then sweeping spiderwebs off the ceiling and a thick layer of dust off the floor with a straw broom. At the same time, Lilah washed off the table and chairs as well as the other pieces of wooden furniture in the two-room house—a rocking chair, a bench with no back, a dry sink, a cupboard, three chests of varying sizes, and two bedsteads.

One of the beds, a narrow one, sat against the back wall of the front room, while the other, larger bed occupied most of the space in the smaller back room. He'd been right. A family had lived here. He wanted to open the chests, to expose the secrets Lilah seemed reluctant to reveal, but both his work and Lilah's presence stopped him. He didn't suppose he'd pry even if those things hadn't gotten in his way, but he sure as hell wanted to.

While he was thinking about this, Lilah opened one of the chests and removed several bedsheets made by stitching flour sacks together. These she stacked on the clean bench. From among the sheets she extracted several small cheesecloth packets. A sweet, clean fragrance wafted across the room.

"Lavender," she said, her gaze caressing the room and a hint of a smile teasing her lips, giving Jesse the impression that she wasn't talking to him at all, but rather to the room itself. "Maw kept a bed of it growin'. Said she couldn't sleep lessen she could smell lavender, 'cause her momma used it and she'd grown up smellin' it in her sleep. She brung some little ol' plants with her when she married Paw. She was raised up over to Homerville, you know."

He didn't know, but he nodded anyway, afraid that if he spoke she'd remember he was there and hush. So, this house had belonged to her family. No wonder she knew so much about where things were. He eased himself into the rocking chair and watched her take the covers and linens off the narrow bed.

"My paw made this upscuddle," she said, pausing in her labor to smooth a palm over the footboard, "out'n cypress."

Jesse could hear his mother calling a bedstead an upscuddle, and he smiled way deep down inside in a place in his soul he hadn't visited for a long time.

"Ain't it purty?"

Again, he nodded, thinking there wasn't anything pretty about the plainly made, unvarnished bed, but he didn't suppose it was ugly either.

Again, she ignored him. She dumped the dusty linens on the floor and popped open one of the sheets she'd taken out of the chest. The scent of dried lavender chased away the final remnants of mustiness. Her wistful look changed to one of sadness, and she fell silent. He wanted to take her in his arms, to fall with her onto the bed and kiss away the sadness.

Telling himself such thoughts were madness, he cleared his throat, which he realized was quite full of compassion. "Are you hungry?"

"A mite. Ye want to rustle us up some vittles, whilst I make t'other bed?"

Her reminder of the second bed annoyed him. And he was further annoyed by the fact that it annoyed him. As he unpacked the canvas bag, he worked at convincing himself

that it really was better for Lilah to sleep in one bed and
him in the other. Without paying any mind to what he was
doing, he opened a jar of berries and dumped them in a
pot, then set the pot on an iron rack in the fireplace. In an
effort to keep his mind occupied, he removed everything
from the canvas bag, placing the items on the table. When
the bag was empty, he sorted it all out, making neat little
piles and groupings of cooking utensils, food packages,
and clothing.

A hiss from the vicinity of the fireplace arrested his attention, and he hurried over to find liquid bubbling out of
the pot. The aroma of blackberries assailed him, and he
laughed—full, hearty, robust laughter that drew Lilah back
into the front room.

"What is it?" she asked. "What's so funny?"

"I'm ... cooking ... berries!" he sputtered.

She frowned. "So?"

"So, do you want to eat berries for supper?"

"Sure."

"Good, 'cause that's what we're having."

She collected tin plates and spoons from the table, then
opened a linen cloth and removed two hard, cold biscuits,
which she crumbled onto the plates. These she covered
with blackberries and juice. "We'uns have to soften them
biscuits with something, if'n we want to eat 'em," she explained. "Mamie Yerby makes the drisomest biscuits in the
swamp, and these is three day old."

Jesse accepted one of the plates and sat down at the table. "My pa used to say *day* and *year* regardless of how
many he was talking about."

Lilah shoved two jars out of the way so she'd have
room for her plate. "And what do you say, Jesse?"

"If it's more than one—*days* and *years.*"

"Three *days* old," she said, dragging out the *s* and holding her spoon poised over the plate. "I'll try to mem'ry
that."

"Please don't," he said, wishing he hadn't mentioned it.

"How come?"

"Because ... because being with you reminds me of home. I'd forgotten how much I missed it."

Lilah shrugged and stirred her berries and biscuit together. "I wish we'uns had some cream to pour on here. I ain't had no cream since I was ... since I lived ..." Her blue eyes misted up, and she looked down at her plate.

"Since you lived here?" he asked, careful to keep his tone gentle.

Her head moved in the slightest indication of agreement, and Jesse didn't push her. He wondered what had happened to her parents, and whether she'd had brothers or sisters. He wondered how long ago she'd lived in this house, and how she'd come to live with Granny Latham. He longed to share her memories and her misery, just as she'd shared his a few days ago. But she hadn't pushed him, and he wouldn't push her. One day, she'd tell him.

They'd almost finished eating their supper when Jesse remembered the can of sweetened condensed milk he'd found in the haversack. Lilah could have had her cream, if he'd just thought of it earlier. He'd bet she'd never tasted sweetened condensed milk before. The thought of introducing her to the thick concoction sent a delicious shiver trickling down his spine.

Lilah rose slowly from her chair and took her plate to the dishpan, which she'd left sitting on the dry sink. She set one of the larger pots of water on the rack in the fireplace, then collected his plate and added it to the dishpan. He noted the sudden weariness in her movements and realized she'd dug a grave, paddled a canoe for hours on end, then cleaned this house—all in one day. It was enough to make the heartiest person weary.

"I'll wash the dishes," he said. "You get some rest."

"I'll be much obliged," she said, taking a pot of water with her to the back room. Her choice of beds surprised him, since he was much larger than she. He supposed it didn't make much difference. He wasn't fixing to go to bed anyway. One of them had to stay awake, just in case.

Although the possibility of One-Eyed Jack finding them here was slim, Jesse wasn't about to take any chances. Not with his life. And especially not with Lilah's.

A sudden, ear-splitting boom awakened him. He shot out of the rocking chair, his pistol raised, his one-eyed gaze searching the shadows for movement. Another boom shook the house and then another.

Thunder.

He took a deep breath and waited for his heart to stop beating so fast. What had he meant, falling asleep? Hell, anyone could have come in. Anything could have happened to Lilah.

A streak of lightning flashed, reminding him that the windows were wide open. Jesse laid his Colt on the table, then hurried to pull the shutters to and latch them. The window over the dry sink was missing a shutter. Jesse cut a piece of jute twine from the bundle Colin had packed in the bag, and tied one end to the wooden knob on the remaining shutter and the other end to a knob on base of the sink cabinet.

With thunder continuing to rattle the house, Jesse moved into the other room, which he'd noted had only one window—on the back wall. He strode toward it, refusing to look at the bed, trying to shut out an imagined picture of Lilah snuggled under the covers, her face softened by sleep. The bed was pushed close to the back wall, leaving barely enough room for him to squeeze by in order to reach the window.

A streak of lightning hurtled to the earth, striking a tall tree near the back side of the house and splitting it asunder. Trees on either side caught and held its divided top as it fell to left and right. The tree burst into flames that leapt along the severed trunk and into the trees that held it. More flames danced along the ground, igniting the under-brush then scampering off to torch other trees into a fiery blaze.

The air hung heavy with the promise of rain, but thus far, not one drop had fallen. At the rate the fire was burning—and without the rain to put it out, the devastating flames would reach the outbuildings within minutes, and from there . . .

A whimper from behind claimed his attention, and he turned to see Lilah rolled into a shivering ball on top of the covers, her arms and shoulders bare above the top of her camisole. From the looks of things, she'd removed only her shirt before falling asleep. Jesse scooped her into his arms and dashed into the front room, then out onto the porch and down the rickety steps without giving even a cursory thought to their deterioration. The bottom step snapped in two as his booted foot left it. Jesse didn't stop until he'd reached the edge of the clearing, and only then because he realized the need to take both the canoe and some provisions. *Damn!* he thought. *Why did I unpack that bag?*

At some point in their flight, Lilah's arms had become entwined around his neck, and she clung to him with the tenacity of a climbing heath growing beneath the dead bark of a pond cypress. Jesse tugged on her arms. She clutched him tighter.

"Lilah, let go!" She didn't respond. "I have to put you down long enough to get the canoe. The house is liable to become a raging inferno any minute now. You have to let go!"

Something he said must have penetrated, because she loosened her grasp enough for him to set her on the ground. "Don't move!" he cautioned, uncertain of what she might do in the state she was in.

Within minutes, he threw some food into the canvas

bag, snatched up the deerskin pouch, and pulled the canoe out from under the porch. Back across the clearing he went, dragging the canoe behind him. When Lilah made no effort to follow him into the woods, he put her in the canoe, along with the bag and the pouch. The weight slowed him down, but he didn't stop until the darkness of the woods engulfed them.

The moment he stopped, exhaustion set in, and Jesse squatted down next to the canoe, thinking only to catch his breath before continuing on to the lake. All around them, animals panted and birds squawked as the creatures of the swamp fled from the fire, which added its roar to the cacophony of storm and flight.

A raindrop pelted his cheek, and then another and another. He relished the sting as hope sprang into Jesse's heart. Cold logic, however, quickly dashed it. The rain, he feared, had come too late.

Chapter Fifteen

The first fat raindrop that stung Lilah's cheek revived her with the potency of the strongest smelling salts. In more than a little confusion, she sat up and took account of her whereabouts. What was she doing in the woods? In the canoe? Where was . . .

"Jesse?"

"I'm right here, darling."

His strong arms encircled her, and he helped her to her feet. She searched the dark shadow of his face, her mind thrusting questions at her so fast she couldn't decide what to ask first. She didn't have to.

"The woods are on fire—dangerously close to the house. I had to get you away from there. We have to keep moving. I stopped only to rest."

"But it's rainin'."

"Too late and not enough, I'm afraid."

She shivered, and he pulled her into his embrace. "I shouldn't a-come back," she said.

"Why?"

"All this time, nothin' happened. And then the night I come back—"

He smoothed an open palm over her hair. "It's not your fault, Lilah. You didn't bring the storm."

"I grew up there."

"I know."

"There was some things"—her voice caught in her throat—"I wanted. Not reg'lar house plunder. Things like Maw's embroidried counterpin and Paw's whettin' stone. Little Jacob's birthin' dress."

Important things, Jesse thought, knowing exactly what she meant. He'd saved a few of those kinds of things himself, had them stored at his sister Alma's in Maryville. He didn't know who Little Jacob was and he didn't want to ask her, not as fragile as she was at the moment.

For a long while, they clung to each other. The rain steadily increased, coming down faster now, beating and tearing the young leaves overhead, drenching Lilah and Jesse.

"Maybe it's not too late," he said.

"Ye reckon?"

Jesse heard the hope in her voice and prayed he was right. Tenderly, he turned them around so he could see back up the trail, toward the house. Thus far, the fire hadn't followed them, but the damp air carried the acrid smells of smoke and charred wood. Wet charred wood.

"Wait here," he said, pushing away from her.

"Nay. I'm a-comin' with you."

He didn't think that was a good idea, but he didn't figure he could stop her. "Then stay close."

Blindly, they ran, dodging trees and scurrying around bushes, slipping and sliding on the wet ground, the rain slashing into their backs. Thunder rumbled so loud the unstable earth trembled. Staccato bursts of lightning illuminated the sky, revealing banks of black clouds dumping cascades of water that reduced visibility to a mere three or four feet, and still they ran.

Jesse ran up on the broken porch step before he realized they'd ever entered the clearing. He reached out and snared Lilah around the waist, lifting her up and pulling her into his side. He had to holler in her ear to be heard above the crash and bang of the storm.

"The back of the house may be on fire." If it were, he reasoned, they should have seen it already, even from the front. There should at least be a glow. There wasn't—but the hint of light spilling out the open door troubled him. Jesse thought it wise to take precautions.

As he moved up the steps, he felt her nod against his shoulder. He set her down on the porch, took her hand, and entered the little house that held so many memories for her. When he saw the source of the light, a long breath escaped him. He'd been in such a hurry to leave that he hadn't extinguished the candle lamp on the table; it burned with a soft yellow glimmer, a fragment of the all-consuming fury he'd witnessed a short time before, yet it held the potential for equal deadliness.

The wind, which was buffeting the front of the house, had been responsible for blowing the porch door open, while firmly closing the door to the back room, since both doors opened into the front room. Jesse closed and barred the porch door, then turned his attention to the back of the house. Certain Lilah would only follow if he asked her to stay put, he led her to the door that blocked their entrance to the back room, where he used his free hand to test the heat of the wood. It was surprisingly cool.

"Stand back!" he ordered, his voice brooking no argument. Assuring himself that she was out of the way, he pulled the door open and encountered gaping darkness. Fearing that part of the room could be burned away, he told Lilah to bring the lamp. Before she even turned aside, a flash of lightning blanched the darkness, its light coming through a neat square on the back wall.

"It's there!" she cried, rushing past him. "It didn't burn!"

He joined her at the window. Together, they watched a few tiny red glimmers, the remains of the fire, flicker and

then disappear. With the wind blowing into the front of the
house, very little moisture came through the opening.

Lilah sniffled, and the sound tore at his heart. "I was so
sceered," she said.

"Me, too," he admitted, surprising and embarrassing
himself. "Uh, I have to go get the canoe before the rain
washes it away."

"Yes."

"Will you be all right?"

"I'll be fine. Now."

"I'll hurry."

"Take the pine knot."

The instant Lilah dropped the bar over the door behind
him, a violent shiver rushed through her. Blaming it on
their ordeal, she hugged herself and realized she was
soaked clear through. No wonder she was shivering! Jesse
must be cold, too. If they weren't careful, they'd come
down with the new mon fever.

She put her shirt back on and tended the fire, then set
a pot of water on the rack and hung two more from hooks.
With the water heating, she dragged out the half-barrel
bathing tub, which Maw always kept in the corner nearest
the fireplace, and proceeded to scrub it as best she could.
Neither the water nor the tub would really be clean, but
that couldn't be helped. At least the house had escaped
damage, and she and Jesse were safe—or they would be
when he got back.

What was taking him so long? she wondered, leaving
the tub to go to the front door. They might not be able to
hear each other, but maybe she could see the pine knot
burning—if the wind and the rain hadn't snuffed it out.
The wind must have really picked up, for it was now hurling tree limbs at the house. They were even coming across
the porch and hitting the door.

Cautiously, she removed the bar and opened the door.
There stood Jesse, his fists raised in preparation for pum-

meling the door again. Caught off guard by his unexpected presence, she yelped and jumped back.

"I'm sorry. I didn't mean to frighten you," he said, his teeth chattering. He stepped inside and barred the door behind him. "I was beginning to think you were never going to hear me knocking. What were you doing?"

His clothes were plastered to his body, and water dripped from his hair and beard and ran down his neck in rivulets. Lilah watched, mesmerized, as one rivulet coursed across the hollow at the base of his throat and disappeared into his shirt. Suddenly, she didn't think their taking baths was such a good idea anymore. When he pulled the shirt out of his britches and started to unfasten it, she knew it wasn't.

"We have to get warm and dry," he said, his voice still shivering.

"I know." She moved toward the fireplace, as much to avoid looking at him as to prepare his bath. "The air's startin' to come off the water, but I have to finish wipin' out the tub."

She squatted down by the tub and picked up the rag again. Out of the corner of her eye, she watched Jesse haul a chair from the table to the fireplace and drape his shirt over the back, then sit down and start to remove his boots. He was close, too close. Dangerously close. So close she could smell the rain in his hair and the masculine musk of his skin, which the heat intensified. She hadn't thought she'd wanted anything more than to be alone with Jesse, but now that she was, now that the crisis of the fire had passed and neither of them seemed the least bit sleepy, the thought frightened her plumb witless. When he stood up and started to shimmy out of his wet britches, she hightailed it to the back room like a flushed rabbit running from a wildcat. His laughter followed her, and she closed the door in an attempt to shut it out.

She'd forgotten about having only the one lamp in the

house, and it on the eating table, but she wasn't about to go back out there now to get it. She stood with her back against the door until her pulse stopped racing and her eyes grew accustomed to the gloom, the open window providing only a modicum of light.

Her work near the fire had served to dry her clothes, but they were filthy, as was her hair, which was only partially dry and extremely tangled. Maw would have laughed and said it was full of rat nesties, then used her large wooden comb to get them out. If Lilah couldn't take a bath right then, at least she could comb the rat nesties out of her hair. Her own comb was in the go-away satchel, which she'd lost along with her canoe, but her mother's was right there in the drawer of the washstand, next to Paw's razor . . .

"Hey, Lilah!" Jesse called. "Come here."

She eased the door open so they could carry on a conversation. "What do ye want?"

"Some soap bush leaves." The splash of water accompanied his request.

She slid the drawer open, removed the comb and the razor, then pushed it shut. "I'll be there tirectly."

"Hurry up. The water's getting cold."

"Can't be. Ye jest got in." She pulled Paw's strop out from the wall and swiped the razor down it, then back up.

"And I need a towel!"

"They's in the chest. Same one I got the sheets out'n."

"Will you get me one?"

Lilah supposed she could interrupt her razor honing long enough to get him the things he needed, but she was afraid that if she went out there without the razor in hand, she'd lose her nerve and not go back with the razor. No, she'd wait until it was ready to be used. "In a bit," she called.

"Look, I'm sorry for laughing at you." He paused, and

she heard his deep sigh. "I'm not some mean old ogre," he said. "Come on back out here."

She pushed the razor harder and faster against the strop. "What's a ogre?"

"Didn't anyone ever read you a fairy tale?"

"What's a fairy tale?"

"A story, you know, where a princess gets herself in some kind of trouble and the prince comes to save her, but then a mean old ogre gets in the way."

"I don't know what ye're talkin' about, Jesse." She carefully traced the pad of her thumb along the edge of the razor and decided it was almost sharp enough. "I never heared of a prince or a princess or one of them ogre fellers. Who is they?"

"Come out here and I'll tell you a story about them."

"I tol' you I'd be there tirectly."

What in tarnation was she up to that was taking so long? he wondered, his imagination spiraling with a plethora of possibilities. The racket from the storm obliterated other sounds and the partially open door blocked his view, but he could just see her in there putting on something soft and feminine. Suddenly, Jesse had a mighty craving to see her in a sheer nightdress, with her curly locks all combed out and hanging to her waist. If she didn't come out pretty soon, he was going in there, even if it meant tracking water across the floor, which they'd been doing anyway.

Besides, he was getting uncomfortable sitting in the half-barrel with his knees up. There was barely enough room for both his behind and his feet on the bottom, and when he leaned back, the rough wood nettled his skin.

"Hurry up, Lilah! This water really is getting cold now."

She came out then, dressed just like she was when she'd gone in. But there was something different about her, something in her eyes, something delightfully feminine and yet devilishly mischievous. She held her hands behind her back. She was hiding something.

"What have you got there? Let me see."

Her gaze on his face, she smiled and stepped closer, but only to within arm's reach of the tub. Though the way she refused to look down or come too close made him smile inside, Jesse didn't dare let her see his amusement lest she dart back into the other room. Slowly, she brought her right arm out, offering him a razor . . .

A razor.

"A razor!" he bellowed, starting to stand up, but catching himself in time. "A razor." He rubbed his bearded jaw and shook his head. "Where—"

"My paw's," she said, waggling it at him. "I sharped it up for you."

"Thank you," he managed, still somewhat dazed.

"Mighty proud I am to have it to give to you," she said, beaming. She turned away then and went over to the chest. "I'll jest git you some soap and a towel. Later, ye can shave yerself. A glass be on the wall in t'other room, right over the washstand."

"Aren't you going to shave me, Lilah?"

The question surprised him as much as it obviously did her. Her head snapped up, and that frightened-rabbit look was back in her eyes. "I ain't never shaved a man."

"I'll teach you."

She closed the chest, collected a branch of soap bush leaves from the pile she'd left on the dry sink, and laid both a linen towel and the branch on the chair beside him. "Ye can shave whilst I'm a-bathin'."

She had it all figured out, he decided as he plucked one of the leaves off the towel and lathered it between his palms. He should have known it was all a connivance. Part of him was disappointed, but another part wondered if maybe it wasn't better this way. He wanted her. There was no questioning that. The more time he spent with the angel, the more he wanted her. The problem was he couldn't offer her forever, and that's what women wanted.

"You'd better put on some more water to heat. I used most of it."

Averting her gaze again, she poured water from smaller pots into larger ones, then took his one extra pair of britches out of the pouch and put them under the towel. "I'll get you one of Paw's shirts. He was big for a swamper. Howsomever, he weren't big as you. I ain't never seed a man big as you."

He smiled again. "Just leave it on the bed. I'll put it on after I shave."

While he was shaving, Lilah washed her hair in the dishpan at the dry sink. All Jesse had to do to catch a look at her was turn his head a bit, and this he found himself doing so often it took him almost twice as long to shave off his beard and mustache as it should have.

By the time Lilah got in the tub, the sun was coming up and the storm had begun to abate. Jesse sat on the chest in the back room, waiting for her to get through, listening to the water splashing and aching all over to peek around the door and get a good look at her breasts. Oh, he'd seen them that day in the lake, the day she'd found his gun in the maiden canes, but that was different. They weren't completely bare that day. He wanted to see if her nipples were really as big and as dark as he thought they were, but he'd promised her no peeking. And he was a man known for keeping his promises.

At long last, the splashing gave way to dripping, which meant she was standing up and drying herself off. Jesse half-rose from the chest, then sat back down and gripped the top edge so hard it bit into his palms. She started to sing, and Jesse recognized the tune as the one he'd heard her singing the first time he ever saw her, the day he'd come to Medicine Island. He'd startled her that day, caus-

ing her to abruptly end the song, but now he leaned back
against the footboard, closed his eye, and let both the soul-
ful melody and the sad words wash over him.

It was a song a man should be singing, a song about a
lady named Greensleeves who rejected a suitor's love and
affection, yet in a larger sense it seemed to belong to
Lilah. And to him, too. The song belonged to everyone
who'd ever had a dream come shattering down.

He'd had a dream once. A dream of raising his sons to
adulthood, of growing old with Martha, of leaving this
earth with the knowledge that he'd left a bit of himself behind and that the world was better for it. A scoundrel
named Jack Scurlock had destroyed that dream and set
Jesse on a path of retribution. Eventually, that path had
brought him to Lilah, the sweetest combination of girl and
woman he'd ever met. A gal-woman, they'd call her in the
hills. Ripe for the plucking. Given different circumstances,
he might have considered starting over with Lilah . . .

He felt her presence and looked up to see her standing
in the doorway, the pale light from the early morning sun
turning her damp curls into a golden halo. Her clear blue
eyes sparkled, and a smile brighter than the sun lit her
face. She wore a pale pink dress sprigged with tiny, darker
pink rosebuds. He suspected the dress had belonged to her
maw. It was as much too large for Lilah as her paw's shirt
was too small for him.

"Are ye as hunger-bit as I am?" she asked, neither looking nor sounding the least bit tired, while he felt like
someone had beaten him soundly and left him for dead.

"I could eat."

"I'm toastin' the last of Mistress Mamie's biscuits."

He groaned.

"But there's honey to drainch them in."

Jesse followed her into the front room. "Where did you
learn that song you were singing?" he asked.

"From maw. She knew all kinds of songs and poems and sich."

"Could yer maw read?"

"A bit. Her paw got sick not long after she started goin' to school, and couldn't pay her way no more. My paw couldn't read a-tall, but he could quote scripture a-plenty. Who teached you to read, Jesse?"

"My mother. She was a far better teacher than I'll ever be."

"Ye're doin' jest fine."

She set plates of split and toasted biscuits on the table. Jesse "drainched" his in honey, just as she'd suggested, and found the fare surprisingly good. "I didn't think there was anything better than sourwood honey," he said, "but this honey has a real delicate flavor to it."

"That's 'cause it's huckleberry honey. They's most always something a-bloom in the Okefinoke, and the bees love ever' one of them flowers. They's cassena holly honey and pick'relweed honey and palmetto honey and lots more. 'Course, they's flavors from more'n one flower in all of it. Ye never know what flavor the honey's gonna be till ye try it, but it's always good. Swampfolks say the Indians was so extree fond of Okefinoke honey that they wed bees to lightning bugs, so they could work in the dark. That way, there was more honey for everybody."

Lilah laughed at the ridiculous tale, but Jesse was so busy wondering what honey would taste like if it were made from the delicately flavored nectar of Lilah's mouth that he missed the humor. His throat went suddenly dry. "We got anything to drink? I'm powerful thirsty."

"Oh! I plumb forgot." She dipped out cups of water from an enamel pot and set them on the table. "Fresh rainwater."

Jesse took a sip, then a long swallow. "Not bad. But not as good as the water from our mountain streams."

"Ye never did tell me about the mountings, Jesse."

"I never did tell you a lot of things, Lilah." He studied his hands for a minute, then looked up at her and pasted what he hoped was a pleasant smile on his face. "What do you want to know about the mountains?"

She rewarded him with a toothy grin and twinkling eyes. "Ever'thang."

Talking about his homeland proved to be a sort of catharsis for Jesse, which surprised him. As he warmed to the subject, he told her about things he hadn't thought about in years—how his father had used ashes to cure pork and how his mother had made lime pickles and blackberry wine. He talked about going to square dances in the fall and making ice cream out of winter snow. He talked about how everyone turned out in the spring and roamed the coves looking for ramps, which he explained were like wild onions.

He talked about the springhouse, which was built on top of the stream with the water diverted into troughs on either side, so that whatever they put in there stayed cold, even in the hottest weather. He talked about his four brothers and three sisters, how the boys teased the girls unmercifully, especially when the girls got old enough to attract the attention of various and sundry young men. That got him to talking about courting, but he carefully avoided mentioning his own love life or anything that happened to him beyond adolescence. He wouldn't allow himself to talk about anything that might lead into a discussion of his and Lilah's relationship—past, present, or future.

Jesse never made promises he couldn't keep. Over their graves, he'd promised Martha and the boys he'd catch Jack Scurlock and bring him to justice. As much as he wished it was all behind him, it wasn't. And after four years of tracking the man and losing his trail again, Jesse carried little hope of seeing an end to this business any time soon.

There could be no future for him with Lilah, not as long

as One-Eyed Jack was alive and free. To lead her to believe that there could, would be unfair to both of them.

She was his angel of mercy. He couldn't let himself become her demon of despair.

Chapter Sixteen

By the time Jesse talked himself out, the rain had diminished to a slow drizzle, and he and Lilah went outside to check on the canoe, which he'd tied to one of the porch piers. Wet leaves, small limbs, and Spanish moss littered the inside of the canoe. They turned it over—and discovered a hole about the size of a silver dollar in the bottom.

"How the hell did that happen?"

Lilah watched Jesse's expression change from astonishment to sheepishness, and she burst out laughing. "Ye don' have to look so shamefaced, Jesse. Ye just shot a hole in it."

"Yeah. And how are we going to leave here without a canoe?"

"We could walk, but it'd take twicet as long." She gave him a long, assessing stare. "Don' ye know nothin' about canoes, Jesse? All we got to do is plug the hole. It's jest a little un."

"Of course. I was ... I'm just ..."

"Ye're tired. Me too."

Thunder rumbled in the distance, drawing their attention. A dark bank of storm clouds was blowing in again. "I don't suppose we were going anywhere today anyway," Jesse said. He shoved the canoe under the porch. "I'll gather some more firewood and stack it on the porch to dry. You go on in and go to bed."

"You need sleep worser'n I do."

Jesse let his shoulders sag—and his spirit drooped right along with them. "No. We both need rest."

"But what about keepin' watch?"

He frowned at the dark cloud bank. "I don't think we have to worry about that. Not as long as this weather holds on, anyway."

Since Lilah could find no argument with his reasoning, she started up the steps while he moved toward the woods. An extreme fatigue she had yet to fully acknowledge measured every footfall. She collapsed onto the small bed in the front room, and fell asleep before Jesse came back in.

Between the storm and the closed shutters, the house was so dark when Lilah woke up that she had no idea what time it was. She lay in bed for a spell longer, watching the firelight flicker and bounce on the floor and snuggling deeper under the covers, while she waited for the groggies to go away.

Covers . . . What was she doing under the covers? Lilah searched her memory, but could not recall ever actually getting into bed. Had she been that tired? She turned onto her side and the lavender-scented sheet skimmed over her bare legs.

Lilah sat straight up in bed. A cool draft skimmed over her back and raised gooseflesh on her arms. She snatched up the covers and tucked them under her armpits. Lord, she was practically naked! No matter how beat all to flinders she might have been, never would she have stripped down to her camisole and drawers, not with a man in the house.

Jesse! He'd done this. He'd removed her clothes and put her in bed. The realization sent a delicious shiver surging through her, yet it frightened her at the same time. What else

had he done? What had *she* done? She recalled the shocking
discovery of the depth of her sensuality and felt herself grow
warm and liquid with longing. She hadn't stopped wanting
him to touch her, but she wanted it to be on her terms—and
when she was fully awake. She didn't want to miss a single
second of experiencing Jesse's caresses.

Where was he anyway?

She looked around for her clothes and spied the rose-
sprigged dress and muslin chemise draped across the footboard. Quickly, she donned the garments, then padded on
silent feet to the door that closed off the back room. Outside, rain pelted the log walls and wood-shingled roof and
the wind tore at the shutters, even those on the back window, which he'd closed and latched, thus shutting out any
light from without. Without a lamp, it was impossible to
see whether he was in the bed.

A snuffle from behind caught her unawares. Lilah
gasped and whirled around. Thin light sifting through the
half-open window above the dry sink spilled onto the eating table. And there, bent over with his head resting on his
folded arms, sat Jesse. He couldn't be comfortable, and yet
she hesitated to disturb him.

While she stood in the doorway, trying to make a decision, he raised his head, then straightened up, and yawned.
"I'm sorry. I didn't mean to go to sleep," he said, patting
at his open mouth.

"I thought ye was aimin' to rest."

"I was, but then I got to worrying . . ." A wide yawn interrupted his speech, but he didn't have to finish the sentence. Lilah understood perfectly what he meant. He got
up and moved to the dry sink, where he splashed water on
his face. "What time is it?"

"Nigh on to supper time, I reckon."

His gaze raked over her in an appreciative sort of way
that made part of her feel beautiful, while another part

questioned the wisdom of her plan to spend time alone with him with little or nothing required of them. To cover her bewilderment, she turned her attention to the fireplace, poking at the coals and then laying on more wood. She heard Jesse puttering around the table, lighting candles and sorting through the provisions Mamie Yerby had packed.

"There's a jar of sweet potatoes here," he said. "Do you know how to make sweet potato pudding?"

"Ain't never made it 'thout eggs 'n' milk, but I can try."

"There's a can of milk here, too."

"For true?" She spun around in excitement. He held up a small can with a commercial label on it, and Lilah practically ran to the table. "I've heared of puttin' milk in cans, but I ain't never seed it before. Ye reckon it's sour?"

Jesse couldn't help smiling at her childlike enthusiasm. "No, I reckon it's good. And sweet, too."

"Sweet? How come?"

"Because they put sugar in it."

She took the can from him and eyed the printed label skeptically. "How do ye know it's milk in here? There ain't no picture."

"No, but there's writing."

"What does the writin' say?"

"Borden condensed milk."

She narrowed her eyes at him. "Condensed? What does that mean?"

"Let me show you." He recaptured the can, set it on the table, and proceeded to take the lid off with a hook-type can opener Mamie had provided. When he'd worked the hook most of the way around the top, he bent the lid back, raked his forefinger across the thick milk, and popped it into her open mouth. Her lips closed around the second knuckle of his finger, and her eyes widened in innocent pleasure.

Jesse's stomach turned to molten desire. He knew he

ought to pull his finger out. He knew that if he didn't, the simple act of her sucking the sweetened milk off could prove his undoing. But he didn't do anything. He ignored the warning and allowed himself to enjoy the sheer carnality of her soft tongue folding itself around the bottom of his finger, of her saliva mingling with the milk, of the gentle suckling until her mouth had absorbed every tiny bit. And still he didn't pull his finger back.

Her lids slid down, masking the fire that had begun to burn in their blue depths. But it was too late. He'd seen it, and he knew it matched his own desire, in intensity if not in expectation. He closed his own eye, and a groan escaped his throat.

She pulled back then, breaking the spell.

"That's good stuff." Her voice was scratchy.

Jesse shivered, dropped his hand to his side, and opened his eye. Lilah was removing a crockery bowl from the cupboard. "Yes, it is."

"But it's too thick and sweet to drank. What do folks use it for?"

For a moment, he couldn't remember. He couldn't seem to think about anything except Lilah's mouth on his finger. When he did remember, he felt like a fool, for he'd stirred many a spoonful into a cup of coffee. "Lightening coffee mostly."

"It oughter make a fine tater puddin'."

The loose shutter flapped against the side wall and the wind, shifting course, hurled what appeared to be a bucketful of rain through the open window. Jesse silently blessed the elements and headed for the door.

"Where are ye a-goin'?" Lilah called.

"To fix the shutter," he called back, snatching the door open and dashing into the pouring rain. There was something else that needed fixing, too, but he was afraid that no amount of cold water could fix it for very long.

* * *

Jesse didn't know how much longer he could hold out. It wasn't that he hadn't been alone with Lilah before— but the aloneness had never felt so intimate. Nor was it that he didn't like her or enjoy her company. On the contrary, he liked her all too well. He liked watching the natural, unaffected grace of her movements, and the animation on her face when she talked. He liked listening to her sweet voice, whether she was chattering or singing. He liked looking at her feminine curves. And he could lose himself in the crystal blue depths of her eyes.

Those eyes now sparkled with unshed tears, making him want to take her in his arms and kiss the moisture away. He'd bet that was what she wanted, too. All he had to do was open his arms, and she'd rise from her cross-legged position on the floor and plop down on his lap. But there were limits to what any man could take, and right now, he wanted her too much to allow her that close, which was why he'd chosen to sit in the rocking chair. The small distance he'd put between them didn't help much, though, not with the firelight turning her unruly blond curls into a lopsided halo, and transforming her tears into glittering diamonds.

He swallowed a groan of frustration and tried to put his mind on something else, but to no avail. He simply couldn't bring himself to remove his gaze from her face, which shone with an enchanting combination of delight and wonderment. And as long as he was looking at her, his mischievous imagination seemed bent on kicking up its heels.

"That's the beautifulest story I ever heared tell of," she said, sucking in a deep breath and batting her eyelids, "but I don' rightly understand how come 'Fairy Tale' to be its entitlement. They weren't no fairies in it a-tall. Weren't no ogre feller neither, like ye said."

A smile tugged at the corners of his mouth. "The title isn't 'Fairy Tale,' Lilah. It's 'Cinderella.' It falls into a category comprised of many stories which are collectively called fairy tales."

"Law, Jesse, ye must have a heap o' book-learnin'."

"Why?"

" 'Cause ye're always a-spoutin' words I ain't never heared before." She smiled wistfully. "Did ye say they's more of them tales?"

"A lot more."

"Will ye tell me another?"

"Right now?"

"I'll let yer tongue take a restin' spell first."

"Thank you," he said on a snorting laugh.

"How come 'em to be called fairy tales?"

"I don't honestly know."

"Is fairies in any of 'em?"

"I suppose."

"And ogres?"

"Yes."

"Ye never did tell me what a ogre is."

He raised his arms, curled his fingers into claws, and snarled at her. "A big, mean, beastly fellow."

She giggled at his silliness. "Ye may be big, but ye ain't no ogre, Jesse."

As her giggles died away, so did her smile. At the same time, a glazed, almost vacant look replaced the twinkle in her moist eyes. She allowed Jesse only a moment to ponder the cause of the transformation, however, before she stood and hurried to the fireplace.

"The puddin' oughter be done," she said, her voice strained.

"What's wrong, Lilah?" he asked gently.

Her shoulders quavered slightly, and he thought he heard her sniffle. "Nothin'," she denied, poking at the pudding with a dinner knife. Apparently satisfied that the pudding was done, she folded a linen towel around the

enamel pan, carried it to the table, and proceeded to set
out bowls and spoons.

As he took his place at the table, Jesse wondered if perhaps he hadn't imagined the sudden change in her. When
she remained unusually quiet during the meal, barely ac-
knowledging his compliments, his suspicions returned.
And when she walked out onto the porch without even
putting the dirty dishes on to soak, he knew something
was definitely wrong, though for the life of him he
couldn't figure out what it was.

Downright peculiar, that's what it was, this crazy desire
for Jesse to follow her, when she'd made it perfectly clear
she wanted to be alone. Until a few days ago, she'd never
acted so queerly, and for the life of her, she couldn't understand why she'd started now.

He'd given her the opportunity to explain, and she was
sure he'd listen to her still. But how could you explain
something you didn't understand yourself? What could she
say? "I'm sceered, but I don't know what I'm sceered of"?
Or maybe, "My thoughts and feelin's keep tumblin' in to
each other"? Neither made any sense a-tall, not even to
her.

She sat down in a creaky rocker and stared out into the
rainy night. But she didn't see the rain. In her mind's eye,
she saw a big mean bully of a man with a dark beard. An
ogre-ish man, wearing a black eye patch. For a moment,
he looked so much like Jesse had looked with a beard that
her heart leapt into her throat, but then he leered at her and
she saw that his teeth were brown-edged, while Jesse's
were pearly white. This man's nose was crooked, too, as
though it had been broken. And the patch was on the
wrong eye.

One-Eyed Jack!

Jesse had fussed at her for being so trusting. He'd suggested he might not be the man she thought he was. The

evening she'd walked into Jack's camp, she'd thought at first that he was Jesse. She recalled the dream she'd had the night Ol' Codger brought Jesse to the cabin, and realized that it hadn't been Jesse in her dream, but Jack. Jack and two other men of his caliber, men she knew she was supposed to know, but couldn't quite place . . .

The bad men who'd kilt her folks! That's who the other two men were. She'd been dreaming about them off and on for years, just as she'd dreamed about the wolf woman over and over again. Now she knew who the men were, and why they haunted her dreams. She wished she understood the other dream, the one about La Loba and the young woman who came to life.

But it wasn't the thought of ogres or outlaws or the wolf woman that had sent Lilah out onto the porch, rather that the crazy womanish yearning had returned to plague her—and it was stronger now than it'd ever been. It lay coiled like a snake in her belly, a-twistin' and a-turnin', jes' rarin' to strike. She knew how to release it all by herself. She'd figured that out the day she'd found Jesse's pistol in the lake. But deep down in the womanish part of her, the part Jesse's kisses had awakened, she knew there was more to it than that. She knew it would take Jesse to take her soaring to the real treetops of pleasurement.

She'd figured all she had to do was teach Jesse how to pleasure her, and then he wouldn't be sorry no more. Now, she wondered if that was such a good idea. In fact, the more she considered it, the less she wanted to try.

She possessed the required grit and daring. And she certainly still had the desire. It just didn't seem to be a wise thing to do anymore. Why, she might embarrass Jesse, even hurt his pride. After all, he'd been married before. What if he found out that he'd failed his wife so miserably? No, she couldn't tell him. If he ever found out, it would have to be on his own.

There was another thing, too. She'd been thinking about

coupling with Jesse as though it were something she could take a bit of pleasure in and then forget about, but suddenly she knew she'd never be able to forget about it once she'd experienced it. No matter how badly she wanted it now, she had to consider the future. She had to figure a way to make Jesse want her back so bad and so often, that he'd never leave her. How she was going to manage that, she didn't know, but she'd think of something. And in the meantime, she'd just have to be miserable herself.

But, law, this was just about the miserablest she'd ever been.

"Does it rain like this all the time?"

Lilah twisted her neck toward the door, through which a tiny bit of light spilled out around Jesse's large silhouette. She wondered how long he'd been standing there with one shoulder pressed into the doorframe and his arms crossed over his chest.

"It rains a heap in the swamp, 'specially in the spring and summer," she said, "but not all the time."

He pushed away from the frame and sat down on a squatty stool her paw had made out of lashed pine boughs. The stool was far too small for a man his size, causing her to smile. He scratched his jaw, which bore the shadow of a beard again. And it had only been a few hours since he'd shaved . . .

"Grows out fast, doesn't it?"

Amazed that he had read her thoughts so accurately, Lilah took a moment to respond. "Ye can keep the razor."

"Thanks."

An awkward silence hovered between them for a spell, while the rain beat a steady tattoo against the roof. And then Jesse surprised her again, but this time with something she hadn't considered a-tall. "Since we seem to be stuck here until the storm passes, maybe we could continue your reading lessons."

She embraced the suggestion with wholehearted enthusiasm, for it provided a solution to her dilemma of how to cope with being constantly alone with him. "There's a bible in Maw's chest," she said, scurrying inside. "And a bit of paper, too," she called over her shoulder. "I'll get them."

Jesse released a long breath and some of the tension left his body. Being at loose ends with Lilah, he'd discovered, wasn't a good idea, but the lessons should resolve that problem.

They didn't. The longer he sat by her at the table, the more his gaze strayed to the play of candlelight upon the golden threads of her hair—and the more his thought wandered to what he'd like to do with the unruly mane. Those thoughts led to others of no less delightful, but definitely more wicked nature. He forced his attention back to the strokes she made with a piece of charcoal on a scrap of brown paper, but instead of seeing the letter she so carefully formed, he focused on the delicate shape of her hand. He remembered what she'd said about his hands being strong—and the feelings her gentle suckling of his finger had evoked. Without conscious direction, his gaze lifted to her pouty lips, which she held slightly open as she concentrated on writing, her tongue caught on her top teeth, its tip barely touching the bottom of her upper lip. His own tongue flickered out, performing a solo dance that demanded a partner.

A groan born of frustration escaped him before he could stop it.

"Did I do it wrong, Jesse?"

She sounded so sweet, so innocent, so totally unaware of the effect she was having on him. He swallowed hard and looked at the letter on the paper.

"No, Lilah. That *t* is about as close to being perfect as any I've ever seen."

She smiled, revealing the gentle curve of her pink, moist

tongue, which now lay in its place on the floor of her mouth. "Tell me a word that starts with *t.*"

"Tongue," he said—and immediately felt his cheeks flame crimson. "And, uh"—he searched his brain for another example—*"toast* and, uh, well, we'll learn some more later."

Seemingly unaware of his sudden discomfort, she proceeded to write an *s*. Thank goodness, that letter didn't conjure a lewd thought. He smiled and started to relax. *"S* makes a hissing sound, like *snake."*

"And like *skin?"*

And there he was, right back where he'd been before, only now he was beginning to wonder if she wasn't intentionally toying with his libido.

"And *r,"* she said, making the letter, "is for *rain. Q* is for—"

"Why are you going backwards?"

" 'Cause I got tired of goin' frontwards. What is *q* for?"

"Quake and *quiver." Which is what you make me do.*

"P is for—"

Oh, God! Not p! He'd had enough of this game. "Past your bedtime."

"But I'm not sleepy."

He wasn't either. Not even a little bit. She had him so thoroughly aroused, he didn't know if he'd ever be able to sleep again, but he wasn't about to let on. Jesse pushed his chair back, stretched, and produced what he hoped was a genuine-looking yawn. "Well, I am."

"We slept all day."

"No, *you* slept all day, while I stood watch."

"You said we was safe long as it's rainin'."

The flicker of fear in her blue eyes tore at his heart. "And we are," he assured her, "which is why we're both going to bed now. But not in the same bed," he hastily added. As her cheeks stained a deep pink, he called himself three kinds of lout, as well as a few other choice appellations.

"Course not, Jesse," she whispered, her voice raspy. "You go on to bed. I want to practice my writin' a bit more. Dream sweet."

Oh, I'll dream all right, he thought as he made his way across the main room, *but all the sweet dreams in the world won't take your place.*

Chapter Seventeen

Without Jesse beside her, Lilah soon grew tired of forming individual letters. By themselves, the letters meant little, and she wanted to start putting them together to make words. She opened Maw's bible, turned the scrap of paper over, and painstakingly copied "In the beginning," without a clue as to what she was writing. She gave the three words a long, hard stare, then said aloud, "Ayn tah-hee bee-gyn-nyn-gah," with no emphasis on any one syllable. It sounded like a foreign language, but it wasn't supposed to be. These were words she was sure she was supposed to know. She had to be pronouncing them wrong, but for the life of her, she couldn't see how they could say anything else. She tried saying them aloud again, with similar results.

A burning desire to hear the words pronounced properly seized her. She glanced at the candle, and decided only a few minutes had passed since Jesse had gone to bed. Maybe he wasn't asleep yet . . .

Jesse clamped his hand over his mouth to keep from chuckling, but that didn't stop his shoulders from shaking with pent-up mirth. First thing tomorrow, he'd teach her those words and others. He'd keep both Lilah and himself so busy with reading lessons, that neither of them would be able to think about what they'd both rather be doing. Lilah wanted to learn more than reading from him. He was sure of that. And, lord, how he wanted to teach her everything she wanted to learn—and more.

A hand on his quaking shoulder abruptly halted his mental ramblings. He'd been lying on his side, with his back to the front room, but at her touch, he flipped onto his back. Only a tiny bit of light came from the front room, but his eye had grown accustomed to the dark enough that he could see the blond profusion of her curls, which seemed to glow with a light of their own.

"Was you asleep?" she asked, bending closer to him, taunting him with her sweet, clean fragrance.

"Almost," he lied, clamping his hands on the covers to keep from reaching up and touching her.

"I'm sorry." She turned away.

"Wait!" Immediately, he wanted to call back the word, but it was too late. Already, she was there, standing expectantly over him, waiting, just as he'd told her to. He closed his eye and fought back the demon that encouraged him to take her in his arms. *Go on,* the voice said. *Touch her. Bury your fingers in her hair and kiss her willing lips. That's what she wants. That's what you want. Do it.* The voice sorely tempted him. Beneath the sheet, his manhood hardened and lengthened. He squeezed his eye more firmly shut and clutched the covers tighter.

"In the beginning," he finally said.

"What?"

"The words you were trying to read. In the beginning."

"Oh."

He waited for her to leave the room, his mind screaming at her to leave now, before it was too late, but her fragrance and the sound of her soft breathing lingered.

"Much obleeged," she said, her voice husky.

"You're welcome." His voice was huskier. Maybe if he

kept his eye closed and breathed shallowly, he'd forget she was there. It didn't work.

"This isn't going to work," he said.

"What isn't?"

"Your being in here this way."

"I'm sorry. I thought ye wanted to tell me something else. I'll go now, and let you go back to sleep."

"I wasn't asleep."

"But ye said ye was 'most—"

"I wasn't even close to being *almost* asleep." He opened his eye, flipped back the covers, and held out his arms. "Come here."

Without hesitation, she sat on the bed, dusted off her feet, and lay down beside him. Jesse turned onto his side, slipped his right arm beneath her and wrapped the left around her, then pulled her against his chest. This was probably the biggest mistake he'd ever made, but nothing had ever felt so right before.

For the briefest of moments, Lilah questioned the wisdom of getting into bed with Jesse, who was obviously naked beneath the covers. But when she snuggled closer, burying her nose in his bare shoulder, she knew this was where she belonged. She knew that whatever happened between them was destined to happen, and that neither possessed the power or the will to stop it.

He slid his right hand up her neck and into her hair. His hand was so big, his splayed fingers covered the back of her head. Gently, his hand lifted her head from his shoulder and brought her mouth up to his, while his left hand cupped her breast. A million tiny tingles of pleasure danced across her skin, raising gooseflesh. In anticipation of his kiss, she opened her mouth, but he ignored it. His tongue traced a fiery path around her lips, then down her chin, down her neck, down to the hollow at the base of her throat. Fire flamed in her belly and coursed through her veins. Her entire being throbbed to be touched, caressed, kissed, devoured by Jesse. And she ached to touch, caress, kiss, and devour him as well. The memory of the night she'd slipped her hand beneath the covers and touched his belly made her bold.

When her palm skimmed down his bare chest and over his ribs, Jesse's own passion flared brighter. And when her hand didn't stop moving until it reached the throbbing tip of his manhood, the fire leapt out of control. His fingers couldn't work fast enough to release the buttons on her bodice and the ribbons that held her chemise closed. As his mouth closed over the straining nipple of one breast, her hand closed around his swollen penis. He gasped in both awe and pleasure.

Never had Lilah imagined how a man's privates would feel, but now that she'd touched him, she didn't want to let go. Instead, she wanted to explore even further. And she wanted him to do the same to her. She wanted him to stroke her and rub her the way she'd rubbed herself that one time. She wanted to experience the explosion of pleasure again, but she wanted Jesse to bring her to that pinnacle. From the way he was moaning and shivering, he must want the same thing for himself.

Suddenly, his hand was on her skirt, pulling the fabric up to expose her bare legs. His palm brushed the sensitive skin on her inner thighs, and when he set the heel of his hand against the mound of her womanhood, Lilah heard herself moan. She didn't have to teach him. He knew what to do. His fingers found and parted the split in her drawers, and she arched her back, straining closer, stroking him faster. Before she realized what was happening, wave upon wave of pleasure crashed through her. And when it was over, a sticky liquid seeped over her hand. So he got wet, too!

"I'm sorry," he said raising his head and planting a kiss on her forehead.

For a moment, she couldn't talk. She gave one final

shudder and clutched him tighter. "Ever-what for, Jesse? Ye done it right."

He chuckled. "So did you. But you'd better let go of me now."

"How come?" She felt him take a deep breath, and then he released it against her hair. That tickled, and she nestled closer.

" 'Cause if you don't let go, I can't promise not to touch you again."

"Ye don' want to touch me again?"

Tenderly, he removed her hand and laid it on his belly. "God, yes, I want to touch you again."

"Then why don't ye do it?"

"Dammit, Lilah!" Jesse winced at the harshness of his tone, but somehow he had to get through to her. Somehow, he had to make her understand that lovemaking wasn't a game, that to him, anyway, it was more than just a moment of pleasure. Suddenly, it occurred to him that she might not be as innocent as he'd thought. "Have you ever lain with a man before, Lilah?"

"Nay. Why would ye think—" Lilah felt herself blush all over. "Was I too forward? I didn't mean ... I thought ..."

Jesse hugged her close. "You didn't do anything wrong, Lilah."

She took some sustenance from his assurance, but it didn't ease all her doubts or answer all her questions. "Why was ye sorry?"

"Sorry?"

She nodded against his shoulder. "That was the second time ye've said so. Was ye sorry ye touched me?"

Jesse supposed he was sorry, at least to an extent, for now that he'd taken her this far, he yearned to make real love with her, and that would never do. "I don't want to hurt you, Lilah."

She laughed. "Law, Jesse, that didn't hurt. It felt plumb

good." She wiggled against him. "I want ye to do it again."

"No!" he bellowed, then immediately attempted to soften his outburst with a gentle kiss against her hair. He didn't dare kiss her on the mouth, no matter how much he longed to. "You don't understand what lying with a man is all about."

"But I want to. Will ye show me?" She rained kisses on his neck and chest.

"Stop it Lilah," he begged, almost at the end of tolerance. When she didn't comply, he pulled away from her. "I mean it. This can't go any further."

"How come? I know ye liked it. I liked it. Ye said I didn't do nothin' wrong." She trailed a hand down his leg, and Jesse bolted from the bed.

"But it isn't right." He plowed a hand into his hair and searched for the right words, words that wouldn't wound. "We're different, don't you see? You're a swamp girl, and I'm from the hills."

"So?"

"So, I don't like the swamp."

"Maybe I would like the hills."

He ignored her protests. "You're just on the verge of womanhood, and I'm already a middle-aged widower."

"Ye ain't old, Jesse."

"And I'm a deputy U.S. marshal. My job brought me to the swamp, but it will also take me out of it. There's no stability in my life."

"But I would be there, Jesse, a-waitin' for you everwhen ye come home."

"No! No, Lilah. I had that kind of life before."

There was a finality in his tone that stayed her tongue, but Lilah wasn't about to give up hope. Not loving him the way she did. And he loved her, too, only he didn't know it yet.

Quietly, she slipped out of the bed and left him standing in the dark, mumbling about duty and honor.

No matter how hard she tried, Lilah couldn't go to sleep. Either the memory of her few minutes of bliss or her plans for securing Jesse's commitment kept getting in the way.

She'd returned to her little bed, the one her father had made for her when she was seven. While she tossed and turned upon the moss-filled mattress, she concocted first one scheme and then another, but none of them pleased her—until she realized she'd never really shown Jesse how much she could do for him, and how much he needed her in his life.

Well, that was easy enough to fix.

But she had to do it now. Time was running out for her. Already, the rain was nothing more than a steady drizzle and the thunder nothing more than a distant rumble. As soon as the storm clouds passed, he'd want to plug the hole in the canoe and take to the water again. She couldn't count on another storm delaying their journey out of the swamp, and once they were in Homerville, he'd leave her with Aunt Agnes and go off chasin' outlaws again. Yep, whatever she was going to do, she had to do *now.*

She got up before the crack of dawn and eased the door to the back room closed, so as not to disturb Jesse. She built up the fire, then put the last of the precious coffee beans on to parch. Just because she didn't like coffee didn't mean she couldn't make it for Jesse. She'd set aside her distaste for fatback, too, and fry some up. She'd make some biscuits, and while they were baking, she'd fix him a nice, hot bath. She'd serve him breakfast in bed, then lead him into the front room, and he'd smile at the sight of the steaming water. She'd scrub his back and wash his hair, maybe even try to shave him this time, and he'd forget all about his reasons for not wanting her.

Inordinately pleased with such a wonderful plan, Lilah attacked it with energy and enthusiasm. First, she collected water from the rain barrel and started it to heating. While she was at the fireplace, she tossed the coffee beans, just as she'd watched Jesse do. Next, she dug through the provisions Mistress Mamie had packed, until she located a greasy, parchment-wrapped package. Telling herself to ignore the queasy feeling the salt-cured meat provoked, she found a knife, laid it near one long edge of the fatty pork, and bore down. Nothing happened. She might as well have been trying to cut it with a wooden spoon.

Not about to let the dull knife defeat her, she upended the chunk of meat, held it firmly with her left hand, and tried sawing down from the narrow end. The knife made a tiny gash, glanced off the slippery meat, and sliced into the first knuckle of her left forefinger. Blood spurted onto the meat, and Lilah yelped in pain, which the salt from the fatback intensified. Since the only water she'd brought in was heating over the fire, she grabbed a tin cup and dashed out to the rain barrel. No matter how many times she washed the cut, it continued to bleed, but at least the water rinsed the salt away.

Back inside, she tore two strips off one of the cleaning rags she'd washed out. She folded and pressed one strip against the knuckle; the other, she wrapped and tied, using her teeth in place of her left hand. The procedure proved awkward, but she finally managed a neat, secure bandage. As she was admiring her handiwork, the smell of burned coffee beans assaulted her nose.

"Oh, no!" she wailed, though not too loud, lest she wake Jesse and spoil the surprise. Quickly, she pulled the pan off the rack, tossed the beans, then set the pan on the hearth. Praying the beans weren't ruined, she rifled through the cupboard until she found her mother's coffee grinder. When she took the top off, a red wasp flew out and stung her on the forehead.

Near tears born of both frustration and pain, Lilah cleaned the grinder and set it on the hearth to dry. She sponged her blood off the fatback, then looked for another knife, but couldn't find one. Jesse had a knife, but it was somewhere in the back room, and she didn't risk rousing him in order to get it. Disappointed, she wrapped the meat back up and set about making biscuits, thinking they would have been better made with sour milk instead of water.

As she was dumping flour into a crockery bowl, she remembered the razor. It was lying on the washstand, just inside the door. And it was plenty sharp. On feet as silent as Bob's, Lilah approached the closed door. The wooden hinge creaked the slightest bit, but it was enough to make Lilah poke her head around the door. Although it was still too dark to see well, she heard Jesse snuffle and roll over. Lilah grabbed the razor and fled back to the table.

With quick dispatch, she sliced three thick pieces off the fatback, taking extra care with the sharp razor. She put the slices in an iron skillet, set it on the rack in the fireplace, and went back to making biscuits. Everything was going to work out now, she told herself. Jesse would be thrilled with the surprise and so pleased to find out what a good wife she could be that he'd forget all about their differences. Without realizing what she was doing, Lilah started to sing.

Jesse awoke to the pleasant sound of her voice and the delicious aromas of coffee, bacon, and biscuits. For a moment, he forgot where he was, forgot that Martha and the boys were dead, and imagined he was back home in the mountains and that it was Martha's voice drifting so sweetly to his ears.

But Martha never sang. He supposed she had once, though he couldn't remember ever hearing her. He'd been drawn to her beauty, not to her disposition. Jesse searched

his memory for a vision of his Martha, his love, his reason
for being for so many years. It had been a long time since
he'd conjured her face, and what he saw now startled him.
She'd been beautiful all right—in a dark, brooding sort of
way—but never happy. Even when they were young and
just married, she hadn't smiled. And she never sang.

Lilah, on the other hand, bore a refreshing difference.
Not only did she laugh and smile and sing, but her beauty
came from within. Even her coloring was totally different.
And she was cooking breakfast for him, not because she
had to, but because she wanted to. Of course, she was
more than likely hungry herself, but she didn't drink coffee or eat meat. Those things she'd prepared just for him.

Careful not to alert her to his awakening, though not
sure why it mattered, Jesse quietly got up and put on his
clothes then tiptoed to the door and peeked out. She was
busy at the table, still singing, her back to him. What a
sight she made in the rose-sprigged dress, with firelight
cavorting on the mass of blond curls trailing down her
back—a pink confection topped with golden icing that demanded to be tasted, demanded to be devoured. A deep
hunger that had nothing to do with food assailed him.

Thinking he'd sneak up on her and surprise her with a
kiss, Jesse opened the door wider. But before he could
take more than a couple of steps, she moved to the side,
revealing a plate of biscuits and fried fatback on a tray.
She added a cup of coffee and picked up the tray. Damn
if she wasn't planning to serve him breakfast in bed, and
he was about to mess it all up.

Quickly, before she could see him, he ducked back into
the room, eased the door closed, then hurriedly removed
his shirt and tossed it on a chair. There wasn't time to get
out of his britches. He barely had time to get back in the
bed and cover himself up before she opened the door.

"Good morning!" he greeted her, sitting up and piling
pillows behind him. "What's this?"

"Breakfast." She grinned as she sidled around the bed and set the tray on his lap. "Did ye sleep well?"

"Yes, thank you."

A warm blush suffused her cheeks, and he wondered if she were recalling their intimacy. In this, too, Lilah demonstrated a marked difference, for Martha had never been so bold—or so sweet—when they made love. Of course, he reminded himself, he and Lilah hadn't actually made love, but, oh, how he wanted to. Right now.

And she wanted it, too. He could tell from the glittering glaze in her blue eyes, and the delightful pucker on her full lips. But that would never do, he reminded himself. He had a job to do. And when he brought One-Eyed Jack to justice, there would be another of his kind to be tracked down. And then another and another. Lilah deserved better than that. She deserved a man who would be home every night, a man who could keep her safe and warm, a man who could protect her from harm.

He diverted his attention to the tray, picked up the cup, and took a swig of scalding hot coffee—and choked on it. He spit it out, spraying coffee all over the embroidered counterpin, the same one Lilah had wanted so desperately to save. Still, he choked, coughing and sputtering and trying desperately to catch his breath. Lilah was beating on his back and asking him if he was going to be all right. He tried to answer her, but couldn't. Water poured from his one good eye, and he was sure he was going to die, right then and there, killed by a swallow of coffee.

Finally, his throat cleared, and he took a deep breath, then another.

"You sceered me," Lilah said, moving around so she could see his face again, a mixture of concern and relief on her delicate features.

"Water," he managed after several attempts at speech.

She rushed out of the room, then came right back with

a dipper and a wet rag, which she used to sponge up the coffee he'd sprayed all over the counterpin.

"Sorry," he said, nodding at the mess he'd made.

"No harm done. Most of it's a-comin' off."

As he sipped the water, he remembered another time he'd choked, back at Granny's cabin when he was drinking red bay tea, and Lilah asked him if he was one of the outlaws. That time, it was her question that had taken him by surprise. This time, it was the coffee.

"Have you ever made coffee before?"

"No. Is it good?"

He couldn't spoil the sweet smile on her face, even if it was the worst coffee he'd ever tried to drink. It was everything coffee shouldn't be: burned, bitter, and full of grounds. And so dark and thick you could almost stand a spoon in it.

"Hot," he told her, taking another—though much smaller—sip and trying not to wince. After a few more sips, he had room in the cup to water it down, but he'd drunk all the water out of the dipper and he hesitated to ask her for more. Instead, he turned his attention to the fried fatback, which was so tough he didn't think he was ever going to chew the first bite enough to swallow it. In fact, the more he chewed, the larger the piece seemed to get.

"Did I cut it too thick?" she asked, hovering over him, eagerly awaiting his response, but there was no way he could say anything with the pork in his mouth—and he didn't dare take it out. Finally, he softened it enough to swallow, then followed it with more of the awful coffee.

"Just right," he said, beginning to feel terrible about lying to her, but sure the truth would hurt her feelings when she'd tried so hard to please him.

"Try a biscuit. I pounded 'em real good."

"Pounded?"

"With a wooden spoon. Makes 'em real tender, Maw always said."

They did look tender—big and fat and golden brown. They smelled good, too. At least she'd done something right. He took a healthy bite and the whole biscuit crumbled in his hand.

Lilah stared in dismay at the crumbs all over the counterpin. "I s'pose I pounded 'em too good."

"I think you used too much lard."

She turned away, but not before he saw the tears in her eyes.

"Lilah, come back here!" he called as she rushed from the room. "It's all right, really. Please, come back and talk to me while I eat."

The front door slammed into the frame. Jesse set the tray aside and threw the covers back. This time, he was going after her, whether she wanted him to or not.

Chapter Eighteen

He *would* follow her the one time she didn't want him to.

"I want to be by myself," she snapped the instant he opened the door.

Ignoring her, Jesse plopped down on the too-small stool. "Why? So you can wallow in self-pity?"

She refused to look at him. "I ain't a-wallerin' in anything. I jes' want to be alone. That's all."

"It wouldn't be fair for you to enjoy this rain all by yourself."

He didn't fool her. Not in the least. There wasn't anything wondrous about the rain—unless you counted the fact that the sun was actually trying to make an appearance. She didn't.

"I appreciate the breakfast."

"Yeah! Ye blew the coffee all over the bed, wore yerself out a-chewin' on the fatback, and needed a spoon to eat the biscuits."

"So? You can't cook."

"I can, too!" she cried, turning her head and glaring at him. "Why, I cooked for Granny nigh on to six year, and she never complained, not one time."

"That's my Lilah!" he said, slapping his thighs.

She blinked at him in more than a little confusion. "What are ye talkin' about, Jesse?"

"Your spunk. Your spirit. You have more of both than the law allows, you know."

She couldn't help smiling at that. "Jes' how much does the law allow, Jesse?"

"Say my name again."

"What?"

"Just do it. Say my name again. I love to hear you say it."

She did.

"Why are you frowning?"

" 'Cause I sound so diff'runt from you."

He watched her features cloud up and figured she was thinking about what he'd said the night before about the other ways he'd said they were different. "It's a good sound, Lilah," he assured her. "Sweet and clear. Quite pleasant to the ear." He laughed. "I made a poem."

When his good humor failed to erase the clouds, he tried a different tack. "You're a very special person, Lilah, deserving of very special things in life."

"That's why I'm a-goin' to Homerville."

Now she was confusing him. "What's in Homerville?"

"My Aunt Agnes. And school. Granny said I should learn to be a lady. Said Aunt Agnes could teach me."

"You are a lady, Lilah."

"No, I ain't. Ladies knows how to talk. Ladies can read and sew and do fancy embroid'rin'. Ladies don' wear britches or fool with critters. They goes to church on Sunday and wears fancy hats. And ladies can dance!" Her eyes took on a wistful gleam. "Did ye know that, Jesse?"

It was all he could do to keep from laughing out loud. "No, I didn't. I don't suppose I know much about ladies at all."

"Well, they can. They can dance and sing and play the pi-anni. Have you ever heared anyone play the pi-anni?"

"Yes."

"Tell me about it. Is it truly beautimous, like Maw said?"

He scratched the stubble on his jaw, and wondered if her mother had been responsible for filling Lilah's head with these crazy notions about the qualities of a lady. "It can be," he allowed, "if the person who's playing it has a bit of talent. But men play the piano, too, Lilah. Does that make them ladies?"

She turned up her nose and pinned him with a look of incredulity. "Does men *really* play the pi-anni?"

"Some men do."

She shook her head in awe. "Shucks, swampmen don' play nothin' 'cept maybe a banjer or a fiddle. Course, they ain't real gentlemen, neither. Now Paw, he liked to strum a bit on Maw's dulcymore, but he wouldn't a-ever let on to t'other men. He said dulcymores was for womenfolk."

"Your maw had a dulcimer?"

She bobbed her head. "It's right in there in the bottom of her chest, I reckon. Leastaways, it was. I ain't really looked for it since we been here."

"Would you see if it's still there?"

A dulcimer! He hadn't played one in years—not because he considered it a woman's instrument, but because Martha had. Before he knew it, Lilah was back, laying the hourglass-shaped dulcimer on his lap. It was a lovely instrument—the top of curly poplar, which was a deep purple in color and made the best dulcimers, and the bottom and sides constructed of black walnut. It had obviously been well cared-for, though it was, naturally, a bit out of tune.

Lilah watched, fascinated, as he plucked the strings and adjusted the pegs, until he seemed pleased with the sounds. And then, quite suddenly, he was playing "Greensleeves"—and she was singing.

The beauty of her voice combined with the haunting melody brought a tear to Jesse's eye, and he made no attempt to hide it. The song ended all too quickly for him, and, he suspected, for Lilah, too.

"You already know how to sing, Lilah. Don't ever let anyone tell you that you don't."

She accepted his comment as fact rather than compliment. "Singin' gives me great pleasurement."

"And listening to you sing gives *me* great pleasurement."

"Where'd ye learn to play the dulcymore?"

"Back home, in the hills. My paw never had a music lesson in his life, but he could play just about anything, including the banjo and fiddle. The dulcimer was his favorite, though." He looked down at the glossy purple wood and drew a caressing hand over the catgut strings. "Paw said some folks call it a gypsy instrument, but they were forgetting that we wouldn't have pianos if we hadn't had dulcimers first. It's an ancient instrument—and so sweet. In fact, its name means sweet song, you know."

"I don' know nothin' 'bout music, 'ceptin' the few songs Maw used to sing and the tunes Paw played. You know any more songs, Jesse?"

"A few. Ballads mostly."

" 'Barbara Allen'?"

He smiled. "Everyone knows that one."

"And 'Little Mohea'?"

"Yep. Bet you don't know 'Get Up and Bar the Door.' "

"And I bet you don' know 'The Piney Woods Boys.' "

"Can't say as I do. How does it go?"

Lilah hummed a few bars, then sang a verse.

> Come all ye sandy girls an' listen to my noise.
> Don' be controlled by the piney woods boys.
> For if ye do, yer portion will be
> It's cawnbread an' bacon is all ye'll see.

She scowled at him. "Well, ain't ye a-goin' to play it?"

"I don't know if I like this one," he teased, picking out the rousing melody on the dulcimer.

"How come?"

"Because it's not very complimentary to men."

"I don' know why not. It's men usually sing it." She waited until he'd finished playing through the tune once, then she sang another verse to his accompaniment.

> When ye go a-courtin' they'll set you a chair
> An' first thang they say is, "Daddy kilt a deer."
> With their ol' sock legs all draggin' on the ground
> An' their ol' cotton hat more rim than crown.
> Say, and don' let the johnnycake bake too brown.

They laughed so hard that tears came to their eyes, but both avoided commenting on the sad truth in the words. When their laughter died away, Jesse taught her "Get Up and Bar the Door." Lilah wasn't surprised to learn that Jesse's singing voice was as deep and mellow as his speaking voice, and when the ballad ended, they laughed themselves silly again.

As they entertained themselves with one song after another, Lilah kept a watchful eye on the rain, which was virtually disappearing, while the sunball started peeking around the scudding clouds. From time to time, she caught Jesse glancing out at the glittering moisture that hovered in the air like dewdrops caught in a spiderweb, and she tried to brace herself for the moment he said it was time to leave. She knew it was coming. She knew equally well no amount of shoring up was going to prepare her for it, so she started praying for more rain.

When they sang themselves hoarse, Jesse handed her the dulcimer. "You'd better put this back in the chest. The dampness will ruin it."

She nodded and started inside, but his next words stopped her cold.

"Maybe one day you can come back for it—and all the other things you wanted to keep. I wish we could take them with us now, but I'm afraid the canoe's too small." He paused, and a feeling of expectancy hung between them. "Since it's quit raining, I'm going to get a green limb to make the plug with. We might as well start preparing to leave."

With all her heart, Lilah wanted to beg him to wait, to give them at least one more day together on the island. One more day with no demands on their time and energy. One more day to laugh and sing and tell stories. One more day . . .

She couldn't halt the inevitable. Eventually, they'd have to leave. But, oh, how she longed for just one more day.

"Come back, rain," she mumbled as she replaced the dulcimer. And then, not caring whether Jesse heard her but wanting to make sure God did, she hollered her prayer at the top of her lungs. "Please, *please,* let it rain again!"

As the day wore on and the sun shone brighter, Lilah became more and more certain that both God and the elements were ignoring her. Jesse, however, appeared in no hurry to leave, and Lilah didn't dare question him, for fear he'd change his dawdling pace.

First, he spent far more time than was reasonably necessary coming back with a green cypress twig. He leisurely whittled out a plug, declared it too small when it looked perfect to Lilah, and proceeded to carve several more before he was satisfied. Once the plug was in place, he took the canoe down to the lake to test it. Again he was gone for a long time. He brought back a large bass he said jumped into the canoe, then gutted it, scaled it, and fried it. As hungry as she was, Lilah barely tasted the sweet meat, for thinking this might be the last time she shared a table with Jesse.

"The canoe is ready and the storm has passed," he said when she was clearing away the dishes. "It's time to leave."

"I know." Her low voice was rife with defeat and heartache, but he didn't seem to notice.

"We probably should have left today, but it's too late now. We'll turn in early and leave before dawn, when it's cooler. Damn, it's hot!"

Wincing inwardly at his detached tone, she piled the dishes in the enamel pan and went to the fireplace to get the kettle. The heat from the fire hit her in a wave, and she realized just how very hot it really was. Hot and sticky. Like they were sitting in the middle of a rain cloud or something. But there were no storm clouds on the horizon, only big, white, puffy clouds—happy, harmless clouds that seemed to sneer at her through the open windows. God hadn't listened.

"How long will it take to get to Homerville from here?" Jesse asked.

"Three or four day, I reckon, maybe five. I ain't never been there before."

"Then how do you know where it is?"

Lilah poured the hot water over the dishes, set the kettle aside, and sat back down at the table with Jesse. "Ever' day-down, Maw used to stand right out there in the clearing and watch the swamp swaller the sunball. She wouldn't say a word, just stand there a-starin'. Paw tol' me onct that all Maw had to do to go home was set out walkin' toward that big ol' sunball, and in a few days she'd be in Homerville."

"Your maw never went home to visit her family?"

"Naw. Kep' sayin' she was goin' to one day, but she never did. After Little Jacob died, ten gators couldn't a-dragged her off'n this island. Maw was always a little crazy after that. Acted like she thought her baby would rise from the bury-hole or something—you know, like Jesus done. Said she had to be here for Li'l Jake. That was what she called him. Li'l Jake."

"Little Jacob was your brother?"

A lump swelled in Lilah's throat, and she answered him with a nod.

"What happened to your folks?"

"They had a . . . acci-dent."

The morbid side of him wanted to know what kind of accident, but he figured that if she wanted to talk about it, she would have supplied the details. There was one thing more, though, that he wanted to know—that he *had* to know—before he took her out of the swamp. "How do you know your aunt is still in Homerville?"

He was rewarded with a smile. Apparently, this was something she didn't mind talking about.

"Maw said Aunt Agnes's feet was as firmly planted in Homerville soil as the roots of the big oak tree that grows in the courthouse yard. Said it'd take more'n a tornado to get her out'n her big fine house on Mulberry Street. I reckon she's still there."

"Did your folks have any other relatives?"

"Paw had a brother, but the new mon fever took him way back yonder."

"And Granny," he added.

Lilah shook her head. "She weren't my real granny. Folks called her Granny 'cause she was a granny-woman."

Jesse had known his share of granny-women in the mountains. Midwives, some called them, but most functioned as the only "doctor" for miles around, regardless of the symptoms or disease or gender of the patient. "Was she ever married?"

"No, but I think they was a man in her life, onct. She never talked much about herself, but she tol' me that her maw was a Indian—Creek, I think—and her paw was a

apper what wandered into the Okefinoke way back yon-
er." She pushed back her chair. "I reckon I oughter do
em dishes up afore the water gets cold."

Jesse sat for a minute longer, wishing he could call back
me ... wishing he was an innocent young buck who'd
ome courting Lilah with his ol' sock legs draggin' like
e piney woods boys in the ballad ... wishing neither
them had faced the trials of life that had ultimately
ought them together—and would, he had no doubt, ulti-
ately tear them apart.

Lilah spent a good portion of the remainder of the day
ing through the contents of the three chests, sorting
ings out according to what she could put to use and what
e wanted to keep. She gave Paw's clothes to Jesse, what
w there were. Most of Maw's underclothes, nightgowns,
d dresses she could wear, once she hemmed them up
d took them in a mite. When she finished sorting, she
acked the clothes into go-away bags they could take with
em, and everything else went back into the chests for
fekeeping.

Talking about Maw and Paw and Little Jacob and going
rough everything that had been theirs dredged up many
memory for Lilah, but these she kept to herself, mostly
ecause Jesse was too busy to listen. He went in and out,
acked the canvas bag, then took everything out and re-
acked it, and kept himself otherwise occupied with tasks
at seemed to get him nowhere.

Just before day-down, Lilah closed the last chest, then
andered out into the overgrown clearing and over to the
lge of the woods, where three sunken spots lay side by
de. She stood there for a long time, staring down at the
raves, trying to understand why anyone would want to
ke the life of another, even in retribution.

Jesse didn't want to kill One-Eyed Jack, just to capture
m, she reminded herself. But when that happened, when

Jack Scurlock was finally brought to justice, he would most certainly be found guilty and then hanged by the neck until he was dead. In the end, he would die, if not by Jesse's hand, then the hangman's. The world would be better off without him, she knew. And yet ... and yet, she wished there were another way. She wished she and Jesse didn't have to leave. She wished they could stay right here forever, neither haunted by their pasts, but concerned only with their future.

Was there a future for them? she wondered. Not un-less—or until—they could lay their ghosts to rest.

Lilah awoke in a cold sweat, her heart pounding in her ears and her breathing labored, as though she'd been running for hours—as though some evil force had been chasing her.

She'd been dreaming about the Wolf Woman again. The dream had come to her at odd intervals for almost as long as she could remember. Outside of her growing realization that the old woman was meant to be Granny and the young woman was meant to be her, nothing about the dream had ever changed.

Until now.

The Wolf Woman built her fire, danced and chanted and shook the bag of bones. She put the bones together, laid on the moss, and the wolf came to life. But this time, the wolf turned on the old woman, snarling and baring sharp-pointed teeth. The old woman screamed and fled, and the wolf followed, its long, lean body stretching out in graceful but deadly leaps.

Lilah tried to turn her face, to hide her eyes, anything to keep from witnessing the old woman's fate, but to no avail. The dream demanded that she watch. The wolf sprang and dug its claws into the old woman's back. The claws ripped through the fabric of her dress and shredded her skin in long, ugly gashes. The old woman's blood poured forth, but she tore herself loose and ran again, while the wolf plopped to the earth and was still.

As she recalled the dream, Lilah felt as though the wolf's soul belonged to her. And for some unexplainable reason, it was the wolf who was dying in the dream, not the old woman. Although she didn't understand the other dream either, at least it wasn't dark. This one was, and it frightened her.

For a spell, she sat on the narrow bed, clutching the covers to her breast and trying to make sense of the dream. Gradually, as she grew calmer, she became aware of the absence of noise from outside. When she'd gone to bed, the noise from the night creatures had been almost deafening, as it often was following a heavy rain. She'd learned long ago to tune the noises out. Now, she was listening, and she didn't hear a single croak. Something was wrong . . .

Lilah rose from the bed and padded across the room to the front door, but caution stayed her hand. She'd wake Jesse, she decided, let him see what the trouble was. Back across the room she went, her heart thudding again. An eerie light, white and silvery like moonlight, but harsh instead of soft, seeped through the cracks in the walls and poured through the open windows. She quickened her steps, not caring now how much noise she made. There was comfort in noise. Comfort that the world was as it should be.

But it wasn't, and no amount of noise she made would make it right. She found little peace in the swish of her nightshift and the faint thumps her feet made against the bare floor. She found little peace in the sound of her voice calling Jesse's name. Deep down inside, she knew that this thing, this force that had thrown the world off kilter, was larger and stronger than either one of them.

Someone crashed into her and she screamed.

"Hush, Lilah! It's me. Jesse!"

She threw her arms around his waist and hugged him tight.

"Whatever's the matter with you?"

"Listen," she whispered, then wondered why she'd whispered.

"I don't hear anything."

"Neither do I."

"So why—"

They heard it then, a shrill whine from some distance away that was rapidly gaining volume as it moved toward them.

"Quick! Get down. Over there, against the wall!" He shoved her away from him and dashed toward the front door.

"Where are ye goin'?"

"Never mind. Get down! And cover your head."

Like a frightened rabbit, Lilah crouched against the wall that separated the two rooms and folded her arms over the top of her head, but she kept her gaze trained on Jesse. A gust of wind sailed through the open windows, snatching at everything in its path, then dying as abruptly as it had begun. Jesse released the bar and snatched the door open. It banged shut behind him, then immediately flew open and crashed against the wall. Wind whipped at the shutters, which Jesse had latched to the outer walls earlier that day. Suddenly, everything was crashing and banging and snapping. Small branches sailed through the door and windows, enamel pots, and pans skipped across the floor, and dishes rattled in the cupboard. The whine turned into a shriek and the shriek into a howl, and still Jesse didn't come back.

"God, don' let anything happen to him!" Lilah prayed, clutching her arms tighter over her head, but refusing to close her eyes until she saw that he was safe.

The fire roared to life in the fireplace beside her and the wind scattered sparks and bits of glowing debris onto the floor, then picked them up and whirled them in the air. Lilah watched in horror as one of the larger pieces landed on a dishrag, which burst into flame. She sat frozen in indecision, not knowing whether she should risk being hit with something while attempting to put the fire out. Better that, she supposed, than burning to death. Just as she started to rise, one of the skipping pots flipped upside down over the tiny fire.

Thunder clapped overhead, lightning popped all around the cabin, and with a loud *whoosh,* a torrent of rain assaulted the log house, but only a part of Lilah acknowledged these things. Most of her watched and waited and prayed for Jesse.

And then, there he was, on the porch, only his legs and lower torso visible, for over his head he carried the canoe. The idiot! He'd risked his life for the canoe. Lilah almost laughed out loud, but he wasn't safe yet. And neither was she.

He made his way across the room on a crooked path, fighting both the buffeting wind and the unwieldy canoe. The wind became a trumpeting roar, wreaking chaos both inside and out, whipping the covers off her bed and ripping the shutters from their moorings, tossing and hurling everything in the room that wasn't nailed down.

At long last, he reached her. Somehow, he managed to sit down and pull the canoe over their heads. "Grab hold of a seat!" he hollered in her ear, yet she barely heard him over the crash and clatter and bang of the storm. She raised her hands, found a seat, and held on with all her might. Something struck the hull of the canoe, and then something else. Soon, flying objects were raining down on them, probably destroying the canoe, but at least not hitting them. The roar mounted to a deafening blast. The pressure on Lilah's eardrums made her so nauseous and lightheaded, she thought she would surely faint.

And then it was over. A pot clattered to the floor,

rocked from side to side, and finally settled on its bottom. And with its silence came an absolute stillness unlike any she'd ever known.

Chapter Nineteen

Jesse gathered his wits, which the storm had scattered right along with everything else. In those few minutes of roaring destruction, he'd felt more frightened, more helpless, more defenseless than he'd ever felt before. Bad guys he could fight, but not the elements. You couldn't punch out the wind or blow a hole in it with a .45. The surge of black humor that mental image evoked almost made him laugh.

"Lilah, we can get up now."

She didn't move, didn't respond, just sat there, frozen. His legs quivering, Jesse stood up, taking his end of the canoe with him. When Lilah didn't let her end go, he gently unclasped her white-knuckled fingers from the cypress board that made one of the seats. Setting the canoe on the floor among the rubble, he turned his attention to Lilah, who had begun to shake. He supposed that was a good sign.

"C-c-c-old," she stuttered, her teeth chattering.

He squatted down in front of her and rubbed his open palms up and down her arms. "Reaction. Perfectly understandable. That was one helluva wind."

He'd seen enough of the damage to the house to know the wind had made one helluva mess, and it was probably worse outside. He'd see about all that later. Right now, nothing concerned him except Lilah.

First, he had to get her warm. Since the cover off her bed lay twisted among broken jars and upturned pots, he took a blanket out of the linen chest. When he came back, she was standing up, her blue eyes wide as she surveyed the havoc the wind had made of the once neat room.

Jesse draped the blanket around her shoulders and smoothed damp tendrils of hair off her forehead. "It's all superficial, I think. I don't see any leaks, so apparently the roof's okay."

"We're alive," she said, spacing the words out. Her voice carried an awe his own heart echoed, but he wasn't ready to talk about how frightened he'd been for both of them.

"It's all over now."

"What was it?"

"A twister, I suppose. I haven't ever been through one before." He wanted to pull her against him, to hold her tight and forget for just a moment how close they'd come to dying, but his clothes were soaked clean through, and she was still shivering. "Will you be all right? I mean, can I leave you here for a few minutes? I want to walk out onto the porch."

"How come?"

He laughed, trying to bring a lightness of his tone. "I don't know. Curiosity more than anything else. Besides, if a tree's fixing to fall on the house, don't you think we ought to know about it?"

"I'm comin' with you."

"I was joshing you about the tree. If one was going to fall, I think it would have already."

"I'm still comin' with you. It's my swamp."

He couldn't argue with that. "Watch your step."

With only an occasional flash of lightning to illuminate the sky and heavy rain hindering vision even then, it was impossible to determine the extent of the destruction, but it appeared that the wind had taken only the very tops of the trees. Small branches and other debris littered the porch floor and clung to the walls. The pine stool was nowhere in sight, but the rocking chair lay on its side next to the rain barrel. A large limb had caved in the roof on the opposite side of the porch, but there didn't appear to be any real damage to either the house or the trees.

Jesse gathered up some of the green branches and took them back inside.

"They won't burn clean," Lilah said, following him.

"I know, but we're out of firewood and I'm cold." He dumped the branches on the glowing coals in the fireplace. "Wet and cold." He started to remove his shirt and heard Lilah's sharp intake of breath. "I don't mind a bit if you stay and watch, but I'm getting out of these wet clothes."

"I, uh, I'll jest check on the back room," she muttered, scurrying through the door. Wearing only the too-tight britches Granny had made, he joined her a few minutes later, bringing a lamp with him. In sharp contrast to the havoc the wind had created in the much larger front room, this room appeared untouched.

Lilah sat on the bed, her palms caressing the embroidered counterpin. "The shavin' mirror's busted," she said.

"Then you're just going to have to learn how to give a man a shave," Jesse teased, finding the prospect of having Lilah shave him rather delightful. When she didn't comment, he set the lamp on the washstand among shards of mirrored glass, then closed the shutters over the window.

"Are you still cold?" he asked.

"Not like I was."

"Well, I am. Why don't we try to get some rest."

"My bed—"

"Your bed's nasty, what's left of it, which isn't much. You can sleep in here—with me."

Lilah couldn't believe she'd heard him correctly. She thought of all the times she'd hoped he'd invite her to his bed. Now that he had, she found herself wanting only his comfort.

Jesse couldn't believe he'd asked her to sleep with him. He thought of all the times he'd lain in this bed, wanting her, knowing she was in the next room, knowing she wanted him and would willingly come to his bed if he invited her. Now that he had, all he wanted to do was hold her close and protect her from harm. He hoped she didn't expect anything else.

While he was searching for the words to explain without hurting her, she slipped off the bed and stood up.

"I can't sleep in this," she said, plucking at one of the many damp spots on the skirt of her full nightdress.

Jesse swallowed hard, thinking, *And I can't sleep with you naked.* "Do you have another gown?"

"This one was Maw's. There's another one in the chest."

Thank goodness! "I'll just . . . wait in the other room," he said, backing out and feeling more nervous than he had on his wedding night. *Reaction,* he told himself as he warmed his hands by the fire. *This has nothing to do with Lilah and everything to do with having just lived through a twister that could have killed us both.* It was amazing that he'd survived at all over the last couple of weeks . . . amazing what both he and Lilah had been through. It was enough to rattle anyone, even a deputy U.S. marshal accustomed to adversity. And certainly enough to rattle an innocent gal-woman.

"I'm dressed now."

The nervousness in her voice helped to ease some of his own misgivings, yet Jesse hesitated to join her. "You go on to bed," he called. "I'm going to sit out here by the fire for a while."

Having finally burned the last of the dampness off the wood, the fire stopped hissing and settled into a pleasant hum. Jesse set a chair upright, lowered himself into it, and stared at the smoking fire. Somehow, over the last few days, he'd lost his focus. Between the rain holding them captive and his enjoyment of Lilah's company, he'd forgotten all about catching One-Eyed Jack. For the most part, he'd forgotten all about being a deputy U.S. marshal. For the first time in years, he'd allowed himself to relax— and it had felt wonderful.

This realization gave him such a mental jolt that he almost fell off the chair. Dammit, it *had* felt wonderful! He didn't know when he'd felt so young, so energetic, so open to life's little pleasures. And here he was, denying himself one of those pleasures. In all too short a time, this idyll would end. He'd go back to the real world and probably never see Lilah again. All he'd have would be the memories, and there were a few more of those he intended to add to his collection.

He banked the fire and hurried to join Lilah.

The longer Lilah lay in Jesse's arms, the more she thought about all the things she'd learned about him—and all the things she still wanted to know. Although some time had passed since he'd come to bed, she didn't think he was asleep yet. She didn't suppose it would hurt to find out, as long as she didn't wake him up doing it.

"Are ye awake?" she whispered.

He chuckled deep in his throat and nuzzled her hair with his nose. "No."

"Ye are so!"

"It's not my fault. I'm trying to go to sleep, but you keep wiggling around. And now, you're talking to me."

"Are ye really sleepy? 'Cause if ye're not, there's something I want to know."

"What's that?"

Suddenly shy about asking the question that was foremost in her mind, she traced the band of his eye patch from his ear to his missing eye.

"Why do I wear the patch to bed?" he asked. "Is that what you want yo know? Truthfully, I forget it's there."

"I must've made it right."

He kissed her forehead. "You did. It's the most comfortable one I've ever owned."

Jesse's apparent ease with the subject helped to erase her shyness. "How long have ye been a-wearin' a eye patch?"

His sigh tickled her nose. "Almost as long as I can remember."

"Was ye birthed without that eye?"

"No, I lost it when I was five. I suppose you want to know how."

"If'n ye want to tell me."

He slipped his arm from around her side and rolled onto his back. "Ma used to read us a story every night. One night Ma read a story about King Arthur and the Knights of the Round Table."

"Who was they?"

"A legendary king of England and his trusted friends. I'll tell you all about them another time. The important thing is that they used swords to fight with. Do you know what a sword is?"

Lilah hated to seem so ignernt, but she wanted to understand what he was telling her, and he had said the sword part was important. "No."

"I don't suppose your mother would have told you about such things. It's boy stuff. A sword is a long, sharp-pointed blade with a hilt. Much longer than a knife and quite deadly. The next day after Ma read the story, my older brother Rob and I decided we wanted to play Knights of the Round Table. Rob must have been seven or eight at the time. He was Lancelot and I was Gareth. We used sticks for swords, and we were thrusting and parrying and shouting words like *forsooth* and just having a grand old time. And then I stepped in a hole and lost my balance. Rob's stick skidded off mine and the end went straight into my eye."

Lilah shivered. "That must a-hurt."

"I'm sure it did. Actually, I don't remember much about the pain. Rob was crying, and when Ma saw me, she went into hysterics. I had clamped my hand over my eye and blood was gushing out between my fingers. Pa put the bridle on the horse and rode me to the doctor, who thankfully lived just over the next ridge from us. Doc Waters said there was nothing to do but take my eye out."

"And he sewed it shut."

"No. Martha did that."

"Martha? Your wife?"

"Yes. I'd always worn a patch over it—there's nothing pretty about a gaping hole where your eye should be. But you have to keep the hole clean. Everytime she saw me with the patch off, she got sick to her stomach. So, one night she was sitting by the fire, mending a hole in one of my shirts, and she said she wished she was mending the hole in my face instead. The next thing I knew, I was agreeing to let her do it."

Lilah suspected there was more to this last part than he let on. There was very probably more to all of it than he let on. She tried to imagine going through life with only one eye, tried to imagine the way people would look at you, people like Aunt Agnes and Mistress Chesser—and Martha. How could his wife have loved him and not loved every little part of him, including the hole in his face? Martha's loathing must have hurt him deeply.

She remembered the first time she'd seen the tiny scar, how she'd traced it with her finger and then kissed the thin ridge. Would she have felt so compassionate if the hole had still been there? Maybe she was being too hard on Martha.

As though he had read her thoughts, Jesse said, "Don't

think too harshly of Martha. She was a good woman—and a good mother to the boys."

The boys seemed to be a safe enough subject. "Tell me about yer boys. What was their entitlements?"

"Matthew and Morgan." The smile in his voice made her glad she'd asked. "They were born less than a year apart. Having Morgan almost killed Martha. He was a big baby, and breach on top of that. We named him after Doc Morgan, who saved her life. It took her almost a year to get over it, and there were no more babies after that."

No more intimacy, either, Jesse thought, but that was something he wasn't ready to share with Lilah. She had asked him about the boys, and here he was talking about Martha again.

"Did they look like you?"

For the first time in four years, Jesse pictured the boys alive—healthy and happy. "Morgan did. Matthew didn't favor either one of us, but he was far more like me in other ways than Morgan was. Matthew said he wanted to be a lawman when he grew up. Morgan wanted to be president. And he might have made it, too. He was smart and charming—and a consummate politician."

"What does that mean?"

"I don't suppose you would know about politicians here in the swamp—professional politicians, anyway. But you must have known at least one unprofessional politician in your life—someone who can play both ends against the middle. A consummate politician does it so well you don't even realize that's what he's doing. Maybe he doesn't even realize that's what he's doing."

Lilah thought about that for a minute. His description reminded her of Colin Yerby. "Ye mean someone who tells you what he thinks ye want to hear?"

"That just about sums it up. It's a talent. Either you have it or you don't. Morgan had it. He was only ten years old. So much of his life ahead of him. Matthew, too. It's a shame . . ." His voice trailed off and he fell silent.

"Ye must miss your family something fierce."

"I do." He rolled away from her then. "Let's try to rest. We have a lot to do come morning soon."

She flinched at the bluntness in his tone and wished he'd allow her to offer him the comfort he needed. At least, she'd made some progress, and if the rain would just keep on a-comin' down for another day or two, maybe she could make some more.

When Lilah awoke, he was gone. For a moment, she panicked; then she heard a clatter and the gruff hiss of a mumbled oath. How long had he been up? she wondered. Between the steady rain and the closed shutters, she couldn't tell what time it was, but it felt late. She yawned and stretched, listening to the soothing beat of the rain and enjoying the luxury of lying abed for a spell far more than she'd ever thought possible.

A gust of wind *whooshed* around a corner and rattled the shutters, creating sounds very similar to those she'd heard moments before. To assure herself that it really was Jesse making noise in the front room and not merely the wind playing tricks on her, she rose from the bed and peeked around the door. He stood at the dry sink, washing pots and pans. The floor was clear of debris and a fire blazed in the fireplace. He'd been up for a while. She smiled to herself and eased the door closed. Taking another of her mother's dresses from the chest, Lilah put it on and went to help him.

"Good mornin'!" she called, her voice bubbling with cheer.

He gave her a cursory nod, and there was only a hint of a smile on his lips. Since he didn't seem the least bit come-at-able, she stopped in the middle of the room and folded her hands together in front of her. "Did ye sleep well?"

"Not really."

"I'm sorry."

"It's not your fault. It's this damned rain."

"I didn't kick you or nothin'?"

He set a clean pot aside and picked up a dirty one. "No."

"I didn't know. I ain't used to havin' someone else in the bed with me."

"I should hope not!"

"I ain't never shared a bed with no one 'ceptin' Granny, and the onliest times I ever done that was when somebody was a-visitin' and needed my bed. Course, she never called it a botheration, but I always wondered—"

"Are you going to stand there flapping your jaw all day?"

He really was in a snit over something. The rain, he said. She reckoned he didn't understand how important it was to their relationship, but he would. Today, she hoped.

She glanced around the room and noted that he'd put the half-barrel tub in front of the fireplace. On the floor beside it were Maw's washboard, a small pan filled with wet soap bush leaves, and a pile of dirty laundry. He'd tied one end of a rope around the crossbar over the door and the other end around one of the short upper posts of her cypress upscuddle, creating a clothesline that hit her about shoulder high. The kettle hung over the fire, and an open pot of water sat on the rack. He'd thought of everything except the rinchin' pans.

While she scrubbed, rinsed, wrung, and hung clothes, she talked. She wasn't the least bit sure Jesse paid any attention to her, since he offered very few comments, but she talked anyway. Talking kept her from reflecting on the short time they had left on the island, and that was something she didn't want to study on right now.

She told him about the night Little Jacob had been born dead. She told him about Granny coming and staying and how their friendship had developed over the years. She told him about all the different kinds of critters in the swamp—what they ate and how they built their nests and when they had their young. She told him how swampers grabbed fistfuls of maiden cane, hauled it into their boats, and used the wee critters hiding inside for fish bait. And when she ran out of anything else to talk about, she started telling him stories she'd heard from Maw and Paw and Granny.

She told him about how the swampers said the black snake could sing the sweetest lullaby human ears have ever heard. She told him tales of demons that lurked on the islands in the dead of night. She told him the Seminole legend about the Milky Way: "Long ago, the Breathmaker blew his breath acrost the sky and made the beautiful white path that leads from the aidge of the world to the land of the dead in the west. They called it the spirit way. The souls of all good people travel this path, but not the souls of the wicked. The bad ones have to stay in their bury-holes. Granny said the path shines brightest for the souls of the very good."

"How can you tell the very good?" Jesse asked.

"Granny called them the dearly beloved. She said they don' lie or steal or kill. They talk kindly and they never get drunk. I reckon Maw and Paw and Granny is now stars up there in the Milky Way, 'cause they was dearly beloved. And Little Jacob. I reckon that's where yer Martha and Matthew and Morgan is, too, Jesse."

When she ran out of room on the clothesline, she sat down and watched him cook flapjacks and told him another story. "Granny's maw was Creek, but I done tol' you that, didn't I? The Indians come here a long time ago, long before the swampers come in. Course, the swampers run most of 'em out, and the rest is mostly dead now. Gran-

ny's maw tol' her there onct was a island here named
Eden. Said some lost and weary hunters jest stumbled on
it one day. There was a band of beautimous women living
on Eden, daughters of the sun, she called 'em. Anyways,
the women feasted the hunters with oranges and dates and
corn cakes and sended them on their way. When the hunters tol' t'other Indians about the daughters of the sun, they
looked and looked for Eden, but they never could find it
again. Some folks, Granny said, is still a-lookin'."

He dumped the flapjacks onto a plate and carried them
to the table. They smelled heavenly. Lilah followed him to
the table, poured honey over the cakes, and talked around
a big bite. "Ain't that a amazing story, Jesse? Kinda like
one of them fairy tales, ain't it?"

"Yes, it is."

His voice was soft and scratchy, and his green eye glittered with a strange inner light. Funny, she thought, how
he was looking right at her, but he didn't seem to see her
at all. He reminded her of the way Granny had looked the
night she called up the speerits to help Jesse, but Lilah
didn't think he was calling up the speerits.

"Are ye all right, Jesse?"

His lips moved without speaking, and as Lilah watched
him, her heart in her throat, a wondrous peace came over
his features, easing her heart but leaving her more confused than she'd ever been before.

Chapter Twenty

Daughter of the sun ... Eden ... Looked and looked, but couldn't find it.

The phrases pierced Jesse's heart with little daggers of realization. Like the sun itself, Lilah's light warmed his heart and stirred his soul to life. Surely if there had ever been a daughter of the sun, Lilah was she. God had dropped him into Eden, the serpent had brought them together, and the devil himself threatened to keep them apart. All the while he'd searched for Jack Scurlock, his soul had searched for Lilah.

Jesse didn't know when he'd fallen in love with her, but he could no longer deny it. He'd been drawn to her from the first time he heard her sweet voice, and his concern for her safety and well-being had colored his every move since. He'd spent most of the last few weeks trying to convince himself that his association with her put her in danger. The reality was that neither of them might be alive right now, if they hadn't been there for each other.

Suddenly, more than anything else in the world, Jesse found himself wanting to spend the rest of his life with Lilah, to love and protect her, to build a home and have a family with her. But that was impractical right now, if not downright impossible. He had to catch One-Eyed Jack first. Even then, it wouldn't be over. There were witnesses to collect and a trial to go through. But once Jack had hanged . . .

What was he thinking about? He'd spent four years chasing the slimy scoundrel, and he hadn't caught him yet. When he got out of the swamp, he had to notify Dan Whitcomb, the U.S. marshal he worked under, of his whereabouts and activities. Dan was liable to send him off after bank robbers or another murderer, and then it would be awhile before he could resume his pursuit of One-Eyed Jack. He might as well face it. He'd lost Jack again. All he could do was wait and hope—wait for someone to recognize Jack from his wanted poster and hope Jack's trail wasn't too cold by the time Jesse got on it again.

Leaving Lilah in the lurch in the meantime wasn't fair. Why, she could grow old and gray waiting for him. And she'd do it, too, if she thought he was ever coming back. He'd come too close already to revealing his feelings. He could never let her know how truly deep those feelings ran. But, god, how he wanted to! How he wanted to take her in his arms and tell her he loved her. How he wanted to make love to her now, while they were still in Eden . . .

"Jesse, are ye all right?"

He blinked and shook his head, not really wanting to let go of the dream, yet knowing he didn't have a choice. "I'm fine."

"The flapjacks are good."

"Thank you." He waved his fork at her. "Eat up. We still have a mountain of work to do, and I want to be ready to leave here the minute it stops raining." The supreme sadness that washed over her face sliced into his heart. "Lilah, I'm sorry things got so messed up."

"Ye didn't bring the storm."

He hadn't been referring to the storm, but it was just as well she'd taken it that way. "I know this house and the things in it are important to you."

"Shucks, there weren't much hurt 'ceptin' Paw's shavin' mirror. The rest'll all clean up, I reckon."

Early the next morning, Lilah stood in the doorway and gave the front room one last sweeping inspection. Eventually, the dusties would again cover the floor and furniture, and the rats and mice and coons would move back in, but for now everything was scrubbed so clean it would shine—if the light could get to it.

As soon as the rain slacked off the afternoon before, Jesse went out and boarded up the windows. Closing them off had made the heat almost unbearable, but Lilah didn't want to leave the house so open to the elements. The blazing fire increased their discomfort, but they'd needed it to dry the clothes. Even the firelight was gone now; its ashes and coals hauled out the door one bucketful at a time until the hearth was bare, thus reducing the possibility of fire.

In the last few days, nature had shown Lilah just how unpredictable and destructive it can be. Concerned that she might forever lose the few items in the house that were precious to her, she asked Jesse if they could take at least some of them when they left. He'd not only agreed, but insisted on helping her pack. Now Paw's dulcymore, Maw's embroidered counterpin, Little Jacob's birthing gown, Lilah's rag doll, and the family bible were carefully stashed in the bottom of the canoe, along with all the vittles they had left, the necessary pots and pans, blankets, rope, and clothes.

Taking a deep breath, Lilah closed the door, pulled on the short piece of rope, and listened to the wooden latch fall into place on the other side. She wondered if she'd ever see the little house again. A cold shiver trickled down her spine. "One day, we'll be back," she said, "me and Jesse both. Maybe only for a visit, but we'll be back." Saying the words aloud eased the ominous feeling.

For a spell, she'd let herself believe that she and Jesse

could live there and raise a family together. For a spell, Jesse seemed to have forgotten about his job, to have forgotten about his vow to catch One-Eyed Jack. But ever since he'd come out of his trance, his every action and every word seemed to be directed toward getting out of the swamp and going back to work. He was at the lake now, waiting for her, eager to be on his way, eager to get out of the swamp and go back to chasing outlaws.

She'd never seen anyone quite so determined as Jesse, but she was equally determined to become his wife. The way she had it figured, all she had to do was convince him she didn't mind being alone while he was off doing his job, that she'd always be there waiting for him when he came home, and that she could take care of herself in the meantime.

She was so preoccupied with devising plans that she didn't pay any attention to the movement behind her, until something bumped her in the middle of her back. She gave a little shriek, but when she whirled around, her panic died a quick death.

"Ye been here all this time, Ol' Codger, a-watchin' out after me and Jesse?" Lilah ruffled the fur on his neck and scratched his head behind his ears. The bear made his happy noise, which was a cross between a grunt and a huff. "Ye sceered me. Course, I ain't never been afeared of you, but I got outlaws on my mind. I was sure that was one of 'em behind me, a-pokin' me with a shootin' iron. Ye really give me a start. But with you here to perteck me, I ain't got nothin' to fret about. Them outlaws'd be plumb foolish to try anything with you around."

"We're goin' to have to kill that bahr," Jack whispered to Red, as soon as Lilah and Ol' Codger moved out of sight. He'd learned to be careful about talking very loud in the swamp, where noise carried a bit too well for his comfort. At least the swamp offered plenty of cover, which they'd taken full advantage of while they watched and waited.

A number of characteristics had contributed to Jack Scurlock's notoriety. Patience wasn't among them. "If we don't kill that bahr, we ain't never goin' to get close to Jesse Redford, and I'm gettin' tired of waitin'. That bahr's been trailin' him and the gal ever since they put Smiley in the ground."

"How you aimin' on killin' it? We ain't got a gun no more."

Jack shot Red a look that would have made a rattle-snake squirm. "We ain't got a gun 'cause that little ol' gal took it away from you. That was plumb keerless of you, Red. I've kilt for less reason."

"We could set a trap," Red quickly suggested.

Jack rose from his spot behind a hurrah bush and started toward the little house. "That's exactly what you're goin' to do."

"Me? How?"

"You figure it out. We could a-done kilt Redford and the bahr, too, if'n you hadn't lost the gun."

His short legs pumping, Red hurried to catch up with Jack. "How come you're goin' to the house? They'll get away."

Without breaking stride, Jack looked over his shoulder at Red. "Sh-h-h! You'll see. And they won't get away. That bahr will lead us right to 'em, same's he's been doin'."

As soon as they hit the clearing, Jack told Red to go through the outbuildings and collect whatever he could use for the trap, plus anything else he could carry that might come in handy. Jack went into the house to do the same. A short while later, they entered the woods again. Red sported several coils of rope over one shoulder, a poke filled with rusty nails and small tools over the other, and several larger tools—including an axe—tied to his back. Jack hadn't fared as well.

"There weren't a drap of food left in that cabin, not even a crust of bread!" he snarled. "They been eatin' good whilst we've been starvin'. Jest wait till I get my hands on Redford."

"And that little filly what's with him," Red added.

"Yeah." Jack licked his lips. "But I got diffrunt plans for her. Real diffrunt plans."

As Jesse and Lilah moved westward, they were sickened by the devastation wreaked by the storm. The tops of many trees had been severed, just as though someone had taken a sharp knife and sliced them off. In places, entire pine thickets had been flattened, and occasionally they saw uprooted live oaks, some with trunks several feet thick. One had fallen on a gator, who died with its jaws wide open. Limbs and leaves, dead birds and other small animals littered the black water.

With all the twists and turns they had to make—skirting cypress bays and small islands, and following winding canoe trails across the prairies—Jesse couldn't decide how far they'd actually come, but he figured it wasn't more than four or five miles as the crow flies.

Traversing the swamp, he decided, was as slow and tedious as mountain travel, especially when the canoe was loaded to the hilt. The extra weight increased the strength and stamina required to paddle it and slowed them even more than the terrain, but he wouldn't dump even one small item, regardless of how much extra time and effort it took them to get out of the swamp. Saving Lilah's special plunder was one of the few things he could do for her now—that and getting her safely out of the swamp. And then, well, and then he supposed he'd leave her with her Aunt Agnes and go back to chasing outlaws. That was

what he wanted to do, he told himself. It was what he *had*
to do. Suddenly, he found the prospect less than appealing.

Regardless, there would be no more chasing outlaws for
him or education for Lilah, if they didn't first get out of
the swamp alive. The way things were going for them, the
elements were as threatening to their continued existence
as One-Eyed Jack and Red were. Concerned about surviving another bad storm without the benefit of proper shelter,
Jesse had been watching the sky all day. Thankfully, the
clouds had steadily moved off to the northeast, clearing the
air, leaving only a few white puffs behind to dot wide
open spaces of blue as bright as Lilah's eyes. If the
weather would just remain fair for a few more days, they'd
be safe.

As the sun dipped low on the western horizon, they
banked the canoe on the boggy shore of a small, relatively
new island—judging from the lack of mature trees—sitting
in the middle of a wide prairie. Jesse wasn't sure he liked
the idea of camping in such an open spot, but there wasn't
another island in sight, and for once, he could see pretty
far.

"You've been awfully quiet," Jesse observed as he
pulled the heavy canoe across the bog.

"Jes' lettin' the swamp do my talkin'."

As usual, the swamp was alive with noises, mostly from
creatures too small or too sly to be seen. But Lilah's silence was unusual, to say the least, and her excuse fell far
short of the truth, in Jesse's estimation. Something was
troubling her—and troubling her deeply.

"Do you want to talk about it?"

"Talk about what?"

"Whatever it is that's bothering you."

"What makes ye think anything's botherin' me?"

This conversation was moving at about the same pace as
the heavy canoe in a prairie choked with water lilies . . . an

inch at the time, and each one a struggle to gain. Jesse decided to let it go, temporarily anyway.

When the bog gave way to sandy ground, he chose a suitable campsite and started to unpack the canoe, while Lilah collected firewood. They were getting low on both matches and food, and they'd been out of coffee since Lilah had burned the last of the beans.

"What do you want for supper?" Jesse asked.

"How 'bout fish."

"We didn't bring a pole."

"Don' need one."

She traipsed off toward the edge of the island, her hips swinging seductively. God! He had to stop seeing her as a full-grown woman. He had to put his longing and his love for her aside, or else he'd go right back to forgetting about his duty to the U.S. Marshal's office and his obligation to Martha and the boys. He turned his back to her and worked at building a fire, but the task was entirely too menial to dilute his lustful thoughts. No matter how hard he tried, he couldn't make a decent case for duty and obligation anymore, not at the expense of losing Lilah.

Groaning, Jesse settled himself by the fire and looked off in the direction Lilah had taken. Although low-growing bushes blocked her from sight, he could hear her laughing and splashing in the water. What was she trying to do? Catch fish with her bare hands? Intrigued, he stood up and stretched his neck, but he still couldn't get a clear view. He glanced at the fire, decided it could go unattended for a few minutes, and set out for the prairie.

She'd angled off to the north just a bit, but all the racket she was making led him straight to her. He broke clear of the bushes, and the scene before him took him so totally by surprise, that he stood gaping like a child at a circus.

Lilah stood knee-deep among a thick cluster of yellow bonnets, her arms held wide and her hands clutching a good-sized piece of fabric, which she was attempting to use as a net to catch an airborne fish. The fish bounced out and splashed into the dark water. Well beyond her, in slightly deeper and less obstructed water, Ol' Codger scooped up another fish and tossed it at Lilah.

She caught that one, gave it a cursory glance, then flipped it off the fabric net and back into the water. " 'Twas jest a wee thing," she called to the bear.

Ol' Codger grunted and shook his head, almost as though he'd understood her perfectly well. Then he ambled forward, his long black muzzle trained on the glassy surface of the water, ostensibly looking for a larger fish.

Jesse returned his attention to Lilah, who made a delicate portrait with the orangey glow of the setting sun turning her hair to apricot and lending a peachy cast to her skin. There was entirely too much of the latter exposed, Jesse noted for the first time. And now that he had, he couldn't take his gaze off her upper body, which was covered only by a thin, sleeveless camisole that dipped low in the back. Soft ringlets spilled from the loose knot at her crown, forming a soft halo around her head and trickling down the slender column of her neck. Tiny droplets of water glistened like a sprinkling of gold dust on her arms and shoulders, and her laughter rang with the clear, sweet voice of an angel.

His breath caught in his throat and his body throbbed with need. An inner voice hollered at him to run back to camp, to put the vision of her ethereal beauty out of his mind, to wash his passion for her out of his heart, to purge his craving for her from his soul. But he couldn't do that. Couldn't or wouldn't. He didn't know which, and at the moment, he didn't care.

Without conscious thought, he started moving toward the water, toward Lilah, but a silvery flash stopped him. It was a big fish, perhaps a bass. She squealed with delight, captured it in her makeshift net, and quickly wrapped the fabric around the flouncing fish before it could flop out.

"Much obleeged, Ol' Codger," she called, turning toward the island, her attention focused on the squirming bundle in her hands. Jesse's attention was focused on the lush curves of her breasts above the low-cut camisole and the rosy circles of her nipples straining against the sheer fabric.

"So that's how you catch a fish without a pole," he said, his voice hoarse with desire.

She looked up and smiled. "Codger got us a big'un."

"So I saw."

"He's the bestest fisherman I know."

As though to prove her right—again—the bear swiped his front paw through the water and another large fish, a gar this time, sailed through the air and plopped onto the shore. With amazing speed, the bear lumbered out of the prairie and pounced on the gar, his weight making the earth tremble and a young pond cypress quiver. He snatched the gar up in his teeth and shook himself hard, sending fat drops of water flying. Then he sauntered off into the bushes to eat his dinner.

Guilelessly, Lilah offered Jesse the fish she'd "caught," which he realized now was wrapped in her blouse. "If ye'll gut it, I'll fry it up."

"Deal," he said, unable to divert his gaze from her bosom. Seemingly unaware of the distraction she caused, Lilah strolled nonchalantly toward their campsite, leaving him standing there, staring after her.

Jesse physically shook himself, much as the bear had done, but his effort failed to dislodge Lilah's spell. Mechanically, he unwrapped the fish, which he only marginally noted was a large-mouthed bass, then he fished his penknife out of his pocket and proceeded to dress the fish.

A mile or so to the east, Red chopped off the head of a fat green lizard, ripped open its belly, and raked its intestines out with a long, dirty fingernail.

"I ain't eatin' another lizard," Jack snarled.

Red tossed the lizard into the stew pot and reached for a small soft-shelled turtle. "Then don't."

"Tell me you ain't goin' to put that turtle in there, too."

"Turtles is good eatin'." He slid the knife around the turtle's side and peeled back the shell.

"You got something against rabbits and squirrels?"

"Nope. Jest ain't got no way to get one, 'ceptin' with a snare. Makin' snares takes time, and then you got to wait for the critter to take the bait." Red scooped a mound of white meat out of the shell and dropped it into the pot. " 'Sides, lizard and turtle meat cooks up fast, and you said we had to put this fire out 'fore good dark." Red stirred the stew with a stick.

"Ain't we got a spoon?" Jack asked.

"Got two of 'em, but they's too short to be much good for stirrin'. You threw the rest of 'em away, said we didn't need 'em and they was jest extree baggage. 'Sides, this here stick smells like sassafras. I'm usin' it to flavor the broth."

"You been studyin' on how to trap that bahr?"

"Yep."

"You figured out yet how to do it?"

"Well, for one thing, we got to move out ahead of the marshal."

"How come?"

Sometimes, Red wondered how much sense Jack Scurlock really had. Jack knew how to make good moonshine whiskey. And he knew how to kill folks. He didn't seem to be good for too much of anything else. "Layin' a trap for that bahr ain't goin' to do much good, if'n the bahr's already in front of it."

"Yeah," Jack said slowly. "I see what you mean. But how're we goin' to know for sure they'll come that way?"

Red nodded toward the setting sun. "They been headin'

due west all day. I figure they'll keep on headin' west till they get out'n the swamp."

"How long you reckon that'll take?"

"Hard to say. Another day. Two, maybe. Three at the most."

"They ain't enough cover here to get by 'em 'thout being seen, and goin' around 'em would take too long." Jack sniffed the steam coming off the stew pot and almost smiled.

"You got a point. I reckon we're jest goin' to have to travel at night. Sure would be nice to have one of them polin' boats. We could travel faster in one of them."

Red fished two tin cups out of their haversack and dipped them into the stew pot. He handed one to Jack along with one of the two short spoons, then set his own portion aside and poured a pot of water over the fire. It hissed and crackled, sent up a final yellow flame, and died down to a few orange coals. At almost precisely the same moment, the sun gave up its last pink ray of light, and a gray darkness swallowed the swamp. Within minutes, the gray would become pitch-black, with only the moon and stars and the few orange coals left to see by. Already, the swamp resounded with critter racket—chirps and croaks and whines that grew louder as the night grew darker.

Red didn't like being in the pitch-black swamp at night, not with big-jawed gators and water moccasins and other dangerous critters everywhere. The dangerous critters didn't make any noise. One of those critters was approaching their campsite even now, coming real quiet and cautious-like, with only a slight tremor of the unstable earth to give it away.

Jack must've felt it, too, because he laid a finger of silence against his lips, set his cup down, and picked up the long-bladed knife Red had been using to dress the meat.

The tremors strengthened. The critter was getting closer. And then it was upon them, coming right into their camp. Jack rose to his feet, and though it was too dark to see much of anything except the glisten of light in the white of his one good eye, Red knew how Jack's face looked. In his mind's eye, he could see the gleam of purpose in Jack's eye, the set jaw and the evil grin upon his lips. He'd seen that look every time Jack prepared to plunge his knife into an unsuspecting victim.

"Thank goodness I fount ye," the critter said. "I been a-frettin' ever since the storm hit."

Neither Jack nor Red said a word.

"Well, ain't ye glad to see me? I fount them bags ye lost, marshal. The least ye can do is invite me to vittles. Smells awful good."

Jack took a step toward the man, and a tiny orange glimmer flashed through the air.

"That you, Jesse? How come—"

A short scream rent the air and reverberated through the swamp, but it was quickly absorbed by the noisy racket of the night critters. Jack wiped his blade on his britches leg, then pulled the man over closer to the dying coals.

"It's that man what was with the gal when they come for Smiley," Red said. "He had one of them polin' boats I was talkin' about."

"Yeah," Jack said, laughter in his voice. "Let's go find it."

Chapter Twenty-one

"Did ye hear that?"

Jesse looked up from his plate. He'd been trying real hard not to look at Lilah, who had yet to put on another blouse over her thin camisole. She sat cross-legged on the other side of the fire, the legs of her damp britches rolled up to her knees, exposing slender calves and trim ankles. Between the flickering light cavorting in her rowdy blond curls and the shadows it cast beneath her full breasts, he didn't know how much longer he could maintain a safe distance from her. The succulent bass on his plate served as his only defense, and now it was almost gone. He swallowed hard to put his mind on listening instead of looking.

"Did I hear what?"

"That scream."

"No. Probably just a panther."

"When cats scream, they scream. This was real short, like it got cut off in the middle."

"Where'd it come from?"

She waved her fork eastward.

"There's nothing out there except prairie," he said. "Last island was a good mile or so back, so whatever it was couldn't be too close."

Lilah set her plate on the ground and stood up. "I'm goin' to look."

"Not without me, you aren't!" She was probably just panicking over nothing, Jesse told himself, but that didn't keep him from remembering that One-Eyed Jack was quite possibly still in the swamp. Funny how a place as big as the Okefinoke could seem terribly small, when you knew someone as evil as Jack Scurlock occupied the same territory.

They stood side by side at the edge of the bog and looked out over the dark prairie. Bright moonlight reflected off patches of clear water, kissed the delicate white petals of the water lilies, and sprinkled its silvery beams over a stand of maiden cane growing close to the island, but no other light was visible. Surely, Jesse thought, if Jack and Red were camped on the tiny island to the east, they'd have some kind of fire going.

He turned toward Lilah, intending to assure her that nothing was amiss, but the play of moonlight in her hair chased all rational thought away. He reached out, thinking only to skim his palms over her curls, and all his resolve evaporated.

The instant his hands touched her hair, the full-growed-woman yearnings rushed through Lilah's veins, setting her skin to prickling and her belly to burning. She turned into his welcoming embrace, slipping her arms around his rib cage and lifting her mouth to his. He kissed her with a fervent need that matched her own, his tongue probing her mouth, his firm lips plying hers, his strong arms crushing her against the solid wall of his chest.

She kissed him back, flicking her tongue over his, molding her lips to his, taking his breath into her lungs. She clung to him as though he were necessary for her very existence, and indeed, she realized, he was. The very idea of having to live her life without him made her cling even tighter.

When he loosened her arms, supreme disappointment squeezed her heart, twisting and turning it, bringing tears to her eyes. She was sure he was rejecting her again, pulling back within himself and denying the passion that sparked between them, just as he'd done before. But then he scooped her up and headed back toward the fire, and a thrill of surprise and delight shot through her.

He set her gently on her feet, and as he spread their blankets on the ground, she found herself wanting to talk to him, to at least call his name and tell him that she loved him. Fear stayed her tongue—fear that the slightest interruption would break the spell, would destroy the dark passion smoldering in his eye. She didn't understand exactly what making real love meant, but she knew she wanted it. She knew Jesse wanted it, too. And deep down in her full-growed-woman's soul, she knew that once he made real love with her, she would be his and he would be hers for true and for everlastin'. The anticipation of this night with Jesse and many more such nights to come bolstered her courage, and she began to undo the buttons that held her britches closed.

As he smoothed out the last corner of the blanket, a measure of trepidation gripped Jesse's heart. Lilah was no soiled dove, he reminded himself, to bed tonight and forget tomorrow. If he took her now, he made her his woman, not only for the moment, but for all time to come. He'd sworn never to do that again, but without even looking at her, he knew she trembled in expectation. How could he refuse her now? How could he explain something even he didn't really understand?

He had to . . . somehow. Somehow, he had to make her understand that she couldn't possibly love him if she knew what demons lived inside of him. He turned around to tell her—and lost both his breath and his purpose.

She stood at the opposite end of the blanket, clothed only in flickering firelight. Until that moment, he'd only imagined how beautiful her body would be. Now that he saw it, all of it, he realized that his mental vision hadn't come close to representing the real thing.

"Come here," he whispered, knowing those words sealed his fate, yet never more pleased with a decision than he was with that one.

She sank to her hands and knees and crawled toward him. "Did I do wrong?" she asked, her voice quavering.

"No, Lilah. You are—" his one-eyed gaze touched her everywhere at once, "magnificent."

She smiled. "It would pleasure me, Jesse, if'n ye took yer clothes off, too."

He shucked them in short order, then lay down beside her on the blanket. "Do you know what we're going to do?" he asked, trailing a hand down her arm.

"We're goin' to make real love this time."

He kissed her on the tip of her nose. "And do you know what making real love means?"

"I know I want you to teach me how to do it."

He nuzzled her hair with his nose and let his hand graze over her nipple. It puckered beneath his caress. "And I want to teach you everything I know, which I expect isn't half of all there is to know about making love. You'll have to teach me the rest."

"But I've never done it afore. I don' know nothin' to teach you."

His hand closed over her breast, and he began to knead it. "Yes, you do. You've already taught me more about love than I ever thought there was to know. We'll just do what comes naturally, and see what happens."

And they did.

Lilah lay in the pillow of Jesse's shoulder, looking up at the twinkling stars and feeling wonderfully whole. It seemed such an inadequate word, but it was the best one she knew to describe the way she felt. Whole. Like she'd been only half a body, half a person before, looking for the other half of herself the way the Creek hunters had looked for Eden. They hadn't found what they were looking for, but she had. Judging from Jesse's shuddering response and his whispered endearments, he had, too.

The one thing he hadn't told her—outright, anyway— was that he loved her. She'd longed to hear the words, longed to hear them still. Maybe he needed to hear them from her first.

"I love you, Jesse."

"Hm-m-m."

His breath tickled her ear.

"I love you," she repeated, louder this time.

"I know." He tightened his arm around her waist and snuggled closer to her side. A cool night breeze fluttered over them, and a barred owl hooted in the distance. She waited for him to echo her declaration . . . waited until his breathing evened out and his hold on her relaxed . . . waited until he fell asleep.

But she didn't give up hope. Maybe he didn't know it yet, but she knew he loved her. If he didn't, he wouldn't care so much what happened to her. And he wouldn't look at her the way he did, or touch her so gently, or kiss her so passionately.

He'd told her that he was learning about love from her. Since she'd never set out to teach him anything, she reckoned she must be teaching by example, by doing what came naturally. She'd been doing what came naturally all her life—loving Maw and Paw and Granny, loving Bob and Ol' Codger and the many critters she'd nursed back to health, and now loving Jesse. She'd just keep on loving him, and telling him she loved him, and one day he'd tell her he loved her, too.

She could wait.

Jesse awoke before dawn. The fire had died down, and he was cold. Partly, anyway. The side of his body pressed against Lilah's soft curves was nice and toasty, but the other side was downright chilled, probably, he realized, because it was completely exposed to the damp air. After all, it was almost summer in the swamp, and warm even in the wee hours before dawn. But it had been more years than he cared to count since he'd slept completely nude—and without cover to boot.

With tender ease, he slipped away from her and folded the blanket over her sweet body. She sighed in her sleep, tucked a hand under her head, and rolled onto her stomach. He pulled on his britches—the too-tight ones—and then his shirt, which he didn't stop to button. Within minutes, he had the fire blazing again and water heating for a rub-down.

While he waited, he sat by the fire and watched Lilah sleep. She looked so young, so fragile, so vulnerable, that it frightened him. He'd taken her maidenhead, and now he owed her his name, his protection, his love. The name was easy, but how he could give her protection and love and remain a deputy U.S. marshal was beyond his ken.

He should have thought about that before. Hell, he did think about it! Thinking about it was what had kept him from claiming her long before now. No matter what, he couldn't regret what had happened between them. Not when it was the sweetest thing he'd ever known.

So, what was he to do now? Abandon his mission to bring One-Eyed Jack to justice? Resign his badge? Move Lilah to Tennessee? Right now, he couldn't do any of those things, not and live with himself afterwards.

The least distasteful option was resigning his badge. He'd been a deputy U.S. marshal for more than a decade, and it was time for him either to move up or move out. He'd been offered a marshal's position not long after Martha and the boys were killed, but accepting it would have required a move to Denver, which in turn would have meant giving up his search for Jack Scurlock. He couldn't allow himself to abandon his search then . . . nor could he now.

Once he'd found the scoundrel, once he'd closed that chapter of his life, then he could resign. At six cents per mile and two dollars per arrest—which averaged out to about five hundred a year—a deputy U.S. marshal's pay was barely enough to support a family. He didn't know what he'd do afterwards, maybe become a farmer, but it would definitely be something that would keep him at home.

Home, for Jesse, had always been Tennessee. He'd told Lilah that he missed his home, and he supposed he did, but not so much as he had at one time. Home, he'd come to realize, didn't mean mountains and valleys and swiftly running streams. Home meant people, especially those you loved.

And he loved Lilah. God, how he loved her! He loved her so much it hurt. That she loved him, too, was nothing short of a miracle. He owed her the declaration of his love . . . and one day, he'd tell her. One day, when the search was over and he was finally free . . .

Amazed at both the playfulness and the loyalty of the huge bear, Jesse watched Ol' Codger splash along beside them. Despite the bear's gentleness, Jesse expected Codger would protect Lilah to the death. From time to time, the bear stopped to swat at a bee or chase a butterfly, but he always returned to his post as point man. Then, seeming to grow tired of the relatively slow pace, the bear bolted ahead, stopping to fish when he neared a black mass that was hardly bigger than he was.

"A blow-up," Lilah explained. "Jest a bit of the floor of the swamp poppin' up. I don' know how come it to do that, but it does. If'n a little ol' tree sprouts up or some buttonbushes takes ahold on it, then it mought grow into a reg'lar house. Right now, it's jest floatin'."

"A house? You mean an island."

"Same thing. Swampers calls them houses—'cause they's finally strong enough to build a house on, I reckon."

"How long does that take?"

"I don' rightly know. There's a batt'ry near Medicine Island that was jest a blow-up when my paw and I used to go there to visit Granny."

Jesse laughed. "You people have the strangest names for things. What's a battery?"

"Atwixt a blow-up and a house."

"An adolescent." At Lilah's frown, he added, "Between a child and an adult."

"I reckon that's one way a lookin' at it."

As they neared the blow-up, Ol' Codger flipped a good-sized fish out of the water and onto the black mass. It shivered and shook, testimony to its instability.

"Do they ever sink?"

"Lots of times. Sometimes, they jest float with the current, till they snag theirselfs on the aidge of a perairie or a bay or another blow-up. And sometimes, a passel of 'em sorta floats into each other and sticks t'gether. If'n enough plants takes root, the blow-up'll maybe grow into a batt'ry, maybe not."

The bear snapped up the fish, then raced off through the water and into a line of pond cypresses some distance ahead. "He'll be a-waitin' for us on t'other side," Lilah said. But he wasn't.

The farther they moved west, the denser the growth of trees became. Most of them were pond cypresses, but an occasional red-leaved tupelo added bright spots of color, and a bald cypress, which was taller than the pond variety, cropped up here and there.

"Why are they called bald cypresses?" Jesse asked. "They aren't bald at all."

"Not now, but this fall, their leaves'll turn brown and drap off, jest like a hick'ry. Pond cypress stays green all the time. I love 'em both, but if'n I had to choose betwixt 'em, I'd take the bald ones."

"Why?"

" 'Cause they're the gran'daddies of the swamp. Some of 'em must a-been here a hunderd year or more. They can stand up to jest about anything. Why, that wind we had last week weren't no botheration to them a-tall."

Jesse had to admit that he hadn't seen a single felled bald cypress.

At times, the trees grew so close together that they completely blocked the canoe's passage. When this happened, they paddled parallel to the trees until they found an opening that was wide enough. Long gray beards of Spanish moss draped the trees, in some places almost completely concealing the limbs and needles, lending an eerie quality to the thick shade that gave Jesse the creeps. It was all his imagination, he told himself. At least it was cooler here. As the day neared an end, however, he began to wonder where they'd camp for the night. He didn't relish the prospect of spending the night in the canoe.

There was a time not so very long ago, he reminded himself, when he would have been thrilled to have the canoe, when he considered the swamp nothing more than a perilous trap. There was no doubt in his mind that the peril still existed, but it had little to do with his reluctance to spend the night in the canoe, and everything to do with experiencing Lilah's sweetness at least one more time before they were separated. Tomorrow—or surely no later than the day after—they'd emerge from the swamp, and heaven only knew when they'd be together again once they reached Homerville.

"Is there an island near here?" he asked, as they paddled by another long line of trees. They'd made so many twists and turns wending their way through the bays, that Jesse wondered if they'd made any real headway at all.

"I don' know. I ain't never been this way before."

"We can always climb a tree." His remark fell far short of the humor he'd intended.

"I wonder where Ol' Codger got off to. Maybe he fount a batt'ry at least."

"Yeah, but are *we* going to find it? We can't even find an opening in these trees."

"There's one!" She pointed to a dark inlet that closely resembled the mouth of a cave. The passage itself was so dark and narrow, that Jesse wondered how Lilah, who sat in the front and navigated, could see where she was going. The canoe bumped against a tree trunk, then ran aground.

"We're goin' to have to get out and drag it," she said. "The water's too shallow to paddle it through."

Recalling his snakebite, Jesse peered over the side and shuddered. "Maybe that isn't such a good idea. Let's go back."

"I thought ye wanted to find a island 'fore day-down."

"I do."

"Well, I think we fount one. I see some light up ahead." She turned around on the seat so that she was facing Jesse and started rolling up her britches legs. "All we got to do is sing."

"Why?"

"To let the critters know we're here. Critters don' 'preciate folks sneakin' up on 'em."

She broke into "The Piney Woods Boys," and he picked up the harmony. Although getting out of the canoe was still against his better judgment, he deferred to Lilah's. She pulled and he pushed, and they both sang the rousing ballad at the top of their lungs. But singing didn't ease his misgivings one whit, especially when he recalled the last time they'd transported the canoe this way. Codger had stepped out of the woods and scared him half to death that time. This time, it might be another critter—one not as friendly as the bear.

Jesse slipped his Colt out of his belt and laid it in the back of the canoe, so it would be easier to get to . . . just in case.

"They're comin'!" Red whispered.

"Get down, you fool!" Jack whispered back.

Red scampered behind a decades-old bald cypress with a base wide enough to hide a good-sized bear. Just a few feet away, Jack squatted behind another one. They'd traveled all night, using a pine knot to light their way and the stars to determine their course. Not long after dawn, they'd poled the punt boat around this cypress bay and discovered a narrow strip of fairly dry land on the other side.

"They oughter get here right at dark," Jack allowed.

"Yeah. This is nigh on to perfect," Red agreed.

Jack tied the boat to a tree and camouflaged it with small limbs, while Red set the bear trap. They scouted the area, selected the most advantageous hiding place where they could see anyone coming from either side, and settled down to wait.

And now, their black souls surging with their first success, they tensed in preparation for the final kill.

"Hesh up!" Lilah hissed.

They were right at the grassy clearing, which was flooded with the last light of day. The hazy rays spilled into the stand of cypresses and cast long shadows behind the trees, making visibility difficult.

Jesse quit singing. "What is it?"

"Listen."

A low, growling moan wafted through the trees. Lilah dropped her end of the canoe. "It's a critter in pain."

"How do you know?"

" 'Cause I've heared it afore." She abandoned the canoe and cut off to the right.

"Where are you going?"

"To see."

Jesse snatched up the Colt and started after her. Out of the corner of his good eye—the left one—he saw a flicker of light. In one fluid movement, he turned, aimed, and fired. Lilah screamed. And through the smoke and the haze, Jesse watched what appeared to be a human form stagger toward her.

Chapter Twenty-two

Jesse aimed and fired again.

The staggering form toppled to the earth while another man or a beast—Jesse wasn't sure which—took off through the trees, running toward the light, but staying within the cover of the cypresses.

Lilah took a step toward the body on the ground.

"Stay there!" Jesse called, moving cautiously around the canoe and keeping the .45 trained on the body. He'd seen too many men get up after being shot—and he remembered how the bullets he'd put in the female gator hadn't fazed the huge reptile. But then, he'd shot the alligator from close range. The bullets probably went right through.

"It's that man," Lilah said, her voice full of loathing, "the one Bob jumped on. The one I took the gun off'n."

From what Jesse could see of the man he'd shot, Lilah was right. He stuck the wet toe of his right boot under the man's hip and flipped him over. It was Red Watkins, all right. The apelike man's eyes stared up at him without blinking, and bright red blood spurted out of the two large, gaping holes in his chest. He wouldn't ever hurt anyone else.

"That must've been Scurlock running off," Jesse said, squinting at the setting sun. "Get the canoe, Lilah. We'll

have to set up camp now, before it gets dark. Can't have
a fire tonight."

When she ignored him, he turned his gaze to the spot
where she'd been standing. She was gone.

Oh, God, no! Jack had taken her! Jack Scurlock, a man
who thrived on cutting and stabbing. It was the flash of
Jack's knife that had alerted Jesse to Red's movement. Images of Lilah's bloody dream-face flashed before his eyes,
melding with his memory of Martha's mutilated features.
A lead weight settled in the pit of his stomach, and he
thought he was going to be sick. Unconcerned for his own
safety, he crashed through the underbrush, calling her
name.

A loud, long wail pierced the air.

Jesse ran toward the sound. A tangle of blackberry vines
tore at his britches and ripped across his bare forearms. He
stubbed his toe on a fallen log and lost his balance, then
regained it before he went sprawling. The wail faded
away, and Jesse thought he was too late. Pain unlike any
he'd ever felt before ripped through him. Then he heard
her sobs, deep, gut-wrenching sobs that tore at his heart
even as they hastened his flight.

He found her then, a trembling heap upon the ground,
her arms encircling Ol' Codger's midsection and her face
buried in his furry chest.

The bear sat with his back against a tree, his staring
eyes as unseeing as Red's, a low moan the only indication
that he lived. But his hold on life was feeble at best. Two
wooden stakes pinned his shoulders to the tree, and his
forelegs hung limply by his sides, dripping blood. Jesse's
gaze followed one of the drips to the ground, and he
watched it plop into the open palm of a forepaw.

Jesse fell to his knees and vomited green, bitter bile.

No one had a right to be that lucky, Jack thought as he
pushed the punt boat away from the bank and into open

water. He'd thought for sure that he had Jesse Redford this time, that he'd be free of him forever. Instead, here he was on the run again. Alone, thanks to the marshal.

One-Eyed Jack Scurlock had never mourned anyone in his life, and he wasn't about to start now. He'd miss Red. No doubt about that. But he'd find another partner eventually. Might even have him a gang again before too long.

First, though, he had to get rid of Jesse Redford once and for all. Otherwise, the marshal would just keep coming after him, and Jack was tired of running. He'd been on the run most of his life, first from his father's whip and later from one lawman or the other. Always, they'd given up the chase—until Redford.

When it was good dark, he stopped poling and sat down on the flat deck of the boat, which was built like a floating campsite. Pretty smart of whoever had built it, he thought, especially since there didn't appear to be another island anywhere around. He supposed he could go back to the one he'd just left, maybe sneak up on Redford and the gal while they slept. But the marshal was too smart for that. He'd be sitting there in the dark, waiting for him with that wicked pistol of his. There had to be another way.

Hungry, Jack reached inside the little cabin, removed Yerby's food pouch, and foraged inside. Instead of the biscuits he'd expected to find, his hand closed over a rolled-up piece of oilskin, and his fingertips grazed a small piece of metal. Confused, he removed his hand and felt the outside of the pouch. Saddlebags! What was Yerby doing with saddlebags, when he didn't have a horse?

He could hear Yerby saying, "I fount them bags ye lost, marshal." Suddenly excited, Jack put his hand back inside and rubbed the pad of his thumb over the engraved piece of metal.

"Jesse Redford," he said, cackling, "your luck jest ran out."

* * *

Lilah was walking death.

She refused to eat, she didn't sleep, and she hadn't spoken since she'd identified Red two days ago.

Until that morning, she wouldn't let Jesse touch her, either. Every time he tried, she fought him tooth and nail. When he'd finished vomiting his insides up, he'd gone to her and tried to pull her away from the bear. She turned on him, a slashing, spitting ball of fury, her face and hair smeared with Codger's blood, and her eyes wild with revenge. A good dousing with cold swamp water had washed off some of the blood and cooled her ire, but she wouldn't let him give her a bath. Perhaps she would, now that she was docile. He supposed it could wait until they got to Homerville.

If they ever got there. Between his dragging the canoe—which was the only way he could think of to transport all the things she'd brought with her from her parent's house—and her slow pace, he was beginning to think they'd have to spend another night on the road.

Jesse glanced back to make sure she was still behind him. She trudged along, her bare feet filthy and her clothes even worse. Her curly blond hair, which he loved so much, fell to her shoulders in a tangled disarray, and dried crusts of the bear's blood clung to the roots. She clutched the coffeepot, which contained Codger's ashes, against her breasts. But it was her eyes, her beautiful, clear blue eyes, that yanked his heart right out of his chest. They just sat in the sockets, cold and lifeless and dull.

And it was his fault. All this time, he'd known his association with Lilah placed her in danger. An inner voice reminded him that his intentions had been honorable, and his actions had been somewhat effective. His protection had prevented her own physical harm. But the fact remained that Ol' Codger would still be alive, if she'd never met Jesse.

The worst part, the part that caused him the most mental

anguish, was that now, when she needed him the most, he couldn't be there for her. More than anything else in the world, he wanted to take her to the hotel in Homerville and stay with her while she suffered through her grief, no matter how long it took. But he couldn't do that. He was too close to catching Jack Scurlock, whom Jesse had decided was the devil incarnate. Someone had to stop him, and Jesse figured no one else on earth had better reason than he did.

Lilah wanted him to go after Jack. He knew she did. He knew that if he stayed around until she started talking again, she'd tell him to do it. But by then, Jack's trail would be cold. He had no real choice.

He'd seen how strong she was. Eventually, she'd get over it, with or without him. At least she had her Aunt Agnes to take care of her. Jesse hoped Agnes wasn't too put off by Lilah's appearance. From Lilah's description of Agnes, he was afraid the woman would be.

"Egads! What happened to her?"

Jesse bit his tongue to keep from asking the screeching woman the same question about herself. The address was right, but neither this woman nor her house came close to fitting Lilah's descriptions. "You're Lilah's Aunt Agnes?"

The woman looked down her hawk's nose at him with something closely akin to disdain, and dipped her haughty chin just the slightest bit. Considering her unkempt appearance and the deplorable condition of the outside of her house, he wanted to laugh out loud at her superior attitude.

"And who might you be?" she asked.

"Jesse Redford, deputy U.S. marshal."

"If you're a marshal, then where's your badge?"

He started to tell her he lost it, then decided it really wasn't any of her business. "I'm here as a friend of Lilah's. If you'll invite us in, I can explain."

Though Agnes's bulk filled the doorway, it didn't block

the commotion from inside—children's laughter, running footsteps, a woman shrieking. Agnes closed the door and waved a hand at a couple of weathered rocking chairs on the porch. He wouldn't have minded being offered a glass of water, but the chair with a sagging rush seat and the paint peeling off it appeared to be the extent of the woman's hospitality.

There wasn't even a chair for Lilah, who was still standing in the bare yard, a mangy cur-dog sniffing at her feet. She seemed to take no notice of either the dog or her surroundings, which was just as well, he supposed. As Jesse sat down, he remembered why Lilah had wanted to come here. How disappointed she was going to be, when she discovered that her aunt didn't know the first thing about being a lady.

"Get on with it, Marshal," Agnes snapped, "and make it quick. I've got a pie in the oven."

A pie! Lord, what he wouldn't give for a slice of pie. He took a big sniff. Apple. With lots of cinnamon. He thrust his hunger aside and concentrated on getting on with the story. The sooner he did, the sooner he could get a square meal in town.

"Lilah's friend—" Jesse realized what he was about to say and clamped his mouth shut. *Lilah's friend, Ol' Codger, a giant black bear* ... He could imagine how Agnes would take that. Why, she'd have Lilah committed to an asylum. He started over. "Lilah's friend Granny, the one she's been living with, passed away."

"So?"

"So, Lilah is without a home."

Agnes turned her head and flicked her gaze over Lilah. "She looks full-growed to me."

"She is."

"What'd you bring her here for? She's got a house in the swamp." Her eyes narrowed then, and she slowly turned her head back until she was facing Jesse again.

"She's lost her mind, ain't she? You mean to dump her on me, don't you? Well, I ain't taking her in, even if she is Merrie's child. Take her back to the swamp. There's folks there what'll see after her."

Jesse signed the ledger "Mr. and Mrs. Redford." Although he didn't plan to remain in town any longer than it took him to find a reliable woman to care for Lilah, he didn't want to try to explain the situation to the gawking clerk—or to argue with the clerk about whether or not he could stay in the room with Lilah in the meantime, which was sure to happen if the man found out they weren't married.

"What in tarnation's the matter with her? She loony or something?"

Jesse was quickly growing tired of hearing those questions—and of people voicing them in Lilah's presence. Ignoring the clerk just as the man ignored Lilah, Jesse pushed the hotel ledger across the counter and held out an upturned palm for the key, which the clerk didn't relinquish.

"That'll be fifty cents."

"We'll need a tub and lots of soap and hot water."

"Cost you another two bits."

Jesse nodded. "And supper. Brought up to our room, please."

"A dollar and a quarter altogether."

Jesse laid his Colt on the counter.

The clerk turned his gawking gaze from Lilah to the pistol. "What's this?"

"Collateral."

"I have to have cash. The boss says so."

"I'll bring you cash—first thing tomorrow morning, soon as the telegraph office and the bank open."

The man looked back at Lilah. "I don't know . . . She

ain't gonna bust up stuff, is she? 'Cause if she is, I've got to get a deposit—"

"What's your name?"

The clerk blinked his bulbous eyes. "Fred. Fred Martin."

"Look, Fred. Besides the fact that this pistol here's real important to me, it's the best handgun made. It's worth a lot more than a dollar or two. I wouldn't be leaving it, if I didn't plan to redeem it."

The bell rattled over the front door. Jesse turned and watched a well-dressed, matronly woman bustle up to the counter without giving Lilah even a passing glance. When he turned back, the pistol had disappeared and Fred was taking a key off a rack on the back wall.

"Did you see that my room was cleaned?" the woman asked, taking her key from the clerk.

"Yes, ma'am. I did it myself."

"You need to hire a maid."

"Yes, ma'am."

Fred waited until the woman cleared the landing before he handed Jesse the key he'd been holding. "You'll keep her in the room?"

"Yes."

"You won't bring her down to supper or nothing?"

"I asked you to bring it up."

"That's right. I forgot. I'll expect to see you in the morning."

"I'll be here."

Jesse had planned to introduce himself to the local sheriff that evening and to caution him to watch out for Jack Scurlock, but that was when he'd expected to leave Lilah with her aunt.

By the time he hauled all their things upstairs, stored the canoe in the hotel's toolshed, bathed both himself and Lilah, then washed Lilah's hair and combed it out, Fred was back with their supper. When Jesse saw the thick slabs of ham, baked sweet potatoes, mustard greens, and big wedges of corn bread, he decided the sheriff could wait.

He managed to coax Lilah into eating a few bites of sweet potato, then tucked her into bed before attacking the food himself. It tasted as good as it looked. He was sopping up the last of the pot liquor from the greens with a piece of corn bread, when someone knocked on the door.

"Coming!" he called, tossing the bite of corn bread into his mouth and gathering up both plates. Fred certainly hadn't wasted any time returning for the dirty dishes.

"Your brother's waiting for you in the lobby," Fred said.

Jesse thought he'd surely misunderstood. "My brother?"

"Yes, sir, Mr. Redford. Looks just like you, eye patch and all."

"There must be some mistake—" *Oh, my God! One-Eyed Jack.* It had to be. But posing as his brother? And coming *to* him instead of running away? It didn't make sense.

Apparently, it didn't make sense to Fred, either, who was eyeing Jesse with sudden distrust. "I mean, I was supposed to meet him later," Jesse hastily corrected, stepping into the hall, then locking the door behind him before he followed Fred down the stairs. This would happen when he didn't have his .45—and he couldn't ask Fred to let him borrow it back, not as suspicious as the clerk already was. He'd have to slip behind the counter and get it. What had he been thinking, anyway, to ever let his gun out of his sight, much less his possession?

Silently, Jesse cursed himself, Lilah's Aunt Agnes, and the hotel staircase, which had been set into the wall, which in turn obstructed his view of the small lobby. But that meant Jack couldn't see him, either. If Jack had his knife—and Jesse was certain he did, he was liable to throw it the instant Jesse appeared.

As soon as Fred cleared the bottom step, Jesse tackled him from behind, throwing both of them to the lobby floor. Before Fred could react, Jesse rolled off of him and darted behind the counter.

The pistol wasn't there!

"Looking for this?" a familiar voice sneered.

Jesse raised up just enough to see over the counter. There stood Jack Scurlock, just inside the door, holding the Colt at his hip and pointing it at Jesse's head. "I thank you kindly for collectin' him for me," Jack said.

Fred got to his feet and dusted off his trousers. "You're welcome, Marshal. Thank you for paying this here man's bill. I knew there was something fishy about—"

"Marshal?" Jesse bellowed. "He's not a—" He spied his badge clipped to Jack's shirt pocket, and knew he'd never convince the clerk. Where in hell had Jack found his badge? And what in hell was he planning to do with it?

He didn't have to wait long to find out.

"Come on out now," Jack said, "and let's mosey on down to the jailhouse. Sheriff's waitin' for you." He tossed a set of handcuffs to Fred.

Jesse did some fast thinking. Overpowering the clerk would be easy enough, but he'd probably get Fred killed in the process. And maybe himself, too. No, his only recourse was to cooperate for the moment and hope the sheriff would see through Jack's charade. Or maybe he could take the gun away from Jack on the way . . .

He stood up and held his hands out.

"Behind your back," Jack barked.

Forget taking the gun away.

Fred snapped the cuffs in place, and Jack motioned him toward the door with the gun. Anger boiled in Jesse's belly, and a sense of doom settled in his gut. This was one fine pickle he was in. But criminals, he reminded himself, were stupid. Sooner or later, Jack Scurlock would make a mistake. Hopefully sooner. There certainly wasn't much he could do right now with the barrel of the Colt pressed against his shoulder blade. He didn't even get the chance to taunt Scurlock, not with the sheriff's office just three doors away. The shingle read, "A. Nester, Sheriff."

A shriveled up, gray-headed man with a paunch awaited them. "So this is the notorious One-Eyed Jack," he drawled. "Never thought I'd get the chance to meet you— not alive, noways."

"I'm not Jack Scurlock," Jesse said, tossing his head backwards. "He is."

"One of his many tricks," Jack said, moving out to stand beside him. "He's tried this one before. You can see how the two of us favors. But who's wearin' the badge, I ask you, and who's wearin' the cuffs."

"I lost it," Jesse said. "Honestly, sheriff, I'm Jesse Redford. I've been a deputy U.S. marshal for over ten years. And I've been chasing this black-hearted murderer here for four of those. If you look real close at the poster, you'll see that it's him."

The man, whom Jesse assumed to be A. Nester, picked up a wanted poster from a pile of papers on his desk and gave it a cursory glance. "Looks just like his picture." Jesse expelled a long breath and started to relax—until he realized Nester was talking to Jack. "Lock him up."

"Wait a minute!" Jesse cried. "Won't you at least ask him some questions?"

Nester slipped a ring of keys off a nail and walked over to the office's lone cell. "You're the one ought to be questioned, not the marshal here. But we'll save that for the trial."

The barred door creaked open, and Scurlock shoved him toward the cell. "Ask him the name of the marshal he works under. I'll bet he can't tell you."

"Dan Whitcomb," Jack said.

Of course! When Jack found his badge, he found his papers, too. There probably wasn't one thing about him or his business that Jack Scurlock didn't know. The bastard was playing the part like a seasoned actor, but Jesse couldn't believe Scurlock was getting away with this. It just wasn't possible. Surely Nester could see—

"How can you be sure which one of us is telling the truth?" Jesse asked, beginning to feel truly desperate. "At least lock us both up until Marshal Whitcomb can come here and make a positive identification."

"And tie up a busy lawman for nought? I don't need no further convincin'." Nester closed the door and turned the key.

Chapter Twenty-three

Lilah awoke the next morning feeling wonderfully refreshed. She stretched and yawned, turned over on her stomach, and then flipped right back over and sat up. Where was she, she wondered, blinking at the sunlight pouring through dingy muslin curtains, and how had she gotten here?

A quick inspection revealed a small, sparsely furnished room. Her gaze slid right over the shafts of sunlight on the wall in front of her and settled on the haversack, deerskin pouch, and packages she'd brought with her from the swamp, which made a neat stack on the floor beside a mirrored washstand. And there, on the top of the washstand, were her comb and Paw's razor, the one she'd given to Jesse.

For a minute she'd forgotten about Jesse. Where was he, anyway? Had he brought her here? Was he coming back?

Lilah racked her brain, but for the life of her she couldn't remember anything beyond her and Jesse leaving the little house where she'd grown up. They were headed to Homerville. Was that where she was? Yes, that must be it. Though she had no recollection of arriving, she figured this must be a room in Aunt Agnes's big, fine house.

Strange thing, this not being able to remember. Had she been sick since then? That must be it. They were probably

real worried about her. She wondered what she'd had . . .
the new mon fever, most likely. It'd do that to you—send
you off in another world for a spell. She took a deep
breath and let it out. No problem with that, so it must've
been something else.

A soft breeze puffed out the curtains and made the sunlight flicker, drawing Lilah's attention back to the wall.
"Law, look at the flowers!" she said in fascination. Tossing the covers back and getting out of bed, she walked the
short distance to the wall and ran her palm over the blossoms, which were different from any she'd ever seen. Up
close, she could see that the large, colorful flowers had
been painted on some kind of heavy paper that was stuck
on the wall. She shook her head in amazement. From even
a short distance, they looked so real, she'd expected them
to have a scent.

Just to make sure, she touched her nose to the wall and
sniffed. Immediately, she sneezed. The flowers had a scent
all right, but it wasn't a very pleasant one.

"Eew! What a funk!" she sputtered, sneezing again and
going to the window for fresh air. Aunt Agnes wasn't a
very good housekeeper.

When Lilah parted the dusty curtains, the first thing she
saw was the glass. Maw had told her about window glass,
but she'd never seen it before. Her fingertips left long
streaks on the dirty pane, and through the streaks she saw
a very short woman walking by a building that had glass
in its windows, too. The dark blue fabric of the woman's
dress shimmered in the morning light, and her full skirts
dipped and swayed with every step. She walked under a
low overhang and practically disappeared.

Seeking a better view, Lilah sat down on her knees and
stuck her head out of the open space at the bottom of the
window—and found herself looking straight down on a
wide dirt path below. She gave a little squeak of terror,
and pulled her head back in so fast she bumped it against

the wooden frame that held the window glass. Was she in a tree house? she wondered. Was that why the woman had looked so short?

Very cautiously, she put her head back out the window and, holding on tight to the sill, looked down again. The wall appeared to go all the way to the ground, and there was another window beneath hers. In front of it was a sort of walkway made with short boards. No yard a-tall.

A bell tinkled, and a man walked out onto the dirt path and climbed onto the back of a four-legged animal the likes of which she'd never seen before. A horse, maybe?

"This must be a dream," she whispered, tucking her head back under the window glass and standing up. That was why she couldn't remember anything. Because she was having a dream. The cure for that, she supposed, was to go back to sleep. And when she woke up again, she'd be in the swamp, where she belonged.

She got back in the bed and unfolded the covers. Why, the sheets were whole pieces of cloth, not patched-together flour sacks like the ones she was used to. She snuggled under the covers, settled her head on the pillow, and closed her eyes. Amazing! Whole sheets, flowers on the walls, glass in the window, a room high enough to be in a tree, strange animals that allowed people to climb on their backs ... But why would her dream have dust in it? And funks? It didn't make sense ...

A sharp rap on the door snatched her out of her ruminations. Her eyes flew open, and she looked around the room. Since it hadn't changed, she figured she must still be dreaming. She closed her eyes again only to be disturbed by another knock. But this time, a voice rang out right behind it.

"Mrs. Redford! Are you in there?"

It was a man's voice and not even vaguely familiar. Where was Aunt Agnes, and why was this man calling her Miz Redford?

She went to the door and called through the panel. "Who is it?"

"Fred Martin."

She'd never heard of him, but then her memory wasn't so good right now, she reminded herself. "Who are ye?"

"Fred Martin. The desk clerk."

Desk clerk? What was a desk clerk? "What do ye want?"

"I need to talk to you, Mrs. Redford. May I come in?"

Lilah stepped back and looked hard at the door. It didn't have a bar or a rope latch, just a dull glass knob sticking out on one side with a little bitty hole beneath it. She put her eye on the hole, but she couldn't see anything through it. "I ain't a-stoppin' you."

Something poked itself into the hole from the other side. She jumped backwards, stepped on the too-long tail of her nightdress, and sat down hard on the floor. The glass knob turned, and the door creaked slowly open to reveal a pair of black shoes so shiny you could almost see yourself in 'em. Lilah's gaze traveled up a pair of brown checkedy britches legs, past a shiny gold chain that just hung in a short loop on one side of a trim waistline, across three shiny metal buttons on a funny-looking garment that didn't have any sleeves, and on up to a crisp white collar with a black ribbon tie at the neck. Above the tie, the man sported a rather prominent Adam's apple, a small, weak chin, thin lips, a long nose, and frowning brown eyes.

"Them sure is fancy-wearin' clothes, Mr. Martin," she said, picking herself up off the floor and dusting her backside. "Must be store-boughten."

The frown slowly faded, but Lilah wasn't sure she liked the smile that replaced it. Made her feel like she was being sized up for gator vittles.

"Are you all right, Mrs. Redford?"

"There ye go again, a-callin' me Miz Redford. How come ye to do that?"

"Why, your husband . . . that man who was with you . . . you aren't his wife, are you?"

Redford . . . was that Jesse's back name? Lilah couldn't remember. "I don' know. Mought be. My mind ain't quite right."

He nodded in a way that said he understood perfectly. "I don't think his name is really Redford, even if he does look like that other Mr. Redford, the one that hauled him off to jail. The whole thing smelled funny to me."

"Yeah, like this room," Lilah mumbled, but her mind was on other, far more important things. Like Jesse being in jail. Or was it Jesse doin' the haulin'? She frowned in confusion and plucked at the worn cotton nightdress. "Law! I ain't decent!" she cried.

Fred Martin's too-short face with the too-long nose turned bright red, and he looked away from her. "I just wanted to check on you," he said. "That man locked you in here last night, and I knew you didn't have a key. I only gave the man one key, and the sheriff brought it back to me this morning." He scrubbed his toe on a splinter sticking up from the plain wood floor and cleared his throat. "Your room's paid till this afternoon, miss. You'll either have to pay for tonight or clear out."

Her room was paid? What was he talking about? "Ye must work for Aunt Agnes."

"I have no earthly idea who your Aunt Agnes might be, Miz Redford, but I can assure you I don't work for her."

"Then, if this isn't her house . . . what is this place?"

He looked back at her with bulging eyes and a gaping jaw. "It's not a bawdy house, if that's what you're thinking."

"I wasn't thinkin' no sich a-thing! Course, I don't know what a bawdy house is, neither."

He didn't explain, just looked mighty discomfited and started to walk away. "If you need some help with your things, just let me know."

Lilah stuck her head out the door and watched him walk down a narrow passageway, then turn a corner. Across from her room, a door opened, and a gray-headed woman came out into the passageway.

"Was that man bothering you?" the woman asked. Her voice was firm but pleasant, and her dark eyes reminded Lilah of Granny's.

"Nay," Lilah said, "but I'm a mite discombobbled. Ye got time to set a spell?"

"I don't have anything else pressing, except breakfast. You hungry?"

"Hungry enough to eat a house," Lilah said, realizing suddenly how empty she was. She glanced back into her room. "But I don't see no way to cook nothin'."

The woman smiled. "You don't have to cook. They'll do that for us downstairs, in the restaurant."

"What's that?"

"What's a restaurant? Lord, child, where have you been all your life?"

"In the Okefinoke."

The woman nodded. "That explains it. No wonder you're a mite discombobbled." She took Lilah's hand and gave it a gentle squeeze. "I'm Mrs. Heywood."

"It pleasures me to make yer acquaintance, Miz Heywood. Lilah's my entitlement. I'd be beholden to you if'n ye mought answer me some questions."

"Why don't you get dressed, Lilah, and I'll answer all your questions over breakfast. Just knock on my door when you're ready."

Jesse jumped to his feet the instant he heard the key turn in the lock.

He'd spent a restless night, tossing and turning on the thin mattress, his mind on Lilah and his predicament rather than on the less than comfortable accommodations at the

Homerville jail. Perhaps without One-Eyed Jack around, he'd be able to talk some sense into A. Nester, Sheriff.

"Here's your breakfast." Nester balanced a napkin-covered tray on his left forearm, while he held the street door open with his right hand and used his toe to shove a wedge under the door.

"Smells good," Jesse said.

"They've got a good cook over to the hotel. Been eatin' most of my meals there since the wife passed on." He set the tray down on his desk, opened a drawer, and took out a pair of handcuffs.

"What are those for?"

"I ain't opening that door without cuffing you first. Redford says you're one dangerous criminal."

Jesse opened his mouth to argue, then changed his mind. Might be better to get his breakfast first. He turned his back and put his arms between the bars, then realized his mistake.

"You do that quite natural-like. I knew you was lying about being a U.S. marshal."

"*Deputy* U.S. marshal. And I wasn't lying. That's how I knew what you needed me to do." The cold steel hit his wrists and two quick clicks secured the cuffs.

"Sure. Sure. And I'm President Arthur."

"Is that what the *A* stands for?"

Nester set the tray on the bed. "The *A*? Oh, in my name? No, it's for Abednego—you know, the one who was with Daniel in the lion's den, along with Shadrach and Meshach. But I expect you don't know 'bout such things, you being a atheist and all."

"Where in the world did you get that idea?" The door closed and the cuffs came off. Jesse sat down on the bed, which was the only place to sit, and lifted the napkin off the tray to see a plate piled with fried eggs and grits swimming in butter, a thick slice of ham, and two huge biscuits on the side. Looking at the food and smelling its mouthwatering aromas made it hard to stay angry about the accusations.

Abednego Nester stuck a tin cup through the bars. "It's just water. I'll get the coffee going in a minute. Got to start a fire first."

"You're being awfully accommodating, considering the fact that I'm a dangerous criminal and an atheist to boot," Jesse said around a mouthful of grits.

"So! You're confessing!"

"That was not a confession of guilt."

"Sounded like it to me."

Obviously, Abednego Nester did not possess a sense of humor—and his other senses seemed to be a bit on the dull side, too. Reasoning with him was not going to be easy. Jesse split a biscuit with his fork and filled it with some of the ham, then considered his next words carefully while he chewed a good-sized bite. He ought to tell the sheriff about Lilah. In her present state, she needed someone to take care of her, but Jesse couldn't quite see Nester taking the part of comforting guardian. And if Nester talked to Lilah now, he'd never believe anything she said later.

If Lilah could only corroborate his story . . . *What a callous, self-serving thought!* he fussed. She needed him far worse than he needed her.

"How long have you been sheriff here?"

"Nigh on to twenty years now."

"And how many prisoners have you had in those twenty years?"

Nester scratched his chin. "Let me see now. Eight—no nine, counting you."

"That many?" Jesse said, trying to keep the sarcasm out of his voice. "Have you ever had a marshal bring in a prisoner and then just leave without giving you any instructions at all?"

"Hadn't ever had a marshal bring in a prisoner before now."

Scratch that line of attack. "Doesn't it strike you just the least bit odd that Jack Scurlock and I look so much alike?"

"Not a bit, seeing as how you *are* Jack Scurlock."

Damn, the man was frustrating! "That's not what I meant to imply. I am *not* Jack Scurlock! I am Jesse Redford, deputy U.S.—"

"Marshal. You keep saying that."

"Because it's the truth. Have you wired Dan Whitcomb yet?"

"Nope. Why should I?"

"Why should you, indeed," Jesse muttered, stabbing an egg and wishing he hadn't stepped so blithely into One-Eyed Jack's trap. This was one helluva mess he'd gotten himself into, and he couldn't see a clear way out. Not without Lilah's help. And the possibility of that right now was bleak.

Lilah pushed a biscuit crumb around on her plate with the tine of her fork, and thought about all the things Miz Heywood had just told her. She knew now that she really was in Homerville, and that this big ol' fine building was a hotel. Miz Heywood explained about hotels and said this one was small, as hotels go, which amazed Lilah, who hadn't ever been in a building so large before. Miz Heywood said it wasn't all that fine, either, and regaled her with descriptions of the Tutwiler in a place called Birmingham, and the Partridge Inn in a place called Augusta.

These places weren't so very far away, according to Miz Heywood, not when you got on something called a train and let it take you there. Miz Heywood said she was a widder-woman whose husband had left her a small fortune in railroad stock, and since she had family and friends scattered to the four winds and liked to travel, that's what she did with her life. She didn't know anyone in Homerville, though. She was just stopping over for a spell of peace and quiet, before she moved on to Macon to see her niece. Now, the hotel in Macon . . .

It was all rather mind-boggling to Lilah, who only wanted to know a few basic things before she went looking for Jesse, but she had a time getting her questions in betwixt Miz Heywood's rambling account.

"What'd that Mr. Martin mean when he said I had to pay or clear out?"

"You do have to pay for your room, dear," Mrs. Heywood said, stirring short-sweetin' into her tea. "How did you manage to stay last night—" The talkative though kindly woman paused long enough to give Lilah a long, piercing look. "You were the girl with that man last night, the one-eyed man who paid for the room with a gun. Fred didn't think I saw that. But you were all . . . how can I say it? Well, obviously you've had a bath since then. And thank goodness you lost that vacant look. I haven't ever seen anyone look quite so . . . so empty."

Lilah thought Miz Heywood's details ought to spark a memory of last night, but they didn't. "There's some of Granny's penetrates in the haversack and maybe a jar of blackberries. Can I use them things to pay for my room?"

"Oh, no, dear. It has to be cold, hard cash. I was real surprised Fred let your man get by with leaving the gun as collateral, even if it was worth more than the room." Frowning, she sipped her tea, then smiled, like she was plumb proud of herself about something, though Lilah couldn't imagine what. "The one-eyed man who brought you here—where is he?"

Lilah chewed her lip, trying to decide how much she should tell Miz Heywood, then realized the widder-woman had probably overheard everything Fred Martin said that morning. "I think he's in jail." She pushed back her chair. "And I reckon I oughter go see. He mought need me."

Mrs. Heywood laid a restraining hand on Lilah's forearm. "Wait a minute, and I'll go with you. A jailhouse is no proper place for a young lady to be going by herself. Just sit back down. I want to finish my tea first—and I've got a proposition for you."

"A propo-what?"

"An idea of how you can earn your keep around here. Have you noticed how dirty this place is?"

"Oh, yes, ma'am! It's so dirty it stinks. I took a whiff of them flowers on my wall, and they smelt plumb funksomey."

Mrs. Heywood came all around choking on a swallow of tea. She pressed her napkin against her mouth until her coughing subsided, then wiped tears from the corners of her eyes with her fingertips.

"Ye goin' to be all right, Miz Heywood? Can I get you some water? My Jesse chokes on tea sometimes, and water seems to holp."

The woman waved a hand in dismissal. "No, I'm fine. It just went down the wrong way." She took a deep breath and let it out in a whoosh. "I was thinking you might offer your services to Fred Martin."

"Offer my services?"

"Cleaning services. As a maid. This hotel could use one."

"Oh, yes, ma'am! I could do that."

"And in return, ask for room and board, plus a small salary. Every woman should have some pin money."

Lilah was horrified. This sounded like something that required a much closer relationship with Mr. Martin than she was willing to allow. "Oh, but I don' want to marry Mr. Martin. I *can't* marry him."

"You don't have to marry him. Just work for him." She opened her purse and laid some coins on the table. At Lilah's questioning gaze, Mrs. Heywood said, "To pay for breakfast. My treat." She stood up, so Lilah did, too. "Let me talk to Fred for you. But first, let's go see your man. What did you call him?"

"Jesse."

Lilah followed Mrs. Heywood down the street a short way to a squatty red brick building with bars in the windows. "They keep critters in here?" she asked, as they started through the open doorway.

Mrs. Heywood laughed. "I suppose you could call them that. Some of them, anyway."

"Lilah!"

His voice rang like the sweetest music in Lilah's ears. She turned toward the sound and cried in anguish at seeing him in a cage. In a flash, she scooted around Mrs. Heywood and ran to the wall of bars.

"Jesse! How come ye're standing back there? Come on out'n there."

"I can't, Lilah. I'm locked in."

She pulled on the door, but it wouldn't budge, so she reached between the bars, took one of Jesse's hands, and brought his palm to her lips.

"Now, now, miss. I'll have none of that in my jail."

"Oh, hush up, sheriff," Mrs. Heywood said. "The young woman isn't hurting a thing."

"This is a jail?" Lilah asked, knowing that it was—now that she'd seen it—and feeling awful about not coming to see him sooner. "When Mr. Martin told me . . . I didn't know . . ."

"It's all right," Jesse said, smoothing his hand over her hair. "How are you?"

Something told her he wasn't exactly asking about her health. "I don' know."

"Do you remember?" he whispered, bending his head close to her face.

She shook her head.

"I suppose it's just as well. Can you tell the sheriff who I am?"

"The sheriff? That man's the high sheriff?"

He smiled and her heart melted. "Please tell him, Lilah."

She turned around and almost bumped into the short, balding man wearing a star like the one she'd thought Jesse ought to have. "This here's Jesse. He's a marshal."

The man nodded. "How do you know?"

" 'Cause he told me."

"You ever seen his badge?"

"No-o-o."

"Seen him with any official-looking papers?"

"No."

"You want me to take your word for it? To believe he's Jesse Redford, because you say he told you so?"

Like flashes of summer lightning, Lilah thought about telling Jesse that all marshals had them stars, that marshals was supposed to have both their eyes. She hadn't believed it at first, might not believe it now if she hadn't spent so much time with him, if she hadn't come to know him so well. But how was she ever going to convince the high sheriff?

Chapter Twenty-four

"But I've met One-Eyed Jack," Lilah said, certain-sure that would convince him.

"Oh, and what does he look like?" the high sheriff asked.

"He's a big man. Real tall. Dark hair and beard. And he has onliest one eye. That's why they call him One-Eyed Jack."

The sheriff pursed his lips and nodded. "Now take a good look at the man there in the cell. What does he look like?"

"I don' have to look at Jesse to tell you. First time I seed him, I said to myself, 'That there's the biggest man I ever seed.' A moccasin'd got him and he was out'n his head. Kep' callin' me 'angel.' "

"Hush, Lilah," Jesse hissed in her ear.

The high sheriff must have heard him. "No, let her talk," he said, smiling almost evil-like.

She thought back over what she'd just said and realized she wasn't making Jesse sound too smart. "Well, he was sick, ye know, and didn't know who he—" She caught herself and took off down another trail. "Anyhow, whilst he was sick, some of the swampfolks come by and tol' us they was some outlaws on the loose and a marshal was a-chasin' 'em. When Jesse here got straight, he tol' me he was the marshal."

"And you believed him?"

"Not at first, but later—"

"And these swampfolks that came by. Did they know the marshal had been snakebit?"

"Naw. They thought he was still out in the swamp, a-lookin' for them outlaws."

"Why didn't you tell them about the marshal?"

"Swampfolks is mighty s'picious. Granny and I was worried they'd think Jesse here was one a them outlaws."

The sheriff grinned again. "But you knew he was the marshal."

"Well, I wasn't certain-sure. I mean, he hadn't tol' me yet."

"And when he did tell you, you just believed every word he said. You didn't question any of it."

Lilah didn't like the path the sheriff's questions were leading her down, but she wasn't sure what to do about changing directions. "I sorta had my doubts, I reckon, but that all changed when I got to know him. And then I ran into One-Eyed Jack," she hastily added, "and I knew he was one of them outlaws. Him and Red. I come upon their camp, ye see, and Jack tol' Red to get me."

"Probably thought you was an accomplice."

"A what?"

"A cohort. A fellow in crime."

"Naw. 'Tweren't that way a-tall! Let me explain—"

The high sheriff shook his head sadly. "You've done enough explaining, young lady. There's enough holes in your story to start a doughnut factory. You can tell it all to the judge, when the trial comes up."

Lilah set the mop bucket in the pantry, straightened up, and rubbed the small of her back. She couldn't recall ever being so stiff and sore—or ever wanting a bath quite as much as she did at that moment. But first, she had to sit down and rest a spell—and admire her handiwork.

As she cast her gaze around the kitchen, she subconsciously stroked the waxed finish on the top of the heavy oak table, her fingertips tracing one of the many deep scars imbedded in the wood. With supreme satisfaction, she noted the warm glow of the lamp bouncing off the painted walls and cupboard doors and its clear reflection on the window glass. Scrubbing the black soot off of virtually every surface in the kitchen had proved a monumental task. The only things she didn't have to clean were the cooking utensils, which made her feel far more kindly toward the cook, an aging dark-skinned woman who went by the entitlement Aunt Susie.

Lilah couldn't find it in her heart to be too harsh on Aunt Susie. Besides not having any help in the kitchen, she was all crippled up with rheumatism. And she'd been a wonderful help to Lilah, showing her where the cleaning supplies were kept, teaching her how to use the cookstove, and answering her questions. Lilah, who'd never seen a person of color before, was fascinated with the coffee brown hue of Aunt Susie's skin, and the whiteness of her teeth. She couldn't wait to see the look on the cook's face when she saw her spotless kitchen come mornin' soon.

Thinking about the mountain of work awaiting her at daybust brought Lilah out of her chair and back into action. She dragged a big washtub out of the pantry, filled it with hot water from the stove's reservoir, replaced the water as Aunt Susie had instructed—"Else the stove'll burn slapdab up," she'd said—and stripped down to her skin.

She got in the tub, laid her head on a chair seat, and let the warm water perform its miracle, easing her aching muscles and relaxing her so much she thought she could go to sleep right then and there and not care who came in and found her. She wished the water could ease her heart and relax her worries as easily—but that would require a solution to Jesse's problem. He was in a fix, stuck in that horrible jail behind the heavy black bars with that ignert high sheriff refusing to listen to plain talk.

She'd slipped out the back door and gone down to see Jesse while Sheriff Nester was eating his supper at the hotel. Aunt Susie had told her the sheriff ate most of his meals there, and that she'd keep watch out for him for Lilah. "He gen'ly takes his time eatin' and visitin', but you doan want him to catch you there by your lonesome, so hurry back!" the cook warned.

Jesse kissed her through the bars. It was a light kiss, barely more than a simple brushing of lips, but it spoke of his hunger—both for her and for his freedom. Lilah took his hand and pressed it against her heart.

"I wish I could get you out'n here."

"You could. The key's hanging right over there, on that nail."

She swallowed a yelp and started to break away from him, but he stopped her. "That would make me look like the real One-Eyed Jack for sure," he said, "and it would make you a criminal—an accomplice. I think old Nester was hoping I'd break out. I caught him eyeing that ring real hard just before he left."

"Why would he want you to break out?"

"I don't know. Maybe he thinks I'm telling the truth, but he's afraid to believe me. At least he finally decided to wire Dan Whitcomb, if for no other reason than he doesn't know what to do with me now that the 'arresting officer' has disappeared. You remember I told you that Dan's my boss. Once he gets here, I'll be out in two shakes of a lamb's tail. Maybe Jack won't have gotten too far by that time."

Lilah didn't want to think about Jesse going after One-Eyed Jack the minute he was free, but she knew he would. She didn't know much about lawmen, but she couldn't understand why another deputy marshal couldn't take up the trail. "How come *ye* have to be the one to ketch him?"

Jesse turned away from her then and walked to the shadows at the back of the cell. His hands curled into fists, and his voice was tight. "Because he killed Martha and the boys! I vowed then to catch the bastard and bring him to justice, if it was the last thing I did."

Slowly, he pivoted back around, and the slanting light from the barred window fell over his face. His expression frightened her. It was the bloodthirstiest look she'd ever seen, and it made her skin crawl. In that moment, he resembled Jack Scurlock so closely that she questioned his true identity.

"It was horrible, Lilah," he said too quietly, too calmly. "He slit their throats and cut off their hands, just like he—"

She didn't know what else he'd said. She hadn't stayed around to listen. She stopped long enough in the alley behind the jailhouse to lose her supper, and then she fled back to the hotel like one chased by demons. Ever since then, she'd had the strangest feeling that she'd witnessed the heinous crime right along with Jesse.

Lilah wiped at the tears streaming down her face and shivered. The water had grown cold, and her body demanded sleep. Quickly, she washed away the grime, emptied the washtub, and put her dirty clothes back on. On feet as silent as Bob's, she slipped upstairs and into her room.

Jesse scratched the stubble on his chin and wondered why Lilah hadn't came with the razor. Nester had been gone almost ten minutes already. If she didn't get there pretty soon, he could forget shaving today.

"I don't know why that man won't trust me with a razor," Jesse had complained. "Says I might decide to slash my throat or my wrists or something. I reminded him that I could just as easily hang myself with my belt or a bedsheet. I think it's just his way of showing me he's in control."

Lilah paled at his words, but at least she didn't run away like she had a couple of nights ago, when he'd told her how Jack had killed Martha. He'd fussed at himself countless times since, about how insensitive he'd been, but the words were out of his mouth before he stopped to think about them. And now he'd gone and been insensitive again.

"I'm not going to commit suicide, Lilah," he assured her. "If I were, I would have done it a long time ago."

She'd promised to bring everything required for shaving while the sheriff was eating supper, but if she didn't come soon . . .

The alley door banged.

"Sorry I'm late," Lilah wheezed. Her face was flushed and beads of perspiration dotted her forehead. "Mr. Martin stopped me in the hall, and I couldn't get away."

She carried a kettle and a pan; she set them on the floor and withdrew the razor, a small towel, and a bar of soap from her apron pocket. When she poured hot water from the kettle into the pan, her hand shook so that water splashed onto the floor.

"Slow down, Lilah. You'll burn yourself."

She set a chair in front of the bars, put the pan on its seat, then took a small mirror off the wall beside Nester's desk and propped it against the back of the chair. Sighing, she sat down on the floor next to the chair and watched him shave. Jesse expected it was the first time she'd stopped to rest all day.

"You're working too hard, Lilah," he said, squatting close to the bars in front of the chair and soaping his face. "You're letting Martin take advantage of you."

She skirted the issue. "It'll be easier onct all the rooms is clean."

"Does Martin do anything anymore?"

"He changes the bed linen ever onct in a while, and sweeps the lobby of an evening."

Jesse stretched his chin up and pulled the razor up his neck, saving his comments for the times he rinsed the razor. The last thing he needed was a nick to bleed, and make Nester realize his prisoner had defied him. Old Abednego was bound to figure it out eventually, but there was no reason to take unnecessary chances. Shaving was about the only luxury left to him.

"That's probably about all he was doing before."

"How do ye like Aunt Susie's cooking?"

"Fine."

"She's teaching me to make fried pies."

"That's good."

"Jesse, I . . . I fount something in the hotel room that I don' understand."

He scraped the razor down his cheek. "What was that?"

"A pot plumb full of ashes."

He dropped the razor in the pan. "You didn't throw them out, did you?"

"No, but . . ."

"Trust me, Lilah. Those ashes are important. Just leave them where they are."

"How come?"

"One day soon, you'll understand. And you'll thank me." He fished the razor out of the soapy water and went back to shaving.

Two more swipes and he was done. He scrubbed his face with the wet towel, then scrutinized his reflection through the bars, turning his face from side to side until he was satisfied that he hadn't missed a spot. When he looked at himself straight on, he realized how confused Nester must be. Damn, if he didn't look just like Jack Scurlock without a beard! He'd always known they favored each other, but he'd never noticed before how much.

"Lilah! Bring me the poster. The one with Scurlock's picture on it. It's somewhere there on Nester's desk."

She scurried to do his bidding, rifling through papers scattered all over the sheriff's desk, then snatching one up.

"Hold it there, beside the mirror."

The resemblance was there, but something was wrong.

"Hand it here, Lilah. Now, hold the mirror up sideways." He stuck the edge of the poster against his cheek—and frowned. "I wish you could see this."

"What?"

"This sketch looks more like me than it does Jack Scurlock."

"Oh." In the one little word he heard uncertainty—and sudden fear.

"You know I'm not Scurlock, Lilah. The artist just got it wrong, that's all. Have you ever noticed how one side of your face is a little different from the other?"

"No."

"Well, it is. Just a little bit. And when you look in the mirror, you're seeing your face backwards from the way everyone else sees it. You don't think about that. I've never stopped to think about it before, but Scurlock's left eye is gone—"

"And yers is the right."

"Precisely." He handed her the poster. "The artist drew Jack's face backwards. Look at it. The patch is on the right eye, but the description very plainly states that Jack's left eye is missing. I'll bet no one ever sewed his lid shut, either. But I don't dare point the discrepancies out to Nester. He'd see them as proof positive that I *am* Scurlock, and probably form a lynching party without waiting to hear from Dan."

Three more days passed before Dan Whitcomb's response arrived via telegraph. In the interim, Jesse chafed at being stuck in Homerville while Jack's trail got colder and

colder, and every time he tried to reason with Nester, he
ended up more frustrated than he'd been before.

Though Lilah visited him every day, she seemed to
grow increasingly distant, which bothered Jesse almost as
much as being in jail. Their conversations centered on the
hotel and the weather and speculation about when Dan
Whitcomb would answer the telegram; and then, once he
had, they talked about how long it would take him to get
to Homerville from Knoxville. Within a week, Jesse assured her, and then he'd be free to renew his pursuit, but
as each day passed, she showed less and less interest in
Marshal Whitcomb's arrival.

"When this is all over, things will be different," he told
her.

"When will that be, Jesse?"

"You know I can't answer that. You've seen how slippery Scurlock can be. But I'm not giving up. I was this
close to having him!" He held up his thumb and forefinger
with only a small space between them.

A cloud moved over her face, and she told him she had
to go back to work.

Jesse wished he could promise her he'd be back soon,
but hell, he couldn't even promise her that he'd be back at
all. He thought she'd understand, even encourage him to
get One-Eyed Jack, after what the bastard did to Ol'
Codger.

That was the one thing they didn't talk about. Jesse was
afraid to broach the subject, lest she lapse back into sleep-
walking, which was the only thing he knew to call her
state of mind following the bear's death. If and when that
happened, she'd need him. So far, she'd given no indication that she remembered. Perhaps it was best that a part
of her blocked the memory.

But one day, she would remember. And he probably
wouldn't be there for her when she did. He'd be off chas-

ing Jack Scurlock and she'd be all alone with her grief . . . just like Martha was all alone when Scurlock—

Why did things have to be this way? Why did people like One-Eyed Jack exist? Why couldn't everyone be kind and decent and caring?

A low growl started in his gut and became a keening moan. Jesse grabbed the bars and yanked hard enough to rattle the mirror on the wall fifteen feet away, but there was no one but him to hear.

Lilah had been studying on going to visit Aunt Agnes ever since she'd found out for sure that she was in Homerville. First one thing and then another got in her way—going to see Jesse, working at the hotel, taking cooking lessons from Aunt Susie, talking to Miz Heywood every time she got the chance—and such things as eating and sleeping and trying to stay clean and smelling good when it was as hot as blazes.

"You doan look so good," Aunt Susie told her one day. "Thin as a pine tree saplin', and pale as a haint. You ain't stopped workin' since you got started. You needs a day off, chile."

"Maybe this wasn't such a good idea I had," Miz Heywood said that evening at supper. She'd started taking most of her meals in the kitchen with Lilah.

"How come?" Lilah asked between bites.

"You're working too hard, that's how come. I'm going to speak to Fred Martin about it."

"Oh, no. Please don' do that. He mought—" She frowned, searching for the word.

"Fire you? I don't think so. Hiring you was one of the best things he ever did, and he knows it."

"He shore do," Susie chimed in, "but that slave driver ain't never gonna say so." She slapped a mound of mashed potatoes on a plate and added a slice of roast beef. "I been tryin' to tell her, Miz Heywood, but she won' listen to me."

"You've got this place clean as a whistle, Lilah. It's time you took a break."

"But I still have three rooms on the third floor—"

"They'll wait."

Lilah got her day off. She pampered herself by sleeping until full light, eating a leisurely breakfast in the dining room with Miz Heywood, and washing her hair with real soap. While her hair dried, she hemmed Maw's best dress—a pale lilac calico with big puffed sleeves and a bit of narrow lace on the collar—and took it in at the waist. Her stitching wasn't as neat as Granny's or Maw's, but it would have to do.

When she was dressed, she twisted and turned, squatted and stretched in front of the mirror on the washstand, try-ing to get a good view of how she looked, but that was impossible with such a tiny mirror. With a flash of inspi-ration, she stood on the bed, which at least allowed her to see the bottom of the full skirt. Delighted at the way it swirled around her ankles, she giggled and kicked out the new hem—and her laughter abruptly ceased.

Shoes! How had she forgotten about shoes? She didn't own a single pair. She couldn't let Aunt Agnes see her without shoes. How much did they cost? she wondered, suddenly glad Miz Heywood had insisted she ask for pin money. She hoped she had enough.

"What'll it take to buy them strappy shoes?" Lilah asked the man who'd been following her around ever since she'd entered the store across the street from the ho-tel. She reckoned he liked smelling her clean hair. "The yaller ones."

He puffed out his thin chest, then let his breath out in a sharp whistle. "Those sandals came all the way from New York. They cost a pretty penny."

Lilah smiled and opened her work-reddened hand. "I got myself six purty pennies here. I reckon I can part with one of 'em."

The man's mouth fell open and his eyes bugged.

"I see ye thank they's purty, too." She smoothed a caressing finger over one of the coins. "Ain't that a purty hawk? I been a-studyin' on how they carved it into this here metal." She flipped the coin over. "And see, there's a diffrunt carvin' on t'other side. It must take 'em a long time to make the pennies so purty. No wonder they's so valu'ble. I worked real hard over to the hotel to earn me these here pennies. A penny a day, that's what Mr. Martin's a-givin' me to housekeep. It pleasures me to know how much they'll trade for. Makes me thank a mite better of Mr. Martin."

The man cleared his throat and cast his gaze on the shoes she liked, the ones he called sandals. Lilah didn't care what entitlement he gave them; she just knew she liked them. She especially liked the way the back came up and a shaft came down. Why, they'd lift her heels right up off the ground, like she was on her tippy-toes.

The store man must not like them, though, 'cause his eyebrows was all pinched up. Or maybe he was just thinking about something that took a heap of figuring. "That's an eagle," he said in a soft, helpful tone, "not a hawk. And they don't carve coins, they mint them."

She didn't have the slightest clue as to what he was talking about, but she didn't want to look any more ignert than she already did by asking him, especially when he was concentrating so hard on whatever it was he was trying to figure out. Suddenly, his frown swayzed and an almost-smile teased a bit of glitter into his eyes. He scooped up the strappy yellow shoes and carried them to the counter.

"You're going to need some stockings to wear with them. Do you have a pair?"

"Oh, I don' want to spoil 'em with socks."

"Not socks. Stockings." He reached behind the counter and pulled a shallow box off a shelf. Inside was some thin, light brown paper that was folded over itself. The paper crackled when the man opened it out, and nestled in the paper was the sheerest pair of socks Lilah had ever seen.

"Why, them socks is skin-colored!"

"Yes, ma'am." He grinned. His eyes were really twinkling now. Lilah was glad he'd gotten over whatever it was that was bothering him.

"These is what ye're s'posed to wear with sandal-shoes?"

"Yes, ma'am." Two spots of color appeared on his cheeks, and his gaze dropped to the counter. "Do you, uh—" He coughed. "Do you have garters?"

His voice was so low Lilah wasn't sure she heard him correctly. Garters . . . sounded like some kind of disease to her. She checked her lower arms and the back of her hands for spots, but didn't see any. Maybe he was talking about snakes. "Garters?" she echoed.

"Sh-h-h!" he cautioned, glancing around the store at the other customers and continuing to whisper. "Obviously, you don't."

He pulled another, much larger box off a different shelf and tipped up the end closest to him, taking care not to tip it very high or slide it very far back. It was snakes for sure, except she couldn't think of a single reason she needed snakes—or why he'd be whispering about them. He thrust his hand inside and came out with two black lacy rings about as big around as a quart Mason jar lid. They did sort of resemble snakes, but Lilah still wondered if garters wasn't some kind of sickness, 'cause of the way he had been so secretive about asking her.

"To hold your stockings up."

Lilah stared at the circles of lace. They looked . . . well, they looked downright wicked. No wonder he whispered!

She opened her hand and looked at the six pretty coins. Suddenly, she didn't care how many of her pennies it took to trade for the stockings and the lacy things to hold them up. She wanted them. "How much?"

Scratching his head through thinning brown hair, the man looked at the pennies and then at each of the items spread out on the counter. His face paled, and he took a deep breath. Maybe *he* had the garters.

"Four," he said, his voice sounding as sick as he looked.

Lilah slowly counted out the coins, making a neat stack of them on the counter. As soon as she was done, he snatched them up and punched down one of the many colored buttons on a big wooden box with a sloped front. Then he pulled a handle on the side down. A bell went *ding* and a drawer slid up.

Lilah gasped in delight and leaned as far forward over the counter as she could in order to get a better look at the contents of the drawer. "Why, it's plumb full of purty coins!"

Nodding, he pushed the drawer closed, then moved down to the end of the counter where a big roll of brown paper rested in a heavy iron bracket and a spool of twine sat on a spindle. In short order, he made a neat package of her purchases.

"I'm much obleeged to you for all yer holp," she said.

"You're quite welcome, Miss—"

"Lilah," she supplied.

"Pleased to know you, Miss Lilah. I'm Leonard Stokes. I own this store."

It was sorta strange, she thought, the way he'd spent all that time helping her, then waited till she was leaving before he introduced himself. In the swamp, that would have been the first order of business. But people in this town were just generally strange. She reckoned that was why swampfolks called 'em strangers.

She hurried back to her room, washed her feet, and took

the stockings out of the box. They fell almost to the floor.
It surely was hot to be wearing such long socks, but she
reckoned Mr. Stokes knew better than she did what womenfolk wore with sandal-shoes, even in the summertime.
Still, covering up her feet and legs with the stockings
seemed to defeat the purpose of wearing airish shoes.

Shrugging, Lilah sat down on the bed and put one foot
into a stocking. She couldn't wait for Jesse to see her in
her new stockings and shoes and those wicked-looking
black things.

As soon as she got the stocking on, she stood up. It fell
right back down, puddling around her ankle. No wonder
Mr. Stokes said she needed the black things. Lilah sat
down again, pulled the stockings back up over her knee,
and stuck an elbow down to hold it to her thigh while she
slipped one of the lacy things over her foot and then her
ankle. There was no way, she suddenly realized, that the
black thing was going to fit around her thigh. It simple
wasn't big enough. She wasn't even sure she could get it
past her calf. She gave it a little tug anyway.

Law, if it didn't stretch! Lilah let go of it and picked up
the other one. She held it with both hands and pulled, then
let one side of it go. It popped right back. Giggling, she
stretched it out again, then set it aside and wiggled the
other one on up her leg to the top of the stocking. When
she had both stockings on and secure, she stood up on the
bed, held her skirt and petticoat up, and admired her
stocking-covered legs in the mirror. The stockings made
her feel so pretty—and the black lacy things made her feel
so . . . so womanish. She pranced around on the bed, kicking her feet out and watching the light shimmer off the
stockings.

And then she remembered the sandal-shoes.

She plopped down on the mattress, picked up one of the
strappy shoes, and looked at it really good for the first
time. The leather looked scaly, like it had come off a

snake. A series of narrow leather straps came out of each side, crisscrossed in the middle, and went into the other side, while a thicker piece at the back supported one long piece of yellow leather. A tiny gold buckle held the ends together to form a circle. The circle, she decided, must go around her ankle.

With both shoes on, she set her feet on the floor and stood up, then fell back against the bed. She tried again, this time taking extra care to balance herself on the high heels. Slowly, she moved around the room, listening to the heels click against the wood floor while she worked at walking without wobbling too bad.

If she was going to be a lady, she supposed she better get used to such things as stockings and high heels. So far, it was fun. And she was sure Aunt Agnes would be quite helpful. Maybe she could move in with her aunt and start lessons right away.

But first, she had to pay her a visit. And she reckoned she'd better get going, if she wanted to find her aunt's house in time for the noon meal.

Chapter Twenty-five

Lilah walked the full length of Mulberry Street three times without seeing one fine house. There were a few fairly large houses, but they were on the godown side of fine. Perhaps Aunt Agnes had moved. Shucks, she might not even live in Homerville anymore. After all, a dozen or so years had passed since Lilah had last seen her maw's only sister, and there had been no direct communication between them since. She'd sent word of her parents' deaths by way of some turpentiners from Homerville, but she couldn't be sure her aunt had been on the receiving end of that news.

Nor could she be sure that she was on the right street. Maybe that was the problem.

She'd gone straight to the jailhouse when she left the hotel, aiming to show Jesse her new sandal-shoes, stockings, and the stretchy black things—and to tell him she was going to her aunt's house for the afternoon and might even stay for supper. But when she passed the window, she saw the high sheriff sitting at his desk, jawing with a man whose head was as bald as a newborn babe's and so shiny it looked like he oiled it. Reluctant even to talk to Jesse with the high sheriff around, she wobbled right on past. She'd just have to refuse—politely, of course—Aunt

Agnes's invite to stay for supper, else Jesse would be worried about her.

She crossed a street, teetered by several buildings with signs on them she couldn't read, and crossed another street before she realized she didn't have the slightest notion where Mulberry Street was. The street she was on ended right in front of her. Facing the end was a pretty little white building with a tower in front. Lilah stopped walking and looked up at the tower, which had a pointy roof and a bell inside. Suddenly the bell started swaying, and a clear, melodious ring filled the air.

When the bell stopped ringing, a tall, thin man dressed in black came out of the building. He was wearing a round black hat and a stiff white collar so tight he looked like he was about to choke, but his step was spry and his face wasn't the least bit red, so he must be all right. He opened the gate at the end of a brick path and walked toward her.

"Good morning, miss," he said, tipping his hat.

"Good mornin', mister," she returned, wondering how she was supposed to return his courtesy, since she wasn't wearing a hat. She made a mental note to go back to the store and trade another purty penny or two for one. "Can ye tell me where I mought find Mulberry Street?"

"Of course." He pointed down the street, back toward the hotel. Lila turned to see what he was pointing at. "Go back up there to the livery and turn right. Then go—" he paused and counted on his fingers, touching three of them, then folding his counting hand around them, "three blocks and there you'll be."

People kept using words she'd never heard before. In the week she'd been in Homerville, she figured she'd added a hunerd or so to her word-stock, most of 'em without having a clear idea of their meanings. This time, she had to ask, even if it risked sounding ignert. "Liv'ry?"

"That big barn over there on the right."

At least she knew what a barn was. She knew what a

block was, too, but she couldn't imagine using a block of wood to mark distance, nor had she noticed a block anywhere. She must not know where to look. This man seemed real nice. Maybe he wouldn't laugh at her if she asked one more question.

"Where do ye stick the blocks?"

He frowned at that. "Stick the blocks? Why, we don't stick them anywhere." His teeth raked his bottom lip, and his chest jiggled like he was laughing inside. Lilah felt her face grow red.

"Thankee kindly for yer holp. I'll find it." She took two unsteady steps toward the barn, then stopped when he called to her.

"You're not from around here, are you?" The kindness was back in his voice.

"Nay."

"Well, then, there was no way for you to know. And here I am being rude to a newcomer. Please accept my apology. I'm Reverend Sawyer."

There he went, too, introducing himself at the back side of a conversation. Lilah wasn't sure she'd ever get used to the way folks here did things. "It's a pleasurement to know yer name," she said. "I like yer front name. I don't thank I ever heared it before."

"My front name? You mean 'Reverend'? Yes, well . . ." He cleared his throat, and she thought he was probably trying not to laugh again. What had she said this time that was so funny? Before she could ask him, he started talking again. "A block is what we in Homerville call the distance between cross-streets. When you get to the third street, that's Mulberry. Do you think you can find it now?"

She nodded. "I'm much obleeged."

"You know someone who lives on Mulberry Street?"

"Aunt Agnes."

"Agnes . . . on Mulberry Street." He pulled on one ear. "Agnes Summerville?"

"Seems like that's her back name."

"Well, good luck to you." The way he said it made her wonder if he wished her luck in finding the street or luck with Aunt Agnes, but she'd wasted enough time talking already. They were liable to be eating the noon meal now, and the hunger bug was biting her.

Following Reverend Sawyer's directions, she turned at the barn he called a livery and counted one-two-three streets. Up and down the third one she'd wobbled in the yellow sandal-shoes, from one end to the other, looking for the big fine house and not finding it. And there wasn't a body in sight to ask, neither. She could feel the sunball, which was directly overhead now, blistering her face and neck, and the straps on her shoes were rubbing blisters on her tired feet. Her feet hurt so bad she could barely walk; twice her ankles gave way and she rebalanced herself just in time to keep from falling. She reckoned she might as well give up and go on back to the hotel.

She was almost back to the street that went by the livery when she heard a whoop and a holler. A boy of no more'n six darted around a house. Right behind him ran another, much larger boy. The little one threw his arms around the trunk of an oak and yelled, "Safe!" That started a fuss, but when the older boy spied her standing in the street, he heshed up real fast and ambled toward her. He was wearing overalls without a shirt and his bare feet were dirty.

"You lookin' fer somebody?" he asked.

"My Aunt Agnes. Summerville's the back name, I thank."

"They live right there." He pointed to the house across the street.

"But that house ain't—" Lilah clamped her mouth shut. There wasn't no point in hurting the boy's feelings. The folks who lived in the ramshackle house might be his kin. She didn't think they could possibly be hers. "Thankee."

"You know old lady Summerville?"

It was the younger boy, who'd walked right up beside the bigger one. There was something about this one's round face, golden-colored eyes, and spiky reddish hair that reminded her of someone she knew.

"If she's my aunt, I do."

"Cain't be no kin of you'n. Why, she's meaner'n a—"

"Hush up, Wyatt." The older boy narrowed his eyes at the youngster, daring him to say anything else. To Lilah, he said, "You be careful now, you hear?"

The boys dropped back to the big oak tree and watched her from its shade.

First Mr. Sawyer and now the boy, she thought as she made her way across the littered yard. Both of 'em knew the woman named Agnes Summerville—and neither of them liked her. As best Lilah remembered, she hadn't liked Aunt Agnes very much herself.

A young woman toting a baby on her hip came to the door. "What you want?" she snapped.

"I come to see Aunt Agnes. Is she to home?"

"Mama!" the woman screamed, moving away from the door and into the shadows without asking Lilah to come in.

Lilah stood on first one foot and then the other, miserable now in the new sandal-shoes. Sweat trickled down her legs and soaked her underarms. She eyed a beat-up old rocking chair on the porch and considered taking a set-down while she waited, but she hadn't been asked and she didn't want to appear rude. Not that she was worried about offending Aunt Agnes anymore. This couldn't be her house. Another Agnes lived here, a woman who wouldn't know her from Eve, but Lilah supposed she owed this Agnes the courtesy of an apology.

A woman appeared in the shadows then—a tall, stoop-shouldered woman whose indistinct features struck a familiar chord in Lilah's memory. But, no, it couldn't be . . .

"What'd you come back for?" the woman barked. "I told that man last week I couldn't take you in."

"Aunt Agnes?" Lilah wished the woman would come out into the light. The light would prove she didn't know this woman. But she knew in her heart that the voice could belong to none other than maw's sister.

"Least you cleaned yourself up. Last week, you looked like you'd been wallowing in a pigsty. Merrie must've been rolling in her grave."

"Ye *are* Aunt Agnes."

"Of course, I am. Who'd you think I was? Oh, I was forgetting about you not being quite right."

Lilah wasn't paying much attention. Her mind was too full of questions. What man? When had she been so dirty? Last week, Aunt Agnes said. Last week . . .

"Go on, now. Be off with you."

The curt dismissal halted her mental rambling. "But, I thought—I mean, ain't ye goin' to invite me in?"

"We're in the middle of dinner, and I don't reckon we've got much to say to each other."

And then she was gone, swallowed by the shadows, as dead to Lilah as Maw and Granny.

Lilah stood on the porch a spell longer, staring at the gaping hole. The door was standing wide open. She could just walk right in. She supposed some folks would. Aunt Agnes would. But she couldn't. She lived by a code Aunt Agnes wouldn't understand. And if Aunt Agnes was a lady, then Lilah didn't want to have anything to do with being one herself.

Having no further reason to wear the painful sandal-shoes, Lilah sat down on the top step and took them off. Then she hiked up her skirt and petticoat and rolled the stockings down her legs, leaving the black lacy things on her thighs. They pinched, but she reckoned she could live with that far easier than the blisters. Besides, the boys were still watching from the shade across the street.

She buckled the ankle straps, strung the stockings through the holes, and tied the two toes to the two thigh bands, making a sort of sling to hold the shoes. This she slipped over her left shoulder so that one shoe hung down in front and the other in the back. She wanted to sling both the shoes and the stockings into the yard with the other garbage strewn there and be done with them, but they'd cost too much money to just throw away.

Sighing, she wiggled her toes and fanned her hot legs with her skirt. It felt wonderful to have bare legs and bare feet again. Made her want to sink her toes into some nice soft grass. There was some at the end of the street—a whole field full of grass and a couple of big old shade trees.

The boys giggled when she started down the street. "I told you!" the little one hollered. "Ain't she meaner'n a—"

The older one clamped a hand over Wyatt's mouth, preventing him from finishing the comparison for the second time. Lilah wanted to know what Wyatt thought Agnes was meaner than.

"I'm goin' down to the field at the end of the street," she told them. "Ye want to come along?"

"There's snakes in that field," Wyatt said, wide-eyed.

"What kind of snakes?"

"Skinny green ones."

Lilah grinned. "Oh, them's jest harmless grass snakes."

The older boy narrowed his gaze. He was a big, burly boy with hair as black as pitch. He seemed oddly familiar to her, too. "You ain't afraid of 'em?"

"Naw." She set off walking down the street. She didn't get far before the two caught up with her. The older one told her his name was Billy and asked her if she wanted an apple. She told him she might, if she knew what an apple was. That got them started talking about the swamp, and pretty soon they were sitting under one of the shade trees in the field eating red, juicy apples—which Lilah loved—and swapping stories. This was far better, she decided, then being cooped up with stuffy old Aunt Agnes in her dark house. She asked Wyatt to finish telling her what he thought about Agnes. "And, Billy, ye let him tell me this time."

Billy rolled his eyes. "You don't want to hear it."

"Yes, I do. Let Wyatt tell me."

Wyatt grinned. "She's meaner'n a bull what just got his balls chopped off."

"See! I told you you didn't want to hear it."

"That's purty mean," she said, holding her laughter inside the way Mr. Sawyer had done.

Billy gave her a long, assessing look. "You know, you're okay—for a girl."

"How do you like your apple?" Wyatt asked.

"It's good," Lilah said around a mouthful. "Granny had one of these in a bowl, but it wasn't real."

"It wasn't?"

"Naw. It was made out'n wax. There's a whole bowl full of fruit I never seed before, let alone et. One summer, it got so hot the pieces of fruit melted a bit, and now they's all lopsided and stuck t'gether."

When they finished their apples, they made a contest out of who could spit the seeds the farthest, and when they ran out of seeds, who could throw the cores the farthest. Wyatt threw his first, and the grass promptly swallowed it up.

"Go stand by it, Wyatt," Billy said, "and watch me chunk mine further."

"I ain't goin' out there with them snakes," Wyatt declared.

Lilah offered to do it, but Billy pointed out that she hadn't thrown hers yet, and then he called Wyatt a sissy. Wyatt said he was not, and he and Billy got into a "yes, you are, no, I'm not" battle. In the end, Wyatt stomped

through the grass until he found his apple core and stayed
there, but his knees were shaking so hard they made the
grass wiggle.

Billy's core fell short of Wyatt's. Lilah suspected Billy
wasn't even trying to beat Wyatt—maybe to give her a
chance to win, but probably to make Wyatt stay there and
face his fear of grass snakes. She tossed hers out, not too
hard either, and it fell at Wyatt's feet.

Wyatt hollered. Billy and Lilah looked at each other.
Lilah smiled and Billy winked. Wyatt kept on hollering.
After a spell, Billy hollered back.

"That's enough, Wyatt. You're scaring the birds."

"Something's scarin' him," Lilah said, moving cautiously toward the little boy. It might not be anything but
a mouse—and it might be a rattlesnake. No sense in taking
chances.

The grass camouflaged the green snake so well that she
didn't see it until its head reached Wyatt's knee. Lilah's
gaze followed its body downward and she understood the
boy's hysteria. The friendly snake had wrapped its slender
body around Wyatt's leg.

"It jest wants to get to know you better," she said, falling to her knees and gently removing the snake from
Wyatt's leg. She held the snake across her palm, showing
it to Wyatt. The snake lifted its head around, laid it on her
wrist, and began a spiraling journey up her arm.

Wyatt's gaze was nothing short of incredulous. "Ain't
you afraid of it?" he whispered.

Lilah stroked the snake's back. "Naw. I would be if'n it
was pizenous, like a rattler or a moccasin. But this here little un don' do nothin' 'ceptin' eat bugs and sich." She
looked up at Wyatt and Billy, who'd tromped through the
tall grass and was watching with equal fascination.
"Didn't yer paw teach you about snakes?"

Billy answered. "All Pa told us was that all snakes is
bad. He takes a hoe to ever' one he sees."

"Does yer paw take a hoe to folks, too?"

"Course not."

"Well, some folks is full of pizen-meanness—"

"Like old lady Summerville," Wyatt said.

And like One-Eyed Jack, Lilah mentally added, shivering in the blazing heat. "That's right. But mostly they's good. Snakes is the same. Ye jest have to learn how to tell 'em apart."

At Lilah's encouragement, the boys took turns touching the snake, then Lilah let it go and they sat back down in the shade.

"I thought it'd be all cold and slimy-feeling," Wyatt said, "but it weren't. I'll have to tell Pa."

"No, don't do that!" Billy said. "Pa'd just get mad and he wouldn't ever let us talk to Miss Lilah again. Tell us some more about the swamp. Does gators really live there? We ain't never seen a alligator."

Lilah told them all about gators, and from there they moved to other critters. When they got to the furry ones, Lilah rubbed Wyatt's hair and told him how much he reminded her of Bob. It was the first time she'd consciously associated the boy with the bobcat, but he did honestly remind her of Bob.

And Billy's size and dark hair reminded her of Ol' Codger.

"Law," she said, "I've been disrememberin' my two bestest friends in the whole world."

"What friends?" Wyatt asked, but she was so choked up all of a sudden, she couldn't answer him. She shook her head, trying to clear away the bad feeling that was slowly seeping into her heart, but it wouldn't go away.

"Come on, Wyatt," Billy said, standing up and tugging on his brother's arm. "We got to go now. Ma'll be lookin' fer us."

"But I don't want to go!" the younger one whined. "I want to hear about Bob and her other friend."

Lilah heard them arguing, but it was as though they were somewhere off way away, instead of right there beside her. Her ears were ringing and her eyes were crying, and her chest hurt like a heavy weight had plopped itself down on her. She lay down in the grass and rolled into a ball, hugging her knees right against her chest and letting the tears flow freely.

Wyatt scooted closer and laid a hand on her shoulder. "I'm sorry I made you cry, Miss Lilah. I hope you won't hold it agin me, 'cause I really do like you."

"You didn't make her cry," Billy said. "You just made her remember something that made her cry, and that ain't your fault. Now come on. We've got to go."

Lilah cried until she had no more tears to shed.

Though she tried to put her mind on other things, now that she'd remembered, she couldn't seem to erase the vision of Ol' Codger pinned to the tree, and she kept hearing his pitiful moans as his life's blood drained out of him.

When she cried herself out, she went to sleep and dreamed about the wolf woman again. This time, the wolf woman called out to the woman who had risen from the bones: "Come back! Come back!" But the young woman ignored La Loba's plea and disappeared into the forest. The wolf woman buried her face in her hands and deep sobs racked her ancient body.

When she woke up, the sunball was hanging low in the sky. Her head hurt and her eyes burned and her thinking was all foggy. She brushed herself off, collected her stockings and sandal-shoes, and trudged back to the hotel.

The moment she walked in the door, Mrs. Heywood jumped up from the sofa in the lobby and rushed toward her, taking her hands and squeezing them hard. "Lilah!" she gasped, her voice breathless. "Where have you been? We've been looking for you everywhere."

"I wasn't aimin' to trouble nobody," Lilah rasped. Talking hurt her throat, and she put her hand on her neck. It was a futile gesture, she knew, but somehow it was comforting, and right now she needed all the comfort she could get. "I was down at the end of Mulberry Street."

Mrs. Heywood looked at her in a way that said she hadn't really seen her before. "You've been crying."

Lilah nodded.

"How did you know?"

"I mem'ried."

The elderly lady frowned. "You remembered? What did you remember?"

" 'Bout Ol' Codger. I mem'ried he was dead."

"So you don't know ..." She tugged on Lilah's hands. "Come sit down. No, better yet, let's go in the kitchen. I'll get Aunt Susie to make you a cup of tea."

Blindly, Lilah allowed Mrs. Heywood to lead her to the kitchen. They sat at the table and Mrs. Heywood continued to hold Lilah's hands until Aunt Susie set cups of tea in front of each of them. "Spirits would be better," Mrs. Heywood said. "You got any, Susie?"

"Not nary a drop."

"Tea will have to do then." She nodded at Lilah's cup. "Drink up."

Dutifully, Lilah drank the tea. Little by little, the fog was lifting—and in its place marched an awful feeling of doom. She could hear its sure, solid footfalls clomping through her soul ... *boom, boom, boom.* Something was wrong, she realized. Something was terribly wrong. "So you don't know," Miz Heywood had said.

"What is it I don't know?"

"We looked for you everywhere. When we couldn't find you, he thought you'd gone back to the swamp."

He? Who was she talking about? Not Jesse, surely. Jesse was in jail. He'd be there until his marshal friend came ... Suddenly, she remembered the bald man at the jailhouse, the one who'd been talking to the high sheriff. She hadn't seen him around town before. She would have remembered that slick, bald head. Could it be—no, he wasn't supposed to be here for two or three more days. She hadn't heard Miz Heywood right.

"He told me all about getting snakebit and you finding him and nursing him back to health. How you hid him from the swampfolks while he was mending, and how he wouldn't have ever gotten out of the swamp if you hadn't guided him. He told me what happened to his wife and little boys and said he hoped you'd understand why he had to go after that One-Eyed Jack fellow."

"Jesse? Jesse's gone?"

"Left about an hour ago. He and that Marshal Whitcomb. They got word that One-Eyed Jack had been spotted in north Georgia, and they figured he was on his way back to Tennessee."

The cold reality of Mrs. Heywood's words was beginning to sink in. "Did he—" Lilah swallowed and tried again. "Did he say when he was a-comin' back?"

Mrs. Heywood shook her head sadly. "Just said to tell you that you were a lady, and you weren't ever to think again that you weren't. He said something about your marrying a man named Colin. And then he said he loved you. He said he thought he always had, and he knew he always would."

Chapter Twenty-six

He'd come back. Lilah knew he would.

All through the hot summer months, she waited. She lived and ate and worked at the hotel. On her days off, she met Billy and Wyatt in the field at the end of Mulberry Street. Through her, they were learning about swamp life—and through them, she was learning about town life. The more she learned, the more embarrassed she became. She'd made a heap of mistakes, but she took some consolation from the fact that no one but her knew about most of them.

Billy was also teaching her more about reading and writing. She was getting better at both, but she still had a long way to go, or so Billy told her.

She started going to Reverend Sawyer's church on Sundays and Wednesday nights. At first, she went with Mrs. Heywood. Later, after Mrs. Heywood left for Macon, she went by herself. She wasn't sure she liked going to church—it required wearing the uncomfortable stockings and sandal-shoes, and she wished she could read all the words to the hymns so she could sing—but it gave her something to do.

She remembered how she'd dreamed of living in town—riding in a carriage, dressing up and going to church on Sundays, attending Saturday night socials on the

arm of a young swain and dancing until her feet hurt. Maw
had put those notions in her head. Maw had grown up in
town and never really liked the swamp. She'd lived there
only because of Paw. She'd never whined about it, just
missed town a bit from time to time. She'd grow real
wistful-like and talk about town for a spell, then go right
back to what she was doing before and maybe not mention
it again for a year or more. Just reminiscing occasionally
seemed to be enough for Maw, but she hadn't thought it
was enough for Lilah. She'd wanted Lilah to live in town.

Lilah wondered if she'd ever be as content in town as
Maw had seemed to be in the swamp, if their roles were
reversed. If having Jesse meant living in town, she supposed she'd choose Jesse over the swamp, just as Maw
had chosen Paw over town. She'd rather have Jesse *and*
the Okefinoke, but that was more'n likely impossible.
Maybe she hadn't given herself enough time yet. Maybe
town was better than she thought it was.

There was certainly enough to do to keep her busy. Just
as Maw had told her, there was a social activity of some
sort most Saturday nights. Lilah seldom lacked for a willing escort. There was Leonard Stokes from the store,
whom she discovered was a widder-man with two small
children. There was Fred Martin from the hotel and J. B.
Thomas, the nice young man from the Western Union office. Even the Rev. Hugh Sawyer—she knew now that
Reverend was a title and not his front name—showed a romantic interest in her. But none of them were Jesse, and it
was Jesse her heart pined for.

At the end of every day, she walked over to the Western
Union office to see if a message from Jesse had come in.
Each day, J. B. told her the same thing: "No, ma'am. No
telegrams for you today. But if I get one, I'll bring it right
over to the hotel." Each day, she thanked him and told him
she'd come by again tomorrow. He'd smile at her and tell
her he looked forward to seeing her again.

From there, she went to the post office on train days, which was twice a week. Mail, she'd learned, came in on the train, so checking in between was pointless. Mr. Estes, the postmaster, always shook his head, smiled sadly, and told her he'd be sure to watch for any letters addressed to her.

Every night at supper, she cornered Sheriff Nester, hoping he'd heard something. Every night he assured her that he'd come running down to the hotel the minute he got wind of any news that might interest her, but so far, he'd say, he hadn't heard a word. Not a single word.

And then one day Mr. Estes brought her a letter that had just come in on the eastbound train. Lilah was so excited she came near fainting. For a moment, she clutched the letter to her chest, and the crackling paper warmed her in a way a quilt never could.

The postmaster's smile was no longer sad. "It gives me great pleasure to make you so happy, little lady," he said.

Lilah handed the envelope back to him and asked him to read it to her.

"Are you sure? I mean, it might say something you wouldn't want someone else to know."

"I'm sure." She thought she might actually be able to read it, but she didn't want to miss a single word just because it was one she hadn't yet learned—nor did she think Jesse would write anything that would make her blush. He'd know she'd have to get someone to read it to her.

Mr. Estes, who was an elderly man with a full head of yellow gray hair and a sweet disposition, took a penknife out of his pocket, used his thumbnail to open the blade, then carefully slit the top of the envelope. Lilah's heart was pounding and her head was spinning. She told her heart to calm down so she could hear what Mr. Estes was saying.

" 'My dearest Lilah,' " he read. " 'Having worn out my

welcome at my niece's house, I've now moved on to Birmingham . . .' "

Mrs. Heywood!

A hot prickle of tears burned Lilah's eyes and her throat swelled up, but she couldn't cry now. She owed Mrs. Heywood the courtesy of listening to her letter. Her daughter had a new house, she wrote, with a big front porch and pretty flowers in the yard and a spare room just for her to stay in when she came for a visit.

" '. . . I don't know when I'll get back to Homerville,' " Mr. Estes read, " 'but probably not before next spring. As much as I would love to see you again, I hope for your sake that the marshal comes to collect you long before then. You have my fondest wishes for a bright and happy future, Lilah. Knowing you has enriched my life more than you will ever know.' "

The postmaster looked up from the letter and studied her face over the rims of the round-framed glasses perched on the end of his nose. "That's it, except for Mrs. Heywood's signature. You must really miss her."

She didn't have the heart to tell him how disappointed she was that the letter wasn't from Jesse. "I do," she said, and she meant it.

She missed a heap of things. She missed Granny and Ol' Codger, though she had begun to reconcile herself to their deaths. She knew now that the ashes were Codger's, and she blessed Jesse for insisting that she keep them.

She missed the swamp and its people and her critters. She missed nights so alive with the critters talking to each other that she couldn't sleep, and days so quiet you could hear the swamp breathing. She missed the reflection of bald cypresses on the slick black water and the graceful flight of the white egret. She missed the dampness of the morning mist on her face, and the way it shimmered in the sunlight. She even missed the isolation of Medicine Island.

But most of all, she missed Jesse.

As the days grew shorter and the nights grew cooler and she still didn't hear from him, she began to despair that she ever would.

One-Eyed Jack's trail led straight back to the mountains of eastern Tennessee. In his wake, Jack Scurlock left a path of death and destruction unmatched by any Jesse had ever known.

Virtually every day, Jesse and Dan found another burned-out house and another group of mutilated bodies, which were usually scattered well away from the house. The bodies seemed to be a boast, as though Scurlock was saying, "Look what I did." In his mind, Jesse could hear screams of terror as the unfortunate victims attempted to run away. He hoped some of them had actually made it, but so many had bullet holes in their backs that he doubted it ever happened. Mixed in with the screams, the sharp report of a gun and the bastard's insane laughter reverberated through Jesse's soul.

Sometimes, the house was still smoldering. Occasionally neighbors—when there were any—would already be on the scene, digging graves and taking care of the livestock. Often a cow bellowed to be milked and penned-up hogs languished from lack of food. Always, a pain as sharp as Jack's blade pierced Jesse's heart. Never was the occurrence any easier to take.

And never would it be. Jesse was convinced of that. With every passing mile and every passing day, he grew wearier of his job, yet more determined than ever to catch Jack Scurlock. And when he did, he was going to retire his badge once and for all. As soon as this business was behind him, he was heading back to Georgia—back to Lilah, if she'd still have him. If she hadn't married Colin yet . . .

He thought about sending her a message. Occasionally, he and Dan passed through a town large enough to have a telegraph office. But what could he tell her? Nothing had

changed. Nothing would change until this business with
Jack Scurlock was over and done with.

Surely, it would be soon.

Please, God, he prayed, let it be soon.

Autumn arrived in Homerville.

Billy and Wyatt went back to school, leaving Lilah at
loose ends on Wednesday, her usual day off. She went to
the field, but it was lonesome without the mischievous
boys to keep her company. She wandered down the street,
kicking pebbles with her bare toes and listening to the
birds sing. The more she rambled, the lonesomer she became.

One Wednesday when she was out on such an excur-
sion, she saw Aunt Agnes sitting on her front porch. Lilah
waved. Agnes jumped up so fast she turned the rocking
chair over. Without stopping to right it, she hurried inside
and closed the door. Lilah laughed until her sides hurt.

For a while, she strolled around town, admiring the few
stately houses in Homerville, but mostly thinking about
how people seemed to have a tendency to destroy the natural beauty of a place. They cut down trees and put up
fences and called it creating refinement, when all they
were really doing was boxing themselves in.

She tried to imagine living in one of the little cottages
on one of the tree-lined streets, spending her days tending
a tiny garden and keeping house for Jesse. She watched a
young mother hanging clothes, while her toddler sat in the
yard and played with a doll. She watched an elderly man
trim a shrub, while his wife sat on the porch shelling pe-
cans. She tried to imagine herself boxed in by town, as
these folks were, with no more view than a dusty street
and the houses close by. Did they really ever *see* the
sunball go down or *hear* the squirrels barking in their
yards? she wondered. They might all have a heap of book-
learnin', but she suspected they missed out on a heap of

other things—things that were far more important to her, she realized, then being able to read and write.

Suddenly, in her mind's eye, she saw the blond-haired woman of her dream, the one La Loba had made from bones and moss. She saw the look of apprehension in the young woman's eyes, and she heard La Loba tell her to go and learn man's ways.

Was this what her dream was all about? Was she the woman made of bone and moss? Was Granny the Wolf Woman? Granny had made her promise that she'd go to Homerville. "See what the world outside the Okefinoke is like," Granny had said. "If'n ye don' like it, if'n it don' suit, then ye can come back. This swamp ain't a-goin' nowheres."

"I've seen it, Granny," she whispered to a big puffy cloud, "and it don' suit. Town mought be fine for some folks, but the Okefinoke is a-callin' me home."

She'd give Jesse a few more weeks. He'd said he wouldn't ever step foot in the swamp again, but if he didn't come back for her—or at least send her a message—then she was going home. She could grow old and gray waiting in town for him. If she had to live her life without him, then at least she'd live where she wanted to.

"This is really strange," Dan Whitcomb said, smoothing a palm over his peeled head just as though there were hair on it. "The man goes on an all-out killing spree, and then just ups and quits. It doesn't make any sense."

Jesse poked at the campfire and watched the sparks fly. "Nothing Jack Scurlock ever did made any sense."

"Where do you think he went?"

"Your guess is as good as mine."

"But you know him better. You probably know him better than he knows himself, Jesse. Don't you have any ideas at all?"

Jesse shook his head. "We're back in his old territory. We've checked the old still site. We've talked to everyone who knows him and a bunch of folks who don't—or won't admit it, if they do. And we're camped right outside the shack he calls home. I'm out of options."

"And I need to go back to Knoxville."

"I can do this on my own, Dan."

"I never doubted you could. I get lonesome for the field sometimes, but I can't say riding with you has been a real pleasure."

Jesse stared off into the darkness and shivered. "I know I've been hard to live with."

"It's not you. It's that damned Jack Scurlock. In all the thirty years I've been a lawman, I've never seen such carnage. Only some kind of deranged monster could take such pleasure in killing. What I want to know is, what stopped him? Why did he get almost back home and then just stop? Maybe somebody killed him. Maybe he's lying in the woods somewhere, with a bullet in his black heart."

"Don't count on it."

For a few minutes they sat quietly by the fire, each absorbed in his own ruminations. Jesse broke the silence.

"You know, Dan, it's the strangest thing, the way Scurlock and I look so much alike. We're even about the same age. Sometimes, I get to feeling all dark inside, like maybe I *am* Jack Scurlock."

"You know better than that, Jesse."

"I suppose I do, but it's not a good feeling, I can tell you that. While I was in jail, all I could think about was getting out so I could kill Jack Scurlock. I've killed a lot of men, but never because I wanted to. All the time before, when I was tracking him, I wanted to see him hang. I wanted to go to court and testify against him. Now, I just want him dead. The sooner, the better." He sighed. "I guess that means it really is time for me to retire my badge."

"I wish I could talk you into staying on, Jesse. You're the best deputy I have."

"Sorry, Dan, but when this is over, I'm gone."

"What if she didn't wait for you?"

"Then I'm coming back here and working my farm. I'm so tired of it all, Dan. I just want some peace in my life."

Jesse stirred the fire again, then lay back on his saddle, and stared at the night sky. The moon was no more than a small sliver of silvery light, but the stars shone brightly in their black velvet heaven. Tonight, he could see the Milky Way, and he recalled Lilah's tale about it being a path to the spirit world. He closed his eyes and conjured up her sweet face—and his heart ached with love and longing for her. Her dream-face smiled at him and her blue eyes glowed—then suddenly dulled, as though she were in pain. The smile faded, and blood trickled out of her mouth.

Jesse jumped to his feet and snatched up his saddle.

"Where are you going?" Dan asked. "It's pitch dark."

"I know where he is." Jesse hauled the saddle up and onto the back of his tethered horse.

"Where?"

"On his way back to the swamp. He's going after Lilah."

"How can you be so sure?"

"I just *know*, all right?"

"Shouldn't you at least wait until morning?"

"My farm is just a few miles from here. I'm going there first—to check on the place and get me some more clothes. It's out of the way, but I may never come back here. I want to see it one more time. I'll rest for a few hours, then head out at dawn." He tightened the girth. "You're welcome to come with me."

"This is crazy, Jesse. Sit down and let's think this through."

"You said no one knows Jack Scurlock better than I do.

Well, this is what my gut instinct is telling me to do, and that's not likely to change." Jesse mounted the horse. "Nice seeing you again, Dan."

"Wait! I'm going with you to the farm, but I'll have to go on to Knoxville from there."

"Suit yourself."

Lilah awoke from a deep sleep.

The dream had come to her again. Never before had it come so many times, so close together. Each time, the Wolf Woman, whose voice and face were definitely Granny's now, grew weaker. Each time, Lilah awoke feeling as though this might be the last time the dream came to her. The Wolf Woman was dying, and when she was gone, the dream would cease to exist.

"Come home. Come home to me," La Loba begged.

Lilah had already waited for Jesse far longer than she'd ever intended. If he truly loved her, as he'd told Mrs. Heywood he did, then he'd find her in the swamp. The swamp had brought him to her once. Perhaps it would again.

A lone tear trickled out of Lilah's eye, coursed down her cheek, and plopped onto her pillow. "I want to come home," she whispered. "I'll leave come mornin' soon."

There was something strange, something eerie about the dark log house sitting on its knoll.

The moment he saw the house, Jesse reined in his horse. Dan pulled his mount up beside him. "What are we stopping for?"

"I don't know. Something's not right."

"This place holds bad memories for you, Jesse. That's all."

"It's more than that. I can't explain. It's almost like an evil spirit is enveloping it."

"Sounds like the beginning of a good ghost story to me."

"You can make light of it, if you want to, but—" A shadow moved in front of a window. "Did you see that?"

"Did I see what?"

Jesse dismounted and tied his horse to a mountain laurel growing nearby, then slipped the rifle Dan had provided out of its leather sheath.

"What are you doing?"

"Going down there. On foot."

Dan cursed softly, got off his horse, and followed. "You're imagining things, Jesse."

"Am I imagining that?" He pointed to the house. A tiny orange glow passed by one of the windows, retreated into the dark bowels of the house, then reappeared at another window. "Someone's in there. Someone who's smoking a cigar or a cigarette. Someone who's nervous."

"How do you know?"

"He's pacing."

Sure enough, as they watched, the glow moved back and forth in front of the windows.

"What's the plan?"

"You go in the front door. I'll go in the back. If that's Jack Scurlock, we'd better be ready for him, so go in with your rifle cocked and ready to fire. Just don't shoot me. Stay low and keep quiet."

Dan snorted. "I know the procedure."

"But you don't know Scurlock."

"Wait for me to get in position. When you get to the front door, count to twenty, then go in."

They made their way down the hill as quietly as two mice in church. Dan took up his position by the front door, and Jesse eased around back, counting to twenty himself as he went. At eighteen, he reached the back door. For a split second, he panicked. What if the doors were barred? What if his little plan got Dan killed? What if the man in-

side was only a drifter? He'd been so sure Scurlock was
on his way to the swamp. They should have taken positions and waited for daylight, waited for the intruder to
come outside.

The front door crashed inward. It was too late now to
change plans. Jesse stepped back and landed a solid kick
on the back door. It banged against an inside wall. Someone opened fire.

For a split second, the discharge lit up the room. Dan
Whitcomb's eyes opened wide in surprise, and he pivoted
a quarter-turn to his left. Darkness engulfed the room
again, then two circles of light blossomed almost
simultaneously—one at the end of Dan's rifle barrel, the
other a mere five paces in front of him. Jesse whirled and
fired at the second light. Then he recocked his rifle and
fired again.

Lord, let it be Scurlock. And let him be dead, he prayed.

Chapter Twenty-seven

Like smoke, the early morning mist hovered over the dark water. Its cloying dampness sent a surge of exhilaration through Lilah, and she stopped paddling to gain the full enjoyment of the moment.

After more than four months of exile, she was home. The word held new meaning for her, and though she'd always been keenly aware of the swamp, even it bore a delightful newness. Never had winter in the Okefinoke seemed so beautiful.

Gaunt and naked, the bald cypresses stood in funereal procession along the waterways, shallower now and darker than Aunt Susie's skin. Not a breath of wind stirred the draping, long-haired moss, and somber tones—tans, grays, and faded greens—marked the brooding landscape. Even the birds' voices were softer, quieter, a reflection of the season.

In a few months, spring would come again to the Okefinoke, bursting forth in riotous splendor, as noisy as it was colorful. But for now, Lilah's mood matched that of the season—a perfect mating of muted hope and the promise of new life.

It wasn't until she'd launched the canoe and set her paddle in the water that she fully acknowledged the life that grew within her womb. As though her child knew that he,

too, had come home, he leapt to life then, teasing her with
tiny flutterings for the first time. She laid an open palm on
the soft mound of her stomach. In time, she knew, her
belly would grow big and firm, like Maw's had when she
carried Little Jacob. Come spring, a new life would burst
forth in the Okefinoke.

A part of her clung to the hope that Jesse would be back
by then, that he would be there to help her bring their
child into the world. Even if he weren't, even if she never
saw him again, at least she had this part of him, this child
to love and cherish. But, oh, how she hoped he would be
there, not only for her, but for himself and their child as
well. Lilah didn't think any man ever needed a child quite
as much as Jesse did.

She took her time, moving the paddle slowly, letting her
mind spin daydreams while her soul reabsorbed the wonder of the Okefinoke. Without consciously choosing to do
so, she avoided the long, narrow island where Ol' Codger
had died, instead sleeping in the canoe her first night back
in the swamp. Late the next afternoon, she docked the canoe on the island where she and Jesse had made real love,
where the child that grew within her had been conceived.
That night, she sat by the fire for a long time, staring into
the leaping flames while she dreamed and planned for the
future.

At dawn, she broke camp, taking great care to spread
the coals in a thin layer and thoroughly dousing them before leaving. At no time was fire a bigger threat than in
the winter.

Although the swamp hadn't burned during the eighteen
years she'd lived there, the old swampers told of a great
fire that had destroyed much of the Okefinoke back in the
fifties. "Ye'd think nothin' this wet would burn, but it
does," they said, "specially when the water's low and the
bog moss has dried out." It was that fire, they said, that

carved out Minnie's Prairie, along with numerous ponds and gator holes.

Lilah continued on an easterly course, paddling straight into the sunball, following the same route she'd taken out of the Okefinoke. An hour or so later, she was skirting a small, almost barren battery, when she spied an upturned canoe leaning against a buttonbush. She called out, but no one answered. Intrigued, she guided the canoe to shore and pulled it well out of the lake before going to investigate.

The earth trembled beneath her feet as she walked barefoot through the dry, brown grass. Why would anyone camp on such unstable ground, when a much firmer island lay so close by? she wondered. She hollered again and listened to the eerie yodel of her voice echoing in the stillness. A long, cold finger of terror snaked down her back.

She was turning to retreat, when she spied the go-away satchel caught in the naked branches of a hurrah bush. It looked just like her satchel—the one that was in her canoe when One-Eyed Jack—

"Oh, god, no!" she breathed, her heart thumping wildly in her chest. For a moment, she stood frozen while her gaze darted left and right. There was no movement, no noise, nothing to indicate that anyone had been there recently. And there was nowhere to hide, not with the few small bushes virtually bare.

Lilah fixed her gaze on the canoe, which, she realized, was covered with pieces of moss and grass. It had been there for some time.

Slowly, methodically, she made her way to the satchel and pulled it from its nest of twisted limbs. From there, she moved on to the canoe, flipped it over, and started dragging it back across the battery.

That was when she saw the skeleton, lying in a bed of dry grass next to a burned-out spot, the flesh either decayed or eaten off by buzzards. But there was no mistaking the clothes. Without a doubt, the patched overalls belonged to Colin Yerby.

She fell to her knees, holding her stomach and rocking back and forth, her voice a keening dirge that rose and fell with each motion of her body. After a while, she rose to her feet, wiped her eyes with trembling fingers, and collected a blanket from the canoe—Colin's canoe. With loving care, she placed the bones on the blanket, tied it in a neat bundle, and set it gently in her own canoe, the one Jack Scurlock had taken. Its presence on the battery could mean only one thing: Scurlock had been there. And he must have had another way to leave, or he wouldn't have abandoned her canoe.

Colin's punt boat.

Colin must have surprised Jack—and lost his life because of it.

Jesse's wife and children . . . Smiley . . . Ol' Codger . . . and now Colin. How many more innocent lives had One-Eyed Jack taken? How many more would he take?

Someone had to stop him.

"Now I understand, Jesse," she whispered. "Ever-how long it takes you, I understand. Jest, please, don't let him take yer life, too."

The Yerbys wanted her to spend the winter with them, but Lilah insisted on leaving the day after Colin's funeralizing. Since Medicine Island lay between the Yerbys and Chesser's Island, the Chessers insisted on following Lilah home.

"Ye can't never be too keerful," Mr. Chesser said. "And I'll tell you straight, Miz Lilah. I don't like the idee of you stayin' all by yer lonesome like ye're aimin' to do. But I reckon if'n I tried to make you stay with us, ye'd jes' up and leave one day. I ain't goin' to tie you down. But I don' like it. No, sir, not a-tall."

"I'll be keerful," Lilah promised.

And she was. Never did she go down to the lake without toting a big stick with her. Never did she go to bed without making sure the shutters and door were secure. Never did she leave the little cabin after dark, no matter what.

Ever so often, someone stopped by to visit and then ended up staying overnight, offering first one flimsy excuse or another as a reason to tarry. Lilah appreciated their concern, but she couldn't live the rest of her life in fear, she told them. Jacob Crews brought her a small caliber rifle and taught her how to shoot it, and she started carrying it with her instead of the stick. As much as she hated guns, she understood now why they were sometimes necessary.

As the winter months passed, her belly grew larger, and her hope that Jesse would return in time for the birthing diminished. Every day, she watched for him—and for Bob, too. She hadn't seen the bobcat since way before she and Jesse left the swamp, and she feared that One-Eyed Jack had added the cat to his growing list of victims.

February arrived, and with it came the bell-shaped white flowers of the highbush huckleberries. Close behind, the hurrah bushes exploded in a mass of pink blossoms. Encouraged by these first signs of spring coupled with no reports of outlaws in the swamp, Lilah started wandering farther and farther from the cabin.

One day in March, she wandered all the way to the meadow where she'd buried Granny Latham. There, the bog orchids, wampee, and old man's cologne were in full bloom, their colors bright splashes among the pale green of new grass. A host of bees drifted from one blossom to another, filling the air with the drone of their busy wings.

Lilah sat down in the grass close to the foot of the grave. "I miss you, Granny," she said. "So much has happened since ye left. I hardly know where to begin tellin' you, but I think I'll start at the back end. I'm goin' to have me a baby. Jesse's baby. I'm happy, but I'm sceered, too.

And I'm sad, 'cause ye're gone, and it don' look like Jesse's a-comin' back. When the baby comes, I'll have someone to belong to again, but for right now, I ain't got no one. Ye was right. It's a lonesome belongin'."

For several hours, Lilah sat in the meadow and talked to Granny. A soft breeze ruffled the grass and toyed with a lock of her curly hair. The air was fragrant with the sweet smell of flowers and rang with the happy chirping of a multitude of birds. As she talked, a strange peacefulness settled over her.

After a while, she felt the warmth of a critter's fur on her bare forearm.

"Bob!" she cried, lying back and allowing the cat to lick her face while she rumpled the hair on his neck. "Where have ye been all this time? Law, I ain't never been so glad to see a body!"

The cat rolled off and limped toward the thicket. Lilah sat up and stared after him. "What's wrong with you, Bob? Ye ain't never tired of playin' that fast before."

He stopped and turned his head, as though he were inviting her to follow him, then took several more limping steps and looked back at her again. "All right, I'm a-comin'. What ye got? A litter of kitties for me to see?"

She followed him through the thicket, but instead of turning toward the cabin, as she expected, he loped off toward the lake. Men's voices drifted up the trail. It was probably just a couple of the swampers, Lilah told herself. Nevertheless, she tightened her hold on the rifle.

Bob broke through the brush ahead of her.

"Did you bring her with you, old boy?" one of the men said.

Jesse! Lord, it was Jesse!

"Jesse!" she called, her heart singing and her blood surging. She dropped the rifle, lifted her skirts, and ran the last few steps—and there he stood. She paused only long enough to fill her heart with the sight of him, then sped into his open arms.

He picked her up and hugged her against him, saying her name over and over, while he rained kisses all over her face.

"I missed you," he said, his voice husky.

Tears streamed from her eyes and she made no attempt to stop them. "I didn't think ye was a-comin' back."

He set her down and skimmed an open palm over her swollen stomach. "Am I too late?"

Hearing the near sorrow in his voice more than his actual words, Lilah choked back her own grief. "I can't brang yer boys back, Jesse, but I thought ye'd be pleased to father another child."

His eyebrow arched above his one good eye. "That's *my* child you're carrying?"

" 'Course, it is. I was afeared our baby wouldn't ever know his papa. I was afeared One-Eyed Jack would stop you afore ye stopped him. And I was afeared ye mought not love me enough to come back, even if he didn't."

Jesse pulled her against him and rubbed her back. "God, Lilah! I love you with all my heart. And a baby . . . *our* baby. It's just . . . it's . . . I'm just sorry I was too late."

It was almost too much to take in all at once. Lilah's head was spinning, and her racing pulse seemed to say "I love you with all my heart" over and over.

"I was too late, wasn't I, Lilah?"

His words finally penetrated, leaving her more than a little confused. "Too late?"

"To marry you. You've already married Colin."

"Ever-what give you that idee? Colin's dead. One-Eyed Jack kilt him."

A deep sorrow washed through Jesse. He'd wanted to find Lilah free to marry him, but not at the expense of another man's life. "I'm sorry, Lilah. I know you loved Colin."

"Colin was my friend, but I didn't love him the way I love you, Jesse. I wouldn't a-married up with him, even if Jack hadn't kilt him and you hadn't a-ever come back."

He squeezed her tighter. "You wouldn't?"

"Nay."

Lilah felt his heart thumping firm and strong against her ear, and she felt her own heart fill nearly to bursting with a joy that was as bright as the sunball at midday. But then a cloud in the form of Jack Scurlock's face darkened her elation, and she pulled herself out of Jesse's embrace.

"How long can ye stay?"

"I've been trying to get back here since the day I left Homerville. Now that I am, I'm not leaving again—not without you."

"But . . . what about One-Eyed Jack? And yer marshalin'?"

"Jack Scurlock is dead, Lilah, and I have officially retired."

"Dead? Ye kilt him?"

"No, though it wasn't because I didn't try. He shot Dan Whitcomb."

"Yer marshal friend?"

"Yes. Luckily, Dan's wound wasn't fatal. He got a bullet into Scurlock first, and I put another one in him, but the scoundrel refused to die."

Lilah frowned in confusion. "But I thought ye said he was dead."

"He is . . . now. It took him three months to recover enough to stand trial, just so we could hang him. That's what kept me in Tennessee so long. But now I'm here, and I'm not ever going to leave again."

It was the second time he'd said it, but she still didn't quite believe she was hearing him right. "Ye're aimin' to stay? Here in the swamp? Ye said ye hated the swamp."

"Forget what I said before. The Okefinoke is your

home, and I'm planning to make it mine. This is where I want to raise my family."

"For true, Jesse?"

"For true." He bent his head then and kissed her thoroughly.

The other man, whom Lilah had momentarily forgotten, cleared his throat loudly.

"You remember Reverend Sawyer," Jesse said, stepping aside so that Lilah could see the minister.

"Yes, but what is he—"

"I came back to marry you, Lilah," Jesse said. "That requires a wedding, and a wedding requires a preacher. I brought one with me."

He took her hand and they walked toward the cabin.

"Could we get married-up in the meadow?" Lilah asked. "I'd like for Granny to be there."

His hand squeezed hers. "I think that's an excellent idea. I'd like for Granny to be there, too."

Author's Note

The name *Okefenokee*, which literally means "Land of the Trembling Earth," bears only slight resemblance to its original Indian name. It was first recorded in 1790 on a Georgia map as *Ekanfinaka;* twenty years later, it had become *Eckenfinooka.* By the 1870's, it had evolved into *Okefinoke,* pronounced *Oak-fin-oak* then, and still pronounced that way by some locals today. In the early part of this century, another *e* was added to the end— *Okefinokee*—and the current, more musical pronunciation was born. Since this book is set in the 1880's, I chose to use *Okefinoke,* its name at the time, throughout.

Medicine Island and Yerby's Island are fictitious, but the other islands, lakes, and prairies named in this story are real. The Lees, Chessers, Crews, and Mizells were also real families living in the Okefenokee in the 1880's. The ballad used in this book, "The Piney Woods Boys," is of Okefenokee origin.

Generations of sturdy, self-sufficient, and gifted people lived an isolated and rather primitive life within the Okefenokee, before the federal government bought them out in the 1930's and turned the swamp into a National Wildlife Refuge. These people represented some of the purest Anglo-Saxon stock left in our country, and bore marked similarities to the residents of the Appalachian

Mountains. In both areas, folks used a regional dialect containing various elements that had survived from Elizabethan times, and have since been dropped from general American usage. I have attempted to incorporate much of this vernacular into the dialogue. Although most of these people were illiterate, they could quote Shakespeare and other Elizabethan poets, and many of their ballads (such as "Greensleeves") were of Elizabethan origin. The line of poetry used in Chapter Three is from Anthony Munday's poem "To Colin Clout."

I have also incorporated as much about the swamp's unique wildlife and plant life as was appropriate to this story, but I have only touched the surface. Sphagnum (bog) moss, the chief component of peat bogs, has been used since ancient times as a dressing for wounds, and wounded deer will wallow in a bed of sphagnum moss. The swampers did bait and torment bobcats. The inspiration for Ol' Codger came from a story about Old Soker, a huge black bear that roamed the Okefenokee in the 1880's. Bears often appear much larger than they actually are. Old Soker was reputed to be as big as a grizzly—and, indeed, proved to be so. When he was finally tracked and killed, he measured eleven feet from "tip to tip." In contrast to Western black bears (which may be black, brown, or cinnamon-colored), Eastern black bears are almost always black.

Bears, I learned, demonstrate many "human" traits: they think analytically, remember, have distinct personalities, often exhibit "human" characteristics, including showing off (some even flex their muscles like a man)—and they have been known to pick up people and other heavy objects and walk off with them. Although both bears and alligators will attack and eat humans, neither prefer human flesh.

I feel, too, that I have only touched the surface in describing this ever-changing swamp, which contains some seventy islands of twenty acres or more each in its thirty-five-mile length. A seasoned swamper could walk it in eight days, but only because of his intimate knowledge of the terrain and his extraordinary strength and endurance. Walking the swamp was the major way of getting around until Josiah Mizell invented the "punt" boat in the early 1870's. This was a utility boat, a floating campsite that could carry two men and their dogs, as well as blankets, guns, and food. The swampers could stay in the Okefenokee for days or weeks at a time in Mizell's boat.

Over the years, natural disasters have played havoc in the Okefenokee. A nineteenth-century hurricane felled acres of pines and uprooted massive live oaks. Severe droughts invite fires of catastrophic proportion about every twenty-five to forty years, but the swamp always rises from the ashes of its destruction, much like the wolf woman rises from La Loba's collected bones. This ancient legend, which forms an integral part of this story, fascinates me almost as much as the Okefenokee does.

Perhaps as you read this book, you, too, will become fascinated with this unusual setting. I hope you will let me hear from you. You may write to me in care of Zebra Books, 850 Third Avenue, NY, NY 10022.

Elizabeth Leigh

TODAY'S HOTTEST READS
ARE TOMORROW'S SUPERSTARS

SURRENDER TO THE SPLENDOR OF THE ROMANCES OF ROSANNE BITTNER!

CARESS	(3791, $5.99/$6.99)
COMANCHE SUNSET	(3568, $4.99/$5.99)
HEARTS SURRENDER	(2945, $4.50/$5.50)
LAWLESS LOVE	(3877, $4.50/$5.50)
PRAIRIE EMBRACE	(3160, $4.50/$5.50)
RAPTURE'S GOLD	(3879, $4.50/$5.50)
SHAMELESS	(4056, $5.99/$6.99)